The Barley Break

The Barley Break

C A HOPE

Copyright © 2019 C A Hope

The moral right of the author has been asserted.

Apart from any fair dealing for the purposes of research or private study, or criticism or review, as permitted under the Copyright, Designs and Patents Act 1988, this publication may only be reproduced, stored or transmitted, in any form or by any means, with the prior permission in writing of the publishers, or in the case of reprographic reproduction in accordance with the terms of licences issued by the Copyright Licensing Agency. Enquiries concerning reproduction outside those terms should be sent to the publishers.

Matador
9 Priory Business Park,
Wistow Road, Kibworth Beauchamp,
Leicestershire. LE8 0RX
Tel: 0116 279 2299
Email: books@troubador.co.uk
Web: www.troubador.co.uk/matador
Twitter: @matadorbooks

ISBN 978 1789017 458

British Library Cataloguing in Publication Data.
A catalogue record for this book is available from the British Library.

Printed and bound in Great Britain by 4edge Limited
Typeset in 11pt Sabon MT by Troubador Publishing Ltd, Leicester, UK

Matador is an imprint of Troubador Publishing Ltd

In memory of my father, the unique and irreplaceable Austin Lawther

PROLOGUE

June 2017

Hospitals... they were not the chillingly clinical places they used to be, Jennifer reflected tranquilly, gazing around the ward with undisguised curiosity. She had recently read a book – complete with many illustrations – about the early days of the NHS. The wards had been positively Victorian-looking, giving little privacy. The decor appeared dismal too, but perhaps that was because a lot of the illustrations were in black and white, she excused. She could recall having her tonsils and adenoids removed, in 1990, which seemed a long time ago now. Her ward had been described by one of the nurses as being 'a wee bit old-fashioned'. It had consisted of two rows of approximately ten beds, dormitory-style, and in between each identical bed had been an identical locker. The beds had each had the same number of pillows, the same colour of counterpane, and bedside tables were uniformly placed. The decor had been bland and uninviting. In contrast, the ward she was visiting now consisted of a series of small rooms, each containing half a dozen beds. It was cosy, homely even, in atmosphere, and the decor was bright and cheerful.

Lying on top of a bed which was covered with a floral pink coverlet, Vi, Jennifer's mother, lounged with the relaxed ease of one who knew nothing was seriously wrong. Secretly she half wished something had been – as long as it was nothing terminal, of course – and then she might have been able to persuade Jennifer and her husband Chas to permit her to permanently move in with them.

'It was a stone in the bile duct which caused the pain,' she explained with a dismissive wave of a hand, the motion displaying immaculately varnished, fearsomely long fingernails to the best advantage, whilst the light flashed from a large sapphire ring. It was the size of Princess Diana's iconic ring, now worn with grace and dignity by the Duchess of Cambridge. If asked, Vi would always tell people it was a real sapphire. It wasn't.

'How can that be? Your gall bladder was removed years ago,' queried Jennifer.

'You can still get stones,' Vi pronounced airily, showing off new-found medical knowledge. 'They can become lodged in the bile duct. It's wonderful all the technology they have nowadays,' she said and pursed her lips into an "O" – a frequent habit which her family found either amusing or irritating, depending upon circumstances.

Somehow she could make the "O" suggest numerous things: disapproval, superiority, ill-humour, to name but a few. On this occasion she appeared smugly superior.

'They removed the stone yesterday, just through passing a camera down my throat!'

She patted her sculptured blonde waves, flattering herself she didn't look anything akin to a woman of pensionable years. Her hair, covered with layers of lacquer, was artificially blonde and as hard as concrete. She had retained the same luxuriously permed style since the 1980s.

'I was really worried, Mum.' Jennifer grasped her mother's hand, at the same time trying to ignore the discomfort of sitting on a hard plastic, unpadded hospital chair. Her bottom felt numb, and it was digging into the backs of her knees. 'You were an awful yellow colour, and when you collapsed with pain I thought it might be something serious.'

Inwardly she wondered if Mum was still jaundiced. Or maybe she was simply wearing a lot of makeup; she tended to apply it generously. Chas always claimed it was as thick as a pancake and likely to crack when she smiled. Also, her jaundiced colouring contrasted violently with her yellow blonde hair. Alternately, it could simply be the overhead lights. A smile suddenly swept across her face.

'All the same, when you talk of cameras, I have a vision of someone trying to stuff a digital camera down your throat!'

She tactfully failed to mention that Chas had voiced a hope that they would do just that. It might shut her up. Vi, who was on the whole a cheerful, good-hearted woman, could also be vocal, domineering and tactless.

As Vi gave a throaty laugh, Jennifer became aware that Sara, her twelve-year-old daughter, was wriggling around on her chair in her usual ungainly fashion. Irritated, she jerked at one of Sara's legs.

'Sit properly, do, and get your shoe off the seat!'

The girl was sitting with one foot on her chair, arms wrapped about her knee, whilst the other leg was flung out at an angle. Why did Sara always look so awkward? She was tall and slim, obviously going to take after her father in this. But surely Chas had never, ever, looked so gawky. He always seemed so in control of his limbs. A keen tennis player, he was well coordinated. Sara was the opposite. Her arms and legs seemed to fly off in totally different directions. And she was so bashful, so gauche with strangers. She was an only child, of course, which might account for something. Jennifer wasn't sure what.

'She's alright.' Vi shook her head in reproof. Jennifer was such a perfectionist, demanding high standards from herself, and Sara too. 'I'm lucky,' she informed Jennifer, directing attention away from the child. 'The poor woman in the bed next to me is not so fortunate,' she nodded knowingly towards the next bed. It was temporarily empty, the floral counterpane turned back, showing crumpled pink sheets. 'She's been taken to have a scan done. Has cancer, you know.' Vi's mouth pursed again, to the size of a hazelnut. 'Of the pancreas. Difficult to diagnose apparently. They've found it too late.'

'How old is she?' Jennifer's face was a mask of compassion.

'About forty.'

Vi was disapprovingly eyeing the woman in the opposite bed, who was lying flat on her back, snoring, making a loud, monotonous sound, her mouth wide open. Snoring was so unladylike. She had never snored… well, if she had no one had dared mention it.

'Just a few years older than me,' whispered Jennifer.

'Yes, it's so sad,' Vi nodded gravely. 'But her attitude is amazing. Two teenage daughters… or stepdaughters, not sure which, but I feel for them. But she is so composed. I can hardly believe it. She's supposedly well-known, you know, but I've never heard of her. Marilyn Hamilton. A writer, apparently.'

'I have heard of her. I've seen her books on Amazon. She writes history… I keep meaning to order one.' Jennifer was impressed. 'But if you say she's composed, maybe she's shocked, or drugged or something.'

She noticed her daughter was now sitting slumped in her chair, long thin legs sprawled out in front of her, feet splayed at right angles. Shrugging aside her irritation, she instead pictured the potential mental pain of a sick mother having to leave her child; but simultaneously she recalled the nick-name Sara's classmates had given her – Olive Oyle. How unfortunately apt. If only the girl would learn to move gracefully.

'I don't know… Here she comes now.'

With undisguised interest, Vi watched as a trolley was wheeled in bearing a prostrate figure. Momentarily the invalid was obscured from view as curtains were briskly drawn about her bed. Amid the sudden activity, the woman occupying the bed opposite was suddenly wakeful, sitting up with arms folded akimbo over huge breasts, nodding knowingly towards Vi and mouthing more loudly than she ought, 'Looks terrible.'

Equally knowingly, Vi, lips pursed yet again, gave a sage nod of her head. Her hair never moved.

Aware it was wrong to set a bad example to Sara, but eager for information, Jennifer leaned towards her mother, whispering in her ear, 'The woman opposite… Did she tell you what they're treating her with? She looks obese and bloated. She must be taking massive doses of steroids.'

'I don't know what they're giving her. But she told me she used to be slim,' was the whispered response.

'Mummy, you're whispering,' rebuked Sara. 'You always tell me it is ill-mannered.' Unconsciously mirroring the posture of the woman opposite, Sara too had her arms folded akimbo.

'Hush,' muttered Jennifer, then, seeing signs of a rebellious retort on the child's lips, crisply added, 'Do as you're told.'

Mutinous, the girl watched as the curtains were pulled back from the neighbouring bed, revealing another very plump woman who was obviously a few years older than Mummy. Her hair was brown and very short. There was a stand beside her bed, with what looked like a bag of water hanging from it, and the tubes coming from the bag were strapped to her arm. Noticing her scrutiny, the woman smiled, illuminating a face which, despite the ravages of illness, remained remarkably pretty.

Returning the smile, Sara's eyes widened with childish curiosity. The girl's high-boned face predicted future beauty. It was thin, lightly sprinkled with freckles, with a neat, straight nose. Her green eyes, set wide apart, were lovely, and her lips were full and well-shaped. One day her smile would be charming but currently it was marred by the steel braces on her upper and lower teeth. Her straight hair, mid-brown and cut into a short bob, ended unflatteringly just above her ear lobes, accentuating the thin face. The thick fringe which accompanied it completed a style which was totally unsuitable for such delicate features. But it was tidy. Very tidy. Her mother hated untidy hair. She hated any sort of untidiness.

'What is your name?' The woman's blue eyes crinkled invitingly.

'Sara,' was the bashful response, accompanied by a vivid blush which spread from the girl's cheeks to her ears.

'A lovely name. Have you seen the film *Dr. Zhivago*? No,' the woman answered the question herself, 'you're far too young. But the heroine is called Lara. It too is a lovely name, and similar to yours. I am something of a film buff. Again the woman smiled, this time wearily.

'What are you called?' Again Sara flushed shyly.

'Marilyn. Appropriate, since I like films.' Seeing the incomprehension in the child's eyes, she explained, 'There was a famous film star called Marilyn.'

Pleased at being talked to as if she was an adult, Sara sat, knees together, elbows resting on her legs, body leaning towards Marilyn.

'Have you any daughters?'

'Yes. Sort of. They're my stepdaughters. One is called Rosie. That comes from another film. An old one… older than

Dr. Zhivago, called *The African Queen*. The other is called Alice. As in *A Town Like Alice*. The old films are the best…'
Marilyn, who had been sitting upright, suddenly sank back on her pillows, closing her eyes wearily.

'I think Marilyn needs to rest,' Jennifer murmured gently.

Surely her stepdaughters ought to be with her now. Marilyn was clearly very sick. But then perhaps they didn't have a good relationship, she supposed vaguely. And what about her husband?

Nodding, Sara was silent, listening as her mother and grandmother chattered inconsequentially, her gaze frequently drifting towards the sick woman. Suddenly, Marilyn raised her head from her pillow, opening her eyes and directing her gaze, with piercing intensity, towards her, before closing her eyes slowly and allowing her head to flop back onto her pillow.

Jennifer, who had listened silently to the conversation which had taken place between her usually shy daughter and Marilyn, had been impressed by the girl's innocent ability to converse with such a sick woman. Adults often found it difficult to converse with anyone who was terminally ill. Suddenly she was taken aback, for Marilyn was looking at Sara with a probing gaze, startling in its penetration and somehow full of wisdom. Then, as sunlight streamed through the nearby window, it looked to her as if a thin vapour emitted from the woman's nose – or was it her lips… or both? – and it was drifting hazily in Sara's direction. It was as if Marilyn was out of doors on a frosty day. But abruptly the sun was obscured by cloud and the moment passed; the vapour was gone. Clearly it had been some sort of illusion. The sick woman was lying back on her pillows, eyes closed, face relaxed and peaceful. It was Vi, who adored anything dramatic, who first realised Marilyn was dead.

CHAPTER ONE

SHAKEN AT HAVING BEEN PRESENT AT THE MOMENT OF death, Jennifer was worried about Sara, not that the girl seemed troubled. In fact, Sara seemed the most calm of the three of them. Perhaps, Jennifer hoped, the girl thought the woman was asleep. Certainly Marilyn *looked* a picture of peace. She and Vi shared the same reaction, which was to protect Sara. Vi quickly pressed her buzzer to summon a nurse, who lethargically approached, reluctant to be separated from the computer, which Vi, in her brisk, no-nonsense way, insisted came between nurses and their wits. However, once the nurse spotted the deceased woman, she hastily pulled the curtains around the bed. By this time Jennifer had hauled her daughter out of the ward.

'Why was she pulling the curtains about Marilyn's bed?' Sara demanded in her high, piping voice.

'Because she's ill. When Grandma was first admitted to the ward, the curtains were always being drawn about her bed. She kept wanting to be sick,' Jennifer explained, sounding inadequate even to her own ears. Why was she finding it difficult to explain to her daughter that someone had died? After all, the girl was hardly a babe in arms.

'Marilyn didn't look as if she wanted to puke,' reasoned

Sara. 'But I expect she'll be feeling better when we come again to see Grammer.'

Grammer. There is was yet again, some kind of in–joke between Vi and Sara, going back to the girl's early childhood when she couldn't pronounce "Grandma". Vi became "Grammer" and seemed to think it hugely amusing. She wouldn't permit any correction, saying it was preferable to Grandma because Grandma sounded ageing. So, she was Grammer, much to Jennifer's disgust There was something immature and silly about it. Suppressing the urge to correct her daughter, instead she muttered, 'I wouldn't be too hopeful about that.'

'Why?'

'They move people from one ward to another. You know, it depends upon the kind of treatment they need,' she stated vaguely. Anyway, she reasoned, surely someone so ill *should* have been placed in a side ward? 'She might be moved to somewhere else.' Her tone invited no further conversation.

Should she say the woman was dead? Jennifer was uncertain. Susan, her neighbour, reckoned that to be an only child was to be over-protected. Well, there was nothing Jennifer could do to remedy that as far as Sara was concerned. Having haemorrhaged badly after giving birth, the solution had been a hysterectomy, since the bleeding simply would not stop. Sara would remain an only child. Anyway, one child was enough. Although they loved her, Sara had been unplanned and highly inconvenient.

Being professional people, Jennifer and Chas had both agreed, prior to their marriage, that children would have no place in their union. Once Jennifer realised she was pregnant, she had seriously considered a termination. It was the logical thing to do. They'd only been married six months. She was twenty-six, a qualified dentist – her doll-like prettiness, her obvious femininity, masked a combination of keen intelligence and ambition – and was a new member of a large dental practice. Chas, then aged thirty, having spent years working and studying, was at last part of a group of solicitors, able to see his name on the signboard above an office: Hill, Philipps and Roseberry. Termination was the answer. She and Chas even consulted a gynaecologist to arrange it… but she couldn't go through with it. Unwanted though the baby might be, it was part of her and part of Chas, who at least had been supportive, if initially unenthusiastic.

'Jen, we will manage financially if you want to keep the baby, and you shall continue with your work, if that's what you want,' he had reasoned. It *was* what she wanted.

'I think we earn enough between us to pay childminders, if not a nanny,' he continued. 'We're young; the big house and big cars can wait. You and I will cope.'

Chas, looking handsome, strong and dependable, had spoken. Jennifer, besotted with him, sighed with relief. Chas would make everything right.

The baby arrived amid high drama. Much to the father's amazement, the tiny infant was cast in the image of both her parents. From birth she had his long limbs and something of her mother's delicate features. Not knowing what to expect from fatherhood, he was not instantly infatuated. It was touch and go initially as to whether Jennifer would actually live. In fear of losing his wife, at the outset Chas barely noticed his daughter. Once Jennifer was safe, he realised the great love he had for his wife was equalled only by his feelings for this tiny scrap of flesh and bone, which was the only description which seemed to accurately sum up his newborn daughter.

As the years passed they lived comfortably. The relationship between Chas and Jennifer continued happily. Both were hugely attractive people, yet, fortunately, both were too absorbed with one another, and their individual work, to be seriously tempted to stray. They both knew they had too much to lose. As for Sara, now aged twelve – rapidly approaching her teens – as far as Chas Roseberry was concerned she was the apple of his eye. Only Jennifer equalled, if not surpassed, her in his affections – his small, petite wife, with her pretty dainty features, green eyes and long, curling dark brown hair, whose image would not be out of place on the cover of a chocolate box. He was satisfied with their sex life too, although Jennifer tended to be modest where nudity was concerned. He didn't mind; it added a certain mystique. They were close – friends as well as lovers – and having seen a lot of marriages collapse – both colleagues and clients – he never took his marriage for granted. People always remarked that Sara favoured him in both looks and physique, but that was always before they'd met Jennifer. Sara's eyes and nose were similar to Jennifer's, in shape. It was because her face, although delicate, was longer than her mother's that gave people the illusion she favoured her father in looks.

As for Jennifer, working in a group practice and used to the compliments of her patients – especially the males – she was comfortable with her looks and her body, even though nudity troubled her. She was physically fit; she and Chas played tennis and badminton regularly – both singles and mixed doubles – with friends. Chas was athletic; she had never known him to be anything else. When they met, she'd been eighteen, impressed by his tall, lean physique, combined with mid-brown wavy hair and blue eyes. Now he was forty-two, heavier than he had been in his twenties but still lean and fit. Sara possessed his long limbs but always seemed at a loss as to how to control them. She had also inherited a portion of her father's easy-going temperament, which was at odds with a sometimes critical, intolerant quality which, Jennifer was reluctant to admit, came from herself. Consequently, mother-daughter relations were often strained. Amazed at the vagaries of genetics, Jennifer often wondered how it had happened that Sara, whose parents both had curly hair, managed to have such a mop of straight hair, which stubbornly refused all efforts to sustain the slightest kink. Vi (whose hair was regularly coloured and permed) said it came from her. Jennifer, whose personality clashed with that of her mother, was unwilling that her daughter should inherit anything from her grandmother – even straight hair. Chas felt likewise.

Having returned home from the hospital, although Sara appeared to be her usual self, Jennifer thought it wise to ensure her daughter was distracted from the hospital scenario. Elsie, the matronly looking woman who was employed as general cleaning lady cum nanny, after being informed of the occurrence, had a suggestion to make.

'Young Simon next door has been getting a kitten. Maybe you should gan in and see it,' she cheerily proposed.

Jennifer inwardly groaned. A kitten! 'Don't come home asking me for a kitten,' she warned. 'I am not having pets in this house.' Some months ago Simon had received a bearded lizard as a gift. That was safe, as Sara hated reptiles. But a kitten?

'Will you come with me, Elsie?' Sara pleaded. Elsie was fun. She had only begun working for her parents a couple of months before, shortly after they'd moved into their current house. But she felt comfortable with the woman, not as if she was constantly in error, as was the case when Mummy was around. Elsie did, however, have a very strong northern accent, which Sara was instructed not to emulate – ever. She was to speak properly.

'Nah, dearie, I canna. I have ta go home. Got to mak dinner for a hungry husband and two teenagers.' Elsie tweaked the girl's nose fondly.

Irritably Jennifer produced her house keys, waving them in Sara's direction.

'Come along, I'll come with you. I need to have a chat with Simon's mother.' Why was it she sometimes felt she was the last person whose company Sara desired?

Simon's house, although next door, was totally different to the one occupied by Chas and Jennifer Roseberry. The small estate where they lived consisted of approximately twenty-five, individually built detached houses. The surrounding area was rural farmland, and all the houses were required to be built in a style appropriate to the character of the locality. The Roseberrys had bought the plot of land, hired an architect and made their own contributions to the design of their home. The result was a traditionally styled, gabled building, which they had moved into just ten weeks before. Chas claimed it reminded him of a rustic Edwardian rectory. He loved Victorian and Edwardian rectories.

One of the problems of holding down a full-time job was that it gave little time to get to know the neighbours. Jennifer knew Simon's parents only because Simon and Sara were friendly, even though they went to different schools. Sara went to a girls-only private school. Simon went to the local comprehensive. This was largely because Susan, his mother, didn't go out to work and they had only one income to rely on. As for the people opposite, they had teenage children who were away at university, and the house seemed to be perpetually empty. Consequently, other than exchanging passing smiles and waves, she knew little about them. Susan was a lively, friendly young woman, with whom Jennifer could have enjoyed a close friendship had she had sufficient time to forge such a relationship.

Chatting amicably to Susan and drinking coffee, she recounted the events of the afternoon, whilst being reassured by Susan's common sense. Marilyn had not died horribly or dramatically, so how could Sara be traumatised by the event?

'Mummy, look at the kitten! Isn't she gorgeous?' Sara's green eyes, so like her mother's in colour, shone with adoration as she held the kitten aloft. 'So small and fluffy!'

Jennifer knew what was coming next.

'May I have one?'

'No. Animals are tying. I told you before we came here, there would be no pets.' Jennifer shook head, her curls bouncing emphatically. 'I might permit a goldfish,' she mused.

'Goldfish aren't cuddly,' was the prompt and accurate response.

'I'm going to call her Snowy because she's white,' Simon, who was a year and a half younger than Sara, informed them.

'Why not call her Sugar? That sounds better than Snowy. Everyone calls white animals Snowy,' Sara proposed helpfully. 'Or else Lily. You know, as in lily white!'

'That's original,' laughed Susan. 'Both names are so original! Simon, call her Sugar!'

'Yes,' agreed Simon thoughtfully.

Original? Jennifer gazed at her daughter in astonishment. Sara was never original. Practical occasionally, sometimes even sensible, but never original. Sara, though she was undoubtedly intelligent, tended to be unimaginative and logical. Like her father.

'Well, sugar is white,' beamed Sara. 'Unless it's brown, of course. So are lilies. You can also say the kitten is called Sugar after the character in *Some Like It Hot*.'

'How would *you* know? You've never seen *Some Like It Hot*,' Jennifer commented.

For a brief moment an adult expression flickered over the child's face, disappearing so quickly Jennifer wondered if she had imagined it.

'Well, I must have seen it, or heard about it, if I know about it,' she stated logically.

'I suppose so,' Jennifer agreed easily.

The Roseberrys lived in Northumberland, the nearest town being Corbridge, some three miles away, where Jennifer worked and Sara went to school. Chas, working in Newcastle, had further to travel. Both of them had been born and reared in busy northern towns, so they relished the rural setting of their new home. However, although she was reluctant to admit it, after having dreamed of living in such a spot, Jennifer was disappointed. She had no desire to move back into a town, but sometimes she felt isolated. There were no shops nearby, and there was no sense of community because everyone, apart from Susan, seemed to be forever at work. But, having always dreamed of living in the country, she was not about to give voice to her misgivings. There was no denying the area was beautiful. Beyond the small estate there were a couple of farms and also a series of elderly rough stone houses with picturesque gardens. There were several pubs within walking distance – hiking distance might be a better description – all of them rustic affairs, oozing with character and plastic plants. Approximately a mile away there was a church, whilst a couple of miles away was the council estate where Elsie lived with her husband and family.

'I think we should start attending church,' voiced Jennifer later in the evening. Chas had returned from work, and they'd all finished eating dinner but were still sitting around the table. 'We hardly know anyone who lives locally, apart from Susan and Elsie. And we only know Elsie because we advertised for a combined nanny and general help.'

Chas grinned, the wickedly suggestive grin which had captivated Jennifer nearly twenty years ago. 'Why not visit the pubs instead? It's a better way to get to know the locals.'

'I'm serious, Chas,' protested Jennifer. 'It's June now. The school holidays will soon be upon us, and poor Sara has no friends of her own age nearby.' Since the girl attended school in Corbridge, and was taken there and back daily by her mother, it meant most of her friends lived in the town itself. 'There must be girls of her own age nearby.'

'We have a large circle of friends. Sara sometimes plays with their children,' shrugged Chas, eyeing the evening newspaper and longing to read it. 'And she's friendly with Simon; they seem to play together happily.'

Somehow Jennifer didn't feel comforted. They ought to try and blend in with the local community.

'I would like to know more girls from nearby,' piped up Sara. 'Simon's alright, but he's a boy. And he's a child. He's more than a year younger than me. Elsie says that during the holidays her daughter Tracy will take me cycling. I can't wait to meet her, but she's quite old. Fourteen.'

Chas ran his fingers through his hair. Never would he admit to any snobbish feelings but, although he was happy enough for Elsie to be the cleaning lady cum nanny, he didn't want his child to mix with Elsie's offspring. He'd met her son Rick – who had several times helped out with some gardening – a tall youth aged eighteen who, had one eyebrow and both ears pierced; the ears were pierced four times each side. His hair was shoulder-length and the badge of the Newcastle United football team was tattooed on one forearm. At least by attending a private school Sara was meeting the kind of children he secretly wished her to mingle with. A clever child, she'd saved her parents much money in school fees by gaining a full scholarship to her school last year. Her parents had been delighted, both with her academic achievement and the money it had saved them.

'I think Tracy will be too old for you,' he protested, convincing himself that this was the root of his objection.

'I would like to go cycling with her! She's a teenager, but I shall be a teenager soon,' mused Sara. 'Maybe when I'm thirteen she won't seem so old. There are no girls my age nearby anyway,' she added. 'Elsie says Tracy is very intelligent, and she often thinks Tracy knows more than her!'

'If we start attending church, and taking Sara to Sunday School, she might meet other girls.'

Jennifer, knowing Chas as she did, knew why he was unwilling for her to mix with Tracy, however intelligent Elsie thought she was. She shared his concern. Having not yet met Tracy, she pictured her as a feminine version of Rick.

'Alright,' said Chas, picking up the newspaper, indicating that the subject was now closed. 'We will give it a try.'

'Good. It's such a pretty looking church, with that lovely little sort of gate, with a roof thing over it, leading into the churchyard. I wouldn't mind going early, you know, before the service starts, so we can look around,' suggested Jennifer, pleased with her success.

'It's a lychgate,' pronounced Sara.

'I beg your pardon?'

Jennifer, poised to load up the dishwasher, regarded her daughter curiously. There it was again. She had not imagined that suddenly adult expression.

'A lychgate,' Sara explained slowly, as if talking to an idiot. 'Many years ago bodies used to lie there prior to burial. Sometimes they lay there overnight. Or longer.'

Opening her mouth, Jennifer shut it again, the words unspoken. She had been about to ask the child how she knew about the lychgate, but her entire manner of speech had been most unchildlike. She must surely be quoting someone.

'Is that what your teacher says?' she voiced at last, bending over the dishwasher, long curls framing her face.

'No,' was the brief reply.

'How did you find out about it, then?' Jennifer began stacking plates and pans with a minimum of noise.

'I don't know,' was the truthful response. 'I guess I read about it.'

'At least you're reading sensible books,' Jennifer commented.

'May I switch the television on?' Sara requested.

'I suppose so.' Troubled, Jennifer studied her retreating daughter. There was something different about her. Maybe the events of the afternoon *had* upset her. Perhaps a good night's sleep would cure it.

As Sara switched the television on, *Look North* was showing. A newsreader was solemnly announcing the death, that afternoon, of the eminent north-east historian and authoress Marilyn Hamilton.

Hearing the announcement, Jennifer scuttled from the kitchen to the living room.

'That's the woman who died today,' she informed Chas.

'Oh... I've heard of her but not read any of her books,' pronounced Chas. 'But she's always spoken of with respect for her accuracy and realism.'

Watching Sara's intense young face, Jennifer tried, and failed, to decipher her daughter's expression.

A couple of mornings later, a Sunday, the three of them trooped to church. The vicar, Alan Reynolds, a friendly and modern young man, was obviously delighted to see a family worshipping together. All too often it was just mother and children who attended. Tea and coffee were available at the end of the service, during which time he not only introduced them to his wife Jilly but also arranged to visit the Roseberrys on the Monday evening.

And so it was that on the appointed evening Jennifer regarded him critically. He didn't look like any vicar she'd ever met before. To begin with, he had long, light brown, curling (but thinning) hair, was in need of a shave, and his clothing was unconventional, consisting of a tee shirt and jeans and no clerical collar. But, probably because of all this, Chas appeared to have taken to him.

'I noticed the service was lively,' Chas was saying, as his wife handed out mugs of coffee. 'I enjoyed it. It was modern, and interesting. Do you play your guitar at every service?'

Alan Reynolds accepted his coffee.

'The early morning service, at eight a.m., is traditional. The evening service at six p.m. is a blend between old and new. The service you attended, at ten a.m., is the liveliest.' Biting into a biscuit, he proceeded to explain, 'You see, we are evangelical, my wife and I. We follow closely the directions for worship given in the Bible. We've set up house groups throughout the parish for the purpose of Bible study and to aid fellowship between individuals. We worship joyfully, using modern songs. But there is also a place for solemnity, as during the giving of Holy Communion.'

A tall, rather angular man of around the same age as Chas, he could not be described as handsome, but his expression was pleasant. He gave a beaming smile as Sara came into the room.

'We welcome children into the congregation. As you observed yesterday, they remain in the church for the beginning of the service, before being taken out to their Sunday School groups.

'I like the way they were given percussion instruments to play, to join in with the first hymn,' reflected Chas. 'Sara really enjoyed herself. She's usually very shy, you know.'

'It was fun,' agreed Sara pensively. 'But there were too many boys in my group. Boys are apt to be silly.'

Alan Reynolds smiled, as if in agreement.

'In the five- to seven-year-old group there are more girls than boys. The distribution is unequal, I guess.'

'We never had Sara baptised,' admitted Jennifer, beginning to find this pleasant vicar exceedingly approachable.

Yesterday, having chatted briefly with his wife Jilly, she found that she too was friendly and approachable, in spite of having frightful dress sense. In fact, she looked nothing like a vicar's wife (her pink skirt and red tee shirt clashed dramatically) but maybe Jilly could be a potential friend. Briefly she wondered about this, before returning to the subject of Sara's lack of baptism, feeling a need to explain the circumstances.

'When she was born, my father and my grandparents were all seriously ill. Subsequently, the three died, and with looking after sick people, plus keeping jobs and looking after a baby, we didn't arrange the baptism. As time moved on, it was something we kept putting aside to do later.'

Lots of children weren't christened, she knew that. But it had always vaguely disturbed her that Sara hadn't been "done".

'Infant baptisms are rather mediaeval,' declared Sara. Again, that disturbingly adult expression was on her face. This time it lingered. 'They used to baptise children in case they died, as they often did in those days. Superstition made them think that if children weren't baptised, they wouldn't go to Heaven. The Bible says nothing about infants needing to be baptised.'

Dumbfounded, Jennifer and Chas gazed at their daughter, each wondering what she had been reading… or watching.

Alan Reynolds looked delighted. 'Quite correct, Sara,' he approved. 'There is no Biblical precedent for infant baptism. But you're twelve now. When you decide you're ready for baptism, tell your mum and dad. They can arrange it with me.'

Gravely the child studied his face. His nose was prominent, his teeth far from even, but it was a cheerful, friendly face, his brown eyes merry.

'I think I'd like to be baptised. I'm ready for it,' she reflected.

'I think we'd better discuss it with you later, Sara,' Jennifer stated warningly. What had come over the girl? She was talking like an old woman! 'When we come to a decision, we can arrange things with Alan.'

'Okay,' nodded Sara, her adult countenance fading. 'I want to go next door to see Sugar,' she declared with childish eagerness. 'I haven't seen her today.'

'Alright,' agreed Chas, thinking regretfully of how his little girl was growing up. She was beginning to sound so sensible. His secretary was forever saying girls grew up more quickly than boys.

At that moment the phone rang.

'I'll get it,' Sara volunteered, as Chas apologised to the vicar that he was expecting a call from a German client and it was important he should take it. Sara's voice was audible as she picked up the phone in the hall.

'Hello? Mr Jaeger? Wie geht es ihnen? Ja… Ich heisse Sara… Ja, tochter. Danke… Sehr gut. Schonen abend noch! Wiedersehen. Daddy, it's Herr Jaeger for you.' She handed the telephone to her father.

Chas, who spoke fluent German, took it, then, murmuring apologies, quit the room to talk privately. How clever of Sara to pick up bits of German. She wasn't learning it through school as yet, so she'd clearly been listening attentively to the recent conversations he'd been having with Herr Jaeger.

Jennifer was dumbfounded.

'How did you learn all that?' she queried as her daughter headed towards the door, bent upon visiting the kitten.

'I don't really know,' she said, her brow puckered in concentration. Echoing Chas's assumptions, she explained, 'It must be through listening to Daddy!'

Sara's baptism was duly arranged, and a date was agreed for mid-July. It was to be held late in the afternoon, before evening service. Feeling guilty, Jennifer refused to admit aloud that she and Chas were using the occasion as an excuse to hold a large party. Not that they always needed an excuse. But by choosing a weekend just before the school holidays, it meant most of their family and friends would be available to attend, before going on vacation.

Chas had a passion for barbecues. Within days of moving into the house, he'd employed builders to construct a large brick barbecue on the patio, near to the conservatory. In turn, the builders were followed by an electrician, wiring coloured lights around the patio area and around the perimeter of the garden. During the past couple of weeks, he'd also arranged for a carpenter to create a rustic-looking shed-like structure around the barbecue, open-fronted but allowing him to shelter from the rain when cooking. By the time the day of the baptism arrived, Jennifer was heartily sick of barbecues. They were dining late most evenings because Chas insisted upon using the barbecue, since it now didn't matter what the weather was like, and it seemed to take him ages to get the food ready. Naturally, some of the food served after the baptism would be barbecued.

'He's talking about getting another one,' Jennifer informed Vi as the family was getting ready to head for the church. 'He wants a gas one, as they're quicker and easier to heat up. And there's room in his new cabin thingy for it. Some of them look like something from a space ship, so I guess, knowing Chas, he'll buy something outrageous!'

Standing with Jennifer and Sara, waiting for Chas to bring his car out of the garage, the older woman looked disapproving.

'I don't like the way he insists on switching those coloured lights on every night. No need for it. Such a waste of electricity. I told him so this morning.' Vi's lips were pursed.

Chas had merely laughed and told her if she didn't like the lights, she shouldn't look out of the window. It was nearly a month since Vi had been discharged from hospital, and she had been staying with the Roseberrys whilst recovering. Having always fancied moving in with her daughter – they had plenty of room – she was unwilling to admit she felt perfectly well now.

As Chas reversed his car out of the garage, Jennifer studied Sara covertly. She was certainly as tall and as thin as ever, but she walked differently. The child had suddenly become more graceful, her posture improved, and she was altogether less ungainly. In fact, she looked totally poised. Amid the flurry of getting into the car, she was saved from responding to her mother's remark. It certainly wasn't comfortable having her around; she was taking over the household, telling Elsie how to do her job, reorganising cupboards and criticising Jennifer's decor. Too few ornaments, Vi had observed yesterday, followed by suggesting maybe she should bring some knick-knacks from her own home. Jennifer and Chas had ignored the suggestion.

Driving towards the church, Chas eyed his wife appreciatively. She looked a vision, wearing a new outfit for the occasion, a short straight skirt, with matching, fitted, short-sleeved jacket in Parma violet. This, combined with a fetching hat in a similar shade, ensured she exuded a dainty elegance. Jennifer certainly knew how to dress, he decided approvingly.

'It's not far to the church. I think we should have walked. Such a waste of petrol.'

The comment came from the back seat, where Vi, her concrete waves immaculate, refused to wear her seat belt in case it creased her pristine white blouse.

'Too hot to walk!' Sara wound the window down, enjoying the breeze. She was wearing a yellow sundress, donned only minutes before getting into the car. Already it was sticking damply to her back.

'You can walk if you want,' Chas informed Vi cheekily.

She was silent for the remainder of the short journey but looked grim as he parked the car outside the Church.

It was cool inside. The thick walls and high lofty ceiling ensured it was always cool. The building was packed with friends and relatives, some attired more formally than others. Having reluctantly bowed to Jennifer's suggestion that Elsie be invited, along with husband and family, Chas spotted Rick, already looking bored, clad in jeans, a black tee shirt with a luminous silver skull of the front, and with his hair tied back in a pony tail. Surely Elsie could have persuaded him to wear something suitable? As for Jennifer's marine engineer younger brother Neil, a bachelor who had loved to defy convention all of his life, he was wearing shorts, a sports shirt and sandals. But at least he didn't have earrings and tattoos. And his hair was short.

With a sense of pride, Jennifer watched misty-eyed as with grave dignity Sara leaned over the font, allowing Alan Reynolds to sprinkle water over her. The girl was improving in looks, largely because her hair was slightly longer, and it was amazing the difference it made. A month ago Sara had pointedly refused to have it trimmed, since it made her face look too long. An extra inch, she stated firmly, would make a great difference. Taken aback at the girl's cool knowing manner, Jennifer had agreed to the suggestion. Sara had also suggested the bulk of her heavy fringe be allowed to grow out and be swept back with a hair slide, with only a light fringe sweeping her brow. Jennifer, slowly approving of the change, wondered why she hadn't thought of it herself. Lately she'd been constantly taken aback at the things the child uttered. In fact, she felt she wasn't talking to a child at all.

After the service, everyone, including Alan and Jilly Reynolds, assembled at the Roseberrys' home. There were approximately forty guests, some congregating in the garden, whilst others, preferring to be out of the heat, sat in the house. The smell of barbecuing food attacked the nostrils of the hungry, whilst Jennifer laid an array of cold meats and salads on the dining room table, along with an assortment of bread rolls. In the fridge the shelves were laden with assorted gateaux and trifles, along with chilled bottles of white wine. Neil, her elder brother, looking comfortable in his shorts and open-necked shirt, enthusiastically opened several bottles of red wine, prior to helping Chas with the barbecue. Out of the corner of her eye, she could both see and hear Vi apologising to Alan and Jilly for the disgusting amount of alcohol being served at a baptismal function. Alan and Jilly, both serenely drinking lager, happily brushed her apologies aside.

Sara, having greeted the children of her parents' friends, felt momentarily at a loss. Until now she'd always enjoyed their company, but suddenly they seemed so childlike, even though some of them were older than herself. She had wanted to be baptised, but now it was done she could only heartily wish everyone would go home. All she'd really wanted was the baptismal ceremony. Her attention was caught by an older girl, of perhaps medium height. She was clad fashionably in a blouse and short skirt, with her gleaming auburn hair caught up in a clasp on top of her head. The girl was approaching and smiling, looking directly into her eyes. For a fleeting moment Sara felt as if something actually skimmed against her mind. She knew what that meant…

'I'm Tracy, Elsie's daughter.' The older girl continued to smile pleasantly, speaking in a voice that was warm and melodious. It was also devoid of Elsie's broad accent. 'You and I are the same.'

'Yes, we are,' agreed Sara cautiously. 'How old are you?'

Tracy gave a rich, mellow laugh.

'Officially, I'm fourteen. The reality… over one thousand years old. I was born in Byzantium in nine hundred and ninety-eight A.D.… or thereabouts. Of course, no records were kept. Charlemagne was already a legend, and my earliest memory is of people talking about him with awe.'

'And I thought I was old,' Sara reflected quietly. 'I'm just getting used to my new habitat. I felt incomplete not being baptised,' she admitted, smiling with sudden relief at meeting a being such as herself. Her smile was now attractive; there was something enigmatic about it, due to the fact she'd just learned how to smile without revealing the braces on her teeth.

En route to the kitchen to find some barbecue sauce, Chas, whose hearing was acute, overheard the beginning of Sara's statement and refrained from giving a delighted laugh. Sara was twelve and thought she was old! He must remember to tell Jennifer about it later!

Feeling it prudent to lower her voice further, Sara murmured, 'I was born in this country, in approximately fourteen forty. No record was made of my birth – probably because I was only a girl. I saw the devastation caused by the War of the Roses.'

'Do you ever feel weary?' For a moment Tracy's bright young face looked worn and haggard.

'Sometimes,' Sara admitted sadly. 'Once I inhabited a body until she reached the age of eighty… which was remarkable considering it was the seventeenth century. When she died I moved into a young woman and was amazed at the surge of vitality I felt,' she mused aloud. 'My last body was that of a relatively young woman, but she was riddled with cancer so she too felt old. When I entered this one I felt renewed, but it's not always wise to inhabit the body of a child. I've lived too long to convincingly act the part of a child. I keep saying the wrong things. But you know how it is – the child's body will soon mature.'

'We have all the time in the world,' Tracy nodded solemnly. 'I too usually avoid the very young, but like yourself I found my former body was ill and weary. I relished the thought of lodging in someone youthful. I went a bit too young though. This body was only eight years old when I began to use it! I am pleased to have found you… one such as myself. We know the past, endure the present, whilst the future is a mystery to us,' she stated poetically. 'I sometimes think that since we cannot die it would be helpful to foresee the future.'

Sara nodded, understanding. 'It would help with the decisions we make, certainly,' she whispered, for Chas was appearing, carrying a bottle of wine in one hand and a bottle of barbecue sauce in the other. Neil, conspicuous in his shorts, remained beside the barbecue. 'It would be wonderful if we could foretell the future. When I was born, it was into a Lancastrian household during the War of the Roses. Henry the sixth of Lancaster was king. There seemed to be perpetual unrest, interspersed with fighting. Then Edward of York was crowned. Financially my family lost so much. It's a long time since I met one such as myself. I am so pleased to meet you.'

'Yes, there are so few of us,' agreed Tracy. Others were encroaching on what little privacy they had. Hastily she squeezed her new friend's hand. 'I'm in contact with an incubus who lives in London. We meet whenever possible. He's famous. He both fronts and narrates historic documentaries on TV. His excellent knowledge of history is very useful!'

An expression of sorrow crossed Sara's young, unlined features. 'I've not met with one of my kind for some years. It's easy to be separated through circumstances.'

'We must meet soon, to exchange memories,' the teenager suggested.

'Yes please.'

'Look at those two; they look like two solemn old women.' Vi, in spite of disapproving of the alcohol, was walking past them with a decanter of sherry and a tray of glasses. Somehow sherry seemed civilised.

Exchanging wry smiles, the girls parted. Turning, Sara saw Jennifer, also carrying a tray laden with drinks.

'I'll help you, Mum?' she suggested.

Jennifer nearly dropped her tray. Sara was invariably oblivious to domestic duties, although she was willing enough to help if asked. But she *always* had to be asked. Then there was the sudden use of "Mum" and "Dad" – no longer Mummy and Daddy. And Vi… Vi was no longer "Grammer" – she was Gran… and didn't like it; she said it made her sound aged.

'There's a small tray in the kitchen. Just load a few glasses of wine onto it and offer them around,' she replied, looking as surprised as she felt.

CHAPTER TWO

A FTER THE BAPTISM, TRACY BEGAN VISITING AFTER school, arriving on her bicycle; she and Sara would then go cycling together. In spite of earlier misgivings, Chas was happy enough for them to venture off together. Tracy seemed a sensible, well-mannered young person, plus it was almost the end of term so neither of them would fall behind with their studies. It was Jennifer who was uneasy about the friendship.

'What can a fourteen-year-old have in common with a twelve-year-old?' she demanded of her mother, early on the Tuesday evening, whilst wondering why was it that Sara always managed to be a source of irritation?

'It's only two years,' shrugged Vi, energetically washing the dinner dishes, her bosom heaving with exertion. She could never bring herself to approve of the dishwasher. 'Less than two years really.' *Really, Jennifer does fuss so*, she reasoned.

'*Nearly* two years is a lot when you're as young as twelve,' frowned Jennifer.

'Well, they chatter away like crickets. Chatter chatter, non-stop. And at least young Tracy doesn't have an accent like her mother. Or "ma" as Elsie would say. You should hear the queer things they come out with. Talking in Latin, they were yesterday, when you were at work.'

'Sara can't speak Latin!' Jennifer exclaimed.

'Can now.' Vi swatted at a fly with a soapy hand. 'She must have learned at school. I might not be as educated as you, my girl, but I know Latin when I hear it. Maybe Tracy's been teaching her.' She gave a triumphant nod, signalling the end of the discussion.

Sighing, Jennifer wondered how to suggest it was time Vi returned to her own home? She was certain her mother was fully recovered from her illness. Although she often complained of indigestion, Jennifer was confident it was due to over-eating and not to a potential relapse. Her mother, she suspected, would love to move in with them and was playing on her recent sickness.

Half an hour later she opened her daughter's bedroom door to find her studying her face in the mirror. There was more curiosity than vanity in the girl's demeanour. She was intently examining her skin, pinching it, then watching with a curious satisfaction as the firm young flesh immediately fell into place.

'Your gran says you've been speaking Latin,' Jennifer remarked.

'I have learned some,' was the cautious response, as Sara unhurriedly turned away from the mirror. 'I'll be learning it from September. In addition to German.' She'd already been studying French during the past year.

'You will be taught Latin properly in due course,' objected Jennifer. 'Tracy might not be… well, she might not be saying it correctly… grammatically, I mean.'

'Have I done something wrong?' The girl's childish face was solemn.

Jennifer felt guilty. *DO I pick on her?* she wondered.

'I don't want you to develop bad habits,' she replied. 'I know from my schooldays how easy it is to develop bad habits with languages, although my school didn't have Latin on the curriculum.'

'Don't worry, Mother, I'll be alright.'

The response was calm and accompanied by a reassuring smile, akin to the soothing smile a nurse might give an anxious patient. It was not the sort of smile a twelve-year-old girl gave to her mother. *Mother?* Since when had Sara begun calling her mother? Feeling as if she was speaking to someone older than herself, Jennifer gave up on the conversation, largely because she had no idea what to say.

At that moment the telephone rang, and speaking on the other end was Elsie, inquiring as to the possibility of coming later than usual the next day. Rick had had one of his nipples pierced, and it had gone septic. She wanted to take him to see a doctor.

'Come whenever you're ready. My mother will look after things.' Jennifer was hardly listening to Elsie's explanation. 'Elsie, by the way, how long has Tracy been speaking Latin?' Her voice was hurried, flustered.

'She canna speak Latin,' was the bewildered reply.

'She's been speaking Latin with Sara.' Jennifer was feeling out of her depth. Lately, where Sara was concerned, it was becoming a habit.

'Oh, well, she must be learning it at school. She never told me owt about it, but then teenagers tell you nowt. She's a clever girl,' was the easy retort. 'The French teacher says her progress is amazing and she has a real ear for the language!' Elsie's voice rang with pride.

It finally registered with Jennifer – *Rick had his nipple pierced?* Shuddering at the thought, she joined Chas who was sitting in the romantically illuminated garden, in spite of it being a cool, damp evening. Just as she was about to report her bewilderment to him, Vi joined them, chattering volubly, suggesting it might be a good idea to paint the dining room a warm pink. The current pastel green was just a touch unwelcoming in her opinion. Sighing inwardly, Jennifer wondered yet again: *How soon can we expect her to return to her own home?* She would certainly have to be back in her own home by the time Chas, herself and Sara went on their family holiday. Much as she loved her mother, Jennifer had no intention of taking her on holiday… or of allowing her to move in permanently.

Late that night, when about to get ready for bed, Jennifer finally managed to chat to Chas, telling him about her unease.

'I'm worried,' she concluded. 'She's changing before our eyes.'

'Jen, what are you saying?' frowned Chas, who was already in bed, reading a murder thriller. Jennifer often teased him about the macabre books he enjoyed for late-night reading.

'I don't know what I'm saying.' Jennifer ran her fingers fretfully through her hair. 'Maybe we should take her to see a doctor… a paediatrician or something?'

'She's growing up, that's all. She's done nothing wrong or destructive, has she?' he reasoned, closing his book.

'Stop being so logical!' Jennifer protested. Turning on her heel, she marched into the bathroom to change into a pretty cotton nightgown. Returning to the bedroom, she perched on the bed, taking one of his hands. 'Chas, nowadays when I talk to Sara I feel as if I'm talking to someone older than myself!'

Chas gave a guffaw of laughter. 'That's because she's heading for her teens.'

'She's still only twelve,' she objected, adding, 'Well, for a couple of months she's still only twelve. As for teenagers, I know they think they know everything. I did too when I was a teen! But until now Sara has always been so young for her age.'

'I told you, she's growing up. Quickly. She's a bright girl. How can she not be? We're both intelligent people. She has good genes,' he soothed.

'Too quickly,' was the brisk retort.

'Well, what do you think will happen if we go to see a doctor?' Chas answered this himself. 'Psychiatric assessment. For us as well as her probably.'

'I don't want that,' was Jennifer's quick reply. 'You know, when she eventually starts looking for a job, her prospective employer might ask if she has any psychiatric history.'

'Jen, I think you *are* heading in the direction of having her assessed by a shrink,' reasoned Chas.

'No, that isn't what I had in mind,' Jennifer mused aloud, adding: 'Well, really I don't know what I had in mind! Anyway, if we take her to see a doctor we might end up with social workers involved and that would be a disaster! They'd probably send her to a foster home or something! I'll just have to think about it,' she concluded, dissatisfied.

'What do you remember most from your early days? Does this ring any bells?'

It was Saturday on the weekend following the baptism, and the girls were at Vindolanda, having been driven there by Elsie, who was sitting alone and contented in the coffee bar, glad to be out of the way of Mrs Roseberry's mother. The woman followed her around the house inspecting her cleaning. If Mrs Roseberry was pleased with her standards, then Vi should be too, in her opinion. She could only assume Mrs Roseberry took after her father. Consequently, she was more than happy to act as chauffeur and take the girls out for a few hours, especially since she was being paid to do so – Jennifer and Chas had arranged a mixed doubles tennis match with some friends. Nor did Elsie believe Vi's claim that she was still too weak to drive. That woman was as sound as an ox, she was certain of it!

Tracy and Sara wandered around, unhurried and relaxed in demeanour. It was not a warm day, but at least it was dry. They both carried jackets, at Elsie's insistence, 'Just in case.' Sara, who had asked the question, was standing on top of a reconstructed Roman fort, gazing at the view. All she knew of the Roman era was gleaned from history books; it was centuries before her time.

Looking around, turning in a complete circle, Tracy studied the landscape and the reconstructed fort.

'I've seen similar things,' she replied, 'but I wasn't born during the great days of the Roman Empire. My earliest memories are of heat in Byzantium. We had a lifestyle adapted to the heat. And of course there was dust. Lack of water was an abiding fear. I don't know when I lost that fear, but it took many years. Centuries. What about you? What are your earliest recollections?'

'Mud,' was the prompt reply. 'I guess you had too little water, and I had too much! It was impossible stuff to walk in, and there was always lots of it, ensuring one's feet were held in an embrace of powerful suction with each and every step. My clothes – and everyone else's, of course – were always splattered with the stuff. Always mud. And cold. I laugh when I see modern Christmas cards. So romantic, with white snow decorating the roofs of thatched cottages, or else with Victorian carol singers holding lanterns. The reality was so different. Mud. Or muddy snow. Or else the ground would be rock hard, and the chill seemed to work its way into one's bones. Trudging to church on Christmas Day with numb hands and feet. And the smells! The smell of tallow candles – so much smellier than modern candlewax. And bodies, unwashed bodies. We were used to that, though. Even though I began to take care to inhabit bodies belonging to people of wealth and education, I still had to endure the mud, the cold and the smells. Probably I smelled no better than the next person. Then there was pregnancy. I was constantly pregnant. Centuries of being pregnant. Except for a few years when I used the body of a nun. That was bliss!'

Gazing into space, Sara recalled her first memorable Christmas, the year she realised she was not quite the same as everyone else.

To begin with, she always felt as if she could easily allow her mind leave her body. In fact, she often allowed it to do so, jumping into other people's minds, if only for an instant. When she left her own body it sat there, inert, looking vacant, making other people wonder what the matter with her was. She was called Maude in those early days. Maude Dubreise, descendent of a wealthy Norman family that had come to England with the Conqueror. With a child's quickness, she realised, or sensed, that other people didn't leave their bodies. Also, it was being commented upon that she was different.

'Maude, you must try to stop looking vacant,' her mother reproved, before the Christmas feast began. Her mother at that time was called Celine Dubreise, a woman who was not a beauty but who possessed the skills to make the best of herself. 'Suitors – bridegrooms – might be put off if they discover their future wife gazes into space like… like…' Words failed Celine. 'You must try to stop doing it, or you shall be soundly whipped. I know your father has a most suitable husband in mind for you in the future,' she whispered mysteriously. 'You must be worthy of him.'

'Yes, my lady mother,' the young Maude solemnly replied.

She was all of eight years old. It was comforting rather than threatening to know the security of a suitable husband awaited her. It did not occur to her to ask questions regarding the identity of her would-be bridegroom.

The Dubreise family lived in a moated manor house near Tewkesbury. Like most of the landowners, their fortunes were currently in decline following the ignominious end of the Hundred Years War with France. The Dubreises' were short of money and short of men to till the soil. Maude heard adults whispering about the defeat, although some people claimed England had won. *Surely they should know if they had won or lost*, reasoned Maude. There had been great battles, which were boasted of aloud; words such as Crecy and Agincourt rolled proudly from people's lips. Both definite English victories; no one disputed those two battles. But child though she was, she suspected France had won, without knowing what it was France had actually won. She didn't really care. She was secure. A husband had been found for her, and she must stop acting strangely.

Having made this resolve, she sat at the festive table, clad in her best gown. The light from the candles, flattering to the complexions of older people, made her mother look like a girl again. By the time the food was served, some mummers and tumblers had arrived to entertain them, and with a child's ability to forget everything but the present moment she gave her attention to the celebrations. That Christmas passed away, but the sounds and smells lingered in her mind.

Years slipped by, and outwardly she behaved like any other child of her class. But sometimes, usually when she was in bed and supposed to be asleep, she would peer curiously into the mind of one of the serving wenches, hired to look after the children. Somehow or other, she knew that if she wished to she could remain there, a permanent lodger, able to absorb the mind that already existed. But if she did, what would happen to her own body?

At the age of twelve she was formally betrothed to Gilbert de Laiche, who, like herself, was of Norman descent. She had met him four times and found him pleasant enough to behold. True, he was not very tall and tended to be overweight, but his features were pleasing. His teeth were sound, which was a huge bonus. He was young too, only three years older than herself. However, the best thing about the union was that she would be living within a half day's journey of her home! The de Laiche family lived at the Manor of Upton, on the banks of the River Severn.

By the time she was fourteen, and her wedding feast approached, she had three younger sisters and three younger brothers. She used to have an older brother, but he'd died of the belly pains, a mysterious and feared illness, which caused a hitherto healthy person to be suddenly bent double with agonising cramps, accompanied by flux. No one, not even the monks at the infirmary, knew how to cure it. Maude herself, tutored by her mother, was knowledgeable regarding the use of herbs and cooking. Herb lore was her especial skill. Spinning, weaving and sewing required effort on her part. Her hands were large, almost like a man's, and she could not apply herself to such feminine tasks with ease. But she could manage. She had to; such domestic crafts were necessary in order to clothe the household. As for reading and writing, they were not part of her education. Such skills were unnecessary for a girl. 'I was never taught and it's done no harm to me,' her mother declared, when Maude once requested to be tutored with her bothers, who could read and write. 'Men hate educated women!' *Men hate educated women*. It was a statement Maude would hear many times throughout the centuries.

At the time of her wedding, which took place only days after her fifteenth birthday, rumours were circulating about the King, Henry the Sixth of Lancaster. Some claimed him to be a living saint; others denounced him for being a weak-minded fool. Whatever the truth was, it was mooted that the Queen, the unpopular Marguerite of Anjou, was in fact ruler of the realm. Maude, still absorbed in her own secure world, didn't care. Her wedding day was approaching fast, and her life would irrevocably change. She would be mistress of her own household, for, although Gilbert's father, Sir Giles, was alive, his mother had long been dead, and his younger sister, who would herself be soon wedded, currently held the household keys. Naively, she failed to see how her future could be affected by the King who ruled the realm. Her only concern was the forthcoming separation from her mother.

As the great day drew ever more near, her stomach churned when she thought of her bridegroom. He looked kind, so perhaps he would be a gentle lover. Maiden though she was, she knew exactly what happened on a wedding night, partly through listening to servants' gossip, but also because there was little privacy in a manor house. Although there was a guest room at the Dubreise manor, only the master and mistress actually possessed their own bedchamber, and even they shared their quarters with visitors on some occasions. Her ability to creep into the minds of others, however, made her more knowledgeable than most maids. She knew some liked the marriage act, others feared it, hated it. But men were usually enthusiastic. In fact, whenever she looked into the mind of a male, it seemed he thought of little else.

The root of her fear lay in the knowledge that she was not a pretty maid. The polished metal mirror in her parents' chamber told her that. She wanted to impress Gilbert, although she knew, because her mother had often told her, that love would come later. Her hair was auburn and truly beautiful. Hanging in two plaits reaching almost to her knees, it gleamed becomingly. But, once married, it meant most of her glorious mane would be covered by a veil. She was plump, but not plump in a comely way. Large-boned, with big, irregular features, she certainly did not favour her beauteous mother in appearance. Apart from her hair, her only other beauty was her teeth. Whilst many a beauty was marred by uneven, protruding or even decayed teeth, hers were white and even. 'Make sure you smile at him,' her mother had advised. Maude knew only too well why she received this instruction.

On her wedding day she looked as well as was possible. Her under tunic was of an amber colour, her surcoat of deep green and trimmed with fox fur. Her hair – worn unbound and without a veil to symbolise her virginity – flowed about her person as if it had a life of its own.

She was unsure of how impressed Gilbert de Laiche was, his features remained impassive throughout the wedding ceremony. But her new father-in-law, Sir Giles de Laiche, was clearly approving.

'There is a mare that will provide fine heirs,' he proclaimed jovially at the wedding banquet. 'If she does not produce sons, 'twill not be her fault,' he nudged his son conspiratorially.

Sons. She had to produce sons. It was expected of her. Mechanically eating, Maude pondered over this new responsibility. Men blamed their wives if they didn't produce sons. Why, her father's steward regularly beat his wife for giving birth only to daughters. Would that be her fate? Such a possibility had never occurred to her before. Her childhood, which she had clung to overlong, suddenly slipped away. She was a wife now, and tomorrow – after spending tonight at her old home – she would move to Upton. And there she would remain. Stoically she chewed on roast swan, a meat she had never favoured but felt duty bound to enjoy. No one would ever dream of criticising the fact that it was tough and dry – even when served with Chaudron sauce – for, after all, it cost more than three shillings for a single bird!

Gilbert de Laiche, clearly as inexperienced as herself, did at least prove, on their wedding night, to be gentle, considerate and as bashful as she. And, of course, they had already met prior to their wedding, which was a bonus. For some newlyweds, their first meeting was at the altar. In consequence, when she quit her home the following morn, it was a sad parting from her mother but not a traumatic farewell. Her mother shed a few maternal tears, for Maude was her eldest daughter and the first to leave. Then Maude, of course, had the security of knowing she would, in the future, at least be able to meet with her parents. Other maids were less fortunate. They had to travel far and never saw their parents again.

'I shall see you soon, most likely for the baptism of your firstborn!' her mother whispered after giving a final embrace.

'Then I hope to conceive quickly!' Maude whispered in reply.

So, riding pillion behind her new husband, she was carried to Upton. Years of familiarity with her old home, accompanied by the fact she had never travelled far and had little with which to compare, made her unappreciative of it. She had never considered how many luxuries it contained. There was a solar for the ladies to retire to, there to work in peace. Her parents had their own bedchamber, and there was also a chamber used for guests, loaned to herself and Gilbert for their wedding night. There was a chapel, storehouses, cookhouse, dairy and buttery, stabling for horses, pens for fowl, and a herb garden. All of this was encircled by a fortified wall and entered via a gatehouse. Surrounding the entire structure was a moat. Upton, however, built upon a beauteous setting on a bank of the River Severn, was smaller, a solitary building, surrounded by a wall.

The ground floor was taken up with the cookhouse and dairy, and a cellar was used as a food store. The upper floor, reached by an external staircase, contained the dining hall. Above the hall, at one end, was a gallery, leading to the only bedchamber. The floor, Maude noted, was covered with foul rushes, looking as if the entire place had not been sweetened for many months. Edith, Gilbert's sister, was clearly a poor chatelaine, but having no mother to teach her it was probably excusable, Maude thought kindly, for Gilbert's mother had died at least five years before. There was an air of neglect about the place, and with the optimism of youth she was undaunted. It could be remedied.

During the following months, speculation abounded regarding war between the ruling House of Lancaster and the great House of York. Richard, Duke of York, fancied himself as King, it was said. And there were many to support him, given the mental weakness of King Henry. Maude scarcely listened. She was happy. She missed the comfort of her old home but had soon adapted to her new surroundings. The house benefited from her expertise – learned from Celine, who was a diligent tutor to her daughters. Edith too benefited. Four months after Gilbert and Maude's wedding, she married and quit Upton, having received much knowledge from Maude herself.

Unafraid of hard work, Maude set about first reforming the lower floor and cellars, sharply berating those who had grown slovenly having had no real mistress to chivvy them. Then she turned her attention to the hall, ensuring it was polished from floor to hammer beam ceiling. It smelled better too, thanks to fresh rushes, changed at least every two months. Tables, chairs and benches were scrubbed, whilst Maude, sleeves rolled up and helping with the work herself, unconsciously won the respect of the servants. Here was a mistress not too proud to work. But she wanted a solar of her own. Also, at night, she and Gilbert had little real privacy. Giles had charitably given them his curtained four-poster bed, which, when the curtains were drawn, at least gave them the illusion of being alone. But Giles himself slept in the same chamber on a pallet, whilst Edith, until her own marriage, slept on a truckle bed underneath the four-poster. As for the servants, a serving man also slept in the bedroom, in case he was required, as did a serving wench. The remainder of the servants slept on the benches in the hall.

For the time being, as a temporary solar, she had a folding screen made, which, when placed in a corner of the hall, gave her something to retire behind. There, with some of the women, she attended to the sewing and mending, whilst Gilbert and Giles conducted their day-to-day business in the remainder of the hall.

Gilbert, who appeared to be getting more and more fond of her, readily agreed it was time to make alterations to the house, and those alterations *should* include a solar. They were not rich, but some changes could be afforded. Giles, who was still head of the family, refused.

'The house can be made bigger when it has cause to be so. When you, my lady,' he stared meaningfully at Maude, 'prove you can breed.'

Blushing, Maude said nothing. After little more than a month of marriage, she was sure she was pregnant. Mattie, a servant who had been appointed as her personal maid, was certain of this too. But Maude, apprehensive yet excited, desired silence on this subject, at least for the time being. However, it was not a fact that could be hidden for long, and soon Gilbert – also excited yet apprehensive – knew he would be a father within ten months of his marriage. 'I told you she was a mare who would provide fine heirs,' was Giles' dour response upon learning the happy news.

And so it was that, within three years of marriage, Maude, who had only just passed her eighteenth birthday, realised she was pregnant for the third time, having already produced two sons. To her great pleasure she was able to inspect some building work being carried out to Upton Manor, which included her much-desired solar. They had been happy years. In spite of her lack of personal beauty, Gilbert, who was not often forthcoming when it came to expressing emotion, actually loved her, whilst she was content with him. This was all she had ever hoped for, for romantic love was something few ever attained. Her old life was growing rapidly distant, and on the occasions when she did visit her old home it was akin to visiting something from a dream. In fact, the only thing she really missed was having a chapel in close proximity to her home. At Upton, there being no chapel attached to the manor, she had to walk to the monastery church a mile away. Being devout in her faith, she preferred to attend Mass daily. It might not be far, but in summer, if she was heavily pregnant, the journey left her hot and flustered, whilst in winter the cold seeped through to her bones. When it rained, she always ended up covered in mud, as did everyone else. It was some solace that when she was due to be confined, the priest, who usually visited the house once or twice a week to save her making the journey, would then visit the household daily to deliver the sacrament. Her husband, impressed by her gentle piety, promised her a chapel in the very near future. 'Then you can have a priest attached to the household and can make confession and attend Mass five times a day if you wish,' he assured her fondly. There was nothing she desired more. She had never aspired to jewels or fine clothes; a chapel was her one desire. She had a kind husband, two sturdy sons, a home that was not magnificent but one that she was satisfied with. She was grateful to God for her blessings, and felt, therefore, that she ought to thank Him. Regularly.

By this time even she couldn't turn her eyes from the fact that there was war within the country: Lancaster against York. Both by birth and marriage, her allegiance was to the House of Lancaster, and she did not question that the rightful King would win. As yet they were hardly affected by outside events, although Gilbert doubted they could remain so. A mother now, fearful for the future of her husband and children, Maude was anxiously aware of how precarious her contented existence was. Yes, she wanted to thank God regularly, but she also needed to ask Him to keep her loved ones safe. They awaited the outcome of the clashes between the two great houses. At the same time, she wondered if she would be perpetually with child for years to come. Certainly she had been happy to conceive for the third time, but after this babe a break of a few years would be welcome. Yet she felt guilty at being weary of her condition, for it was a woman's duty to conceive and bear children. At least Gilbert didn't turn to serving wenches, which many men, including her own father, did when their wives were great with child. She had heard that if a woman nursed her own children, it guaranteed freedom from pregnancy. She had nursed both of her sons herself, and had, on each occasion, fallen pregnant whilst doing to. Mattie said it was miraculous.

Rumours filtered through to them regarding the King. He was known to be a pious man, given to spending hours in prayer. But some claimed he was a lunatic. Indeed, during the few months when Richard Duke of York was Regent, the King was reputedly clean out of his senses. Then came word that the King had regained his sanity, and Richard of York was banished from court. Next, there was news of a battle between the houses of York and Lancaster at St Albans. Whilst this made Gilbert uneasy, at Upton the event did not touch them, for as yet there was no levy of money or men required from them. It was not until Maude was nearing twenty, married for nigh on five years and with child for the fourth time, that rivalry between York and Lancaster developed into open warfare, leading to a battle at Wakefield and yet another battle at St Albans. The House of York was defeated, and Richard Duke of York executed.

There was celebratory banqueting at Upton, for the Lancastrian cause was theirs. After all, Henry was an anointed King. He ruled by God's will. They owed him their allegiance. This time they had paid money into the Lancastrian coffers, and men had been dispatched to fight, leaving farmlands short of workers. Anxiously they hoped most of them would return.

Giles was now dead – having rejoiced in seeing no less than three grandsons born to the de Laiche family – and Gilbert was Lord of the Manor. Were it not for an injury, Gilbert – who, according to his status, was trained for knightly combat – would have been required to fight for the House of Lancaster. The injury had occurred some time ago and was due to what had begun as a trivial incident. Giles, still alive and determined to celebrate the baptism of his third grandchild, had done so liberally, encouraging Gilbert to do likewise. Gilbert had awoken in the night with a need to visit the garderobe. Returning to bed, having relieved himself, he had fallen. He'd then clambered into bed feeling as if no injury had been sustained. However, the next morning, he could barely move, so painful was his lower spine. In time the pain had eased, but Gilbert was unable to sit on a horse. 'I must needs travel in a litter like an old man,' he grumbled. Maude silently blessed the injury, and equally silently gave thanks to God for it. At least Gilbert could not go to war; were it otherwise, he would surely have done so. Gilbert would always do his duty.

A few more years sped past, and by the time she was twenty-one Maude was mother of four boys, and yet again with child.

Childbirth, so hazardous to many women, seemed to come easily to her, and this time she accepted her fate without question or resentment. Like Mattie, the local midwife, in awed admiration, had told her, it was mightily unusual to fall pregnant whilst still nursing. Unusual or not, Maude knew now that she was likely to spend most of her married life in such a condition. Fortunately, unlike many women, she actually increased in energy whilst breeding (at least until the last few cumbersome weeks) and having an aversion to submitting her babes to a wet nurse, as many women of her station did, she hoped to be able to continue feeding her precious infants herself, whilst effortlessly continuing with her duties as she did so.

As her fifth child grew within her, money in the de Laiche household was scarce. By this time Edward, son of the executed Richard of York, had seized the throne, and the cause of Lancaster was lost. Or so it seemed for the time being. They had heavily supported the cause and had lost both money and men. Notwithstanding the losses, Maude remained content. Her sense of being different to other people – owing to her strange ability to move into the minds of others – had receded. It did not occur to her that this was due to having little time to ponder upon the matter, or even to try to investigate the minds of others. Every day was full; she worked hard and willingly. Her figure, lamented as a girl because of her large frame, was a blessing, just as she had once blessed Gilbert's injury. Adversity sometimes had its uses! The Lord God, she decided, had not designed her for a ladylike purpose. It was not her destiny to sit upon a chair and embroider. She was tall and strong; her fate was to work. Gilbert was not destined to go into battle. God was good.

The manor had continued to change since her marriage. An extra wing had been added, whilst the outer walls had been strengthened. Also, at last (to her huge delight) she had her chapel, and her own confessor attached to the household. There was further work still to be done but the depleted coffers meant it must wait. Throughout the neighbourhood she was becoming renowned as a wise, good and pious woman, meaning that many came to her seeking advice and prayer. Gilbert, approving of her piety, jokingly suggested that maybe they should request payment for her advice and prayers. But he was proud of her, thankful for the peace that marriage to a good and pious woman had brought to him.

Rumour circulated, stating that the old King, Henry the Sixth of Lancaster, wandered the realm a fugitive, but it was the Queen and her son to whom Lancastrian supporters now looked, and it was claimed they were safely in France. They rejoiced that the young prince was growing fast, for his monk-like father – dismissed as either saint or lunatic – was unfit to rule, even in the opinion of his most loyal supporters. All looked to his son. But, as ever, at Upton life continued quietly, in spite of turmoil in high places.

A decade later Maude was in her thirty-first year. Her eldest son, turned sixteen, ought, according to custom, to have been sent to some neighbouring castle, there to learn the art of chivalry and skill in armed combat. But Gilbert, following that seemingly trivial accident, was becoming more and more an invalid. He had little feeling in his left leg and walked with the aid of a stick. In consequence it fell to Giles, their firstborn, to attend to much of the day-to-day running of the house and lands which would one day be rightfully his. Geoffrey, their second son, had been away for more than a year now and wrote regularly – letters which Maude could not read – telling of a life that seemed filled with excitement to her unsophisticated mind. If Giles was envious, it was well hidden. He had inherited his parents' amiable disposition, except when it came to the matter of marriage.

Nearly a year ago Giles had fallen in love with the daughter of a Tewkesbury blacksmith. Notwithstanding her lack of dowry, he pleaded with his parents to permit marriage between them. Gilbert, in his good-natured way, eventually agreed, after giving the matter some days of contemplation… although that was merely outward show. Maude, privy to her husband's thoughts, knew he was of a mind to permit the match, in spite of the lad's youth; after all, his parents had married young. The hesitation was simply his way of displaying parental authority. The girl would bring no dowry – which would have been so beneficial to them – but Giles was clearly determined to wed the maid; there was a mulish look upon his good-humoured face which bespoke of potential rebellion. He would wed with or without parental approval. Maude meanwhile hoped mayhap an heiress could be found for one of their other sons.

A beauteous young maid called Alice was residing within the household for the purpose of training in domestic skills. It was now intended she should be betrothed to Geoffrey instead of Giles. Negotiations were in progress. The girl came from a moderately wealthy family, so her dowry would be modest – akin to that given to Maude herself. Still, she pondered placidly, they had plenty of sons. Surely one of them would revive the family finances!

After nearly seventeen years of marriage, Maude had produced twelve children. Gilbert might have had a debilitating injury, but until recently it had not prevented him from attending to his marital duties, Maude realised wryly. As always, she had accepted the inevitable pregnancies with resignation. Two had died in those critical weeks immediately following birth but fortunately ten had thrived, surviving infancy and childhood ailments. Eight sons in succession Maude produced – two of them being the deceased infants.

Mattie claimed that no other woman had ever given birth to eight sons in a row. Then, to her joy, she produced one girl then another, before finally being delivered of her last two sons. It was unlikely she would conceive again, she told herself. Her courses, once so regular, were becoming less frequent. Gilbert, suffering increasing pain, was less amorous. Her youngest child was six months old now, and her husband regularly apologised to her for being, as he termed it, less than a man.

Less than a man! Maude felt a lightness of spirit. She had been fortunate enough to be a woman who, for the most part, enjoyed the marital act. As for her husband, he felt himself blessed in having a wife who welcomed his advances. But after being with child for the best part of her marriage, she felt she had more than done her duty, and less of the marital act was something she could face with equanimity. Gently she assured her husband that none could doubt his manhood – they had ten living sons and two daughters to prove it! Also, vaguely – she gave the matter little thought – she knew her own health was declining. Her last pregnancy had been more difficult than the others. She had remained active throughout but not with the energy of previous pregnancies. She had moved with a less than sprightly gait, whilst her hands and feet had swelled to an alarming degree as she became great with child. She had assumed it would remedy itself once she gave birth, but even now, six months later, her legs and ankles continued to swell. At the end of a busy day they were large; when she pressed a finger to them, an indent remained for some minutes. She also suffered strange palpitations. But then, she excused, she was no longer a girl. Consequently, she gave little thought to her own ailments. After all, she had many other, more important, things to think of.

Calamity came to Upton. There was another clash between York and Lancaster at Barnet, and then came news that the

Queen and her seventeen-year-old son, Prince Edward, had landed at Weymouth and were gathering forces. The newlywed Giles, showing the stubbornness a placid personality could occasionally display, insisted upon answering the call to arms, joining the army of Jasper Tudor, Earl of Pembroke, as did his brother Geoffrey. York and Lancaster met at nearby Tewkesbury, and the result was a terrible defeat for Lancaster. There was no mercy from the Yorkist contingent. Fleeing Lancastrians were cut down, and amongst the slain was young Prince Edward, plus Giles and Geoffrey de Laiche. The conflict which had so far only affected the finances of the family of Upton Manor suddenly brought deep tragedy. The nearby villages suffered too, also with loss of men, slain like Geoffrey and Giles for supporting the wrong side. The spectre of famine loomed due to lack of people to farm crops.

Consumed with grief, Maude tried to take comfort from the knowledge that her daughter-in-law, Lottie the blacksmith's daughter, who had become very dear to her, was with child. Her first grandchild. Gilbert, in his grief, resumed his attentions to his wife, notwithstanding his physical discomfort. As a result, Maude, having believed herself past childbearing, was also with child. She valiantly tried to rejoice in this, proclaiming the child was a blessing from God. But weariness assailed her, as did bouts of dizziness as the pregnancy advanced. Thankfully, her daughter–in–law was able to deal with the household duties Maude had once attended to with such zest. Lottie gave birth to a daughter, whom she called Maude, and was delivered of the babe as easily as the senior Maude. But days later, six months into her pregnancy, the older Maude's labour began. She was too weary to fear for either the child or herself. As her pains began she felt a strange detachment, as if her mind was being forced from her body. Never before had it occurred to her that Maude de Laiche could die, yet her spirit would not die; it would live on, using another body. In the past she had been able to leave her body according to her own will, and return to it, again by her own will. Curiously, now she was being all but forced out, and it was as if her old body was bolted and barred. She could not return.

Her mind, separated from its old home, could now see a sick woman, bloated and prematurely aged through work and childbearing. She had spent much of her life pregnant or nursing, sometimes simultaneously. Most of her teeth were missing, the remainder unattractively blackened. Her cheeks were lined and sagging, hair streaked with grey and eyes sunken. *Never again will I lodge in a plain body*, she vowed to herself, looking around the anxious women in attendance, seeking for one who was suitably beauteous. It had not been an unhappy life, living in the body of Maude Dubreise, later Lady Maude de Laiche; she had indeed been fortunate. But beauteous women had a very clear advantage over those of more homely appearance, she decided. Beauty could mean power over men. Maude had never enjoyed admiring glances from anyone, not even her husband, even though her marriage had been happy. Her gaze fell upon Alice, whom she had hoped might be a bride to poor Geoffrey. With an effortless leap – the first time she had attempted such a thing for many years – she reached out to Alice and entered her mind. Through Alice's eyes she saw the body she had occupied for thirty-two years, knew the love the girl felt for kindly Maude. Bloated and gasping, Maude lay, then was still. The babe, newly born, was hastily baptised, then he too gasped and was also still.

Suddenly aware of a keening wail, she realised it came from herself, Alice. To her great surprise she discovered many others had also loved her. Always Maude had felt herself too plain to be the deep object of anyone's affection; yet throughout the household, and throughout the countryside, people were shedding tears for her. Maude the Good, they called her. It was gratifying to know.

The burial was simple. The family had no money to raise a monument, which Gilbert would have preferred. Instead she was buried in the nave of her beloved chapel, the place where she had worshipped so devoutly every day. Her dead infant son lay with her.

'One day,' Gilbert declared, 'when our fortunes revive, she shall have the monument she deserves.' For now, a simple slab was placed over the grave.

She quickly absorbed all that had been the mind and spirit of Alice, adding the girl's knowledge and experiences to her own. And there came a sense of renewal, for Maude's body had been worn out. Over the centuries, with the relentless passing of the years, every time she quit an older body for that of a young person she experienced that same quickening of the senses, an increase in vigour. But, upon leaving Maude's sick body, she had no knowledge of how long – how many years – she could exist. She had met none such as herself, and it was a lonely, isolating feeling. She dared discuss it with no one, not even Gilbert who mourned his wife so terribly. Often she longed to tell him that she lived; he just needed to talk to Alice and there he would find Maude. In fact, although he often commented that Alice had adopted many of Maude's ways, she dared not. He would think her possessed of madness. Or a demon. So, in Alice she continued to live.

CHAPTER THREE

ON THE FIRST SATURDAY MORNING OF THE SCHOOL SUMMER holiday, Jennifer decided to attempt some weeding on the front garden of the house. The larger rear garden she decided to leave for Chas – currently he was playing golf, which he disliked, with a business partner – or more likely for the gardener who visited every fortnight. Working at one side of a bow-fronted window, she could command a view of the drive without being immediately visible herself. Sara came into view, pushing her bicycle out of the garage, ready to ride to Tracy's house to meet her friend. At that precise moment, a group of girls and boys, around six of them, all possibly in their early teens, came cycling along the road and came to a halt at the top of the drive.

'There's jaws!' shouted a boy, pointing towards Sara. 'Got a gob full of metal!'

'She rides around wi' Tracy,' shouted a tough looking girl, clad in tight Lycra shorts, cropped top, and sporting pierced ears, nose and naval. 'Saw 'em tergether yesterday. Didna know you came from this posh estate, kid! Show us yer teeth!'

Unaware of Jennifer's presence, they stood laughing. Putting down her fork, heart pounding in anger, she was about to intervene, to tell them that nearly every girl of Sara's age had braces on her teeth, then, glancing towards her daughter, Jennifer registered amazement, for the girl was calmly studying the group.

'Nothing wrong with my braces,' Sara announced cheerfully. 'Mind you, with a mouth full of metal I have to be careful if there are any magnets about. Beauty is painful,' she shrugged.

The good-humoured reply stunned the teenagers, all of whom expected the girl to burst into tears, which had been the object of the exercise. Jennifer was no less nonplussed. In fact, knowing Sara as she did, she too had expected her to turn away and rush weeping into the house.

'Nice bike,' observed Sara pleasantly, taking charge of the situation and addressing the youth who seemed to be leader of the little group. 'Had it long?'

'About a year,' was the reply. 'Where you going? Give you a race?'

'To see Tracy. No use my racing against you; I'll never win. You're tall!' Sara's voice showed just the right hint of admiration to appeal to his ego.

Flattered by her seemingly ingenuous response, the leader gave a delighted grin. 'Come on then, kid, we'll take you to Tracy's house and see yer get there safe.'

Watching them disappear from view, Jennifer realised she was standing motionless, the dropped fork lying beside her on the ground. What was happening to Sara? The girl had applied psychological tactics by startling her adversaries with her nonchalant response. In fact, she had turned it into a joke. Then, by targeting the leader, she had made him her ally.

'He was so flattered by her little display of admiration, I swear he just about rolled over to have his tummy tickled,' stated Jennifer, having recounted the scene to Vi.

'Wise girl. She'll go far,' observed Vi.

Recently she had figured out how easy it would be to have a granny flat built for herself. Her current bedroom could be extended outwards, over the garage. This would give her a bedroom and a generously sized sitting room, so she could entertain friends. It would also give her space for a decent bathroom. Her room, as it was at present, had its own en suite lavatory and shower but no bath. If she wished to soak in a bath, she had to use Sara's en suite. That would have to be changed if she moved in permanently. If she sold her own home, it would pay for the extension to Jennifer's house and there would be money left over.

'But Mum, that is simply *not* Sara. Just four weeks ago someone teased her about her braces, and she sobbed all night. We had difficulty in persuading her to keep on wearing them,' protested Jennifer.

'Well, you obviously did a good job,' was the calm retort, which failed to sooth Jennifer's concern. 'Anyway,' Vi could not resist adding, 'I don't know why she wears braces. Her teeth always looked alright to me.'

'I'm a dentist, Mum,' Jennifer spoke through clenched teeth. 'I know if she needs a brace or not!'

The following evening, a few days of good weather ended abruptly with a thunderstorm. Tracy, who had spent all afternoon at the Roseberrys' house, was invited to stay for the night. She was to sleep on a sofabed in Sara's bedroom. There were five bedrooms in the house, which meant that, even with Vi in situ, there was ample room for a guest, but the girls felt it would be more fun to share.

'In other words, you want to talk all night.' Chas gave an impish grin in the direction of his daughter.

They were gathered about the table eating dinner. His much-desired gas barbeque had arrived that afternoon and he was eager to try it out. Such was the downpour of rain, he was outvoted in the matter. Uncorking a bottle of red wine, he proceeded to offer glasses to the adults present.

'They talk all the time anyway,' voiced Vi, wondering how to introduce her idea of extending the house to create a granny flat... although, with five bedrooms, an extension could be avoided if Jen and Chas didn't want all the upheaval. One of the other rooms could be altered to be her sitting room. Perhaps she could swap bedrooms with Sara, who preferred a shower to a bath? That en suite was too big for a young girl anyway. Sara's room would first of all need redecorating of course. At present it was a bit girly for her own taste.

'I hope you haven't seen those boys and girls who were teasing you yesterday,' frowned Jennifer. 'I really ought to have stopped you from cycling away with them. They looked rough.'

Privately she was ashamed of her lack of presence of mind. She ought to have had sufficient sense to deal with the situation promptly and with authority. Instead, she had been little better than a zombie.

'Oh, they're no trouble, Mrs Roseberry,' Tracy pronounced dismissively. 'They do no harm; they just like to tease people sometimes.'

'They looked pretty rough to me,' Jennifer persisted.

What was it about Tracy? She talked and acted like an adult. There was nothing of the teenager about her. Elsie kept praising the intelligence of her daughter, but it was more than that. She wasn't just intelligent, she was astonishingly mature. Just like Sara. It was unnatural.

'Tracy was so funny when we all arrived at her house.' Sara gave a girlish giggle. 'The leader's called Brad. Tracy came out of the house, and said to him, "*Podex perfectus es*". When he asked what it meant, she told him it meant he was good-looking!' The two girls roared with laughter. So did Chas.

'What's so funny about that?' Vi was baffled, jolted out of her dreams of the extension.

'It's Latin, Vi.' Chas took an appreciative sip of red wine. 'Roughly, it means "You are a total asshole".'

'Oh!' Vi's lips pursed more tightly than usual.

'So, you baffled them with science,' grinned Chas, adding, 'Well, maybe not science... learning!'

'Knowledge rules,' beamed Tracy.

Feeling as if she'd donned a mask, Jennifer smiled too, but inwardly was thoughtful. Tracy was fourteen. Was that the type of remark a fourteen-year-old would make? Maybe, but not in Latin. She stared into her wine glass, as if seeking inspiration. They didn't teach Latin at Tracy's school. She knew that fact through talking to a patient, just this morning, who happened to be in Tracy's class. Jennifer had stated that she must be glad not to be doing Latin homework during the holidays. The girl had looked dumbfounded, and stated, "We don't do Latin." Reflecting on that conversation suddenly made her aware of another disturbing fact. Elsie, her husband and Rick all had strong regional accents, so why exactly was it that Tracy didn't? How had that happened? Was Tracy trying to iron out her accent or something? She couldn't resist mentioning it to Tracy there and then.

'How is it you have an accent of sorts but not a strong local accent?' No longer hungry, Jennifer was pushing her food about her plate.

'Mum mentioned that the other day, Mrs Roseberry,' Tracy replied politely. 'I haven't noticed anything different,' she shrugged calmly. 'I believe I've always talked like this.'

Yes, thought Jennifer. *I heard you talking at Sara's baptism. It didn't strike me at the time.*

'I guess you have,' she agreed, smiling mechanically.

Something had happened to Sara. It was easy to try and blame the influence of Tracy for the changes happening in her daughter, but then she'd noticed changes occurring before the two girls met. Suddenly weary, she wondered why she was so apprehensive? The youngsters were sensible, mature for their ages, they weren't chasing boys or behaving inappropriately... *Just why am I worried? What is there to worry about?*

The meal finished, unbidden, the girls rose, cleared the table and loaded the dishwasher, both of them handling the dishes deftly and not like amateurish youngsters, observed the watchful Jennifer.

Overhead, a deep rumbling of thunder was followed by a flash of lightning. Then came the staccato patter of rain. Chas, who was now sprawled in the conservatory to glance at the newspaper (out of the way of Vi, who hated the conservatory because it didn't have a television set), shouted, 'My goodness, you should hear the noise in here! Sounds like peas rattling off a tin!'

'May Tracy and I go upstairs and play chess?' asked Sara, peering into the conservatory.

Chas had tried to teach her over the Easter holidays, but at the time she'd showed no great inclination for the game.

'Of course,' nodded Chas, who adored chess. 'Keep practising, then when either of you becomes proficient enough I shall have a partner to play with.'

Jennifer, to his regret, was a hopeless, very defensive player, anxiously guarding her king to such an extent there was nowhere to manoeuvre the piece to when threatened. He could checkmate her in six moves.

'If either of you wants help, just give a shout to me.'

'Thanks!' The girls disappeared rapidly.

Sara's room was decorated in a pleasantly girlish fashion, with pale pink and white wallpaper and coordinating pink frilled candy- striped duvet and curtains. Tracy set up the chessboard, whilst Sara took down a series of Justin Bieber posters.

'I've been longing to do this. He's a bit infantile looking. I'm not too keen on current music, though Muse and the Foo Fighters are pretty good. Now, the 1980s... that was a great era. Ultravox, Duran Duran, Paul Young...'

'Culture Club,' added Tracy.

'Bon Jovi.'

'Rick Astley.'

'Roxy Music,' mused Sara.

'Now you're talking. I saw them in concert.'

'I did too! Where did you go to see them?'

'France!' squealed Tracy. 'They were touring.'

'Oh, I saw them at Newcastle City Hall. How music has changed through the centuries!' Rolling up the Justin Bieber posters, Sara, in a high clear voice, began to sing, 'It was a lover and his lass, with a hey and a ho and a hey nonny no, with a hey nonny nonny no—'

'Morley!' Tracy exclaimed with delight. 'They certainly don't compose songs like that that anymore! Mind you, a lot of people would probably say it's just as well. Did you meet him?'

'No, I didn't actually get to meet him properly. But I did hear him play quite often. During the Elizabethan era he played at St Paul's. Old St Paul's. Another famous composer of the time was William Byrd. He composed madrigals. I used to play them on the virginals. Are you familiar with his work? *The Barley Break*, for example?' Sara's face was suddenly but briefly solemn, almost tragic. She was now briskly rolling up a poster of Lady Gaga. 'I quite like her music, but I don't want to look at her picture,' she explained.

'I can't remember. I don't know much about Byrd really,' was the slow reply. By now Tracy had the chess pieces arranged.

Putting the posters aside, Sara moved to an electronic keyboard placed beside the bedroom window. Switching it on, she proceeded to play a few bars of music.

'Yes!' shrieked Tracy. 'I know it! Play some more.'

Sara played for a few minutes and then stopped. 'That's *The Barley Break*. Or at least some of it.'

Standing outside of the door, guiltily listening to the conversation, Jennifer turned and unwillingly tiptoed away, fearful of being caught eavesdropping. What were they talking about? Were they just making it all up? Was it some sort of game between them? In the bedroom she shared with Chas, she rummaged amongst some items on a shelf in the wardrobe and found a digital voice recorder. Muttering 'One two, one two,' into it, she found it worked perfectly. *This is very underhand, but as soon as I get the opportunity, I'm going to record one of their conversations*, she decided unrepentantly.

'When did you first meet one such as yourself,' questioned Tracy.

The two girls were sprawled on the candy-striped duvet, the chessboard lying unheeded between them.

'During my second body.' Sara picked up and examined the queen reflectively. 'I was called Alice then and had been betrothed to the second son of Maude, my first person – or body, if you like. Maude was plain, and as Maude lay dying I vowed never again to inhabit the body of a plain woman. Beautiful women have an advantage, even in this century, although I think it's frowned upon to admit such a thing.

'Alice was beautiful but came from only moderately wealthy parents. Her dowry wasn't huge. Like most women of that time, she was a pawn. Geoffrey, her intended, was killed during the Wars of the Roses, and it was considered perfectly in order to give her to John, who, to use modern parlance, was an utter prat. His IQ and shoe size were possibly the same.'

Some memories were so painful they never faded. The memory of that marriage remained fresh.

Sir Gilbert de Laiche survived his wife Maude by only three years, and perished despairing of his son John, who behaved in a boorish fashion, drinking, wenching, beating Alice for being childless – for a childless state could only be the fault of the woman. Angry at being reproved, Alice once made the mistake of pointing out to John that none of his mistresses had borne him children either. The result was a loosened front tooth. Stunned by the blow, and overcome with resentment, Alice had learned to hold her tongue. Women were barren, men were not. John was nothing like his gentle father, and she learned this to her cost.

Money was scarce because John had no idea of monetary matters. Unable to accept responsibility, he blamed Alice, claiming: ''Tis her extravagance with household expenses which leaves the coffers depleted.' He beat her soundly and often, but still money remained scant. Notwithstanding this, he insisted upon holding a sumptuous twelfth night revel at Upton. On this night Alice found herself being stared at earnestly by a youth of perhaps twelve winters, who possessed a curiously adult stare. And not just an adult stare; he seemed to peer into her mind. Something about him made her hang her head (she was tall, but so was he for his age) to hide a bruise beneath her left eye.

He approached her, gently taking her arm.

'Come, Lady,' he said and began leading her from the great hall, with its noise, smell and press of bodies. 'You and I have matters to discuss, and I think the Lord of Misrule is occupied enough not to notice our absence.'

John had been elected Lord of Misrule, and as such ordered the entertainments and games of the evening. Presently he was sufficiently inebriated to order the evening's entertainment with wild abandonment.

'You and I are the same,' the lad declared when they were seated in the chapel, once beloved by Maude.

On the altar three candles burned, symbolising the trinity. In a nave lay the bodies of Maude and Gilbert, side by side, and over them was their simple memorial plaques on the stone-flagged floor. She, who had once been Maude, listened with amazement to people who declared her saintly; in fact, recently a woman had claimed a miracle had been performed at Maude's grave – she had asked Maude to grant her fertility, and it had happened: the woman had given birth to a son. They maintained that Maude ought to be canonised. Knowing Maude's faults as well as her virtues, Alice viewed this with wry amusement.

'What is your name, young master?' she inquired quietly, lowering her voice instinctively in this hallowed place.

'Geoffrey,' was the equally soft reply.

'I was once to be betrothed to someone called Geoffrey. He was killed at the Battle of Tewkesbury. I loved him well.'

It seemed so long ago. Seven years had passed, and she could no longer recall his face. Geoffrey – her Geoffrey – had been gentle, as his parents had been. Unlike John. Hastily she crossed herself. It was sin to hate one's husband.

'Do you know how old I am, my Lady?' the youth questioned, making no reference to the sudden genuflection.

Gazing at his beardless face, skin taut and unlined, a faint down showing above his upper lip, she replied promptly, 'Twelve winters mayhap. Possibly thirteen.'

'This body is twelve years old. I am actually much older. Two hundred years, my Lady. I think you do understand me. You too are not as young as you seem.'

His eyes, full of knowledge, gazed directly into hers and she knew he spoke truly.

'But how can it be?' whispered she, nervously picking at the edge of her shabby, much-repaired mantle. 'Why did I not die with Maude?' She nodded towards the grave in the aisle.

'Aaaah, my lady, I see you were once Lady Maude de Laiche,' Geoffrey nodded, wise with sudden understanding. 'This is only the second body you have lived in.'

'Aye, Master... Geoffrey. I cannot understand why I could not die with her – not that I really wanted to; I wanted to go on living. But others die.' In her confusion the words were rushed. But he clearly understood.

'You see, my Lady, I am an incubus. Even as you are also—' he began explaining.

'Indeed I am not, Master Geoffrey,' she interrupted, much distressed. 'I am no evil creature—'

'Nay, Lady Alice,' he in turn interrupted, gently laying a hand over hers. 'We are not evil. You and I, we are not evil. But some are, hence our reputation. Some use the power to take over a person's mind for their own sinful intentions. There are few of us, and how we come about I know not. I was born to a lowly family that lived in the Welsh Marches. I was fortunate in meeting with one of my kind during my boyhood, in my first body. He was a priest, wise and good, over a century old, and he recognised me for what I was... and am. He taught me many things, including how to regard my state as a gift, and to use it for the good of myself and others. It is not easy for us to die, for as the body we inhabit withers it no longer sustains us, and it beholds us to move out.'

'Did you know the priest for very long?'

It was a relief to know something of what she was. And a greater relief to know it was not unholy to be thus.

'Nigh on forty years. I believe he possibly did die. He was aboard a ship bound for France. It never reached its destination and his body drowned. I had learned, from him, that under certain circumstances we can die. We can exist for some time without a mortal body, and the older we are the longer we can do so. We can travel without our bodies, but when young we are limited as to distance. That ability too increases with age. We need a body to live in to survive, and sometimes circumstances are such that a living body might not be available! He may have survived, I hope he did, but we were separated. I still miss him sorely; it is a goodly thing to have a friend. One such as myself…' the lad admitted, wiping his eyes roughly, as if ashamed of his emotion.

In the chapel all was still, the noise of a rising storm buffeting the outside walls, drowning the murmured conversation of the occupants. The candles guttered for a moment, disturbed by a sudden draught as if the door had opened, and all but went out. Upon seeing no one entering the chapel, Alice and Geoffrey remained bent upon their conversation, both simultaneously realising the wisdom of kneeling as if in prayer.

'So, it is dangerous for us to travel by sea,' mused Alice, patting his arm with gentle sympathy. 'Mayhap he did not die. He could have been near the French coast and entered the body of a Frenchman.'

'Mayhap,' he agreed, unconvinced. 'I have met others of our kind, very few, Lady, and once again circumstances have caused us to be separated. But whenever I meet one I do try to maintain contact.' The lad squeezed her hand in a brotherly gesture. 'It is good to have company. And I think you have much to ask, Lady Alice,' he allowed himself to smile.

'I assume you have met with an evil one?' Alice inquired with some alarm, wondering what she should do if it should happen to her. Would she immediately know he or she was evil?

'Aye, about eighty years ago. He was old, very old; more than a thousand years and therefore very strong. He could leave his body and take on an illusion of a shape, without entering and using another body! I too can do that now, but he could make it look human or animal, as he wished. This he could do for hours, a day even, without needing to return to his own body for nourishment. But of course he could, if he wished, briefly use any body he wished for replenishment. We may do likewise, and withdraw before bonding with that new body. However, he could do what the Church believes and fears about the incubus. He could seduce a woman to his own satisfaction and her shame. The Church only recognises our evil brothers and sisters. The only incubi (or the female form, a succubus) the Church chooses to know of are the ones who go out and seduce a man or woman, usually while they are sleeping. The others are not acknowledged, the harmless ones.'

'You mentioned a succubus... I ne'er heard of such a being... or creature,' amended Alice.

'A succubus. A female version of the incubus,' he explained.

'I felt great renewal when I left Maude's poor body and entered this one,' murmured Alice. 'But I feel such... such...' It was her turn to weep, angrily dashing the tears from her eyes.

'Your present life is unhappy. I need only consider your husband to know it cannot be anything else. But ponder this – in time you will leave your present body, it will perish. Look about, contemplate your next body carefully, and choose wisely,' he urged.

'Do you?' Alice rubbed her chilled hands together. The chapel was bitterly cold.

'Aye, Lady. Always. For my own comfort I never choose the body of someone poor or infirm. I have had many wives, some I have loved dearly, but thus far none of them have given birth to a creature like me. My wives have all died and caused pain. Likewise my children have all perished. Yet I continue and move on. I chose this body a year ago.' Taking her hands, Geoffrey chafed them between his own. 'I chose it because the people who are parents of this body are both wealthy and good. It is wise to surround ourselves with good people, and to enter and use the bodies of those who are also wise and good. By doing thus, we ensure we improve as the years roll past. My parents have placed me in this household, temporarily, to begin acquiring knightly skills and courtly manners. I but arrived this day. It clearly was a poor choice on their part – although I beg you feel not insulted at this. My parents believe Sir John to be better than he is. And also wealthier than he is. I perceive – again, apologies, Lady – that Sir John is not a man of means. But at least I have found one such as myself. I will not be here for long; I am to move to Ludlow Castle sometime in spring.'

'It must seem strange occupying the body of a lad,' she reflected. 'Have you occupied the body of a maid?' She was curious, certain she would not wish to inhabit a male body herself.

'I have, briefly, and it was not to my liking,' he stated dismissively. 'But we are, I think, made male and female in the natural order of things. My advice to you is to find someone young, or relatively young, when you move on, for the young mind is easily grasped and taken over. Older people carry a great deal of information, and it takes longer to absorb the essence of the person. But that is not a problem, should you feel moved to use that body. If possible, take time to consider well your choice.'

'You are teaching me much.' In spite of the cold, Alice felt happy. John was elsewhere, and she was in this peaceful, holy place, with someone with whom she felt totally at ease. 'Suppose I leave this body, what will happen to it?'

'It will die. If you leave it for an hour, others will think you are sleeping deeply. But to leave it for a long time, a day... I know not how long.... it will sink and perish.'

'Shall not Alice – the original spirit of Alice before I moved in – remain, and leave me to move on?'

'No, for you have been here some years and have absorbed all that is her essence. You are bound to her. Maybe during the first days – again I know not how long – you could have left, and a small part of her would remain and recover. I once left a body after six months. Jesu, my life was intolerable, one of oppression. I separated myself from him and leapt into the mind of another. But I took much of his knowledge and memories with me, what was left ought to have been a twenty-year-old man, but so much of his mind was missing, he was little better than a breathing corpse. I had taken with me everything of worth. We come to value the bodies we occupy, to know them and the people who surround us.' He gazed upon his lovely companion with sympathy. 'I pity you, mistress.' Gently he touched the bruise beneath her eye. 'But it will not last long,' he assured her kindly. 'You will go on, he will not.'

'You give me much hope,' she admitted.

Sometime later they quit the chapel, entering once again the great hall and mingling with the guests. Surely they could not have been missed, Alice reasoned. Most folk were sorely inebriated. The next morning she awoke, finding herself alone. It was often so; her husband was no doubt with another woman. Wrapping a fur blanket about herself, she peered out of the narrow slit of a window. There had been snow on the ground at Christmas but that had melted quickly. Now, on this first day of the New Year, the sky outside was heavy and misty grey. Now a new white blanket of snow lay there, of some depth; this time it would not melt quickly. Snowflakes still whirled dizzily; it was morn but could have passed for twilight.

'This weather looks fit to last for days,' sighed she, hearing the door open, thinking it to be her tiring maid entering.

A strong masculine hand gripped the back of her neck.

'I hear you shamed me last night. Whoring in the chapel with a callow youth!' Her husband's sneering voice hissed loudly in her ear.

'My lord, I was not. He is but a boy. Only twelve, and we were... we were praying,' she gasped, fearful of the violence he might commit, for he was clearly still drunk.

The sour stench of his breath, combined with the smell of his body, was nauseating. He was tall, strong of physique, for in build he took very much after his mother Maude, although his features bore nothing of her kindness.

'Well, he is out on the roads now. I have sent him away. I would gladly have hanged him, but his parents are powerful enough to seek revenge. Suffice to say he will probably perish on his way home. And you, my lady wife, shall be soundly beaten and sent forth from this place too for being the whore you are.'

Still holding her by the throat, he delivered several sound blows to her head, then released her so abruptly she fell heavily, dazed by the force of the repeated impact.

'Get up, whore, and pack your bags! You shall return to your family, and all will know you for the harlot you are.' He kicked her several times, in the stomach and head.

Feeling the taste of blood in her mouth and the wet trickle of blood pouring into her eyes, Alice was unable to defend herself. Trying to curl up to protect her stomach, she wrapped both arms about her head to cover her face.

'Harlot!' Again he kicked her viciously, this time in the back.

She was vaguely aware of people entering the room and someone attempting to restrain her husband. Then came shouts for help, as more blows were rained upon her person. At last the attack ceased, and what happened to her husband after that she knew not. Someone lifted her onto the bed, and for a while she could focus on nothing but the all-engulfing pain. In desperation she freed herself from the body of Alice, her spirit moving freely about the room, eventually observing events from the vantage point of the ceiling. By the end of the day Alice was dying. This she knew because she could no longer re-enter her body. As it had been with Maude, so she must now permanently leave Alice. Geoffrey had instructed her to choose her next body well, if possible to choose the next person well in advance, in order to be ready when the time came. But how could she have known Alice was to die so quickly? It was not as if she had been ill. In a corner of the room stood a couple of nuns, praying for the dying woman. Both nuns, the eldest being the abbess, hailed from Waltham. They were returning to their abbey and had, accompanied by a suitable entourage, for some months been on a pilgrimage. Seeing the lowering skies and the threat of snow, wisely they had all sought shelter from the inclement weather at Upton yesterday. They must have been mightily horrified if they had witnessed last night's revels, Alice surmised.

Feeling a desire for the peace and seclusion of a holy establishment, she studied the two veiled women. The younger was attractive. *I shall become a nun,* she decided quickly, looking down at the battered and bruised form of Alice and surveying the bloodied, broken features of the once beauteous woman. *If I am a nun, no man will dare to use me thus!* Without further ado she moved into the mind of the younger nun.

'I remained at Waltham for fifty years,' Sara reflected. 'In fact, I was abbess for approximately forty of those years, in two different bodies of course. I was there when the Wars of the Roses reached an end, when Richard the Third was killed at the Battle of Bosworth Field. Then came the Tudors. Henry the Eighth destroyed the monasteries, but by then I was ready to move out into the world again. I was happy during those years, but I knew in my heart it was time to leave. We move on, do we not?'

'We do,' agreed Tracy, nodding reflectively. Between them the chessboard still remained unused. 'What happened to the young Geoffrey?'

'His body was found in the snow. He no doubt moved on to another body, but I don't know whom he chose; to my knowledge he didn't return to Upton in his new form. As my husband John predicted, he never reached his home. As a result his parents, who were powerful, descended upon the Manor of Upton, and my husband was himself hanged for the joint murder of his wife and the youth. Given the laws of the time, John would probably have been excused of murdering his spouse since he claimed she was a harlot. But the double murder was his undoing.' Sara gave a satisfied smile. 'It's possible Geoffrey returned to Upton in a new body, but by then I was installed within the confines of Waltham Abbey, I suppose.' She picked up a pawn and studied it absently. 'I am glad you and I have met. The best friends are always those who are of the same kind.' She offered a hand to Tracy, who took it in a warm grasp.

'We must make sure we don't allow ourselves to become separated. But nowadays it's easy to maintain contact, with the internet and so forth,' Tracy mused aloud.

'I wish it had always been so,' Sara murmured, sad for a moment, pushing certain memories aside with an effort, determined to be cheerful. 'I'll play something modern, really up-to-date.' She waved a CD disc in the air.

Sensing her friend's need for diversion, and wise enough not to inquire further, Tracy gave her attention to the disc.

'What is it?'

'Mumford and Sons. You know of them I'm sure! They really are good. I like their music.' Sara placed the disc in a small, portable music centre, offering the case to Tracy for examination.

'Yes, I've heard a few tracks from this,' Tracy nodded as music blared from the speakers. She gave a quick, wry smile. 'They are very, very good. Music has moved forward over the years. I remember the days when the organ was considered progressive!'

'I can recall listening to some priestly chants at Old Saint Paul's Cathedral, and during the recital someone's cattle were herded through one side of the building to the other! Few thought strangely of it; it was regularly used as a shortcut! Imagine that happening today in the new St Paul's!' Sara gave a hoot of laughter.

Downstairs, Jennifer decided the school holiday was already turning into a nightmare, and it was only the first Sunday! The holiday, technically, hadn't even begun. Much as she loved her mother, Vi was outstaying her welcome. It was hard to tell her to go, but since she showed no inclination at all to do so some plain talking was going to be necessary. Then there was the problem with Sara. Flicking through a dictionary of music, she checked the names she'd heard the girls mention. Morley and Byrd. She loved music, was a talented musician herself; at one time she'd played the piano skilfully. Now, although she still played, her standard had slipped but was still reasonable, she supposed. But she had insufficient time to practise. Classical music was her favourite, but she hadn't heard of the two. Yet the dictionary of music informed her they really were genuine and, furthermore, Morley had been organist at St Paul's. How had Sara known that? Sara too played the piano, she attended lessons, but was not a natural musician, nor was she particularly interested is anything classical.

Thankfully they would be going on holiday in the near future, just for a week, or possibly two. This would separate Sara from Tracy for a while. They'd decided not to go abroad this summer and hadn't even made any hotel bookings, but Cumbria was a likely destination. Possibly they might venture into Wales. She and Chas enjoyed touring, generally deciding on the spur of the moment where their next day's destination should be.

It was, she reasoned inwardly, no use talking again to Chas about her fears. Especially since she didn't yet know exactly what it was she feared! He was so rational. He would find an explanation for everything, whilst she knew instinctively that there *was* no rational explanation. She only knew something was wrong, with both girls. She longed to have a heart-to-heart chat with Elsie regarding Tracy but had no idea how to approach the subject. Maybe if she could put her finger on just what the matter was with Sara, she could talk to Elsie. Nor could she take Sara to see their family doctor. What could she say to the doctor? That her daughter seemed to have matured well beyond her mental age in a matter of weeks? Chas had mentioned a psychiatrist, and she definitely didn't want that. Nor did he. The best solution she could come up with was to separate Sara from Tracy for a short while, then see what happened. Maybe it would be wise to extend their holiday to three weeks. She suggested it to Chas.

'Darling, we agreed not to have an expensive holiday. We've spent a vast amount of money on this house and the garden, and I'm collecting the new car, the Alfa Romeo, in a couple of days,' he protested.

'I know what you mean,' Jennifer agreed hastily. She wanted the Alfa Romeo as much as Chas did. Well, she excused, they needed one big car. Her Micra, which she was fond of, was too small for family outings in her opinion. 'Well, we could go and visit my brother for the third week,' she proposed.

Chas looked mutinous. Neil currently lived at Scarborough; he was sick of visiting Scarborough. They'd been considering the Lake District, and Scarborough was on the opposite side of the country. Then he remembered the new car.

'Well, it would be good to let the Alfa stretch its legs, metaphorically speaking,' he considered, the mutinous expression fading. 'We could visit Scarborough then go to the Lake District,' he mused. 'Not sure about three weeks though, Jen, getting time off work for that length of time...' his voice faded.

'Yes, I know what you mean,' she sighed.

Three weeks could be justified perhaps if they were going to the US or Canada. But for touring the UK? No, her colleagues at the dental practice wouldn't be pleased about that. So, two weeks it would have to be.

'Perhaps, as a compromise, though, we could both take off the following Monday and Tuesday and go back to work on the Wednesday... Two and a half weeks might be acceptable to our colleagues... Plus the holiday will be a good time for trying the car out,' she added cunningly. Chas would happily take her anywhere in order to enjoy his new vehicle.

Chas was wooed. 'Good idea. I'll have a word with the boss folk tomorrow. You decide on the itinerary. As long as we don't take your mother.'

Tonight Vi had suggested that maybe he and Jennifer ought to consider economising; she thought they spent too much money on readymade meals (which were a sheer extravagance in her opinion), and far too much alcohol was drunk in the

Roseberry household. They had wine regularly, Vi had stated disapprovingly. With difficulty he'd refrained from giving a sharp retort, his patience wearing thin. In fact, he only just refrained from commenting that they needed alcohol to endure the criticism of his mother–in-law!

'I think we should take Tracy too; she'll keep Sara company,' he proposed, pleased with the notion since it would enable himself and Jennifer to spend a maximum amount of time together.

'No!' Jennifer almost shouted.

She most definitely did not want Tracy with them. The conversation she'd overheard tonight had been odd. Disturbing, in fact. Separating the girls was the only solution she could currently think of. Anyway, she had the voice recorder ready to surreptitiously use just as soon as the opportunity arose. Once she'd recorded a conversation as strange as the one she'd overheard tonight, she could play it to Chas.

'It's too much responsibility to take another girl. Anyway, I prefer us to go as a family,' she declared firmly.

CHAPTER FOUR

'Have you ever been famous? Famous as in a historic person who was a beacon for future generations? Florence Nightingale, for example? Edith Cavell? Violette Szabo?' Sara inquired.

'I was a well-known cook once, famous in my time, but my fame didn't survive to go down through the centuries. My recipes have been plagiarised – that is the correct description – by many succeeding cooks and chefs,' mused Tracy. 'And I've been married to a Prime Minister. I thought it might be a more powerful role than it was. I was Hester Pitt, wife of William Pitt the Elder, no less. He never allowed me to rule the country. What about you?'

'No, I've never been famous in my own right. I was once a poet called Daisy Gardiner.' As Tracy gave an undignified honk of laughter, Sara joined in with the mirth. 'Yes, I agree; who's heard of the Victorian poet Daisy Gardiner? And for your information, that was indeed my name. Yet there is a volume (a small one!) of her work in the British Museum if you would care to look! It lies beside the work of such luminaries as Emily Bronte, Elizabeth Barrett, Robert Browning and Charles Dickens! Did you ever *meet* anyone *really* famous?'

'Yes, quite a lot over the centuries,' nodded Tracy, who was seated cross-legged on a sunlounger in the garden. After the thunderstorm of the previous night, the weather was dry but not hot. Both girls, sitting side by side on loungers, wore jeans and sweatshirts. 'I've glimpsed a few monarchs, you know, in procession. And as wife of a Prime Minister I met George the Third, and also Queen Charlotte, plus a lot of statesmen too. But most often those whom I actually met, you know, to talk to, at the time I met them, weren't famous, and I didn't know how famous they were going to be. Take Charles Dickens. I saw him several times when he was only a journalist. He regularly called into a tearoom in London, near to where I was then living, and drank tea or coffee there. What about you?'

'Mmmm,' Sara mumbled indistinctly, busily eating a peach. Wiping her mouth with a tissue, she announced, 'I not only saw Lord Nelson, I spoke with him. Ugly man. At the time I *knew* he was famous, everyone was talking about him, but I couldn't see what Emma Hamilton saw in him. It was clear she was smitten... as was he with her. Modern historians often neglect to comment on how fat she was. Plump women were considered very desirable to men in those days. But she was *fat!* And he – Nelson – had a queer kind of smile. Eventually I discovered it was because a lot of his teeth were missing, mostly from one side of his mouth. So, in common with many folk with missing teeth, he used to stuff his mouth with rags. I once used to do the same myself... I am so thankful for modern dentistry!'

'Not a very glamorous look,' observed Tracy, peeling a banana. 'I too used to stuff my mouth with rags. Also, I've used teeth taken from cadavers; a procedure that was all the rage at one time amongst those wealthy enough to pay for it.'

'Yes, I had some Waterloo teeth,' nodded Sara. 'A set of false teeth where the actual teeth were taken from cadavers from the battle. They were of no use to them, so it seemed like a good idea at the time. Shame to waste them!'

'I saw Queen Victoria.' Tracy took a hearty bite out of her banana, munching steadily for a short while before continuing to talk. 'I saw her whilst she attended the Great Exhibition. What an ugly woman she was. She might have been attractive in her youth.' Dubiously she added, 'I hope so, for Prince Albert's sake!'

'I saw King James the First in 1603.' Sara was still having difficulty with the peach; it was ripe and very juicy. Again dabbing her mouth, she added, 'I was living near here at the time, in Durham, and had done so for some year… you know how it is, in more than one body. There was no reason to move away. In those days one didn't often venture far from one's roots, unless it was because a marriage had been arranged which took one to another district. I was with the crowds in Durham city, in Silver Street to be precise. There we watched King James the First of England (formerly James the Sixth of Scotland) as he progressed towards London to claim his crown. He was heading for Durham Castle, to spend the night there. He was another dull-looking person. Not at all dashing. There was a huge banquet given that night. I attended, with some good friends, and was dismayed to witness the King actually dribbling as he ate. Most discomfiting,' grinned Sara, throwing the peach stone away. 'I've achieved a good imitation of him whilst I ate that peach!'

'I lived in France several times, for approximately a century on one occasion. I saw the Sun King. My, was he handsome! Not a let-down like your Lord Nelson. Even by modern standards, with complete with nose jobs and dental work, he was good-looking. He had a prominent nose, but it didn't look ridiculous, it looked masculine! But the first famous person who really, really impressed me was Joan of Arc. I was in Rheims when she was burned. I was there,' Tracy's voice was soft, reflective, as the years rolled back. 'She knew I was a succubus the moment she met me. But unlike those who are frightened and unknowing, she realised I wasn't evil. She was a good woman. Well, not a woman, a girl really,' she amended. 'I admired her enormously, yet was in awe too. A woman... in a man's attire! It was unimaginable then.' As Sara nodded in understanding, Tracy continued, 'I didn't want to see her die, but I knew I had to be there for her at the end... when they burned her. There were rumours she wasn't well treated in prison, that the guards were brutal. I suspect they probably raped her. They often did that to female prisoners back then. I don't know if she saw me when she was led to the stake. I like to think she did. She was looking here and there at the crowd, a bit like a frightened animal, although in other respects she was fearless enough. She died courageously.'

'Did you know she would burn, or was it a surprise?' Sara gently inquired.

'Yes and no. My then husband was a powerful man who wanted to keep her as a valued hostage. But he informed me that, for political purposes, she would possibly burn. I hoped she would be spared, but as we all know now, she was not.' Tracy shook her head despairingly. 'Even after all this time, I feel bitter about it. I can't even recall her features, but I remember her honesty and innate goodness.'

'It's terrible to outlive husbands, children, acquaintances, friends and those whom we admire, whether they're killed or die naturally. Their life spans are so short. As for burning...' Sara gave a shudder. 'I experienced that for myself. Although I made sure I left my body before the flames scorched it. We feel the pain, mental and physical, of those whom we inhabit. Unfortunately.'

'You were burned? Why?' Glad to be distracted from Joan of Arc, Tracy waited to be enlightened.

'Nowadays people might have a vague idea of what an incubus or a succubus is, although the internet and reference books don't describe us at all accurately,' reflected Sara. 'They're not commonly used in plots for films and theatrical productions. In fact, I'm not sure if there *are* any films about our kind...' She looked askance at Tracy, who shook her head doubtfully. 'Vampires and werewolves, of course, there are hundreds of books and films about them. But incubi and succubi are in the minority. Maybe it's a good thing... maybe.' Dreamily, Sara lay back on her sunlounger, gazing upwards at a heavy grey sky.

'But,' Sara continued, 'in the seventeenth century, when everyone feared demons and witch fever raged, a clergyman turned witchfinder sensed I was different. Then someone betrayed me to him, confirming his notion that I was different. By coincidence, his surname was Reynolds, like that of our current vicar, although if they're related it matters little now. I explained the true meaning of the incubus and succubus to him but it did little good. I stressed that a succubus, like any human, can be good or evil. We absorb the identities of those whom we inhabit. We are influenced by those with whom we associate. But we grow stronger as we progress from body to body, less likely to be influenced for the bad. Most of us are good. But those who are bad, are bad indeed... pure evil. And it is they who give us such a terrible reputation. But he wouldn't accept my definition and insisted I couldn't be anything but evil.'

Incubus or succubus, brooded Sara, move from body to body, infiltrating the mind of the host, taking over the host's identity, filling the mind with many years of knowledge and experience. This is always baffling at first for the host. After all, where did all of this sudden knowledge and strange memories come from? But, as the spirit of the host is absorbed by that of the incubus or succubus, the questions cease and the knowledge is accepted. Always the host retains some characteristics of his or herself. It has to be, for the spirit, the essence of being, remains. But the incubus or succubus, especially the older ones, are composed of many such spirits, all compounded into one. Whilst a new host might show traits of a former self, changes are inevitably obvious right from the start, and it's difficult to disguise the huge amount of accumulated learning. Such was the cause of Sara's downfall in the seventeenth century.

Brows drawn together, she pieced together the events. The woman who'd attended the banquet given in honour of King James the First was in fact dying. By this time, the succubus who had originated as Maude Dubreise was nearing two hundred years old. In spite of the fact a quarter of her life had been spent sequestered in a convent, her wisdom in worldly matters had grown considerably. Also, by this time, she easily recognised the signs of approaching death in a human body. Within a few months of that banquet she knew that once again she would move on, being worn out with bearing fifteen children. Her next body would be, she decided, a young woman who chanced to be the daughter of one of her very good friends. She was also betrothed to a wealthy merchant.

Rosalind Lowther was young and beautiful, possessing a quick wit and keen intelligence; all very appealing to a succubus in need of a new body. She was born of wealthy Roman Catholic parentage, which was the only drawback for a succubus who was, by this time, decidedly Protestant in faith. Rosalind was related on her mother's side to the mighty Percy family of Northumberland. Admittedly, her future husband, Sir Robert Bingham, was lacking in aristocratic connections, but wealth meant power, and he was exceedingly wealthy.

Rosalind was tall and blonde, her figure curvaceous, guaranteed to turn the heads of many a male. It was a sad fact that a beautiful woman, if she used her advantages well, enjoyed more success than the less attractive members of her sex. Having once been the plain and lumpish Maude, it was sound sense to use an attractive body and use it well, for good looks didn't last indefinitely.

Rosalind was, at the time preceding her betrothal, and prior to her mind being entered by a succubus, a modest creature, uninterested in feminine fashion. Robert Bingham was a tall, darkly handsome man, possessed of great charm, smooth talk and elegant attire. He'd been instantly attracted to the demure and beautiful Mistress Lowther, having first beheld her at a banquet given by the Lowthers at their home, situated on a bank of the River Wear. It had been held on the eve of May Day, given in honour of Edmund Neville of Latimer, who ought, most people claimed, to have been rightfully in possession of Raby Castle. The Nevilles had lived there for generations, but unfortunately the previous Earl of Westmorland, Henry (father of Edmund) had been a supporter of Mary, Queen of Scots, during the reign of Elizabeth the First. Owing to this allegiance, Raby had been forfeit to the crown, and thus far no one else possessed the land – largely because the profits were currently helping to fill Crown coffers. In vain did Edmund Neville visit Scotland to offer support to King James, when he succeeded to the English crown, and petition him for the restoration of his estates, stating his family had loyally supported the King's late lamented mother, but to no avail.

Listening to Neville's tale of woe, Sir Robert Bingham shrugged his shoulders, a wry smile playing about his lips.

'Well, might you beg the new King to listen to you. I have heard that King James listens only to his own counsel,' he stated, addressing the Earl but keeping his attention focused upon Mistress Rosalind. For certes, she was a beauty. 'He does claim he is no apprentice in kingship, having been King of Scotland for many years prior to his coming to England.'

'How know you of such gossip?' demanded Mistress Lowther, detecting, with pleasure, the glances which the merchant gave towards her daughter.

The Lowthers, being landowners whose fortune had originated in rearing sheep and trading in wool, were wealthy but not as wealthy as they had once been. Largely this was due to a carefree squandering of money and an almost complete rebuilding and refurbishing of the family home, combined with a propensity for gambling. Recently they had made vague attempts to economise. A rich merchant as a son-in-law would not go amiss.

'I am recently returned from London, my lady,' Robert Bingham bowed respectfully, showing just a hint of admiration, knowing well how to be deferential and appeal to the vanity of the fair Rosalind's mother. Women whose charms were fading were, he knew, susceptible to a show of admiration. 'There is much talk of how His Majesty spends money as if it is mere dross, lavishing presents upon his male favourites, whilst his wife behaves with less wisdom still. Jesu, she is a fool!' His tone suggested Mistress Lowther would not be such a fool.

Mistress Lowther, however, whilst accepting his homage, was less than interested in the King's affairs.

'Tell us of the fashions!' she exclaimed. 'We do hear the farthingale is not well favoured now.'

'Madam, alas I know nothing of fashion,' stated the elegantly clad Robert Bingham, again bowing gallantly towards his hostess. Mistress Rosalind, being simply and modestly attired, looked as if she cared little for outward show, so it would not appeal to her if he blatantly admitted worldly, frivolous inclinations. 'All I can say is this: in my opinion, Mistress Lowther, you may appear without shame at His Majesty's Court. And of course these other ladies too,' he added, as if in afterthought.

Smiling, Mistress Lowther accepted the compliment, priding herself on being as fashionable as any London lady.

Having wooed the mother, Robert Bingham turned his attention to Rosalind's elder brother, head of the household since the death of their father. Subtly impressing him with sly allusions of his personal wealth, he described a house he was having rebuilt not very far away, being desirous of establishing a home for himself. Next, having wooed the brother, he turned his attention to Rosalind.

The Lowthers, although they possessed no title, were well connected, thanks to Mistress Lowther's Percy heritage. So, should he unite with the family, they would be well able to advance his social standing. The fact they held no title was due to their Catholic sympathies. Bingham himself was born of a tradesman father of modest wealth who had ensured his only son was well educated from an early age. Robert was astute enough not to waste that education and had been an apt pupil with a clever eye for seizing chances. His substantial fortune was due to his own endeavours. Now aged twenty-eight, he was rich and in need of a wife. The invitation to dine with the Lowthers had been cunningly contrived. Having heard of the loveliness of Mistress Rosalind, he had a notion to woo her. Bingham desired to wed above his station and had sufficient sense not to look too high. The Lowther connections would ensure they were accepted into the houses of the nobility. The daughter of the house would well suffice for a wife. Especially since her much praised beauty was not exaggerated… If it had been so, he would have looked elsewhere.

Her modesty too was enchanting. He contrived to speak with her alone, but with her mother and brother nearby it seemed an impossible objective. However, some minstrels duly arrived, and dancing commenced. The hour was late when finally he managed to dance with her, and his patience was rewarded by an exchange of a few hurried words.

'Mistress, surely you will be attending the fair, to be held in the Market Place tomorrow, will you not?' he inquired hopefully.

'Why, yes, everyone will be there,' smiled she, blushing as she encountered his bold gaze and hastily lowering her eyes.

As he turned to her again in the dance, he informed her, 'Last year I attended the May Day holiday in Canterbury. There were mummers aplenty, bear-baiting, cockfights, jugglers... I knew not where to look first. I am sure there will be as much revelry here. I love this part of the country, which is why I intend to make it my home.' Keenly he observed her countenance. Here was a true maid, innocent and well sheltered by a doting mother and older brother.

'You must travel much,' murmured she, her voice scarcely audible over the music, unintentionally giving her companion the opportunity of inclining his head to hers. 'I heard you say you were planning upon purchasing a home near Durham.'

'Aye, that I am. But I am a merchant, and it is necessary for me to move around the country from time to time. I do much trade in the northern parts, yet still I must travel. I long for a time when I can settle in one place. Permanently,' he sighed, regarding her eloquently.

'It must be wearisome to journey constantly,' replied she. 'Here one day, gone another.'

Unconsciously she gave a glance of regret in his direction, for the dance required she must turn to the man standing on her left, thus ending the conversation.

The following day, Bingham ensured a meeting with Rosalind at the May Day fair by carefully observing her home for more than an hour – keeping himself well hidden – until she departed in the company of not only her elder brother but her younger brother also. Following them at a safe distance, eventually he waylaid the group as they watched a band of travelling players enact a play depicting Robin Hood and Maid Marion – the latter being played by a fair-haired lad.

The result of the encounter was an invitation to sup again with the Lowthers that evening. Before the night was ended, his manners and gaiety brought an invitation to dwell with the family, instead of residing in a hostelry, whilst business kept him in Durham. A favour which was earned not only by his manner, but also by the discovery that he too was of the Roman Catholic faith. The Lowthers were devout Catholics, a fact they tried to keep secret. Such secrecy was necessary as there was much anti-Catholic feeling. But rumour had always surrounded the family. Queen Elizabeth had been reasonably tolerant of Catholics during her long reign, but anyone convicted of heresy still stood to be dispossessed of his lands and even confined to goal. As for King James, no one was entirely certain, as yet, of how lenient he was going to be. There were people who had either lived during the time of the persecution of Protestants, or had heard reports from parents and grandparents of the horrific burnings which had taken place during the reign of Queen Mary which ensured there was always fear of a Protestant backlash. So, all things considered, wise Catholics worshipped as secretly as possible. But servants gossiped. The truth was, nearly everyone gossiped.

'I am sure you will be more comfortable with us,' fussed Mistress Lowther, delighted by the discovery of his faith.

Before a week passed, Robert Bingham had wooed and won Rosalind Lowther, and not only she but her mother and brother too. He was elegant and handsome, his charm irresistible. Rosalind was infatuated. She was unworldly enough – in spite of her wealthy upbringing – to gaze with amazement as he showered her with gifts, such as bales of damask and sarsenet, while her mother received precious spices. He sent eloquent letters describing his devotion and even composed songs to her. The betrothal took place at Lammastide, and she confessed herself to be the happiest of women, for not many young ladies of her station were able to wed where they loved. As for the wedding, it was to take place at Michaelmas. So delighted was her family, it never occurred to any of them how little of his personal history was known. They heard skeletal facts pertaining to his family, his place of birth and his education. It did not seem to matter. It was actually the besotted Rosalind herself who first made mention of this, shortly after the betrothal.

The family were, at that time, grieving over the death of a dear friend, a woman who was not actually a blood relative but one whom the younger generation regarded as a revered and wise aunt and whom Mistress Lowther considered to be akin to a sister, in spite of the fact the woman in question was devoutly Protestant. In autumn of the previous year, Lady Margaret Farrer had attended a banquet at Durham Castle. This had been given in honour of King James, who stayed there whilst en route to London, whither he was journeying to claim the crown of England, after the death of Queen Elizabeth some months previously. At the time Lady Margaret admitted to feeling ill, and although she did not admit as much it appeared certain her condition was grave. Her skin, seemingly overnight, developed a yellow tinge, which deepened by the very hour. In spite of subsequent ministrations by the most skilled doctors, she failed to improve, and in July, shortly after Lammas, was carried to the Lowther household, there to be looked after by her loving friends, for it had been her sad fate to outlive husband and children, all having perished of plague.

Robert Bingham was never to meet this much-loved family friend, for she expired a day before he returned to the Lowther household, following an excursion to France to obtain merchandise. Upon his return, he found his adoring Rosalind excusably distressed, yet, although she shed tears over Lady Margaret Farrer, his intuition told him there was an underlying calmness of spirit amid her grief. Certainly she was nowhere near as distraught as her mother, who had taken to her bedchamber, claiming to suffer from a nervous humour. Bingham could remain with the family only a few days, and he quit the house, again on business, the day after the funeral. But he sensed there was something different about Rosalind, and it had nothing to do with her grief.

To begin with, when she regarded him with those glorious eyes there was something amiss in her gaze. The adoration had changed. The young woman who gazed into his eyes seemed now to read his soul. It was a disquieting experience, for there was much of his soul he wished to remain illegible; such as a wife in Brittany, a poor but beauteous woman who had piously refused to bed with him until matrimony had taken place. She still lived, but the marriage was childless. There was also a mistress and two bastards in Dover. Nor was he Roman Catholic. Having heard rumours about the Lowthers faith, his admission had merely been a ruse to ingratiate himself.

'I wish dear Robert had remained here for a few days longer; his presence would cheer us,' sighed Mistress Lowther on the evening following his departure.

'You are pensive, Sister,' observed Rosalind's older brother, Christopher. 'We all grieve, but we must remember, Margaret suffered during her final months. We must be thankful she is with God now,' and reverently and unselfconsciously, he genuflected.

'I agree.' Usually Rosalind would have copied the gesture. Now she did not, but no one noticed the omission. 'But it was Robert whom I was thinking of. Brother, it strikes me we know naught of him.'

'We know he is rich,' declared Christopher, whose wife, presently great with child, was carefully embroidering the collar of the bridal gown with exquisite stitches. 'His house may be old, but it has been totally restored... virtually rebuilt. Jesu, you will have a home many will be envious of!'

'I was not thinking of his wealth,' mused Rosalind. 'I was thinking of his character.'

Christopher, being closer to his sister than anyone else, had also sensed a change in her during the past few days. Dismissing this as being clearly pre-wedding nerves, he soothed, 'He is a good man. A devout Roman Catholic. You are fortunate, Sister,' he squeezed her hand reassuringly. 'You will be a happy woman, for he is clearly gentle of character, not quick to wrath, and in short will make an amicable lord and husband.'

'Mayhap we are so overjoyed by his wealth and religion, we overlook too much,' she mused.

'Well, the betrothal is done, 'tis binding, and you must set your fears aside. Be guided by myself and your lady mother, and you will be happy,' her brother fondly advised.

Mistress Lowther, beguiled by her spice chest, now filled with all manner of exotic substances, nodded her agreement. Bingham was a gem of a son-in-law.

There was nothing Rosalind could do but accept the betrothal as binding. For both incubus and succubus, such things were usually accepted patiently anyway. What else could they do? A human body lives but a short while, and trials and tribulations were to be endured. One body died and was discarded, sometimes with regret, whilst a new life commenced in a new host. Rosalind was, so far, a satisfactory host.

Bingham, on the day of his marriage, was an uneasy man. The Rosalind to whom he had been betrothed now possessed a different personality. The air of innocence was gone, as was her utter adulation of himself. His young bride gazed upon him with a cool appraising stare; it was disconcerting. He missed those adoring glances; they had been so delightful to encounter. As for their wedding night, it was a puzzlement.

Undoubtedly Rosalind was a virgin; her upbringing had been such she could not be anything else. But – and he could not adequately explain this – she seemed to be experienced. He had lain with virgins before and, however enthusiastic they were for him to dispense with their virginity, they had been eager yet apprehensive. Rosalind was neither. She was virginal, but she was calmly accepting of her fate on that wedding night. So calm, it dampened his manly enthusiasm.

The newlywed Binghams lived in the home Robert had purchased months before meeting Rosalind. At great expense – which Bingham never tired of mentioning – the old manor house had been restored and extended. Their marital residence, Harrociff Park, was situated outside the village of Harrofeldt, which in turn was but three miles from Durham. Now a house of some consequence, Robert had plans to rename it Bingham Park. Like many great houses, it was built on the bank of a river, in this instance the River Wear, for it was easier to transport furniture and goods by river than by land. The Harrofeldt family, who gave their name to the village, resided in a larger house, called Harrofeldt Hall, lying north of the village, and proudly they claimed their name came from Viking forebears. Impressed by this, Robert visualised the name "Bingham" surviving for centuries. But it could only survive if his wife proved fruitful.

Unfortunately, Rosalind persisted to have a curious affect upon his manhood. Never had he encountered problems before when dealing with an attractive – nay beautiful – woman. But his wife's cool, knowing gaze was enough to dampen anyone's ardour, he reasoned resentfully. Thinking back to his first meeting with her, of her evident admiration, he wondered how he could have been so deceived.

But however aloof Rosalind's gaze might be, that of her personal maid was definitely not lacking in enthusiasm. Anna was decidedly attracted to him and, finding her interest flattering compared with the indifference of his wife, within weeks of his marriage he not only possessed a wife but also a mistress. The situation was uncomfortable, for though he had no qualms about taking a mistress, he would have preferred to be associated with someone not of his own household. However, Anna was pretty enough, though not as lovely as his wife. But at least she was a total contrast, being small and dark, as opposed to Rosalind's tall fair beauty.

Inevitably, during that first year of marriage Rosalind remained childless. As for Anna, she confided to her lover she might be with child.

'There is a man who will marry me,' she whispered to Robert one night, as they lay furtively in each other's arms in her small room, separated from Rosalind's chamber only by a communicating door. It never occurred to Robert, but this very furtiveness enhanced his desire for the servant. 'He loves me well, and although the child is not his – I have lain with none but you – he will gladly give his name to the babe.'

This was a dilemma for Robert. The babe was his, and Anna was talking of marrying someone else, which meant the infant – which might be a boy – would bear another man's name. His protests were waived aside by his companion.

'You have taken many light women in your time, during your travels. You are virile and your seed will have borne fruit, yet you have known it not. Why be so concerned now?' she demanded in what appeared to him a guileless manner.

This was something he could not argue with. Silenced, he pondered upon the situation. He had a dream of founding a dynasty; without a son, a legitimate son, it was an impossible dream. Anna, his paramour, was with child. Rosalind was not, nor ever would be. With her, he was impotent. But Rosalind was well connected, well brought up. Attributes which could never be applied to Anna.

Anna was not as detached as she outwardly appeared to be. She was pleasing to look upon, fruitful, but a serving maid nonetheless, who spoke truly when she claimed there was a man who would be glad to marry her. Indeed he would, but he was penniless, and she had no desire to marry a penniless man. With covetous eyes she gazed upon her mistress, whilst closing her ears to the love and respect Mistress Bingham evinced from the remainder of the household.

Particularly loyal to Rosalind was young Mol, a kitchen wench. Mol, Anna fancied, was a cunning hussy; there was something sharp and knowing about her. When she mentioned this to Robert, he failed to agree with her. Mol, he stated, was very adoring of Rosalind, who ensured she was not ill-treated by her fellow servants. As for Anna and himself, they had been careful regarding their relationship. But he was worldly enough to know how easy it was for the truth to be discovered. An unconscious gesture, a sidelong smile... it did not take much for servants to be suspicious. Could it not be that Mol had guessed the truth? Perhaps she resented Anna for taking the place of Rosalind in her husband's affections... and bed. He explained this to Anna, who unwillingly admitted this might be so, but, she informed him, it hardly mattered. Soon she would be married to her suitor, a strolling player. At least she would be when he returned home, for currently he was elsewhere. In fact she knew not where.

Rosalind, being no fool, was quick to suspect her serving maid was with child, and it was easy to guess at the name of the child's father. Robert was not as cunning as he believed himself to be. He had always singled Anna out. No doubt, Rosalind thought wryly, he imagined he was being very circumspect in his behaviour. But the infidelity of a husband, whose shallowness failed to earn her respect, troubled her not at all. Other matters did. The new King was reputed to live in fear of demons and witches; indeed, it was rumoured he was an expert on the subject. So much so, he had penned a book called *Demonology*. In consequence, His Majesty's subjects were becoming fearful of witches and demons. Her intuition told her the entire county would be swept with witch–fever.

Her fears were justified. Very quickly, it seemed, everyone looked askance at their neighbour, looking for signs of witchery. It was a sad state of affairs, Rosalind decided regretfully, hoping she was exaggerating this in her mind. Perhaps it was not as serious as she thought it was.

Several weeks later, an old lady, resident in the village of Harrofeldt since birth, was taken for questioning. Her crime, in Rosalind's opinion, was none other than being old and eccentric. She was found innocent, and freed, but her mind was never the same again. Terrified by her ordeal, she went insane, drowning herself in the River Wear within weeks of her release. Rosalind now realised that anyone who appeared different to others could be looked upon as being a witch or warlock. For herself she feared not. She was a succubus and therefore would outlive the body of Rosalind Bingham. Her fears were for others, so anxiously she observed events. People were on the lookout now for witches. Very quickly it was as if an epidemic raged. Folk eager to appear caring and responsible, and those eager to be rid of foes or rivals, could whisper their fears, whether true or false, to members of the clergy. With zeal, the clergy investigated all reports. If they did not, they too could be accused of being in league with dark forces.

She noticed with mild concern that Henry Reynolds, the local vicar, began visiting her home regularly. He singled her out for his especial attention, his reason for so doing, he claimed, being her reputation for wisdom. Rosalind Bingham was renowned as a wise and knowing woman, knowledgeable beyond her years in the ways of medical lore and human nature. This was hardly surprising, she supposed wryly. Her body might be youthful, but she had been around for several hundred years. Try though she might to seem no different to anyone else, it was a truly difficult task. She *was* different. Nor was it challenging to surmise who had reported her to the vicar, for someone had surely reported her to him, otherwise he would not be so interested in the state of her soul. It was Anna, her maid. Unknown to the latter, she had overheard her commenting to her fellow servants that Mistress Bingham was a strangely discerning woman, and knowledge such as hers was surely beyond normality.

It was possible, of course, that Anna and Robert might be in agreement with one another, their purpose being to betray her to the authorities. Only two nights ago, Robert had cursed her for being an enchantress, filling him with desire for her beautiful face and body, whilst at the same time repelling him, rendering him unable to use her body as was lawful for a husband to use his wife. But some deep intuition told her that although Robert was shallow and a philanderer, he valued her for her status; through her he achieved respect, and even envy, from other men. So, he would not personally cast her to the newly created witchfinders, even though his paramour carried his child.

Henry Reynolds, the vicar, spent much time talking to Mistress Bingham. He was a thin man, with a hawk-like nose and pale, piercing blue eyes, which he allowed to linger longer than was comfortable in the direction of her modestly covered bosom. Rosalind's choice of attire had never, ever, included daring necklines. Everything about him repulsed her, from his cold, empty eyes, to his thin, white hands. He took much time to examine her views upon the Church, marriage, motherhood, and life in general.

He had observed, he informed her, that she adopted a tolerant view of human nature, seeming to anticipate that all men and women were prone to faults, she included, therefore she was willing to excuse the faults of others, anticipating they would excuse her own shortcomings. This was surely not a Christian view? Faults, Reynolds felt, must be purged. As must all sin. By torture if necessary.

It was possible, of course, that Reynolds visited their home for another reason, Rosalind told herself. It could be because he suspected her family was of the Church of Rome. The irony was that she no longer celebrated the Mass. Some days after their wedding, Robert had admitted he was really Protestant and had forbade her to worship according to the rites of the Roman faith. Rosalind in turn had explained that she too was Protestant but had celebrated the Mass simply out of respect for her family. Reynolds would find no evidence of the Mass being celebrated in the Bingham home.

However, a new vicar was appointed to take over the parish, and Henry Reynolds was then officially created Witchfinder, and therefore her fears that he suspected her of worse than Catholicism intensified. Uneasily she believed Reynolds was now ready to accuse her of witchcraft.

There were numerous ways of identifying a witch. They had secret nipples, which they used to suckle imps. They had moles which did not bleed when pierced with sharp pins. When submerged in water witches did not drown. If branded with red-hot irons, their skin did not burn. Witches were to blame for all manner of calamities, from a cow losing its milk, to a sudden drought or deluge. Witches caused crops to fail, cream or ale to go sour.

Her fears were justified. One of the skills of an incubus or succubus was the ability to look into the minds of others, something which these days she never undertook lightly, believing the thoughts of others were sacred to themselves and not to be examined for her amusement. One autumn evening, as Rosalind supposedly slept, she left her body reclining on her bed and ventured to the home of Reynolds. There, looking into his mind, she saw what she already suspected – a twisted and ambitious man. The word "evil" was one she hated to apply to anyone, but Reynolds came close to it. She knew what was planned for her; that when Robert was away from home, she was to taken away and borne to the home of Henry Reynolds, there to be formally accused.

Wildly she considered returning to her childhood home. But if she did so, what might happen to her mother and brother? They too would come under suspicion. Apprehensively, she accepted her fate. A couple of days later, Robert set out for France, and almost immediately she was arrested according to Reynolds' plan.

'Madam, one of your servants, who shall be nameless, declares you to be a witch, for you know too much by far. She doth claim you predict household events, knowing who will marry whom and whether that marriage will be happy or no.' Reynolds' cold, lizard–like eyes watchfully regarded her.

As he uttered this, Rosalind knew she had been guilty of being too open. She had lived for many years now, and this present decade was not a time to show knowledge. Especially from a woman. She should have realised this. Truly it took no witchery to predict the success of a marriage, simply a sense of how one personality would suit another, and she had had many years of experience regarding human nature. More so than anyone else. She had not been sufficiently discreet, and it was a lesson she had better learn quickly, lest when she seized upon another body the same fate might follow. As for Reynolds, when first he had met her she knew he had looked upon her with lust. When looking into his mind, that suspicion had been confirmed. That lust had not been returned, so he considered himself spurned and would seek to destroy her. She also knew the identity of her betrayer. That person was Anna. To be certain of her suspicion, she had looked into Anna's mind.

'What manner of witch are you, madam?' he demanded an hour later, pale eyes gleaming. Her body had been stripped naked and pierced with pins, but his assistants had found no sign of a witch spot upon her.

Overcome with shame and embarrassment, she pulled her petticoat about her person, covering as much of her bleeding flesh as she could. They could find no witch mark, but she was surely doomed to die. Knowing she was to perish as a witch, there was no harm in telling this man the truth.

'I am Maude Dubreise,' she stated once alone with him. This name, her first name ever, was the one she always regarded as being her true identity. 'I am more than two hundred years old,' she informed him evenly, through teeth chattering with cold and fright. 'But I am not evil. I thrive on that which is good. As does most of my kind.'

'You are a succubus,' he guessed instantly and correctly. Then incorrectly added: 'Therefore you thrive on that which is carnal.'

'That I do not,' she insisted truthfully.

'There is a preference now that a witch should hang, not burn. I think, madam, one such as you should burn. You are possessed by an evil spirit. Your servant informed me of your evil ways, and when first I met you I knew you had the mark of the evil one upon you. You struck me as being a woman of much knowledge, none of it wholesome.'

'Do as you wish,' Rosalind's reply was weary.

Anna had betrayed her in order to become Robert's lawful wife and bear him his child in holy wedlock. As for Robert, he was weak but not ruthless. She had by this time looked into his mind, learning of his earlier marriage, which made this marriage unlawful. She knew also of his bastard children. The whole betrayal of herself had been formulated by Anna, without his knowledge. She, Rosalind – once Maude Dubreise – now knew which body her spirit would next occupy.

'But it is beyond your skills to destroy me,' she assured the witchfinder confidently. 'I abhor all that is evil and am a servant of the true and living God. I worship the Lord Jesus with penitence and adoration and believe in the divine power of the Holy Spirit. I am Protestant and worship according to the liturgy of the Protestant Church. I speak truly to you, sir, and throughout your future career methinks you will never forget my words…'

'She is about to curse you!'

She had thought herself alone with Reynolds, but a rough henchman had silently entered the room at some point, unnoticed, a man who had recently prodded her with pins. He struck her roughly about the mouth. 'That I shall not do,' she spoke indistinctly, tasting blood. Running her tongue experimentally about her teeth, she felt a few of them had been slackened, if not broken. Wincing with pain, she added, unable to raise her voice above a whisper, 'I give you a blessing, sir, in the sure knowledge that if you are undeserving it will return to me. I will pray for you.'

'I do not require the prayers of one such as yourself,' Reynolds icily informed her.

'I think you need a great deal of prayer,' Rosalind whispered meaningfully.

And so it happened that four days later, on a wet morning, she was taken by cart to Durham marketplace, and there beheld the scene of her intended execution. The stake, surrounded by faggots, stood dark and sinister... and wet, therefore the faggots would smoulder rather than burn. An excited, interested crowd had gathered, and glancing quickly about she ascertained that Robert was not a spectator. It was unlikely he could be as he was not due to return from France for several days yet.

Anna *was* amongst the crowd. Gloating no doubt, Rosalind surmised, noting the woman was wearing ample skirts to disguise her condition. Henry Reynolds was there too, clutching a prayer book and praying aloud, one hand grasping the book, the other raised in entreaty, pleading for the soul of the woman who was about to be burned. *Hypocrite,* she thought contemptuously. *You are more evil than I.*

Her captors, handling her roughly, bound her arms behind her back, nearly jerking her shoulders from their sockets and causing her to wince with pain. Then she was chained to the stake. What manner of man was Reynolds? Surely he knew she was innocent. The only witch test they had performed upon her had been to prick her, which had been unbearably painful and undignified but had only served to proclaim her innocence. They had deprived her of sleep for two days, trying unsuccessfully to force a confession of witchcraft. Yet now he and his assistants were bent upon burning her for the crime of admitting she was a succubus. According to Reynolds, there was no distinction between the two. *I should not have admitted to him that I am a Succubus,* she mused. Yet, without doubt, the Witchfinder was determined she should die anyway. What difference did it make?

The faggots were lit and, instead of blazing, smouldered as she had known they would. The flames did not rise healthily, but flickered, and were she not a succubus her death would have been slow and painful indeed. Eyes watering from the smoke, she gazed intently upon Anna, whose countenance was anguished, not gloating, which was the reaction she expected. Assailed by a fit of coughing as smoke entered her nostrils, she knew it was time to leave the body of Rosalind Bingham to its fate.

Anna saw the intent glance, the fit of coughing, and then beheld the once beauteous body of her mistress sag, overcome with smoke. Silently she prayed she would not regain consciousness to endure the agony of the flames. She had wanted to be rid of her mistress but had not anticipated how badly she would be treated, or that she would actually be burned. She had simply envisaged Robert divorcing his wife. As she stood watching, Anna felt a strange sensation, a stirring within her very head. It must be due to her condition, for she could think of naught else it could be.

The smell of burning flesh filled the air, turning her sick. Hastily she quit the scene. Rosalind's body still sagged at the stake, and it was clear she would never awaken. She had died quickly, without suffering, which was a blessing.

By the time Anna returned home, Maude Dubreise (or Rosalind Bingham) discovered two new and unsuspected items. She had not examined Anna's mind for long enough to unearth the whole truth. The babe was possibly Robert's, but mayhap not. Anna had not come to Roberts as the virgin she claimed to be, but had given herself numerous times to the strolling player.

Also, Anna had not worked alone. She had persuaded Mol, the kitchen wench, who was badly favoured with a crooked nose and overly large forehead, to be the person to report Rosalind to the witchfinders. Mol was willing enough to do so, being assured by Anna that the witchfinders would look with favour upon her for so doing, and it could be that one of them might actually wed her. Her apparently deep love for her mistress was not as deep as she'd proclaimed it to be.

A few days later, Robert returned home to find himself widowed. He had the boldness to declare his wife was no witch, but then contradicted himself by informing Reynolds he had actually been bewitched, for he could not consummate his marriage. For sure he was not impotent; the serving wench was with child by him after all.

Anna suddenly found herself regarding him knowingly, recognising him for the weak philanderer he was. Her mind was suddenly filled with a huge amount of knowledge, and she knew not how it came about. Over the course of the following days she discovered the source.

'So, Rosalind burned,' reflected Tracy. Horrid death. Witches were usually burned in Scotland. In England mostly they were hanged. Which was pretty horrid too. In reality, they choked to death. It wasn't quick and clean, then.'

'No,' agreed Sara. 'The humane long drop had yet to be invented. And I have to admit, I still feel uneasy at the possibility that I might have been bigamously married to someone!'

'But you're a woman, and in those days if you weren't married you had no status. You had little choice but to marry him. He was a better proposition than the strolling player, or pedlar… whatever he was,' Tracy stated logically.

'I never saw *him* again,' Sara explained.

'Well, you acted wisely, then! But what happened to Anna… and to Mol, the kitchen maid?' Tracy demanded.

'Anna lived to bear Robert eleven children. I recall that one was stillborn, two died in early infancy, and three died of childhood ailments. Five survived into adulthood. Robert Bingham clearly didn't find Anna as threatening to his manhood as Rosalind. As for his wife in France – well, I have no idea what happened to her. There was plague in the town where she lived, so it's probable she died. But I was uneasy at possibly being bigamously married to him.

'Mol, the kitchen maid, was dispatched from the house. I must admit, it had never occurred to me to examine Mol's mind, so her betrayal came as a surprise. In fact I was quite hurt, because I treated her kindly. She actually did quite well for herself, all things considered. She married a miller, which meant she wasn't rich but she never wanted for the necessities of life, which so many people lacked in those days. After all these years I can still manage to recall her face. It's engraved in my mind!'

'I kind of hoped you'd say she came to a bad end,' sighed Tracy. 'She deserved a ghastly fate! You know, Sara, you don't seem to peer into people's minds as much as I do,' she reflected.

'Well, I like to respect people's privacy. I took it too far back then. In spite of being two hundred years old I acted foolishly! But when necessary, I take a look. Thinking about bad deeds, I think bad people are always punished, somehow, sometime.' Sara smiled broadly, the sunlight glinting, briefly, from her brace. She hated the brace, but fortunately it wasn't permanent. She was a succubus. She had time, and knew how to wait.

CHAPTER FIVE

C HAS, SEATED OPPOSITE HIS DAUGHTER WITH THE chessboard on the table between them, surveyed her intent face. What concentration! Amused, he confidently awaited her move, anticipating a speedy victory. When playing against his daughter, usually he tried not to demoralise her by winning too quickly; and by protracting the game he hoped she would improve her own game. Certainly she was taking this game seriously. *Chess ought to be taken seriously.* He could think of no other game which depended solely on skill and left nothing to luck. It was all about strategy. She was looking very pretty too. She and Tracy, having spent much of the day in the garden, in spite of the poor weather, were both rosy, causing Jennifer to spout remarks about melanomas over dinner. As the game progressed he realised Sara was certainly improving; he was having to think before each move.

'Check, Dad,' she declared eventually, moving her bishop.

'What!' He sat bolt upright, studying the board with as much intensity as the girl. Quickly he moved his knight, protecting his king from Sara's bishop. Briefly he noticed she'd called him "Dad"; he wasn't "Daddy" anymore. A momentary spasm of regret assailed him but was sternly suppressed by the strategy of the game.

'Check,' she announced again, some minutes later, tactically moving a castle.

Amazed at feeling under pressure from his daughter, whose ability at chess he had thought to be abysmal, Chas took rapid stock of the situation, then moved his king out of danger. An excellent player since boyhood, he knew he ought to be thrilled by her sudden improvement, but although he refused to admit it he hated losing.

'Checkmate.' Sara again moved her bishop.

Stunned, Chas realised he'd been beaten. It was surely a fluke. The game had lasted less than an hour!

'You and Tracy have certainly been practising,' he stated, trying to recall the moves of the game. 'Yes, you got off to a really good start; that does show practice,' he mused aloud, realising he must concentrate more when he next played his daughter. *I do tend to assume the game will be easy,* he ruminated.

'Do you want another game?' beamed Sara.

'Yes, if you wish.' Chas was anxious to regain supremacy, especially against a twelve-year old.

This time the game lasted considerably longer, continuing long past Sara's bedtime, not that it mattered since the summer holiday had begun. He had been casual about the previous match, but to his total shock the outcome was the same. Sara won. Her concentration, he noted, was intense. She was growing up so fast; there was something unchildlike about her. Looking into her eyes as she announced 'Check' he felt, uncomfortably, that there was something knowing and aged about those unlined, clear eyes. Had Jennifer looked like that when arriving at puberty? For the first time he wondered if Jen's worries were justified. But she was just a child…

'I like chess,' she announced, packing the chess pieces into the case, disturbing his train of thought. Unconsciously she echoed his own earlier thoughts. 'Chance doesn't come into it. It must be the only game in the world where that doesn't happen. You know something, I've been fancying playing mah-jong; maybe you and Mum should buy it.'

'Maybe,' Chas nodded, torn between outrage at being bested and pride in his daughter. His unease was abating.

'If you have had enough of chess, I'm going to have a shower.' Blithely she quit the room, singing some song he'd never heard before. He assumed it was Lady Gaga, because the young people in his office seemed to like her.

What had gone wrong? How had Sara managed to win? She *was* improving intellectually of late.

'Don't bother me, Jen,' he announced, hearing his wife come into the room. 'I've had a bad evening… beaten at chess.'

'I've not exactly had a good evening either,' Jennifer declared.

In fact, she'd had a terrible evening. Some hours ago Chas had informed her mother that it was time she returned to her own home. As a result Vi was upset, having apparently entertained plans to actually move it. Move in! Much as she loved her mother, Jennifer could not bear the idea of permanently sharing a house with her. 'Of course you're welcome to come and stay, Mum,' she had assured her, 'but you must see it's better you keep your own home. Independence is best,' she'd said, trying to be as gentle as possible.

The end result of the conversation was that Vi, with an air of injured martyrdom, intended to return to her home after tea on Sunday. But Jennifer felt ashamed, as if she'd let her mother down by refusing to give her a permanent home. It just wouldn't work, she reassured herself. Much as she loved her mother, it had to be said that she and Vi bickered. Then there was the interference. Yesterday Vi had gone out and bought some duck egg blue paint for the dining room, without first consulting anyone. She'd even contacted a decorator to undertake the work! But what had really annoyed Chas had been the discovery that Vi had sacked Elsie that afternoon, without discussing the matter with him or Jennifer. Jennifer had rushed to Elsie's house directly after dinner to make peace, placating her with the promise that Vi would soon be moving out. So, if they all lived together permanently, it would be a recipe for disaster.

Following her visit to Elsie, Jennifer had quietly and furtively prepared to listen to a discourse between Sara and Tracy, which she'd recorded. Feeling disturbed by the conversation overheard the previous evening, she'd set up the voice recorder, attaching it to the patio table, since the girls had announced they planned to sit outside. At lunchtime she'd returned home, feeling like a criminal, to discover the two chatting together in exactly the place she'd discreetly placed it.

Aware this was being underhand, but too perturbed to care, she switched on the voice-activated player. It commenced inauspiciously enough, the girls chatting pleasantly. *But they don't talk like young girls,* she thought uneasily, her recent unpleasant exchange with her mother forgotten.

"Have you ever been famous? Famous as in a historic person who was a beacon for future generations? Florence Nightingale, for example? Edith Cavell? Violette Szabo?" It was Sara's voice, childlike in tone yet mature in speech.

Next came Tracy's voice. "I was a well-known cook once, famous in my time, but my fame didn't survive to go down through the centuries. My recipes have been plagiarised – that is the correct description – by many succeeding cooks and chefs," mused Tracy. "And I've been married to a Prime Minister. I thought it might be a more powerful role than it was. I was Hester Pitt, wife of William Pitt the Elder, no less. He never allowed me to rule the country. What about you?"

Sara spoke again. "No, I've never been famous in my own right. I was once a poet called Daisy Gardiner. Yes, I agree; who's heard of the Victorian poet Daisy Gardiner? And for your information, that was indeed my name. Yet there is a volume (a small one!) of her work in the British Museum if you would care to look! It lies beside the work of such luminaries as Emily Bronte, Elizabeth Barrett, Robert Browning and Charles Dickens! Did you ever *meet* anyone *really* famous?" she inquired.

Feeling dizzy, Jennifer realised she was holding her breath. Sitting cross-legged on her bed, forcing herself to breath regularly and deeply, she continued to listen, hardly able to believe what she was hearing.

"Yes, I had some Waterloo teeth," Sara's voice. "A set of false teeth where the actual teeth were taken from cadavers from the battle. They were of no use to them, so it seemed like a good idea at the time."

How did she know about Waterloo teeth? Of course, that could be from history lessons at school, mused Jennifer.

Tracy's voice. "But the first famous person who really, really impressed me was Joan of Arc. I was in Rheims when she was burned. I was there."

Jennifer realised she was holding her breath again. Then the voice recorder began crackling as sudden gusts of wind distorted the sound. But she managed to make out Sara's voice saying:

"Vampires and werewolves, of course, there are hundreds of books and films about them. But incubi and succubi are in the minority. Maybe it's a good thing… maybe." There came more crackling and distortion. Then again came Sara's voice. "I stressed that a succubus, like any human, can be good or evil. We absorb the identities of those whom we inhabit. We are influenced by those with whom we associate. But we grow stronger as we progress from body to body, less likely to be influenced for the bad. Most of us are good. But those who are bad are bad indeed... pure evil. And it is they who give us such a terrible reputation. But he wouldn't accept my definition and insisted I couldn't be anything but evil."

Feeling sick, Jennifer tried to surmise that it surely was some sort of fiction the two girls had cooked up. They were working on a school project or something. But then, she reasoned, they went to different schools. Bewildered and numb, for some time, nearly quarter of an hour, she remained seated on her bed, wanting – yet not wanting – to replay the whole thing again. Incubus. Succubus. She'd heard of the former, but had no clear idea of what it meant. Sara had spoken accurately when she'd stated that most modern people knew, or were familiar with, the term incubus but had no idea what succubus meant.

Rousing herself, she switched the recorder on again and listened to the full dialogue. The entire conversation wasn't recorded; its memory was inadequate for anything above a half hour. But what she heard was disturbing enough. Clutching the recorder, she went downstairs and there found Chas alone in the dining room, frowning at the chessboard.

She collected a large dictionary from the sitting room bookcase then, sitting opposite to him at the dining room table, she spoke tersely.

'Listen to a piece of recording, Chas,' she instructed. 'It's part of a conversation between Sara and Tracy. I've listened to it once and need to do so again. I think you should listen with me.'

The fact she'd gone to the trouble of actually recording the conversation surprised Chas; it seemed an extreme and intrusive thing to do. But perturbed by the urgency of her tone, and the tension in her face, he withheld any comments and silently listened to the voices. Stiffening with surprise, he heard his daughter say, "I not only saw Lord Nelson, I spoke with him. Ugly man. At the time I *knew* he was famous, everyone was talking about him, but I couldn't see what Emma Hamilton saw in him. It was clear she was smitten… as he was with her. Modern historians often neglect to comment on how fat she was. Plump women were considered very desirable to men in those days. But she was *fat!* And he – Nelson – had a queer kind of smile. Eventually I discovered it was because a lot of his teeth were missing."

Shaking his head in bewilderment, he touched the pause button.

'They're having some kind of jest! How did you manage to record this?'

'I hid it, and I guess I was lucky enough,' she shrugged helplessly, 'if you can call it lucky, to catch this. Keep listening for a while longer.' She switched the machine on again.

Resting his elbows on the table and his chin in his hands, Chas continued to listen.

"I lived in France several times, for approximately a century on one occasion. I saw the Sun King. My, was he handsome. Not a let-down like your Lord Nelson." Chas recognised it was Tracy who now spoke.

'Please keep listening,' begged Jennifer.

Chas, responding to the distress in her voice, grasped one of her hands; the reassuring warmth of the contact made her feel more cheerful than she'd felt during the whole of what had been a traumatic evening.

After the recording ended abruptly, Jennifer opened the dictionary.

'I've looked up incubus and succubus,' she announced. Reading aloud, her voice hurried, she intoned, 'Incubus – an incubus is a male spirit, essentially evil, who is believed to assume a male body and has sexual relations with women whilst they sleep.' Flicking forward through the pages, she found the word succubus. 'Succubus,' she read. 'A succubus is an evil spirit which assumes female form and has sexual relations with men as they sleep. In ancient times it was believed that a succubus would seduce warriors on the eve of battle in order to render them weary and unfit for combat.'

'Jen, you're not saying our daughter has become a succubus?' Distracted, Chas ran his hands through his hair. 'It's ludicrous. Impossible. These things do not happen.' There was an edge of pleading in his voice. 'Everything has a logical explanation. There must be one, surely?!'

'I know,' Jennifer nodded, unconsciously mirroring his action, pulling her hair wearily away from her face. 'But I don't know what to think. There's something wrong. I know it. She is *not* my daughter. I know Sara, and what we have now is *not* Sara; she only looks like Sara. Only, there are times I feel she even looks different.'

'Let's listen to the rest of the recording,' he suggested, squeezing her hand, hoping this might provide an explanation for the situation. 'Maybe we're being over–imaginative.'

'I hope we are,' Jennifer managed a wry smile. It failed to reach her eyes. 'But if you tell me that girls mature more quickly the boys, I swear I shall… well, I shall hit you, Chas!'

She managed another wry smile. This time there was a steely glint in her eyes. Some girls maybe did mature quickly but Sara was not one of them. Until recently, she'd been *immature* for her age.

'Alright, Jen. But I keep saying that to make me feel better.' Pulling her close, he rubbed his cheek against her hair. 'Whatever's wrong, we can sort it together. Right?'

'Right.'

Comforted by the affectionate gesture, Jennifer was about to switch the machine on again.

'Wait; this needs a gin and tonic.'

Chas briefly disappeared, returning with two full glasses, complete with ice cubes clinking invitingly.

'I think you read my mind.' Jennifer accepted her drink. 'Maybe Mum's right, perhaps we do consume too much alcohol!'

'For medicinal purposes.' Grimly Chas switched the recorder on again and silently they listened till the end, when, annoyingly, it stopped mid sentence.

Helplessly, they exchanged distraught glances.

'She sounds like Shakespeare.' Jennifer felt inadequate to deal with the situation. Each time she listened to the recording, it simply endorsed the fact something was gravely amiss. 'Her vocabulary includes words like mayhap and methinks.'

'I wanted to hear more,' admitted Chas. 'I found myself listening to it as if it were a talking book. Yet at the same time I was disturbed, knowing it was my daughter describing the events. The woman whom she talks of, Rosalind; we can presume she died by being burned alive. Sadly we don't have the entire conversation.' As an afterthought he added, 'That is, if she ever existed.'

'Do you believe it?' Jennifer demanded.

'I *cannot* believe it, I don't want to. But I do seem to recall reading somewhere that the Scots burned witches. The English hanged them. I don't know if that's correct or not.' Feeling the need for another supportive glass of gin, Chas resisted the impulse. Going to work tomorrow with a hangover was not an inviting prospect. 'Jen, if we believe what's being said on that tape, do you know what it means?'

Jennifer was mute; she simply gazed into the bottom of her now empty glass, as if seeking inspiration.

Chas answered the question himself. 'It means, if we believe it, we have to accept our daughter is possessed. I never believed in such a thing in my entire life! Possession is for films like *The Exorcist*!'

'I wish I knew what to do.' Jennifer felt sick. 'And there's something I haven't told you. I thought – you know, with my going on about Sara not being Sara – that you would think I'd lost the plot. But one night, a week ago, I saw something in our room. I woke up and saw a woman. I wasn't frightened somehow; she wasn't scary. But a woman nonetheless. I could make out she had long plaits. Her features were indistinct but I felt she wasn't a pretty or glamorous woman. I saw no clothing, but her form was so shadowy. Like vapour. I've kept quiet about it… In fact, I've not allowed myself to think about it until now.'

It had been a strange experience, weird, yet somehow she'd not felt frightened. Years ago she and Chas had stayed in an old hotel, and during the night she'd felt as if someone was in the room with them, someone not very friendly, causing her to shake Chas, waking him up, and even he – who didn't believe in ghosts – admitted the atmosphere in the room felt unpleasant. Neither of them had gone back to sleep. But this recent apparition had been different altogether. Whatever it was just seemed to dissipate and drift through the bottom of the door, like smoke.

'You should have told me.' Chas's tone was gentle, not reproving. 'But unless I way it myself, I *would* probably have thought you were dreaming or something at the time,' he admitted.

'I'm sorry, I should have said something. But I hoped it was a dream. In fact, I still think it could have been a dream. What do you think?' Jen leaned her head against his shoulder.

'I think you *want* to think it was a dream. In fact, it surely *was* a dream,' he replied logically. 'If it happens again you *have* to wake me up, darling. I think we should have some caffeine.' Chas disappeared again, returning this time with two mugs of coffee. 'It was Sara, yet not Sara, whom I played chess with,' he reflected aloud. 'As for the recording, I don't know where she could have obtained all that information, you know, about witchfinders and so forth. I wish the entire conversation had been recorded. And the language... She's too young to know how to talk like that. You and I can. We've both enjoyed numerous Shakespearian plays. It's only a month since we went to the Theatre Royal at Newcastle to see *Hamlet*. We've also read the likes of Chaucer and Beowulf, which are yet more complex. More... well... archaic... than the way Sara spoke. But then she was supposedly speaking as someone from the seventeenth century. Far later than Chaucer and Beowulf.'

'Sara doesn't know Shakespeare, although she has heard of him of course. She might even have heard of Chaucer and Beowulf.'

Jennifer sipped her coffee. There was something relaxing about a hot drink. *Maybe that's why people drank so much tea during the Second World War,* she reflected inconsequentially.

They sat in silence for a while, each feeling a sense of union. They would deal with this together. Reaching for Chas's hand, Jennifer took another drink of coffee, again appreciating the warming effect. Her knees felt curious, as if they were turning to rubber. *Must be the gin*, she decided. Wine, which she was used to, didn't produce this effect. Unless of course it was shock.

'Maybe we should talk to Alan and Jilly Reynolds,' she suggested, wondering what, if anything, the Reynolds might be able to suggest.

Slowly Chas nodded in agreement.

'I think they should listen to the tape. We'll sleep on it and come to a decision tomorrow. We mustn't rush into something we might regret.' Glancing at his watch, with surprise he realised it was past midnight. 'Let's go to bed,' he sighed. 'Maybe we'll ring Alan Reynolds in the morning.'

'I feel tipsy; that gin must be powerful stuff,' Jennifer observed.

'Well, I poured out substantial amounts – to save having to get up to do a refill.' Chas managed a half smile. Jennifer had no head for spirits.

Helping her up the stairs, he thought he heard a faint clicking noise, the sound of a bedroom door surreptitiously shutting. Had Sara been listening to them talking? Probably not, he decided. It was unlikely she would be awake this late. More likely it was Vi – she had a penchant for surreptitiously listening to him and Jen talking; in fact, he'd caught her in the act more than once. At least something positive was going to happen – Vi was leaving!

The following morning, following a brief conversation with Jennifer, Chas rang the vicarage, finding Jilly on the other end of the line. Alan was busy all day – he had a funeral to conduct and a number of meetings – but they could certainly arrange to meet the Roseberrys that evening, especially as it sounded urgent. Tactfully Jilly refrained from remarking that Chas Roseberry sounded very uptight, and inwardly she hoped this wasn't due to marital problems. They seemed such a nice, close family. It would be tragic if Chas and Jennifer were contemplating splitting up.

'Of course. You could come to us?' Used to being confronted by all manner of crises, Jilly's voice was controlled, friendly but calm.

Chas thought rapidly. He and Jennifer had never thought to discuss where the meeting should take place. Perhaps it would be best held in their own home, then if Alan Reynolds wanted to speak to Sara she'd be around.

'Maybe you should come to us. Is that too much to ask? You would be doing us a great favour.'

'No problem. How about eight o'clock?'

Jilly's voice, Chas decided, was warm and kindly. No wonder many parishioners took their problems to her, notwithstanding her awful dress sense. In fact, he believed he'd never seen a woman who wore such dreadful clothes.

'That'll be fine. Whatever time you choose.'

Instinctively, he felt there might at least be some chance they would believe him. They would perceive that something was strangely affecting his daughter. They wouldn't simply dismiss it as adolescence or, worse, suggest it could be something akin to schizophrenia. He hardly dared admit it, even to himself, but he was terrified his daughter might have some mental malady. The only one he could put a name to was schizophrenia.

He'd telephoned the vicarage from work. Currently seated in his office, through the frosted door window he saw the outlines people walking along the corridor, whilst his secretary, in her little office next door, muttered to herself as she sat at her computer. What would his colleagues say if pressed for an opinion? Would they believe anything about an incubus or succubus possessing Sara? He didn't seriously believe it himself, but it was better than admitting the child was mentally ill. He knew Jen well enough to guess her thoughts; and although she hadn't admitted it aloud, he realised she believed the girl was possessed. If fact, she seemed to have suspected as much for several weeks now.

As they were eating breakfast that morning, Elsie had arrived to begin her work. Trying to quiz the cleaning lady, he'd remarked, with an air of innocence which he hoped would appear genuine, that Tracy was certainly growing into a smart, very intelligent young lady. Elsie's reply had been a breezy, 'Oh, she's bright alright is Tracy. Sometimes the hubby and I joke it's like she's been here before! You should hear some of the things she comes out with!'

Maybe we worry too much, Chas reflected hopefully.

Finishing work early, Jennifer indulged in some shopping. Retail therapy. Using the fact she needed new holiday clothes as an excuse. The truth was, she loved new clothes; they always cheered her up if she was upset or worried. And currently she was both. She didn't know whether to be flattered or offended by the remarks of the assistant.

'You really suit that skirt and jacket,' the young girl remarked. 'And they can be worn at any time – for the office or in the evening. Are you a secretary?'

'No, I'm a dentist,' Jennifer absently replied, her mind on other matters.

'You don't look like a dentist,' the assistant responded artlessly, sweeping a stray lock of lank hair from her eyes.

Jennifer wondered, *Do dentists have a certain look?*

'I don't carry the tools of my trade with me,' she acidly informed the assistant, instantly regretting her tone.

Upon returning home she took her packages upstairs, not bothering to do more than shout a greeting to Sara, who was in the garden, inevitably with Tracy, a fact which irritated her beyond measure. Desperately she was hoping that Sara's strange talk was all due to the older girl's influence; but a rational portion of her brain told her that if Tracy left, permanently, the problem would continue. Pushing the matter aside with an effort, Jennifer began opening her bags, intent upon studying the garments in the mirror. Sometimes items looked different when tried at home... probably something to do with the lighting in the shops, she supposed vaguely.

Sometime later she stood in front of her cheval mirror, clad in a new peach-coloured shift dress, with a chain belt hanging loosely at her trim waist. It looked undeniably good. Pleased with the effect, she donned a pair of peach and white sandals. There was a gentle knock and the bedroom door cautiously opened. Sara's face appeared.

'May I come in?' she inquired uncertainly.

As Jennifer nodded, Sara sat down on the bed.

'Tracy's gone. She's going to a barbecue with her parents.' She studied her mother with interest. 'You look great.'

Pleased by her daughter's response, Jennifer held up another shift dress, this time a mauve, floral affair.

'I'll wear this belt with both dresses. Real retro sixties,' she grinned. 'I nearly bought some platform sandals but decided that that was going too far with the sixties look!'

'That would be in the seventies,' Sara replied absently, peering into a well-filled carrier bag. 'You've had a good shopping trip. I love this shirt.' Heedless of the expression of frozen stillness on her mother's face, she pulled out several brightly hued tee shirts. 'You've bought four of them! But they're not all in the same size!' she observed.

'Two are for you,' Jennifer managed to announce.

How did Sara know platform sandals were from the seventies? Of course, she excused, the girl could have read it in a magazine. *I'm always looking for signs of strangeness,* she decided, feeling momentarily penitent.

'The shop assistant told me I don't look like a dentist. What's a dentist supposed to look like?' she demanded.

'Clinical maybe. Smelling of disinfectant perhaps. You don't look clinical, nor do you smell of chemicals, thank goodness. Dad would hate it,' was the prompt reply, followed by, 'Funny how fashion always seems to come full circle. I wonder how long it'll be before punk comes back in. I think the punk clothes were really creative. I hope they'll reappear before I'm too old to wear them.' Sara held a tee shirt against herself, studying the effect in the mirror. 'Thank you for the tee shirts. May I have some new shorts, Mother? I would like some.'

'Of course.' Jennifer suddenly sounded strangely wooden. 'I'll take you shopping at the weekend.'

'Wonderful,' she said happily, waving her tee shirts in the air in the act of departing from her mother's bedroom. 'These are great! See you later.'

'Sara!' Jennifer called as her daughter's hand rested on the door knob. 'Why have you begun to call me "Mother"? What's wrong with "Mummy" or "Mum"?'

'Well, "Mummy' sounds a bit infantile now. After all, I am growing up. And I'm not too sure about "Mum", but if you prefer it so be it!' beamed Sara, eyeing the tee shirts with satisfaction.

'I think "Mum" sounds more friendly than "Mother".'

'So be it, Mum,' was the placid response. 'It'll be fun having a girlie shopping day on Saturday. I'm so looking forward to it.'

Suddenly deflated, Jennifer sat heavily on the bed. Was she being paranoid? Was it normal or abnormal for a twelve-year-old to know about sixties' fashion and make comments about fashion turning full circle? It could be she was repeating something she'd overheard. Children did things like that. Taking a neat cotton three-piece suit – consisting of contrasting shorts and skirt, plus a three-quarter sleeve matching jacket – from a bag, she hung the items in the wardrobe, uncharacteristically without trying them on. Maybe she would do so later. At Sara's age, would she, Jennifer, have made such a remark? Maybe

Vi should be consulted... Well, maybe not. She answered this herself. She didn't want Vi interfering. As for Sara, usually she wasn't interested in clothes. At least she hadn't been in the past. It was a character trait Jennifer had previously found irritating. Now the girl suddenly seemed to be interested... which was also irritating, because Sara had changed, and she, her mother, couldn't figure out why. Well, she could, but she didn't like the explanation.

Alan and Jilly arrived punctually at the appointed time, having walked from the vicarage. Feeling a great need to indulge in a glass of wine, Chas wondered whether or not to ask Alan and Jilly if they wished to have a glass of Bardolino. Maybe it would be best to stick to coffee, he decided.

At first the atmosphere was distinctly stiff and embarrassed. Jilly, tall and gangly like her husband, was seated next to him on the sofa, their long legs splayed in differing directions. Jilly could have been a devastatingly attractive woman but, for reasons Jennifer would never understand, she was uninterested with either clothes or her appearance. Her hair, mousy and shoulder-length, was worn loose apart from a tortoiseshell Alice band, and it hung, lank and flyaway, in need of conditioner. As for her clothes, Jilly scoffed at the notion that there were colours that simply did not mix. She wore whatever colour combinations she chose. This evening she was wearing cropped slacks of an uninteresting pale boiled cabbage colour, blue canvas shoes and a loose, mauve, baggy tee shirt, much worn and stretched around the hem, with 'I Love Jesus!' emblazoned on the front. Her appearance could best be described as scarecrow. She hated tight clothes; so, consequently, her garb was usually too big, enhancing rather than hiding her lanky physique.

Offering her a cup of coffee, Chas realised, not for the first time, that Jilly possessed fine, intelligent eyes. They were olive in colour, bright and warm, illuminating a thin, pale face. Never did it occur to Jilly to wear make-up, but her face was arresting and her smile warm, showing white even teeth.

'Thanks. Just what I need,' she said, accepting the coffee.

'Just what I need too.' Alan Reynolds accepted his mug, balancing it on a bare, bony knee. He was wearing khaki shorts, which, like his wife's attire, seemed too large for him.

Jennifer, sitting primly in a neat skirt and blouse, wondered how they could ever introduce the subject of Sara, who, at the very last minute, had received an invitation from Simon to a barbecue next door. At least she was nearby if they needed to chat with her.

Vi was no longer in the house. Instead of waiting until Sunday, she'd abruptly returned to her home that morning, by taxi, shortly after breakfast, wearing an air of injured dignity. *Elsie had been supported instead of herself.* That, thought Jennifer, was certainly for the best, as it was probable Vi would have tried to gatecrash and interfere.

Chas too was wondering how to reveal the purpose of the arranged meeting. Seating himself next to Jennifer, who seemed remote and rigid, he endured a few moments of silence, as the Reynolds both gazed at him expectantly. Glancing downwards, he beheld an unexpected sight. Some alabaster eggs had fallen from Jilly's spacious but grubby fuchsia pink suede handbag.

'Did you lay those yourself?' Chas grinned impishly.

Jilly leaned backwards, giving forth a pleasant carillon of laughter.

'I've been to the Children's Club – we hold it once a week for the younger children. They were for an egg and spoon race!'

Scooping up the eggs and replacing them into the vast cavern of her bag, she rapidly took stock of Jennifer. A good judge of character, and able to do so without actually passing judgment, she'd long since deemed Jennifer to be earnest and well-meaning, but basically just a tad uptight. She liked Jennifer but longed to be able to tell her to relax and enjoy life. As yet she didn't know her well enough to do so.

'We need to talk to you about our daughter, Sara,' Chas explained, feeling it was easier somehow, now that everyone, including Jen, had burst out laughing. 'Jennifer spotted changes in her before I did... Well, I spotted changes but thought they were because girls grow up more quickly than boys. Jen, darling...'

Jen took the hint and began describing recent events, sometimes referring to a notebook, into which she had precisely dated and described varying incidences. Alan and Jilly listened attentively, not interrupting, and reserving questions until Jen had ceased speaking.

'You said you taped a conversation,' prompted Alan, when Jennifer paused for breath and fortified herself with a sip of coffee.

'Yes. We think you should hear it... or at least some of it.' Chas produced the digital recorder and pressed the start button. 'You'll notice the sound is not of the best quality, distorted by gusts of wind and sometimes birdsong.'

The Reynolds listened to all of the tape, occasionally stopping it to ask questions when clarification was needed. Eventually it finished, leaving the four adults sitting in contemplative silence.

'Anyone fancy a glass of Bardolino?' demanded Chas.. To his relief, everyone nodded their assent. 'Do you think Sara is mentally ill?' he demanded. The words had been uttered aloud. Mentally ill. A glass of wine was definitely required.

'I'm no doctor, but she sounds rational enough to me.' Alan Reynolds rubbed his chin gravely. 'But if she has a problem, then the other girl, Tracy, has a problem too.'

This had not occurred to either Chas or Jennifer.

'She seems to believe the stories she's telling,' Chas remarked, feeling a sudden surge of relief. Yes, Alan Reynolds was correct. If Sara had a problem, so did Tracy, and surely to goodness they both couldn't have the same mental issues.

'She seems to believe in what she's saying but doesn't appear to confuse it with what's happening in the present time. I'm no expert,' Alan Reynolds shrugged apologetically, 'however, she seems stable enough to me.'

'Could she be possessed?' demanded Jennifer. 'Is it possible?'

'It is possible. The Church admits such things do occur, although thankfully I've had no experience of such a thing. That is, up till now. I have colleagues who have,' Alan mused aloud. 'But what about the poet, Daisy Gardiner? Have you checked up on her?'

'Yes, we googled her this afternoon.' Chas opened up his laptop. 'Early Victorian, born 1838, died 1861, only lived to twenty-three, died probably of tuberculosis. The only example of her work... the book of her verses... is in the British Museum.'

'So, she *did* exist,' mused Alan.

'Yes. Who in the world has heard of Daisy Gardiner the poet? How did she find out about her?' demanded Chas. 'Of course, she could have tried a search on obscure Victorian poets, I suppose.'

'Have you talked to Sara?' Jilly inquired.

Chas and Jennifer regarded her in surprise, before gazing at each other in astonishment. No verbal reply was needed. No. They hadn't talked to Sara, and it had never occurred to either of them to do so.

'Maybe you should. Or, if you wish, I could. Sometimes it's better to talk to an outsider,' Jilly proposed.

'I don't know how to talk to her about it,' Jennifer miserably confessed. 'She's no longer my Sara; she seems to be older and more knowing than I am.'

'Would you talk to her?' Chas leaned forward in his seat, facing Jilly earnestly. 'As you say, an impartial outsider is sometimes best.'

'Of course,' Jilly agreed.

'But you do think there's something odd about Sara?' Jennifer demanded. 'We're not imagining it? Forgive me for asking this, but have you heard of an incubus or a succubus?'

Alan Reynolds drained his glass and glanced at his watch. Nearly midnight. The evening had flown.

'I *have* heard of both. As for having experience of either of them, the answer is negative. There is certainly something unusual happening. I'm sorry I can't give you an explanation right now, but I will try and help you. I have a colleague, a good friend actually, who is very competent in dealing with cases of possession and the paranormal. Not that I am, as yet, of the opinion that your daughter is possessed. I know this is certainly irrelevant to Sara, but he also deals with people who are trying to come into Christianity, leaving behind them a background of satanism and witchcraft. If he can deal with such people, he can surely help your daughter, should his help be necessary.'

'Thanks for listening.' Chas warmly shook the vicar's hand.

'And for believing us.' Jennifer gladly allowed Jilly Reynolds to give her a hug. 'It sounds too absurd for words.'

'It is unusual... but not absurd. We'll be in touch soon,' promised Alan Reynolds, setting off to walk back to the vicarage with his wife, two tall rangy figures, silhouetted hand in hand in the moonlight.

'It never occurred to me to speak to Sara,' mused Jennifer.

'Nor me.' Chas wrapped an arm about her shoulders. 'I guess it's called *avoiding the problem*. If you mention it out loud, then it exists. Ignore it, and you can pretend nothing is wrong.'

'Well, we have mentioned it out loud now.' Jennifer leaned her dark, curly head against his shoulder. 'We have well and truly accepted it exists.'

'And that means we can fix it,' Chas stated stoutly, realising he was beginning to believe it could be fixed.

'I feel a bit better now,' Jennifer admitted.

'Me too,' Chas agreed truthfully.

CHAPTER SIX

TRACY HAD GONE TO HOLY ISLAND FOR THE DAY, IN THE company of an older cousin, plus his wife and children. This was a long-standing arrangement, made before the friendship between Sara and she had taken off. Tracy would have liked her friend to come too, but there was no room in the car.

Since Tracy wasn't available, Sara passed the morning gardening, a favourite pastime for many years. Centuries, in fact. Gardens had changed so much over the decades, she reflected. A century ago they were, on the whole, used for cultivating vegetables. Only the wealthy could afford to have large expansive flowerbeds. Ordinary people who grew flowers (usually in small patches to brighten the front of their houses) grew different plants to the ones now currently popular. Clothing was not the only thing to be subject to fashion, flowers were too. Her recent pleasure in gardening was, she knew, worrying the Roseberrys. Clearly they knew their daughter was different. They were aware something had changed within her, and it was all due to that perpetual problem: she no longer knew how to act as a child of twelve ought to act, and it was difficult to pretend. Always cautious when it came to peering into the minds of others, she had, nonetheless, thought it expedient to do so. Consequently, late yesterday evening she'd taken a sneak peek into Jennifer's mind. It was only the second time she'd done so. On the first occasion, she'd wondered whether or not it would be a wise idea. Eventually, deciding it *would* be sensible, she'd gone into their bedroom and, before she departed, Jennifer happened to wake up. But at least she didn't seem terrified to see a vaporous being in her room. As for last night, she'd learned of the outcome of the visit from the vicar and his wife. Not that it was a particularly dramatic outcome. Chas and Jennifer were seeking assistance from the clergy. She gave a faint, half smile. Much good would it do them!

Jennifer arrived home from work early, anticipating a short visit from a friend who'd moved to Wales a few years ago. The friend was a certain Denise Smythe, who had trained with Jennifer and was briefly visiting old acquaintances in the north-east before travelling to Scotland with her fifteen-year-old twin daughters, there to enjoy some hiking.

Sara, having met Denise and her daughters during previous visits, had, in the past, thought the twins' names were romantic – Maria Elena and Maria Theresa. Now she thought them simply cumbersome. Each girl received her full title; no shortening was permitted. She half expected Jennifer to dismiss herself and the twins to another room, to play games or chatter. That had happened before. On this occasion the dismissal didn't come, and Sara guessed the reason why. Jennifer was trying to compare her conduct with that of the fifteen-year-old twins. She hadn't failed to notice the look of concern of Jennifer's face when she returned home to find her daughter busily pulling out weeds, having suddenly acquired an encyclopaedic knowledge of gardening. Clearly her explanation of botany lessons at school was inadequate.

It was a hot day, but with a pleasant breeze, preventing it from being too sticky. In short, it was too nice to remain indoors, so the group moved outside, clutching cold drinks and helping themselves from a selection of salads Jennifer had placed on the wrought-iron garden table shaded by a huge candy-striped umbrella.

'What is this, Jennifer?' Denise, who had been enthusiastically vegetarian for a year, dubiously examined a dish Sara had just brought from the fridge.

'Coronation chicken,' explained Sara, offering the bowl.

'No, thank you.' Denise recoiled as if stung. 'Do you not realise these pieces of chicken *were* once living creatures?' She heavily emphasised the word "were".

'I sincerely hope so,' Sara replied, smiling and keeping her tone polite. Jennifer often seemed uptight but Denise was even more so. And not only was she uptight but, Sara judged, also very jealous of Jennifer.

'How are you coping?' Jennifer inquired of her friend, unconsciously asking a question that would satisfy Sara's curiosity.

'I manage. Fortunately I have a good job, like you. Dentistry pays well. But the girls miss their father.' Denise helped herself to a large portion of green salad.

'I don't miss him. It was he who chose to leave us,' Maria Elena contradicted, unable to disguise the bitterness in her tone.

The twins were replicas of their mother, being tall and slim, with tightly curling auburn hair cut unflatteringly short, with no fringe, showing off exceedingly high foreheads. They had pale freckled complexions and long, inquisitive noses, inclined to be pink at the tips. They also seemed devoid of eyebrows and eyelashes, which gave them a permanently startled look. All three of them combined their unbecoming hairstyle with unflattering clothing. They wore cropped trousers, displaying a length of unshaved, pasty leg, visible in the gap between trouser and trainers – their combined choice of footwear. They were also all wearing sweatshirts, all well-worn garments. Denise had holes in both elbows. The sweatshirts and trousers were worn several sizes too large. Sara felt a twinge of pity for them, especially the twins. The potential was there for them to look attractive, if they took the trouble. Given the glances she and Jennifer were receiving from Maria Elena and Maria Theresa, she felt certain the girls wanted to make the most of their assets.

'He left us for that awful woman, and we don't want to see him,' declared Maria Theresa.

They're hurting, Sara thought compassionately. *All of them. Little wonder Denise is uptight.*

Jennifer searched for something to say before Denise started talking about her ex-husband, well knowing how vitriolic she could be on the subject, and managed to utter, 'I hope your holiday is lovely.' That sounded safe enough. 'It is such a pity you could only spend an hour or so with us. Maybe on another occasion you could stay longer.' *I hope not,* she added inwardly. Denise and she had been friendly once but never close. They were not kindred spirits. Also, Denise was a difficult guest, with her vegetarian diet and avid recycling habits.

'We all enjoy walking.' Denise heaped tomatoes, cucumber and olives onto her plate, then liberally splashed salad dressing over it from a pretty glass jug. 'What kind of dressing is this?' she demanded abruptly.

'Olive oil, vinegar and garlic,' replied Jennifer, surprised by the sudden aggression.

'I don't like garlic.'

Sara leapt to her feet. 'I'll take your plate away and give you a clean one. Then you can start again.' Poor Jennifer. She wasn't enjoying this reunion at all. As for the girls, they at least were enjoying the food Jennifer had prepared that morning before leaving for work. Clearly the guests were a family dominated by a demanding, humourless mother.

Returning with a fresh plate, Sara heard Jennifer asking the twins if either of them had boyfriends.

'I do,' replied Maria Theresa, 'but we've only been seeing each other for a few weeks. Maria Elena had a steady boyfriend; it lasted six months.'

'We finished a week ago. I found out he was also seeing someone else,' added Maria Theresa. 'He wants us to get back together, but I'll never forgive him.'

They're very passionate about their beliefs, reflected Sara. *Maybe I was like that once. When I was young.*

'She's best off without him. My husband wanted me to come back to him, but infidelity is unforgivable,' Denise added caustically.

Jennifer was silent, lost for words. Denise had that effect on her.

'I think there are worse things than infidelity,' announced Sara, taking pity on her mother. 'There are many kinds of infidelity. Having an affair can cause issues regarding trust. However, giving too much time to a career and therefore neglecting a partner, that can be as destructive as seeing another person.'

Startled by the maturity of the comment, Jennifer grasped a bowl of couscous like a life raft and thrust it in Denise's direction.

'Couscous,' was the approving response. 'Very good for you. Girls, have some too,' Denise instructed, forking couscous into her mouth and munching steadily for a moment before turning to address Sara. 'I don't know where you get your ideas from, young lady, but I think you've been eavesdropping on other people's conversations. You shouldn't repeat such things.'

'Sara is mature for her years,' defended Jennifer. 'She thinks a lot.' Her daughter's statement had astonished her, but then she was getting used to being astonished by Sara.

'Well,' Sara tried to shrug the subject aside, 'I think people often regret giving up a relationship because of infidelity. It's not only trust that's the problem but hurt pride. But a bit of work can make the relationship better than before.' She half wished she could share her own past experiences with this very young, very immature group of humans. Instead she informed them, 'It improved the marital relationship between James Garfield, the American President, and his wife. She forgave him and they tried again. They were happy together... at least until he was assassinated.'

Following this, conversation was stilted. Denise, convinced her friend's daughter was a twelve-year-old prig, felt she needed to be taught to keep her mouth shut. As for Maria Elena and Maria Theresa, they were so disconcerted by the young old philosopher, they hardly knew what to say, and concentrated on the food instead. It was all very delicious, far removed from the unimaginative vegetarian fare their mother usually served at meal times. They too were vegetarian, but only because there was no other choice in their household. Hence they enthusiastically made the most of everything, including surreptitiously partaking of the Coronation chicken. There was cake for dessert too. As a dentist, Denise frowned upon sweets and biscuits and was surprised Jennifer didn't do likewise. In lieu of biscuits, Denise provided cream crackers for her girls.

Poor girls, what a dismal household they must come from, thought Sara, watching the cake disappearing with energetic enthusiasm.

Jennifer felt suddenly weary and hardly noticed the conversation flagging. She'd arranged to get in touch with Jilly, who intended to have a chat with Sara, but realisation was dawning that it was her responsibility to do so. After all, she was her mother. And the conversation this afternoon had given her an idea of how to approach Sara. Suddenly it didn't seem difficult to take the bull by the horns, metaphorically speaking. In addition, she was truly grateful to Sara for her obviously supportive presence. *Why in the world do I bother with Denise?* she wondered sadly. But the answer was obvious – she felt sorry for the woman.

Denise had been eyeing Jennifer's long hair with disapproval throughout the meal, which Sara hadn't failed to notice.

'Do you think you're pandering to male opinion by having long hair?' Denise demanded coolly as they were preparing to take their leave.

As Jennifer blinked in surprise, Sara sprang to her defence.

'My mother is a professional working person, contributing to the family finances. I think there are some feminists who are frightened to be feminine. Women should celebrate femininity, not disguise it.'

Denise gave a gasp of shock whilst Jennifer tried not to smirk. Goodness, Sara had defended her like a tigress!

'The length of my hair does please Chas, but I like having long hair, so there's nothing wrong with that,' she managed to say.

Denise and her daughters departed, and Jennifer waved as they drove away.

'Revolting woman,' Sara voiced, having also waved politely until the visitors' car was out of sight. 'I was worried in case they invited me to join them!' Giving a dramatic sigh of relief and a mock wiping of her brow, she went indoors.

'She's even more difficult than I remember her being,' sighed Jennifer. 'She wasn't vegetarian when we met at college.

Not that her dietary preferences are the problem. I haven't seen her for something like two years. The last time was just after her husband left her,' she calculated rapidly.

'I'm not surprised he left her, stupid mare.' It was Chas who spoke, having arrived just as Denise and her daughters were moving off the drive. 'I'm glad I missed them!' He flung an arm around Jennifer. 'Not a good afternoon?'

'No.' Having given Chas a peck on the cheek, hesitating, Jennifer drew in a couple of deep breaths. 'Actually, I was so glad of Sara's company. Her support,' she informed him, 'was not the support of a twelve-year-old.'

Sara had wandered into the kitchen and was deftly clearing up the detritus of the meal. Leaving her to deal with it, Jennifer and Chas sat on the patio.

'I'm going to phone Jilly later and tell her I'm going to talk to Sara myself. I'll nip upstairs and use the bedroom phone,' Jennifer spoke quietly since the kitchen window was open.

'If that's what you feel you want to do, that's fine,' Chas said, pulling at the knot of his tie and nodding his approval, preferring that Jen should be the first to speak with Sara, rather than Jilly. He would never have pushed Jen into confronting Sara, but it struck him as being appropriate that a mother and daughter chat should come first, and he respected his wife for deciding to try to deal with it. He doubted it would be easy. 'But what about food, woman, is anything left for me?' he cheerfully demanded whilst giving her a warm hug.

Jennifer chuckled. 'They ate like horses... At least the girls did. They ate as if they hadn't eaten in a month,' she informed him.

'Probably haven't.' Chas picked up a newspaper. 'We were once invited to her house, when she was still with her husband. The food was inedible, as I recall. Her now ex–husband probably thought she was trying to poison him!'

'Just as well you married me,' Jennifer informed him sweetly.

'Well, I admit, woman, you *can* cook,' he grinned.

Jennifer smiled, careful not to remind him that much of their food came ready-made from a supermarket.

'This is a democratic household,' Chas continued, giving his wicked grin. 'You do the indoor cooking, I do the outdoor.'

Sara, who had come to join them on the patio, caught the latter part of the conversation.

'Why is it men seem to like cooking outside, I wonder?' She frowned, as if deep in thought. 'Maybe it's the danger aspect. They never know if they're going to set themselves on fire!'

Chas roared with laughter. 'Is that your theory? Cooking in a kitchen is too mundane? No danger factor? I think you might have a moot point there!'

―――

It was later in the evening, when Sara was in her room reading, that Jennifer telephoned Jilly Reynolds, informing her that she had decided to speak to Sara herself. Mother to daughter. 'But I – we – would like to meet up with you to discuss the outcome, if you don't mind,' she suggested.

'Fine. How about tomorrow, or is that too soon?'

'That would be helpful.'

'Why don't Alan and I drop by tomorrow evening?'

There was something pacifying about Jilly's tranquil, pleasant voice. Pleased with the arrangement, she went to join Chas, who was in the conservatory.

'I'm going up to see Sara.' She patted his cheek lightly. 'I'll give you a full report.'

She headed upstairs, her curls bouncing, then paused outside Sara's door before rapping gently a couple of times –

something she never used to do – and entering upon hearing a soft, 'Come in.'

'Hi, may I sit down?' Again, this was unusual.

'Of course, Mum.' If Sara was surprised by the formality she didn't show it.

Seating herself in a wicker chair, Jennifer surveyed the room. It had changed. Once there had been numerous soft toys, but most of them were gone now. The wall posters were missing too.

'Where did you put Justin's poster?' she inquired curiously.

'I put them all in the recycling bin; I've outgrown them,' Sara shrugged, putting aside a book she'd been reading and lounging casually on the bed.

'Who do you like now?' Jennifer was curious to know.

'I'm starting to incline towards the heavy stuff. The new heavy north-east band VPL. They're excellent. So too is Queen Anne's Revenge, as well as AC/DC.'

'Queen Anne's Revenge? That was Blackbeard's ship,' Jennifer interrupted. 'Are they a male or female band?'

'All male,' smiled Sara. 'I think it's a very original name.' There was a stillness about her, an air of anticipation, of knowing there was a purpose in this visit.

'You saved up for those posters,' Jennifer reflectively remarked. They hadn't been cheap. 'Who else do you like? Tell me the truth,' she looked squarely into Sara's eyes, daring her to be honest, whilst she wondered what the reply would be. Would she begin talking as strangely as she did to Tracy? Would she mentioning long-dead and all but forgotten Elizabethan composers?

'Elvis Presley.' Sara's wide-set eyes were steady and truthful.

'Elvis?' Somehow this was not what she had imagined.

'He changed music forever. I am also partial to Bach, Strauss, Vivaldi, Roxy Music, Beethoven, The Shadows, Bon

Jovi, Vaughan Williams, Iron Maiden, the Foo Fighters and Led Zeppelin. Not necessarily in that order. I dislike jazz.'

Digesting this, Jennifer studied the calm, self-possessed child in front of her. Sara. Yet so much *not* Sara.

'This afternoon you talked with assurance about adultery and hurt pride. You cannot possibly know about such things yet. I believe I'm contradicting myself here, but I think somehow you do know about it. What's happened, Sara? Tell me. The truth.'

There was hesitation in the girl's manner, a faltering in her gaze.

'Do you really want to know?' Her voice was almost a whisper, seeming to come from far away.

'I want to know the truth. Something's happened. You've changed. At first I was frightened in case you were mentally ill. But I don't think so now. I don't really know what to think. I've been more than a little crafty and deceitful, and I make no apologies for that. I love you dearly and that is explanation enough. I've listened at your bedroom door when you've been with Tracy; I also recorded one of your conversations. When you were both in the garden. I heard words bandied about which I know nothing of, so you certainly shouldn't know of them – words such as incubus and succubus.'

'Aaah,' Sara nodded musingly, looking as if she was rapidly reaching a decision. 'Whilst I was at the barbeque, you played it to the vicar and his wife, didn't you?'

'Yes, and I don't apologise for that either.'

Jennifer's knuckles were starting to ache, her fingers were clenched and the nails dug into the palms of her hands. She was beginning to wish Chas was there.

'Some things never change. I'm still Sara. I still love you and Dad. But you want the truth, and that is what you shall have.' Abandoning her casual pose, Sara sat upright. 'I knew about your plan to record our conversation. I saw inside your mind.' Seeing Jennifer was about to speak, she gently lifted her hand, gesturing for silence. 'Many years ago, I was in a situation similar to this, and the persons concerned handled it very well. Year's earlier still, again in a situation akin to this, the news was not well received. So, first allow me to state that if you overreact and start taking me to doctors and psychiatrists, I will deny everything, and they will think it is you who is being overly anxious.' The words were uttered gently, but a steely and totally unchildlike expression appeared on the girl's face.

'Just tell me the truth.' Jennifer felt breathless, as if nearing the end of a vigorous session at the gym.

'I like Elvis because I was around when Elvis was first heard on the airwaves. I was around when Glen Miller was all the rage too,' again lifting a hand, seeing Jennifer was about to interrupt, she continued, 'You know what a succubus is. I know that.'

'An evil spirit who seduces men,' Jennifer uttered through suddenly dry lips.

'You've been reading the dictionary,' the fleeting smile Sara gave was forgiving. 'I am a succubus... a female incubus, if you like. But I've never done anything like that. I probably could if I wanted to, but basically there's no point. Tracy is a succubus too, and she's not evil either. The older we are, the stronger we are. I'm not as old as Tracy – she's one thousand years old. I was born in fourteen forty. My name is, or was, Maude Dubreise. You saw me, Jennifer, when I was in your room. I have to say, I don't do that very often, so don't worry about my being a nuisance. But I needed to know what you were thinking, you see. It's a lot for you to take in, eh?' Reaching out, she took one of Jennifer's trembling hands. 'I still think of myself as Maude Dubreise. Her life was hard, but I was happy.

I didn't realise then that I would just keep on living... using other bodies.'

Jennifer snatched her hand away, as if stung.

'I want you to leave my daughter... We shall... we shall exorcise you if necessary.'

Her expression one of compassion and sadness, Sara shook her head. Eventually she stated apologetically, 'I'm afraid that won't work. I need to survive. Maybe it was a mistake to choose such a young subject. I've not been a child for many years and find it difficult to act like one. But really, whichever body I choose to use, there will be differences, and eventually they will be detected. Most often, I find family and friends tend to accept them without question, as if they're part of the maturing process or something. People are often like Elsie and her husband, proud of their suddenly clever offspring. In Tracy's instance, her brother Rick is close to guessing the truth, we believe.'

'I cannot accept this. I *will* not... I want my twelve-year-old daughter back. As she was,' Jennifer insisted vehemently.

'But I won't hurt Sara... My knowledge will actually help her! And she will live on forever, because years from now Sara will move with me to yet another body, then another, absorbing knowledge along the way! That is what an incubus or succubus does. Yes, some can be wicked, just as ordinary mortals can be wicked.'

Gently, Sara began explaining, at length, exactly what she was.

The information was received silently, without interruption, then Jennifer protested, unconvinced, 'But you are evil, you must be!'

'I am not evil. Feel my spirit... I am not evil.'

Sara was looking at her with disturbing intensity, then Jennifer felt strangely as if something brushed against her mind, a sudden movement of knowledge and experience, a spirit of calmness and illumination, which passed into her mind and then out of it.

'But why Sara? Why *my* child? If you can do that to her, surely you can move into someone else… There are plenty of other young girls,' Jennifer pleaded.

'I need a permanent home,' was the reply, also pleading in tone. 'Please understand, you have not lost your daughter.'

Jennifer gave a hollow laugh. 'That's what you would like me to believe. That I've not lost my daughter but instead gained a kind of elderly spirit! What…? I mean, how many… other bodies have you taken over in this way during the past nearly six hundred years?'

'I've lost count,' was the simple response. 'Nearing a hundred surely. During times of war or famine I've inhabited several bodies in one day! As I've already explained, each time I enter someone I absorb what is theirs, adding to the knowledge which is already mine, and I become stronger. When I briefly touch someone's mind – as I've just demonstrated – I enter and leave quickly. If I stay longer, then gradually I become part of that mind and body. I unite totally with them, which is why I cannot leave Sara. If I leave her, only her body will remain, which would, in fact, soon die, or at least be reduced to a vegetative state.'

'What about Tracy? Her family… Are they not worried about her?' Jennifer toyed with the idea of perhaps chatting with Elsie, a woman who was in the same unique position as herself.

'Oh no,' Sara smiled, eyes sparkling with sudden amusement. 'As I've already said, they're terribly proud of her accomplishments. Rick suspects something but so far hasn't challenged her about it. But he is more astute that his parents. Also, a brother's position is less nurturing that that of a parent. So, if he suspects anything, he will be less eager to find a remedy.' The amusement subsided quickly. 'Perhaps I ought to have chosen a less enlightened and intelligent household.'

'Perhaps.' Wearily Jennifer ran a hand through her long curls. 'But intelligent or not, I can't see how anyone, not even someone as easy-going as Elsie, can fail to notice and worry over dramatic changes in their offspring.'

'Sometimes people believe what they want to believe. Elsie boasts that at last someone in her family might go to university,' Sara reasoned.

'But… are there many of you? Incubus or whatever?' Jennifer clutched her throat; it felt dry, constricted and parched.

'Not many. I've met a few of us over the years. I've been married many times, given birth to many children – none of whom have been like me. They all died in due course.' An adult sadness crossed Sara's face.

'I need to talk to Chas.'

She felt a sudden need to distance herself from this strange being, who was her daughter yet not her daughter.

'Good idea,' Sara nodded equably.

Having almost stumbled down the stairs, Jennifer found Chas in the kitchen opening a bottle of wine.

'Oh, I so need that,' she sighed, rushing to him to enjoy a firm hug, 'But I need this more.'

They stepped through the conservatory to the patio, which was, as usual on an evening, illuminated with garish, jolly, multi-coloured outdoor lights. The heat of the day had given way to a cool evening, almost chilly in fact, so they didn't linger out of doors but returned to the conservatory, where Jennifer explained everything that had been said.

'I'd like to talk about this with parents who are in the same position as us.' Chas refilled both of their now empty wine glasses. 'But with the best will in the world, we cannot approach Tracy's parents. I once met Elsie's husband in the supermarket and he asked me if I could tell him how to cook ready-made Yorkshire puddings. They're a pleasant bunch of people, I suppose, but let's face it, they'll accept the changes in Tracy without demur.'

'I guess you're right,' Jennifer agreed, curling up next to him on the sofa and resting her head against his shoulder, feeling him rubbing his chin against the top of her head. 'It is such a…' she searched for words, '… weird situation,' she stated inadequately.

Sara walked purposefully into the conservatory clutching a glass of water.

'There are no support groups for parents in your position,' she quietly informed them. 'I have come to show you what will happen if I leave this body. You really need to know.' Her voice held a warning note.

In unison, Chas and Jennifer nodded, sitting bolt upright, feeling curious yet somehow not threatened. There was nothing menacing about Sara's manner, nor was there any drama. She sat in an armchair, and briefly both Chas and Jennifer thought they saw a faint emission of what looked like vapour coming from her nostrils. Then there was a sudden movement as the girl's head sank downwards and her shoulders slumped. Quickly, Chas rushed to shake her, horrified as she crumpled, her breathing stertorous as her head swung backwards. She would have fallen had he not caught her, picked her up and deftly placed her, prone, upon the sofa which Jennifer had hastily vacated. Her breathing, now regular, was peaceful, as was her entire countenance. She looked asleep. A gasp from Jennifer made him look in his wife's direction. Jennifer was pointing to a doorway, where there now stood the image she had described to him, a shadowy, steam-like column, identifiable as a woman, even down to the long plaits. Then it rapidly dispersed. He persisted in shaking and trying to obtain a response from Sara. Jennifer, who held her wrist, was reassured by at least being able to feel a steady pulse. Then, just as they were both beginning to believe the succubus had permanently departed, leaving their daughter in a vegetative state, they observed a quick sliver of vapour seeming to re-enter Sara's nostrils, then her eyes opened, staring solemnly into those of Chas.

'You see... You have seen what you would be left with. As for me, I need a body,' Sara stated firmly.

At breakfast the following morning, as if nothing had happened, Sara requested permission to visit Tracy. It was readily given, although Jennifer wryly wondered how she could refuse. Her daughter was, technically, close to being six hundred years old. Certainly she was wiser than herself. But physically she was only twelve, and as such she was vulnerable. This was a situation which, potentially, could cause tension between them, although, to be honest, Jennifer knew there had always been a degree of tension. She, the perfectionist, had demanded high standards from her only child, which poor Sara had been unable to meet. The sad fact was, she would now give anything to have the old Sara back again, with her gawky manner and dreamy ways. *Why did I not accept her for who she was?* With penitent regret she hoped Alan Reynold's friend could restore her daughter to her again, whilst inwardly she vowed never to utter a word of criticism against Sara if he managed to do so.

Throughout the course of the day Jennifer found herself wondering, with increasing curiosity, about the spirit that had taken over Sara, an old spirit that had inhabited numerous bodies. Trying to keep her mind focused upon her current task, a root canal filling, she found a brief but interesting notion passing through her mind. Sara must surely have plenty of stories to relate regarding dentistry! She would have seen dentists at work in previous centuries. She would also have personal experience of their gruesome handiwork. It would be interesting to speak to her about it. And, if she'd lived in numerous bodies, there must have been a series of husbands and children. Last night Sara had explained that she had borne children but sadly none of them had been like herself. They had all died in the natural human fashion. That was sad, she found herself thinking sympathetically. Perhaps the creature was to be pitied. In fact, she would, personally, be quick to pity her, if only she ceased inhabiting the body of her own daughter.

A competent, conscientious dentist, Jennifer was noted for being pleasant to staff and patients but not talkative. She preferred to work quietly. However, the dental nurse assisting her on this particular day had known her for several years and felt that today Jennifer was totally withdrawn. Then, at lunchtime, when asked if she would like a cup of coffee, she had totally, and uncharacteristically, ignored the question and dashed out of the building.

Jennifer's errand was to visit the library. She wanted to find some illuminating literature regarding the incubus and succubus, but she was disappointed to find nothing she didn't already know. Maybe tonight Alan and Jilly's friend might provide, or suggest, something more satisfactory. She sincerely hoped so. She returned to the surgery unsatisfied.

It seemed a long time before evening when Alan and Jilly arrived. Sara had already cycled to Tracy's home, promising to return before dark since she didn't have a light on her bicycle. It had struck both Chas and Jennifer that, now Sara had nothing to hide, she was no longer even trying to act like an adolescent. During the course of the day Sara had performed pruning tasks in the garden and had prepared a meal ready to simply push into the oven when her parents arrived home. This was all very nice… but the former Sara would never have thought of doing any of those tasks.

Jilly and Alan arrived in their battered car and emerged from it clutching vast piles of magazines and books. Without preamble, Alan informed his hosts that he'd spoken to his friend, a man called Terry Richardson, of the unusual situation. If they were agreeable, Terry wanted to see them, and obviously Sara also. As she and Chas nodded their agreement, Jennifer took stock of her visitors' clothing. They were both wearing combat trousers and black tee shirts.

'This isn't a warzone,' Chas quipped.

'These are comfortable garments,' beamed Jilly. 'As for these books and magazines, we've found some articles and paragraphs which might be interesting to you.'

'Some articles only refer to the incubus… but obviously this includes the succubus also, since they are the same.' Alan placed his pile of books on the coffee table.

Chas eyed the books and magazines; all of them had pieces of paper sticking out, where Alan and Jilly had clearly found a reference. He felt touched; they had clearly gone to some trouble to be of help. Alan and Jilly, however, thrust his and Jennifer's thanks aside.

'We are glad to give help when needed,' they both declared dismissively. 'But if you read nothing else tonight, you must read this.' Alan gave an old, yellowing magazine to Chas. 'I've marked an interview for you to look at. It involves a person who claims… or I should say claimed… to be an incubus.'

'What!' Jennifer leaned over Chas's shoulder, avidly reading the interview. The print was small but still legible. Poignantly the interview, headed, "I wish I could die", was from a man who claimed to be eight hundred years old, and it described his aching loneliness. He longed to belong to a community with others of his kind.

As they drank coffee – no one wanted anything stronger, and even Chas was glad to give his liver a rest – and continued searching through the literature, both Chas and Jennifer felt a sense of exhilaration. These journals were all paranormal in nature, and usually neither of them would have paid any attention to them. They certainly would never have read them. But suddenly they realised Sara's situation was unusual, but not unique, and it must therefore be something that could be treated.

'You may keep these things for a while,' Alan informed them, glad to see the sudden air of confidence his hosts were displaying. 'And I shall organise a meeting for you with Terry,' he promised.

Reading an entry from yet another magazine, Jennifer gave a sigh of satisfaction. Last night she'd seen her daughter limp and comatose. There must surely be a way to separate the small piece that was Sara from the huge piece that was the succubus. She glanced upwards and saw Chas looking at her, his eyes shining with new optimism. They both knew, they were absolutely certain, they were going to get their daughter back.

CHAPTER SEVEN

THE FOLLOWING MORNING CHAS GOT OUT OF BED BOTH looking and feeling unwell, plus he'd been awake most of the night complaining of abdominal pain and nausea. Since he seldom complained of any kind of ailment (Jennifer usually joked that he had the constitution of a buffalo) she suggested the unheard-of ..... he should take a day off work. Chas, priding himself upon his reliability, informed her that she was uttering obscenities. Trying to be optimistic, Jennifer supposed aloud it might only be wind.

Grabbing the cordless telephone, she began dialling the number of the doctor with one hand, whilst at the same time steering Chas towards the sitting room sofa with the other. Being a natural pessimist, her suggestion that it might only be wind veered suddenly towards a more sombre supposition. Chas might be seriously ill. Supposing it was bowel cancer. He might have some sort of obstruction which was causing the pain. He might need a colostomy!

Sara, wandering into the sitting room, took one glance at Chas and, darting over to him, deftly conducted a brief examination. Chas was too startled to object.

'Appendix, I think. Highly probable.' Noting the stunned features of her parents, she murmured, 'I used to be a doctor.

Well, several times actually. I was one of the first female medics!' Her voice rang with pride. 'But it was a long time ago. However, some things never change. You have appendicitis, I'm pretty certain of it.'

By the time the GP arrived, Chas was feeling much better, the spasm of pain had abated, and Jennifer, whilst much relieved, guiltily informed the doctor it might indeed be a false alarm. Impressed by her petite charm, the doctor was initially paternally reassuring; but after examining Chas thoroughly, he eventually declared he was certain it was acute appendicitis. Chas was now once again feeling sick and the pain had returned. He needed admitting to hospital, declared the doctor. The solution was going to be surgical, particularly since Chas reluctantly admitted he'd actually been suffering from abdominal pain for some days but had dismissed it.

Jennifer's pessimism led her to wonder what would happen if the surgery went wrong. Fighting to remain calm, she wondered what she would do without Chas. So immersed was she in her thoughts, it was Sara who was practical.

'Doctor, we're insured. I think you should contact the local private hospital, see if a consultant is available to sort Dad out,' she suggested quietly.

Sara, having now flung aside all pretence at behaving like a child, proved to be a tower of strength. A few telephone calls later, Chas was admitted into hospital and, having undergone an abdominal scan, was scheduled to go to theatre late that afternoon. Jennifer and Sara sat with him in his private room, both feeling hungry, but not wishing to indulge their appetites whilst Chas had to remain without food. As soon as he was wheeled to theatre, Sara seized a menu from the bedside table.

'Jennifer... er, Mum... we can order food from this. How about it?'

'I noticed the menu but didn't care to look whilst Chas was lying there. According to this, all we have to do is telephone the kitchen and they'll bring it to the room.' Jennifer eagerly scanned the menu. 'Oh my, what an excellent selection. What a pity I'm driving; we can even order wine!'

It was early evening by the tine Chas returned to his room, by which time his wife and daughter had enjoyed a hearty meal. He was awake, seemingly pain free, and had a drip attached to one arm.

'Smells like a restaurant in here,' was his first remark. 'Typical…' he sighed dramatically, and then fell asleep.

Whilst Chas slept off his anaesthetic, Jennifer made a series of telephone calls. She felt as if she'd spent the entire day using the telephone. Firstly to the dental practice where she worked, updating her colleagues of the situation and thanking them for their understanding – they had totally supported her regarding taking compassionate leave that day, and the following few days if necessary. Then she'd had to update Chas's legal partners, who had been naturally concerned about him. Chas, who was never ill, needing surgery? Incredible. Then there had been the calls to the medical insurance team, who spoke with professional and, she was certain, totally insincere sympathy. Finally, she'd telephoned Vi, appraising her of the situation. Bracing herself to refuse Vi's offers to come and stay (which would be typical of her), she was nonplussed when an offer was not forthcoming. Clearly Vi was still offended.

'I think you should both go home,' Chas suggested sometime later, opening one eye and yawning. 'I'm not going to be of much use conversationally, so both of you go home and rest. Immediately.'

At that moment a nurse walked into the room, accompanied by the surgeon who had performed the surgery.

'It was a very straightforward surgery,' the surgeon proclaimed. 'Having heard what has just said, I think both of you ladies should depart.' He winked at Sara, pleased with himself for including her. He prided himself on his patient—relative rapport. It was good for business. 'He'll rest more easily alone. Nurse here will keep an eye on him. As for you, my man, I'll see you tomorrow, and you can probably go home if I'm happy with your wound.'

'Fabulous,' beamed Jennifer, gracefully gathering up her jacket and handbag, then stooping to give Chas a kiss. 'Sleep well, darling, I'll be here first thing in the morning. Come along, Sara, let's go.'

'That drip has run its course,' Sara addressed the nurse before following Jennifer from the room, choosing to ignore the surprised glances the surgeon and nurse were casting in her direction.

'Here… you deserve it; you were a tower of strength.' Jennifer held out a glass of wine, offering it to Sara.

'I'd best dilute it. Twelve-year-old bodies get drunk easily.' Sara liberally added soda into the glass. 'I'll turn this into a spritzer. Marilyn, my previous body, was tee-total until I moved in,' she stated wryly.

'I know I want my twelve-year-old back, but I couldn't have got through this day without your help,' Jennifer admitted ruefully. Her expression changed to one of alarm. 'Oh shoot, maybe I should have informed Alan and Jilly. Vicars like to be told about these things.'

'I phoned them,' Sara spoke apologetically. 'I thought it was a good idea. I forgot to tell you. Jilly said she'll be in touch, and she's praying for you and Chas. And for myself also!'

Jennifer eyed her speculatively. In no way did it now sound strange hearing Sara refer to her father as Chas. 'You said you've been married yourself,' she stated curiously, hoping to elicit information.

'Oh yes, many times,' smiled Sara.

'Do you fall in love regularly? I mean... you know, you take over a new body when the old body dies. So, with each new life do you fall in love? I'm not expressing myself very well; it can't be the wine, I've hardly had any,' Jennifer tried to joke.

She'd barely sipped at her wine as yet. Chas was a pernicious influence, she decided fondly. He adored wine, and insisted that once a bottle was opened it was unwise to re-cork it.

'It's difficult to actually fall in love with a man whose knowledge and experiences are limited to one lifetime, and who is destined to live only a short while,' Sara mused aloud. 'I did *love* my first husband, when I inhabited my first body, that of Maude Dubreise. But I wasn't *in love,* if you know what I mean.' As Jennifer nodded, Sara continued. 'It was an arranged marriage. I knew then that I would keep on living, and so it became more and more difficult to emotionally commit myself to a mortal man. I very much loved someone only once. It began during the nineteenth century. He was like me. An incubus.'

'Then he must be still alive,' breathed Jennifer, her romantic interest aroused. Rising from her seat to venture into the kitchen to dilute her own glass of wine with soda – just in case she needed to drive back to the hospital that night – she returned to the lounge, where they'd been sitting, and found herself utterly startled by the desolation written upon the face of her daughter. 'Do you want to tell me about it?' she inquired gently.

'It's a long story.' Sara managed to compose her features.

Jennifer shrugged. 'I'm too overwrought to be sleepy, so there's no point going to bed. As for you, you've no need to get up early in the morning. But you don't have to talk about it if you don't want to.'

'The past one hundred and fifty years have been the most exciting – as far as progress is concerned,' Sara mused aloud. 'Trains. Cars. Aeroplanes. Bombs. Silicon chips. New resins for bonding teeth.'

'And the Channel Tunnel,' added Jennifer. 'A marvellous idea; I would love to give it a try and go to France. But Chas is inclined to avoid tunnels. He prefers to be on top of the water, not underneath it.'

'Ah yes, today's inventions are regarded as clever. We take them all in our stride! But in the mid to late 1800s, everything was met with absolute awe,' Sara assured her listener. 'You can have no idea of how suspicious people were of anaesthetic when it was invented! Some problems are laughable now – such as when women needed anaesthetising. There were doctors who refused to give anaesthetics to women, as they worried lest females, when befuddled with ether, might utter obscenities! Nowadays you take an operation like the removal of an appendix for granted. In 1870 we dared not attempt invasive surgery unless it was totally certain the patient would die without intervention. When there was intervention, frequently they succumbed either during the operation or soon afterwards.'

Jennifer carefully noticed the use of "we".

'Anaesthesia, primitive as it was, had been successfully used… and sometimes unsuccessfully too. But people mostly died of sepsis. Surgery was more or less kept to things like amputations.' Sara gave a faint, involuntary smile. She had a captive audience.

Jennifer was all but open-mouthed with astonishment. Of course, during her dental training she'd learned about asepsis and Lister's contribution, but hadn't thought deeply about the earlier conditions endured by doctors and patients. Sometimes she vaguely considered the plight of bygone patients, having teeth extracted without pain relief in any shape or form, but she didn't dwell on it with any amount of interest. Jennifer was more interested in the here and now.

'I had better start at the beginning. I was living in Hampshire, not very far from the famous Buckler's Hard, on the Beaulieu River. For years I was the only child of a wealthy baronet, a shipyard owner. It was the latter half of the nineteenth century, and I was called Nancy when I met him, an incubus. I had occupied Nancy's body from the age of twelve – same age as this body I now have.' An amused tone crept into her voice and, eyes half closed, Sara reclined against the well-upholstered back of the sofa, lost in recollection.

From the age of twelve, Nancy Denley had seemed to rapidly increase in wisdom, to such a degree that her parents, and the household servants, were awestruck. She quickly changed from a noisy child, often corrected by her governess, to a quiet, grave young lady who was happy to peruse her books, and for whom games of leapfrog – for which unfeminine pastime she had often been chastised in the past – no longer held any charm. Overnight it seemed she had become a model child: calm, quiet, obedient, sensible; a miniature adult. The Victorian ideal. Her parents felt the change happened overnight and could pinpoint when it occurred. Her governess verified the timing. It coincided with the sudden demise of a much-loved relative, the child's aunt, Lady Anne. The governess proclaimed the shock had changed the child forever.

On that tragic day, Nancy had been whipped shortly after breakfast, on account of having already torn her dress whilst romping. She was despatched forthwith to her room, there to read her Bible and remain until sent for. From the confines of her room she could hear servants scurrying around, followed by the rumble of a carriage drawing up to the front of the house. There she saw the family doctor, a hugely overweight man, extricating himself with considerable difficulty from his brougham. Poking her head outside the door, she managed to claim the attention of the sympathetic upstairs maid, who was hurrying past clutching a bowl of hot water.

'What is wrong? Is it Mamma?' gasped Nancy.

'No, it's Lady Anne,' was the brief reply. 'Taken ill, all of a sudden like. I can say no more as yet. The doctor is here.'

'I know that,' murmured Nancy.

For some considerable time Nancy (who had been baptised Anne, in honour of her much-adored aunt, but was called Nancy to avoid confusion) sat forgotten in her room. Late that afternoon, driven by hunger, she eventually dared to open the door, creep to the kitchen and beg some food from Cook, who did not believe growing youngsters should fast. They needed, in her opinion, regular, wholesome food and plenty of it. Supplied with the same, Nancy hastily returned to her room, guessing momentous events were happening, for the household was now hushed. In the past, such a hustle and bustle was sometimes followed by the bawling of an infant and in due course she would be informed that she had a new brother or sister. Sometimes there was no bawling to be heard, simply a quiet announcement that her baby brother or sister had gone directly to God. This occurred at least once a year. Sadly, none of them survived infancy, and after each death Mamma looked ever more sad and lined, her lips drooping, cheeks sagging. Only Nancy, the firstborn, had survived.

The maid had said that Lady Anne was ill, Nancy mused. But surely it could not be so; Aunt Anne was known to not enjoy good health, but had looked well enough yesterday, so possibly the maid was mistaken. It *must* be another baby arriving.

She awaited the noise of a bawling infant. But prior to a baby arriving, Mamma increased in girth, and at present she was as thin as a rail. Papa was keen to have a son, she knew that. She had heard him often remark, aloud, that it was such a pity Nancy was not a boy. Prone to eavesdropping, she had also overheard the servants commenting that young Miss Nancy would, the way things were going, become a considerable heiress. She was uncertain of what a "considerable heiress" was, but their tone suggested it was a very good thing. Her upbringing had been strict, solitary, almost cloistered. She mixed with very few other children; her education was solely supervised by a governess. Mamma was fearful of her one surviving child mixing with other children, in case of contagion. Nancy was also uncertain of what "contagion" was, but it sounded a fearful thing. Occasionally Mamma would fiercely hug her only child, almost knocking the breath out of her slight body. But hugs were infrequent. Mostly, Mamma would issue a flogging, lest Nancy should become proud or worldly. Flogging was beneficial for children. Both Papa and Mamma were unanimous regarding this.

But a son was needed, to be trained to take over Papa's shipyard. One day, vowed Nancy, *she* would take over. Why not? What could a boy do that she could not?

Following the deaths of each of her babies, Mamma had cried for weeks; deep, wracking sobs, which caused Papa to reprove her soundly, saying she must not weep at something which was God's will. Nancy, an early observer of human nature, felt this advice did not appear to help Mamma very much.

Plucking up her courage, she crept downstairs, pausing outside the drawing room. The door was partially open and the sound of muffled sobs drifted from the room. Tentatively she peeped around the door, fearing another flogging, to behold Mamma, sitting alone, clutching a lace handkerchief.

Glancing towards the door, she noticed the small, tense face of her daughter.

'Papa's younger sister, your dear Aunt Anne, Lady Nusiat, died today,' pronounced Mamma, dabbing at her eyes. 'She shall be sorely missed. She was so wise. I never knew anyone so wise!'

Nancy felt a sharp pain stab in the region she believed to be her heart. It was in fact her abdomen, but she deeply felt the loss of a kind relative. Cautiously, lest she should be committing a gross error, she walked over to Mamma and placed her arms around her neck, tentatively hugging her. Lady Anne had been an ally, a compassionate and gentle friend, one who was ever ready to spend time with a lonely child. Like Mamma, Lady Nusiat had once been a handsome woman. Also like Mamma, she had given birth to a number of babies, none of whom had survived infancy, leaving her thin and worn too. Her fine golden hair had lost its lustre. It was said that once it had been thick and curly, but Nancy could not recall it being anything other than thin and lank and invariably hidden beneath a prim lace cap. Papa appeared approving of her aunt's barren state. She had once heard him remark that it was a good thing, since Anne, who had been widowed over a year ago, possessed a large fortune which would be inherited by himself, her only brother.

Mamma, Lady Denley, who had been genuinely fond of her sister-in-law, whose temperament was totally unlike that of her older brother, was both surprised and warmed by the gesture. It was soothing to hug that warm little body. It was wrong to cuddle children frequently; it caused weakness. But on this occasion she could give free reign to maternal affection, take comfort and not worry lest she was spoiling her child.

'At least your aunt did not suffer for very long,' whispered Mamma.

Silently, Nancy read between the words, deducing that dear Aunt Anne's death *had* involved some suffering. In fact, she did not know how, but she simply *knew* that Aunt Anne's death had involved a gripping abdominal pain, and her aunt had been glad to be free of it.

At breakfast the following morning, it was evident that Nancy was changing for the better. She ate her breakfast with dignity, spilling nothing (she had been prone to spills), and afterwards, in the schoolroom, attended to her lessons with grave interest. The little hoyden had abruptly gone for good. A few members of the household mourned the loss, for she had been a spontaneous and merry source of entertainment. However, the model young lady was a supreme comfort to her poor Mamma, whose health was rapidly failing. Six months after the death of the beloved Lady Anne Nusiat, she again gave birth, and yet again the child, a daughter, was puny and pale, unlikely to survive the night. The midwife gloomily commented that each time Lady Denley gave birth, her health weakened and did not ever fully recover.

'I think you should bear no more children,' the youthful Nancy declared, when seated in private with Mamma, echoing the words spoken by the midwife just a short while before.

Wearily, Lady Denley regarded her only child, opening her mouth to reprove her for introducing a subject which was singularly inappropriate for a child to speak of. But no words tumbled forth. Instead she found herself considering Nancy as if through new eyes. Her black curling hair, dark eyes and thin face... the girl was the image of her father. She would, one day, be very attractive. Yet her personality was becoming increasingly akin to Anne Nusiat's, which was hardly surprising since the latter had been her aunt. It was good to know the child was of similar temperament to that wonderful, sensible, kind, woman. Oddly enough, Anne Nusiat herself had been wont to proclaim that childbearing was too much for her dear sister-in-law and maybe Frederick, her brother, ought to recognise the fact. But it was a woman's duty to bear children, and Lady Denley must therefore attend to her duty. Just as Lady Anne had done.

The changes in Nancy were welcomed by Papa, Sir Frederick Denley, who insisted it was all due to the good effect of discipline. Her wit was sweet, never cutting; common sense and wisdom were qualities which were becoming increasingly evident, especially since, just a few days after being delivered of a stillborn daughter, Lady Denley herself also died.

Barely had he emerged from mourning, when it became evident that Sir Frederick Denley would remarry. He did so fourteen months after the death of his first wife. Nancy, now thirteen, received the knowledge with equilibrium. 'Men such as Papa do not remain alone for very long,' she gravely proclaimed when informed by her governess of the forthcoming nuptials. The governess had then hastened to inform the housekeeper, who informed the cook, who informed the butler, of Miss Nancy's latest profundity – a habit which was becoming ever more frequent. Where did the child get it all from?

The new Lady Denley, Charlotte, was tardy in showing signs of fertility. As least the late Lady Denley had diligently done her duty. Privately, Nancy hoped Sir Frederick did not reproach his new wife for this error. Certainly the new mistress of the household was lovely, her face a mask of sweetness, combined with auburn hair and kittenish green eyes. Her manner was guileless; she was full of inconsequential chatter, anxious not to offend anyone in the house, no matter how lofty or lowly a servant's status might be.

Lady Charlotte Denley's days were mostly spent reading romantic fiction, choosing books with a happy ending. Noting this, Nancy recognised the need for escapism. Her stepmother was not a happy young woman. Her early intention of making her union with the impressive but older Sir Frederick, a truly ecstatic marriage, a shining example to her friends of what a happy marriage ought to be, soon withered and died.

Indeed, she was unable to please him. During their brief courtship, her beauty and charm had been sufficient; but whilst still a new bride, her inability to grasp household matters wrought from him a brusque, 'Madam, my thirteen-year-old daughter is capable of running the household. Since you are incompetent, I suggest you permit her to be your advisor.' This early reproof had caused her to weep for days. Nor did weeping soften his heart. In romantic novels men were always touched by a woman's tears. Life, she was discovering, did not mirror novels. Admittedly he visited her bedroom regularly, but even she had to confront the unhappy fact that it was merely to procreate an heir. Desire for her person did not bring him hither. But, in the early days, she hoped that all might be well eventually. Oddly enough, the person whom she found most helpful and supportive was her stepdaughter, who, as the years passed and the third year of her marriage drew to its conclusion, was still only sixteen years old.

One day, shortly after breakfast, Lady Denley and Nancy sat in the morning room, Nancy industrious, Lady Denley making no pretence of employment. Nancy, studying the proposed menu for the day, made several amendments and then placed the sheet of paper on the table.

'The McAuleys dine with us tonight. Papa wishes to undertake some serious business with them. We need to impress. I hope you shall approve the menu, I think it suitable. It awaits your signature.' She passed the paper over to her stepmother, who merely glanced at it, automatically nodded her approval, then scratched her name on the foot of the sheet.

Nancy expected nothing more. Retrieving the menu, she was about to ring the bell for the housekeeper, but instead her hand was arrested by that of her stepmother, who clutched it shyly.

'Promise you will not tell anyone,' she blushed as she spoke, 'but I so need to talk with someone, and I feel very isolated. I see so very few friends nowadays.'

Nancy nodded slowly. That was true enough. Papa had not encouraged the first Lady Denley to accept frivolous visitors. Unless, of course, it furthered his business. The Denleys worshipped regularly at a local church, so it followed that only the vicar, his wife, and staunch (wealthy) members of the congregation, were truly welcome to pay social visits to the lady of the house. His first wife had been a sensible woman; he certainly did not wish for his giddy second wife to entertain guests as foolish as she.

'I am glad to listen to you,' she responded, giving the plump, soft hand an encouraging squeeze. 'And I do not gossip,' she added. 'Whatever you have to say shall go no further.'

'You know, I feel I am with an adult when I am with you. As if *you* were the stepmother!' Lady Denley gave a girlish giggle.

'Well, you are not very much older that I,' Nancy stated. 'You are very young, only twenty-two. It is appropriate we should be friends.'

The words were warmly uttered, for she deeply pitied the fluffy little creature who was married to Papa. Really, she ought to be married to some plump, merry old buffoon, who would at least be kindly and tolerant. He might also appreciate her inconsequential chatter and girlish giggle.

'I find myself wondering if you are about to become indisposed... you know...'

'You have guessed!' Lady Denley looked anxious. 'I am so frightened.'

'Papa, he will be pleased. And concerned for your welfare,' pronounced Nancy, studying her companion sagely and seeing the young woman's expression brighten.

'Oh yes. He shall be pleased. I am so glad I have done something to earn his approval at last,' she gasped. 'I do hope you will not be put out if it is a boy.' Again she timorously squeezed Nancy's hand. 'You have been a great help to me, and I am fond of you. But I know you expect to be your father's heir.'

In truth, Lady Denley had initially found her capable stepdaughter only marginally less formidable than her husband, although it took very little time to discover that the girl was an ally she could depend upon. Swiftly overcoming her awe of the girl, she was soon very fond of her.

'I will be most happy should you produce an heir. I have plans of my own which I would like to fulfil. If you give my father a son, then Papa might approve of my own wishes,' Nancy mused aloud. 'I have a notion to study medicine. If not, then I would wish to become a nurse. It is a respectable profession nowadays, since Mistress Nightingale made it so during the Crimean wars.'

'A nurse!' Lady Denley gasped and fell silent. *A nurse! Or else a doctor. Women did not study to be doctors, surely.*

Sensing her thoughts, Nancy murmured, 'There are women nowadays attending medical school. Admittedly they are a minority, only a very few, but one day their numbers will increase, I am sure of it. I do not wish to spend my life in a gilded cage. If Papa has no sons, then it is my duty, as his eldest daughter, to marry suitably so a man can take over the business. I have no desire for that. I am pleased you are in your current condition, and Papa, well, he will be very happy. You shall have the very best of care, be assured of that.' Nancy again gripped her stepmother's hand reassuringly, then suddenly felt moved in inquire, 'Does he know of this news?'

'No,' Lady Denley shook her head. 'I don't know how to tell him.'

'Just blurt it out,' smiled Nancy.

Her prediction was accurate. Sir Frederick did indeed ensure his wife had every care and attention. Warmed by his suddenly benign approval, Lady Denley became relaxed and at ease, even daring to read her novels when in his company. However, in case she incurred a rebuke, she always ensured a Bible was also nearby, within her grasp.

On Nancy's seventeenth birthday, Lady Denley gave birth, after a long, arduous and difficult labour, to twin sons – both fine, healthy boys, who howled lustily and seemed likely to survive. Congratulating her stepmother, Nancy's compassion for the artless creature increased. If only her father would be happy with his two boys and permit his wife to remain healthy and strong, instead of being constantly worn out as the previous Lady Denley had been. The present Lady Denley was too fragile a creature to endure frequent childbearing.

Having ascertained the well-being of her stepmother, Nancy then knocked on the door of the study, to congratulate her father. As anticipated, he was seated in front of a large leather-bound ledger, the birth of two sons being no excuse to cease work. But he looked more benign that ever she had seen him. They exchanged a warm handshake – an embrace was out of the question.

'Congratulations, Papa.'

She did not actually like Sir Frederick Denley, but could not help but admire him for his intelligence and foresight.

He was a stern man, apt to be humourless and preoccupied. Nor was he warm of nature, although she believed he cared for his daughter as much as he was capable of caring. She recognised that this was because he saw that she was herself clever, beautiful, sensible and wise. Obviously he could not know that her wisdom was deeper, older, than anything he could imagine.

'Papa, I need to speak with you, and today is as good a time as any,' she informed him gravely, accepting a glass of water poured form an elaborate decanter. Excessive use of wine or spirits was disapproved of in the Denley household. Conversely, when desiring to impress guests, alcohol was very much in evidence! 'Had not a son arrived, I would have been prepared to be your obedient daughter. However, the business – the shipyards – will have males to take over in due course, which is as it should be. For myself, I have always desired to follow in the footsteps of Mistress Nightingale. I would like to be a nurse. Or else, if you permit it, I would prefer to be a doctor.'

Sitting back in her chair, she watched him cast the idea around in his mind. If he was startled by her audacious suggestion, he did not show it. Nor did she expect him to.

'Women tend towards nursing. The supposition is that female brains are not sufficiently capable to hold the learning necessary to become a doctor,' he mused aloud, then fell silent. As the silence lengthened, she was about to speak but remained mute as he raised a hand. 'Some women *are* incapable of the necessary concentration. Your stepmother, for example,' his voice sharpened with disapproval. 'But I know you to be of a different calibre. I shall tell you what I have decided. You wish to be of service to society, I believe?' As she nodded, he added, 'I trust you shall never behave like those fearful women who flaunt their learning and independence. Most unfeminine. But you have been sheltered, and I think you should see the inside of a hospital before any decision regarding your future shall be made. Therefore, I shall arrange for you to partake of a visit to the local infirmary. As you know, one of the trustees dines regularly at this house. A visit will either add fuel to your aspiration or end it completely.'

'I thank you Papa.' Draining her glass, she replaced it unctuously upon a polished silver salver, preparing to take her leave. 'And if I should wish to proceed with my ambition… even after visiting the hospital?'

'I shall expect you to instruct your stepmother in the intricacies of running the house. And forthwith you shall be given the opportunity to study as a doctor. I shall ensure that you attend a university, and you shall reside with respectable people, perhaps belonging to the clergy. Anything other is unthinkable. Meanwhile, we shall see how you conduct yourself during your visit.'

'You do not seem surprised by my request, Papa,' she observed, coming close to performing the unthinkable – planting a kiss upon his be-whiskered cheek.

'You are a remarkably assured young person. Unlike any I have ever seen,' he informed her gruffly, permitting a glimmer of pride to show in his countenance. 'I do not believe in idleness. What you desire is unusual – but not foolish. I do not doubt some will disapprove of my decision though.'

Smiling, she took her leave. His suggestion was excellent and would not curb her plans for the future. She had lived for five centuries now and had seen bodies twisted and maimed from battle, illness and everything else life could inflict upon them. This was why she wished to study to be a doctor. Nothing any hospital or infirmary had to offer would offend her sensibilities. It was time she entered a new phase. Something new and exciting.

So, nearly eight weeks later, she found herself accompanying her father in the carriage, bound for the nearest infirmary. Anxious not to give anyone the appearance of being a frivolous creature, she had dressed carefully. Her hair, as dark and curling as that of her father's, was dragged into a neat but severe bun, with no wisps permitted to stray. Studying herself in the bedroom mirror prior to departure, she was pleased with what she beheld. She looked businesslike; the sober austerity of her garb was a more effective foil for her beauty than any finery could be. Tall – as was Sir Frederick, whom she obviously favoured in appearance – her height added to her air of maturity. Lady Denley, hovering in the vestibule as the carriage was brought to the front of the house, clutched Nancy's arm anxiously.

'I hope nothing distresses you, my dear,' she whispered anxiously, lest her husband should rebuke her for fussing needlessly.

'I shall be perfectly composed throughout,' proclaimed Nancy calmly.

'I do believe you shall.' Lady Denley managed a tremulous, admiring smile. Sickness was something she could not cope with. But then, there were many things she could not cope with, including her precious babies. Thankfully there was a competent nanny to deal with the twins on her behalf.

As they neared the hospital, the carriage turned from a wide, respectable-looking cobbled street, passing through wrought-iron gates standing open. An avenue of trees led to a large brick building, imposing but bleak in appearance. This was a new hospital, modern, mooted as being a model for other hospitals. She had heard that it consisted of a series of long wards, each with beds flanking either side, plenty of windows, and wards set apart from those designated as being "fever wards". Florence Nightingale had been very much consulted regarding all of this.

Nancy and Sir Frederick walked into a commanding entrance hall. It was gloomy, full of shadows, with a wide sweeping stairway, and furnished with items of dark-stained wood; but a glimmer of light, hailing from a stained-glass window somewhere in the upper regions, shed a weak, insufficient illumination into this spacious foyer. Slowly she took in the impressive stairway, polished oak floorboards, and walls adorned with portraits of stern, majestic-looking individuals. And there was something else. A pungent smell. Possibly beeswax combined with another somewhat familiar odour, which she thought might be camphor. A woman came hurrying to greet them, a creature of stately appearance, nearly matching that of Sir Frederick's. She was tall, handsome, brisk of manner, and clearly competent. Her dress was black, the only ornamentation being a gold watch pinned to her spacious bosom.

'Good afternoon to you, Matron,' Sir Frederick greeted the woman.

Matron, having shaken hands with Sir Frederick, bowed in Nancy's direction.

'You are very young. But I am assured by your father that you are desirous of embarking upon what is now considered a very noble profession. I will instruct one of my senior nurses to escort you around the female wards,' she announced graciously.

'I wish my daughter to see as much as is decent. Including men's wards, if possible,' Sir Frederick proclaimed decidedly. 'She is no fainting creature, I assure you. I wish her to observe and learn from this visit.'

At that moment, a young man approached whose appearance initially impressed Nancy. With fair curling hair and light blue eyes, he was of equal height to Sir Frederick but slight of physique and therefore less imposing. But he was undeniably handsome. However, as Nancy met his gaze, his appearance, fetching though it was, became of secondary importance. She realised she was face to face with an incubus. As they stared at one another, mutually recognising their similarity, Nancy barely registered his name as Matron formally introduced them. Eventually she realised Papa was tugging at her sleeve.

*****

'I had to enquire of him, later, as to his name. I did not take it in....' Sara's voice trailed away as she smiled reminiscently.

'So, it was love at first sight?' Jennifer interposed, staring at the childlike figure in front of her. Sara. Yet not Sara. Suddenly wishing the creature *was* Sara, the *old* Sara, she swallowed a sudden rush of bitterness.

'I have many memories to treasure. But if I could move backwards in time and choose only one moment to relive that would be the moment. I hate to sound like a soppy novel, but for an instant time did stand still. I don't think for one moment it *was* what romantic poets would describe as love at first sight. We recognised one another for what we were... are... and mutually approved. It would not have mattered if he had taken a body which resembled an ape. Incubus and succubus are aware that each body is transitory. But the fact he had selected a handsome form was an added bonus. I had chosen a handsome female shape. He shared the same opinion as I: handsome, wealthy people are the most desirable bodies to occupy. The year was somewhere in the mid-1870s. We were separated during World War Two. Seventy years together, approximately. Not a long time retrospectively, considering how long I've been around,' Sara reflected solemnly.

'No, I suppose seventy years is a short time for you,' mused Jennifer. 'For Chas and I... well, for us it is a long time, and I sincerely hope we both survive to see our golden wedding anniversary. I cannot imagine being without him. Life would be empty.'

'Yes. One adjusts. But *empty* is the most worthy description,' agreed Sara.

'Tell me more about it, please,' begged Jennifer, realising at that moment that she had now totally accepted the strange reality that her daughter was possessed by an ancient spirit and, though it was regrettable, no longer did it seem strange or improbable.

CHAPTER EIGHT

Chas was discharged from hospital the day following his surgery. With dismay he recapped his instructions.

'No driving for two to three weeks, depending on when I can do an emergency stop,' he protested. 'I can do an emergency stop now, I'm sure of that!'

'I doubt it,' predicted Sara. 'Although it's over forty years since I last removed an appendix, and techniques have moved on since then, I still doubt it! But although you don't have much evidence of surgery – just a few tiny scars – you have still have some internal trauma, and need rest.'

'Yes,' agreed Jennifer, suddenly perturbed by the notion that someone, outwardly twelve years old, could remove an appendix. *Will I ever get used with this?* she wondered.

'But what about our holidays?' protested Chas.

'I've thought about that,' Jennifer announced. 'How about a coach tour? I saw one advertised this morning. Instead of our old plans, we can scrap them and visit my brother when Sara has her half term, October time. I fancy Gloucestershire. The tour takes in Tewksbury—'

'Tewksbury,' breathed Sara.

'It takes in the abbey, varying sights of Gloucester, er... I need to find the article.' Jennifer rummaged for the newspaper.

'It's a luxury coach, excellent hotels, and the abbey I'm sure is included in it—'

'Tewksbury Abbey.' Again Sara sounded breathless. 'I've not been there for years!'

'How many years?' Chas wanted to know.

Jennifer had collected him from hospital, leaving Sara at home. She'd wanted time alone to acquaint him with the conversation she and Sara had had the previous night.

'Well,' Sara did some mental arithmetic, 'a couple of hundred. No, not that long. But over a hundred and fifty.'

Chas was silenced.

They were seated in the conservatory; the late afternoon sun was weak, nothing as strong as it should be for midsummer, and there was the threat of rain, but the room was warm enough. Chas was lounging on the sofa, whilst Sara was sitting on the floor cradling a guitar, which she had just tuned to her satisfaction. No one now bothered to wonder how she managed it. The Sara of old had never struck a chord. Now she could.

'Here,' Jennifer produced a creased newspaper. 'Have a look at it and see what you think. But I quite fancy a trip that doesn't require driving. We can't go abroad – you've just had surgery and can't be insured – and I think our original plans will be too much for you.'

'I agree,' nodded Sara. 'And in late August, VPL are doing an open-air concert somewhere in that area… Not sure where. Might actually be near to the abbey. I'll check up on it if you'd like to go.'

'VPL?' frowned Chas.

'Girl band. Heavy metal,' Jennifer enlightened, having previously talked about them with Sara.

'Not sure I want to see them – or hear them, for that matter,' Chas protested. 'I am not familiar with their music. But VPL?' He looked bewildered. 'Does it stand for something?'

'Visible Panty Line,' smirked his wife.

'The lead singer is called Gentian de Barke. It's their first tour for well over a year because both Gentian, and Paradise Beam, the drummer, went on holiday to somewhere in South America, and one night they got completely stoned and visited a dubious tattoo parlour, adding a few bits of body artwork to their collection. Afterwards both were admitted to hospital with septicaemia as a result. In fact, one of them, I think it was Paradise, was not expected to live.'

'Is this Paradise Beam her real name?' demanded Chas.

'Allegedly,' Sara nodded. 'Sounds really cool, yes?'

Jennifer hesitated. 'I suppose it does.' She sounded doubtful.

'Can't bear tattoos,' grumbled Chas. 'I hope you don't start wanting one,' he warned Sara.

'The youth of today,' Sara chipped in.

Chas laughed aloud and regretted it. 'Ouch,' he winced as he clutched his midriff. 'I was thinking of maybe calling into work tomorrow. I hope they don't try to entertain me with jokes.'

'Perhaps you should wait a few more days,' suggested Jennifer. 'My colleagues have been very good to me the past couple of days; I don't want to take time off to drive you there.'

'I'll get a taxi, and I'm sure someone will be kind enough to deliver me back home,' Chas predicted.

'I can drive,' beamed Sara.

'Don't make me laugh,' protested Chas. 'It would look fabulous in the newspapers. *Lawyer found in passenger seat being chauffeured by twelve-year-old daughter.* Oh yes, that would make my career soar!'

'He requested to be permitted to show me around the hospital, and Matron agreed, though reluctantly. She would perhaps have preferred that my escort be a nurse, but they were all busy. Thankfully,' Sara smiled reminiscently.

Chas, feeling weary, had gone to bed shortly after seven p.m. Jennifer was eager to hear the rest of the story of Nancy Denley.

'He was younger than me. I'm talking in incubus years, of course, so it was not a huge amount by our standards. Approximately half a century younger. He was originally one of the Earls of Northumberland, of the fabled Percy family.'

'Not Harry Hotspur?' gasped Jennifer, trying to work out the date of when Harry Hotspur had lived and died.

'The fabled Harry died in fourteen hundred and three,' Sara answered Jennifer's question. 'You might recollect that some years later Anne Boleyn was betrothed – before she captured Henry the Eighth's attention – to a young man called Harry Percy.'

Jennifer nodded eagerly, quickly recalling her Tudor knowledge. 'Wow! Your companion was engaged to Anne Boleyn!' She sat bolt upright with excitement. 'I adore reading about Anne Boleyn; she has always been a kind of heroine of mine!'

'Strange heroine,' smiled Sara. 'Not a very nice woman, really, when you think about it. She had no compunction at all about stealing another woman's husband!'

'I suppose not. But she paid a huge price for her brief few years of fame,' nodded Jennifer, as if this excused Anne's behaviour.

'Indeed she did,' agreed Sara. 'But no. Not that Harry Percy,' she shook her head apologetically. 'My Harry Percy was his father, the fifth Earl of Northumberland, also called Harry Percy. He was the Lord Percy who conspired with Cardinal Wolsey to have the betrothal ended. As a mere Boleyn, she was unworthy of the great Percys. But by the time I met him he was a doctor. His name was David Royale.'

'But how did you realise he was an incubus?' Jennifer wanted to know. 'I mean, suppose you should meet another, would it be the same as when you met Tracy? You've told me you each knew what the other was – or is.'

'It's... well, it's an aura,' Sara mused aloud. 'It is as if the head cannot entirely contain the mind... something I – and others like myself – feel. We know and recognise it. And, of course, it takes a few years, using more than one body in my case, to actually develop this instinct. It's not a good description, but it is as accurate as I can get,' she stated apologetically, adding, 'I failed to recognise the first incubus I ever met. The ability to do so developed with time.'

'So, you were – are – a Percy?' Nancy mused aloud.

'Yes. And you were – still are – Maude Dubreise. I've heard of you. The fabled Maude. When I came into the world your name was spoken of reverently. You were canonised, in fact!'

'Yes, shortly before the Reformation! People claimed miracles occurred at our grave. It seems strange to me that we were so revered; we were just ordinary people; we did nothing particularly special!' mused Nancy. 'It is still there, my grave. *Our* grave. I think no one was sure which of us was performing the miracles, so Gilbert was canonised too. I saw it around fifteen years ago when travelling in that area. The graves were – are – within a private chapel. The original graves were very simple. A stately monument was raised above them, following the canonisation, to receive gifts and make a profit, but it did not remain there for long. Less than ten years, in fact. The Reformation came and it was dismantled, leaving just the grave slabs again. The house is there too. Bigger than when I resided there – it was extended over the years. But the core of the place, where I spent happy years, bearing children, running my home, is recognisable. I did not realise I would keep on doing much of the same for centuries.'

'I don't just say this because you are here with me, but Maude was certainly regarded as being the saintly person. I think the Pope probably felt her virtues were due to her husband's good guidance,' David Royale speculated gravely. 'As for me, I fought battles, as Harry Percy, little knowing I would keep on fighting battles over the centuries.'

They were slowly walking through the hospital, she trying to give the appearance of being absorbed in every aspect of the building, its routine, its occupants, and he trying to assume a sermonising air. In truth, they merely wished to compare experiences. Finally, as they eventually emerged into the garden, they could speak freely.

'Is that why you are now a doctor?' she inquired sagely. 'The reverse of your earlier activities?'

'Indeed, yes,' he agreed. 'Indeed, yes! I weary of bearing arms! This is the opposite. This is a good time to be a doctor. So many new things are happening. I intend to go to London soon, to be at the centre of it all,' he acknowledged frankly. 'There is a very good dissection studio at St George's Hospital, near Hyde Park Corner. The lab is not exactly at the hospital but at Kinnerton Street. I am eager to learn more.'

'That is what I wish to do. But as a woman it is not so easy for me,' she reflected. 'I have been alive for so long, and have seen so much, dissecting a cadaver does not horrify me. Of course, I do believe that since the Anatomy Act of 1832, there are more cadavers available.'

'Yes,' he nodded in agreement. 'At one time only executed criminals were dissected. Now any unclaimed body can be used. It has made a marvellous difference apparently. At least, that is what I have heard.'

'And it has ruined business for the resurrection men!' she added, a tinge of wry humour in her tone.

'We must not lose each other,' he whispered urgently, for Sir Frederick and Matron were now approaching. 'When can we meet again?'

'Leave it to me,' she advised, adding, 'I live at Denley Lodge. It is a well-known address.' As an afterthought, she added, having studied him intently, 'I must admit, you have chosen a comely body to inhabit.'

Indeed he had, for not only was he handsome but there was something good-natured in his aspect. He was also bewhiskered, as was fashionable at the time. Few men were not.

'As have you,' he returned the compliment, equally impressed.

'Well, child?' demanded Sir Frederick, fixing his daughter with what appeared to be an uncompromising glare. Nancy, unlike most persons, could delve beneath it. It hid concern.

'I am well, Papa. And I have learned a great deal. So much so, it inspires me! Doctor Royale has given me so much to ponder over; I am quite overwhelmed with excitement. I think it would be an excellent plan if he, and of course the good Matron here,' Nancy smiled gently and politely towards the dark, regally handsome figure, 'would do us the honour of dining with us in the near future. I shall much profit from her wisdom,' she concluded, seemingly ingenuous.

Matron, flattered by the invitation yet nonplussed by the strangely self-possessed young girl, could only nod her agreement.

'Well, this Saturday evening would be excellent,' agreed Sir Frederick. 'The Lord Lieutenant with his wife are to join us, as are Sir Nigel and Lady Redvers, plus one or two others. It will make an interesting gathering.'

Matron abandoned her regal air and suddenly displayed the radiant aspect of an awestruck schoolgirl. 'Splendid. Of course, we are delighted to accept,' she pronounced without consulting Dr Royale. Dinner... at the esteemed Sir Frederick's home! And with such august company too. It would give her something to talk about for weeks.

'But please come into my office to partake of some sherry wine before you depart,' she found herself saying, managing to regain some composure.

Nancy now knew what the odour was that had initially so assaulted her nostrils in the vestibule. Certainly beeswax and camphor, which she had recognised. But from her tour of the establishment, she now realised it included the acrid fumes of vinegar. They used vinegar everywhere. The belief was that it gave protection from contagion. It seeped into every corner, including Matron's office. In parts of the hospital the aroma was strong enough to sting both the eyes and the nostrils. But it was a small price to pay for deliverance from contagion.

In her office, Matron, now endeavouring to become acquainted, directed Nancy's attention to a pianoforte.

'As well as aspiring to study, do you enjoy music, Miss Nancy?'

'I do,' Nancy affirmed.

'Are you familiar with the work of William Byrd?' David Royale's eyes held a mischievous glint.

Of course, she knew of the Elizabethan composer. Before she could reply, Matron, kittenish with delight over the invitation to the august Sir Frederick's home, suggested perhaps Dr Royal might entertain them briefly before the guests departed.

'This is called *The Barley Break*. It is a sweet piece of music. You will recognise it, I am sure,' he addressed everyone, but Nancy knew it was aimed at herself.

She knew it well but had not heard it for many decades. A century and a half, in fact, if not more. But at once the one-time familiarity of the piece flooded back to her.

Matron smiled benignly, trying to assume an air of being well acquainted with the piece. Sir Frederick merely gave a snort of dismissal. Music was well enough, in his opinion, but something he merely tolerated.

Later, in silence, Nancy sat beside her father as they headed homeward. She had half expected some sort of interrogation, but he clearly did not feel so inclined. His nature was usually uncommunicative. She presumed he believed her determination to pursue a medical career remained a fact, since she had shown no repugnance when confronted with the sights and smells of the hospital. Since he asked no questions, she deemed it prudent to remain mute.

The following day her spirits soared. Unable to wait until Saturday to meet with her again, David Royale had sent a note to her home requesting they should meet in the early evening, in a nearby park. The timing of the meeting was providential; it would take place before she dined with her father, stepmother and several visitors. It was not a social gathering, purely business. Had David Royale suggested a later time, a refusal would have been unavoidable.

They met with a degree of bashfulness on both sides, gravely greeting one another with surprising formality given the number of years each had lived. Both were equipped to deal with any situation, but this was unique. Not just a meeting of fellow incubi, but a meeting of like souls who were instinctively drawn to each other. Within fifteen minutes they were totally at ease, walking aimlessly about the park, arm in arm, in earnest conversation. Exchanging histories was a lengthy subject. At first hand they had experienced events which now provided subject matter for history books and lessons.

'I once visited Richard the Third's grave,' Nancy informed her companion, following a discussion of the Wars of the Roses. 'I was of a Lancastrian household, but since I was visiting Leicester it seemed wrong to ignore the grave of one who had been anointed king. People used to discreetly visit it, although it was supposed to be a secret. But often flowers and offerings would be deposited there, until the abbey church was pulled down. I would not know the site now.'

'So many monarchs we have encountered,' mused David. 'Well,' he amended, 'maybe not encountered personally. But we have lived with the results of their reigns. My family fell into disgrace through making bad decisions – such as supporting Mary Queen of Scots.'

He had occupied his current body for nearly a year, he informed her. However, he had been a doctor for nearly twenty years, using another body. As had been stated at their previous meeting, his interest had sprung from the battlefield. Years of fighting had led to him desiring to make people whole again, reattaching partially severed limbs, stemming the tide of blood, attempting – usually without effect – to relieve pain, seeking to cure noxious illnesses and endeavouring to be not discouraged by failing to achieve a good result.

Finally, checking the watch pinned to the bodice of her blouse, Nancy realised it was nearly time to return home. Only then did David broach the subject of matrimony.

'I take it because of your age that you are free.' He squeezed her hand, an expression of regret fleetingly passing over his face.

'I am,' she nodded affirmation, 'but I suspect you are not?'

'Alas, I am betrothed. I am relatively new to this body, and he was already betrothed when I came to use it. But this sense of oneness is new to me. I feel as if I have met… have met… part of my own soul. How can I wed another?' he mused aloud.

'Yes… how?' she nodded in agreement. Breach of promise was against the law, and it would damage her own reputation, as well as his, permanently, should she stand between David and his betrothed. They were silent, clutching hands, contented but not entirely at peace.

'It requires some thought. There must be a way. Even if I have to leave this body and take up another one,' he suggested.

'Or I could take over the body of your fiancée,' she considered the notion. 'I would rather not – should this body perish it would pain my father. Although he would recover from that blow, I very much suspect,' she mused aloud. 'Also, as is usual, I like inhabiting this body, as no doubt you have grown used to yours,' she considered options aloud.

'Yes, we do, quite often, become fond of these bodies and become attached to them. At least until they become very old and infirm. But we must both think it over,' he affirmed. 'We meet again on Saturday. There is no immediate necessity to arrive at a decision.'

'We can wait,' she agreed. 'We know better than to be hasty. But I must go now. We have guests coming shortly and I must change my attire.' Nancy glanced at her watch in alarm.

Hurrying, he walked with her, almost to the very gate of the handsome Queen Anne mansion inhabited by the Denleys. Flushed, Nancy sped to her room, hastily unbuttoning her garments and shedding pins. Hot and flushed, she dismissed her maid, desiring above all things to compose her thoughts before facing guests. But just as she was wrestling with the buttons of her evening gown, and regretting having dismissed her maid, there came a light tap on the door, and Lady Denley entered.

'You have been missing for some time… and, oh my, you look flustered! Where have you been? I don't wish to intrude, but I wonder…' Her girlish voice trailed away.

'I have been in the park. Walking,' Nancy admitted, turning to allow Lady Denley to fasten the minute buttons on the back of her gown.

'Alone?' The question was flung lightly but was deep with meaning. Lady Denley was profoundly romantic.

'No.' Nancy was reluctant to be dishonest.

'With a man?' Noticing a flush sweeping over the younger girl's countenance, spreading downwards over her neck, she exclaimed, 'With a man! Whom, pray?'

'I met a doctor at the hospital. David Royale. We met at the park, merely to talk. He is betrothed. Please do not envisage anything inappropriate between us.'

'But you like him. Unrequited love can be… is… painful. I would not wish you to be hurt, dear Nancy. Is he handsome?' Lady Denley sat on the bed, hands folded daintily in her lap, waiting to be enlightened.

'Tall, with curling fair hair and whiskers. His eyes are blue and his nose is most noble,' smiled Nancy.

'A man should always have a noble nose. As for a woman, a pert, neat nose is desirable.'

Complacently, Lady Denley considered her own exceedingly pretty nose in the glass. It was such a comfort. She could not have coped with an unshapely nose adorning her face, and felt sorry for those who did. Dear Nancy did not have a pert nose, but it was neat and suited her lovely face.

'You shall meet him on Saturday. He comes to dine, along with Matron. Please do not tell Papa I met him today.'

Satisfied with her appearance, Nancy gathered up her fan and reticule, ready to leave her room.

'You know I shall not. But will he bring his betrothed?'

Lady Denley patted an imaginary stray lock of hair into place.

'No. Only he and Matron are invited.'

'Take care. Please do not be hurt, dear Nancy.'

'I can promise I shall be sensible,' she briskly assured her stepmother.

THE BARLEY BREAK

Saturday passed in an unusual manner in the Denley household. In the morning, the custom was for the carriage to be sent for. Then Lady Denley would undertake her morning calls, leaving household matters to Nancy. However, Sir Frederick was now adamant she should learn household organisation herself, but it was such a bore. If Nancy left home, surely the housekeeper would deal with it all. Dear Nancy wasted her time needlessly running the house, and she had fondly reprimanded her for it. Men did not like women if they knew too much, or were too practical. But on this particular Saturday morning, she persuaded Nancy to accompany her on a shopping expedition. The girl had such good taste when it came to selecting clothing. Especially hats. And Lady Denley fancied she needed a new hat.

'What do you think, Nancy?'

They were in Lady Denley's favourite department store, a new edifice in town frequented by everyone of wealth or status. Nancy found herself peering at a large hat of navy blue, decked with navy silk flowers. Amid the flowers lurked some bright pink feathers.

Blinking in surprise, Nancy managed to profess, 'I think the pink feathers would be better employed on a straw summer hat. It is garish in effect.'

Lady Denley liked the pink feathers.

'I am sure more appropriate feathers could be brought and secured in the hat,' Nancy suggested to an assistant who stood patiently nearby.

Awaiting replacement feathers, Lady Denley beckoned a second assistant.

'May I view some gloves from the next department?' In reality it was an instruction, not a request.

'I will have some brought for your approval. What manner of gloves do you require, my Lady?' was the formal, respectful inquiry, accompanied by a bobbed curtsey.

'Navy blue. Silk, please… or should I have kid?' She looked askance towards her stepdaughter, but Nancy was clearly not paying attention.

'I will ensure both are brought to you, madam. Will you require a cup of tea?' Another curtsey accompanied the question.

'Yes. Thank you. For both of us,' Lady Denley glanced towards her stepdaughter again. She still seemed absently preoccupied. 'Nancy… is all well?' she demanded.

'Yes. I am merely contemplating the seating plan for this evening,' she admitted.

'I am contemplating my clothing account. I am terrified of displeasing Sir Frederick by overstepping my budget,' Lady Denley admitted, adding with a deep sigh, 'and I *have* overstepped it, I fear.'

Nancy was well aware of how feckless her stepmother could be.

'Since the arrival of the boys, he will forgive anything of you,' she assured her stepmother, inwardly hoping this was indeed true.

An assistant arrived bearing a tray of tea and some biscuits, followed by the other assistant returning with new feathers, of a pale blue colour, to be affixed to the hat.

'Oh, that is so much better,' Lady Denley admitted, surprised. 'You were so right, dear Nancy! And here comes the selection of gloves too!'

Happy as a child, Lady Denley squealed and exclaimed over each pair, eventually hovering between navy kid trimmed with squirrel, or navy silk trimmed with pearl buttons.

For her part, Nancy remained quietly reflective. What would become of David and herself? One outcome was certain; they would not permit themselves to lose contact with one another.

'Which do you think?' With one of each pair of gloves on either hand, Lady Denley extended her arms towards Nancy.

'Oh, buy both,' was the easy reply. 'They are both exceedingly wearable. Are the hat and gloves intended for any particular occasion?'

'The bishop's wife will be holding her annual garden party soon. I already have a navy gown with a white silk collar which I have not worn.'

'And navy trimmed with white becomes you,' Nancy approved. 'Perhaps you should also purchase a pale blue collar for the dress and some white feathers for the hat whilst you are here,' she suggested, as if indulging a well-loved child. 'It is a practical idea; you may wear white with white, or pale blue with pale blue. In effect, it gives you two outfits! I shall inform Papa of this if he objects.'

Reassured by her stepdaughter's words, and enchanted by the suggestion, her ladyship agreed.

'Oh yes! You are so wise, Nancy!' She needed forays such as this. Not being introspective, it didn't occur to her that they provided yet another escape from the disappointment of marriage. Shopping distracted her thoughts from her husband, whom, she had come to reluctantly perceive, still failed to fall in love with her. Once upon a time she had imagined herself to be in love. Now it was replaced by a fearful apprehension. He was not physically violent, yet his disapproval was palpable. The arrival of the twins had brought about a tolerance on his part. But she desired more than mere tolerance. He remained distant and aloof. She sincerely hoped dear Nancy fared better in the marital situation. But then she could not imagine anyone intimidating Nancy.

They returned home and, following her usual habit, Nancy proceeded to summon the housekeeper, bent upon ensuring all was running according to plan in the kitchen. The housekeeper often wondered whether, if Miss Nancy was less capable, would her ladyship have learned to reign over the household before now? She was uncertain.

By evening, everything was ready. For Nancy, however illustrious the guests might be, it was merely a matter of routine. She felt calm and competent, albeit quietly excited. Lady Denley kept shooting glances and half smiles in Nancy's direction as they awaited the arrival of the guests. She was eager to see this Doctor David Royale who had so impressed her cool, competent stepdaughter. Nor was she disappointed when he finally arrived. He had, she decided, *an air of distinction*.

Dinner proceeded smoothly; the conversation was vivacious. One of Lady Denley's virtues was her ability to make small talk, ensuring every guest felt welcome and not neglected in any way. Nancy had once remarked to Sir Frederick that her stepmother was a charming woman. He had simply responded by saying anyone could be charming if they so chose. Therefore, Lady Denley's one skill passed unlauded, utterly dismissed by her husband.

During dinner Nancy and David were able to talk quietly, as she had adroitly ensured they sat next to each other, but both were aware that their preference for one another had already been observed, as several guests were exchanging amused, indulgent glances in their direction.

'Which faith do you prefer?' he inquired quietly, as Matron's attention was taken by the helpful Lady Denley.

'I have not been Roman Catholic since the Reformation,' Nancy informed him. 'I embraced Protestantism with a passion. You, of course, being a Percy, are no doubt devoted to the Church of Rome.'

He shook his head vehemently. 'I don't belong to anything very much at all,' he reflected aloud. 'In days of old one had to take sides. Often I have taken the wrong side. But I was never seriously inclined towards anything religious. I suppose I learned to sway with the tide of religion and politics. Used whatever I could to my advantage! I am not proud of that. I merely state a fact.'

'It is what most people did,' she shrugged. 'At times, I had to hide the fact I was Protestant. It was self-preservation.'

Adeptly she turned to the person sitting on her other side, to exchange pleasantries, wishing she could talk to David Royale and no one else.

'Nancy, you must show Dr Royale the gardens later in the evening,' suggested Lady Denley, who had been chatting amiably with him. 'He says he is wondrously fond of gardens.'

Smiling acquiescence, Nancy could have kissed her.

'I would show them to you myself,' prattled Lady Denley in her kindly manner, 'but I feel a little fatigued, and Nancy is so very knowledgeable about plants, I am sure you will be kind enough to excuse me.'

Throwing her stepmother a grateful glance, Nancy accepted David's arm and accompanied him out into the mild, evening air. The time they had to speak with one another must necessarily be brief. A long private exchange would naturally be construed as inappropriate flirtatious behaviour on her part.

'After our last meeting I met with my fiancée,' he informed her, running his fingers through his hair distractedly. 'It was painful. Obviously she has noted I have changed. I am not the man to whom she was betrothed just over a year ago. But whilst she has observed the changes, she has accepted them. I hate to sound conceited, but she does harbour some feelings for me. It was because of this partiality that she immediately suspected my affections were engaged elsewhere!'

'So you had to admit the truth?'

Nancy casually pointed to varying plants, so the ever-vigilant Sir Frederick would assume she was demonstrating her knowledge of horticulture.

'Yes,' he said, and following her cue he too indicated in the direction of some healthy looking bushes. 'I begged her to consider releasing me from our betrothal. She requested time to think upon the matter. She does not desire to make a scandal by taking the issue to the courts for breach of promise. However, our engagement has been published in the press, and it will cause embarrassment to all parties concerned. Particularly to her. What she does request is to maintain a public facade for two weeks. I am to accompany her to the launching of a ship, which will be followed by a particularly grand party, and invitations have been issued to her family, and my name has been added. It is a significant social event, and she desires I do not cause her humiliation by requiring her to attend alone, apart from the company of her parents,' sighing, again he ran his hands through his hair, all but making it stand on end.

'She has no desire to be attached to a man who prefers the company of another woman. If I do this, she feels she can release me… if her parents also agree. They are respectable people. I know not if they will permit it.'

'The ship which is to be launched is *The Lady Anne*.' Nancy's voice was almost a whisper. 'Named after myself and my late aunt of the same name'.

'*The Lady Anne*,' he nodded. 'Yes, that is the very ship.'

'I shall be there too. Maybe it would be best if I were to take over your fiancée's body. Much more simple,' she pondered aloud.

He detected a lack of enthusiasm in her tone.

'Victoria, my fiancée, will surely be introduced to you and your family. Her father is the owner and governor of The Grey

Coat School.' This school was a local, much lauded provider of education for the sons of wealthy citizens. Sir Frederick had attended it in his youth.

'I already know of the family of the woman to whom you are betrothed. The Furness–Youngs. Her parents have dined here.'

Nancy, still making a show of helpfully pointing to plants, felt a sudden surge of pity for Victoria Furness–Young. Optimistically, she hoped the woman was not so deeply enough in love as to allow the separation to ruin her life. The fact was, during her long life she had never felt such affinity for anyone, whether mortal or incubi, as she did for David Royale.

'Before your body was inhabited by an incubus, you must have felt deeply for her,' she speculated.

'I *liked* her,' he admitted. 'But I was not in love with her. She was a very suitable wife for an ambitious doctor. I was then, and am now, ambitious. But I cannot permit myself to feel deeply for a woman who will perish… perhaps in childbirth, perhaps because of illness.'

She recognised the truth of this.

'And yet I think I am jealous of her,' she smiled.

'She is a fine young woman. I realised that when deciding to marry her. I *need* to marry. I inhabit a male body and…' His voice trailed away. He regarded her anxiously, wondering if she was embarrassed.

'I know what you allude to.' Her smile allayed his fears. 'I have been married many times! And have given birth to many children. As for Miss Furness-Young, I have seen her at social gatherings but have not actually been introduced.'

Nancy could picture Victoria Furness–Young. Pleasant, tall, homely in appearance. Yet, the truth was, although she had a preference for using an attractive body, beauty never lasted for very long. The freshness faded quickly. But it *was* wonderful while it lasted! And over the years she had become very artful at using cosmetics, giving an illusion of prolonged youth. She shook her head in bewilderment. 'I have lived a long time and yet find myself in a unique situation. Whatever I do, I shall forever wonder if I acted wisely. If I take over her body, I pain my father, although he will recover, I am sure. If I don't, Victoria will be disappointed...'

'Similarly, I could find a different body, belonging to someone suitable for you to wed,' David pointed out. 'Then I too would cause distress to my parents.....'

'But we cannot just lightly discard these bodies. We have a duty toward them and to those who care about us,' Nancy quietly interrupted.

At that moment Sir Frederick could be seen heading directly towards them.

'I cannot but be jealous,' she whispered as her father approached. 'Your fiancée can meet you openly. In fact the people gathered here will be wondering why she has not accompanied you. But if I do not see you again soon, at least I have the knowledge that you will be at the launching in less than two weeks!'

'We must meet before then. Like yourself, I have never been in this situation before. Often I have longed for something new, something unique, and when it arrives I find it unsettling.' Then, as Sir Frederick drew near, added, 'Aha, Sir, your daughter has more knowledge of medicinal herbs than I,' he declared heartily.

'She is very educated when it comes to plants. I suspect her mother taught her,' Sir Frederick replied amiably. Matron had informed him that this young man was engaged. Nancy seemed to like him, and until now she had never displayed any preference for anyone. Therefore this attraction must immediately be nipped in the bud.

The late Lady Denley had known little about plants, and Sir Frederick had known little about his wife, mused Nancy. 'I must venture indoors to talk with our guests,' she stated primly, suspecting that as soon as she moved away her father would surely have questions to ask of Dr David Royale. He had certainly deduced she had a preference for him.

CHAPTER NINE

'Did you marry David Royale?' Jennifer very much hoped all had turned out well between the two.

'We did marry,' Sara nodded. 'It's nearly midnight, though, and I think it shall keep until another time. It's a long story. But suffice to say I didn't take over Victoria's body. It might seem the obvious thing to do, but it felt immoral, to me, to just wantonly abandon one body and seize another, merely for the gratification of my own wishes.'

'Did you have children together?'

Jennifer began the usual night-time checks, ensuring doors were locked and lights switched off. Turning to look at Sara, she witnessed an expression of pain on that very youthful face.

'Yes. Sort of. I was pregnant twice; I miscarried both times.' Sara stooped to switch off a table lamp. Her face momentarily hidden, she added, 'We had hoped that with both of us being the same, we might at last produce one such as ourselves. But, as he pointed out to me, to be like ourselves might not be a blessing for anyone! It can be regarded as the reverse. But it didn't happen, and perhaps it was for the best. Later, with both of us using different bodies, I did become pregnant, and gave birth more than once. They weren't like us, and eventually of course they died.' Her tone was bitter. 'Anyway, science being as it is... much as I love children, I shall now probably never conceive again!'

Thoughtfully, Jennifer washed, cleaned her teeth, then pulled on one of her dainty nightdresses. *Not that Chas is in any condition to fully appreciate the vision*, she realised wryly. But they were fortunate; things could have been so much worse, and he was safely home now.

'Do you need anything, darling?' she asked, climbing into bed and noticing he was bleary-eyed but awake.

'Glass of water... Aha, I see a glass on the bedside table. My private nurse has anticipated my needs!' He drank deeply.

'This particular private nurse didn't,' Jennifer admitted. 'Sara put it there.'

'What have the two of you been talking about? It's nearly midnight,' he noticed with surprise, glancing at the digital display on his alarm clock.

Jennifer gave a brief resume, then added, 'I feel sorry for her, Chas.' She lay back on her pillows and switched the bedside lights off. 'She mentioned, just before we came upstairs, that she and her fellow incubus had children together. They all died in due course. She looked so sad, I nearly cried for her. She obviously can't help but love them, and they die. It sounds wonderful to live, to go on forever, yet it's really not very nice at all. Small wonder she's pleased that modern contraception is so good; she intends not to have any more children. I don't blame her. What do you think, Chas? Chas?'

Chas had fallen asleep.

Two days later, during the afternoon, Alan Reynolds arrived, asking after Chas and wishing to know if he could be of assistance in any way. Sara, who had answered the door, thanked him courteously, explained that so far they were managing very nicely, and since Chas was relaxing in the conservatory (Jennifer was at work) he would be very happy to enjoy some male company.

The vicar felt slightly nonplussed by the self-assured teenager. He knew her... he wondered what to call it. Her history? Her situation? Well, he knew she was unusual. Best to just leave it that way. She *was* unusual. He entered the conservatory to find Chas discussing the Spanish Civil War with another teenager, a red-headed young lady who looked slightly older than Sara. Frowning, he tried to place her. He'd seen her around the village.

'Alan... sorry, I can't get up easily.' Chas extended a hand to shake. 'This is Sara's friend, Tracy.'

'How do you do, Vicar.' Tracy shook hands with the new arrival. 'My mother's in the kitchen. Would you like her to make a cup of tea for you?'

'That would be lovely. I could do with one too,' Chas replied for both of them. 'I suspect Sara might be already sorting it out,' he added.

'I'll help her,' Tracy murmured, before discreetly withdrawing.

'What a sensible young girl,' remarked Alan. 'I know her face... I've met her before. I know! She attended Sara's baptism.'

'She's the same as Sara but much older,' whispered Chas. 'You know... the other girl in the tapes. Hence our discussion about the Spanish Civil War. She was killed during the conflict. Her mother doesn't know about her though.'

Alan Reynolds silently wondered how any parent could not be anything but aware when their offspring suddenly began acting differently. As he briefly pondered, Elsie herself came crashing in, literally, all but dropping a tray onto the coffee table, which juddered dangerously.

As Alan managed to stop the table swaying, Elsie boomed heartily, 'Good to see you, Vicar. How about a nice ham sandwich? I can easily mek one; there's both brown and white breed in the kitchen. Tek your pick.'

As Alan declined politely, but Chas felt a sudden pang of hunger, the first since having surgery.

'*I* would like a sandwich,' he pronounced. Then, teasingly imitating her accent, added, 'I would like white breed, but don't tell my wife! She disapproves.'

'Can I not persuade you, Vicar?' Elsie demanded.

'Well… er… yes. White for me also.' Alan needed little persuading. 'Incidentally, it is good to see your eldest, Rick, attending church. He's a splendid young man. Wants to be a care worker,' he informed Chas.

Chas was silent. *Splendid* was not a description he would readily apply to Rick. But to be fair, the lad seemed nice enough, once you looked past the multiple piercings, chains, and goth attire. And also there was the very visible presence of his tattoos.

On cue, Elsie cheerfully informed them, 'He's nowt so good the day though. Had another nipple pierced a couple of days ago. The first one got itself infected, and so has this one. His da insisted he should go to the doctors' this morning. Needs antibiotics again.'

'Thank goodness he only has two nipples,' Chas muttered fervently. 'It's enough to make me queasy.'

'I've just seen your daughter. I recall I saw her at Sara's baptism party. She seems a very sensible girl,' Alan Reynolds fished for further information.

'Oh, we always keep saying she's been here afore,' Elsie assured him heartily. 'You should hear her talk sometimes. Her da is ever so proud. It looks like she'll mek university. No one in our family has done that afore! We'll find a means of helping her out. Nowt is going to stop it! There're both good kids. Our Rick is going to college in September! To get qualified for 'is youth work! I think he'll do as well as Tracy – in his own way.'

Turning abruptly, she strode sturdily from the conservatory, with Alan's assurance of, 'I'm sure he will,' echoing pleasantly in her ears.

Later, having eaten the sandwiches, the two men, momentarily silent, studied the two teenage girls, both of whom were now steadily working in the garden, deftly dead-heading and pruning. Each appeared totally competent.

'At this rate we can dispense with the gardener,' Chas remarked drily. 'Sara has her own herb garden now; she likes the thought of cooking with our own basil, coriander or whatever, instead of supermarket-bought plants. Not sure what the difference is. Probably even a gourmet wouldn't be able to tell,' he speculated. 'I suppose it's the satisfaction of having grown it personally.'

'Are you still agreeable for Sara to meet my friend who specialises in matters supernatural?' Alan Reynolds rubbed absently at an insect bite on his leg. In spite of spending a lot of time wearing cropped trousers, or cargo shorts, his legs were lily white.

'I guess so,' frowned Chas at length. 'But I can't see a solution. To be honest, if this incubus... succubus, or whatever it is... leaves Sara, there will be nothing of Sara left. It has bonded with her. She showed us just yesterday evening. She left Sara, and all we were left with was a comatose girl!'

It'd been horrific, he reflected. They'd been sitting in the conservatory, and Jennifer had begged to see what would happen if Maude, or whatever the being was, left Sara's body. She had obligingly demonstrated. The evening sun was streaming through the windows. Had it not been so, they would have missed seeing what appeared to be a thin stream of vapour emerging mistily from Sara's nose and mouth., akin to vapour produced when it was frosty. Except, of course, it wasn't frosty. The vapour had dispersed, and they thought it had disappeared. Meanwhile, Sara had flopped sideways in her armchair, looking like someone in a vegetative state. They had shaken her, and there was no response, apart from her eyelids fluttering. Then suddenly Jennifer had gasped and quickly pointed towards a column of vapour organising itself into the hazy outline of a woman. It was obviously the woman Jennifer had described when talking about the strange "being" she thought she had seen in the bedroom. The facial features were barely distinguishable, but the shape was unmistakably female, and Chas had thought he could detect she had two long, waist-length plaits.

'Okay,' he'd informed the column of vapour. 'I think you'd better go back to where you came from.' It had then proceeded to quickly dissipate into Sara's nose and mouth. Within seconds his daughter was awake and returned to normality. If you could call it normality.

'How do you feel about it?' queried Alan Reynolds. He and Jilly had no children; they'd been offered IVF, but since neither of them was particularly enthusiastic about parenthood, by mutual agreement they remained childless. As Jilly was apt to state, 'If it happens it happens. If it doesn't it doesn't.' They were satisfied with that. But it did sometimes make it difficult to fully identify with, and appreciate, the anxiety parents felt when their children were threatened.

'I suppose I'm getting used to the situation. The positive thing is, whatever happens to Jen and I, Sara will always be able to fend for herself. She will, theoretically, never die, and will always go on – in another body. We cannot lose her. She's clever; she shall, I do not doubt, end up with a very good career – whatever that chosen career shall be. She *wants* to work. She's not idle. As for intelligence… she has it in abundance. And her knowledge base…' He gave a low whistle. 'She finds inhabiting a child's body difficult but says she can cope with it as she'll not be a child for very long! That is true enough. So, you see, there are positives in this!'

'It sounds as if you're accepting it,' Reynolds nodded slowly, ruminating upon Chas's words.

'I want Sara back. Make no mistake about that,' Chas proclaimed grimly. 'But I have to accept that that cannot be. As for Jen, I believe she's likewise inclined, but as yet, she cannot, or will not, admit it.'

'Hmmmm,' mused Reynolds. 'Tricky.'

'To put it mildly,' agreed Chas. 'As for your friend-cum-colleague, maybe we should meet with him. Frankly, I don't suppose Sara, or the being inside Sara, will mind either. Although she's adamant about remaining in situ, and we well know what will happen if she moves out. But he might be able to think of something perhaps.' Chas felt he couldn't foresee any solution, but this "expert" might be of help. 'How soon can we see him?'

'He only lives in Hexham. I'll text him and see when he's free,' beamed Reynolds, glad to be of help.

Extracting his mobile phone from one of the large pockets in his baggy cargo shorts, he proceeded to rapidly fire off a text. Watching, Chas found himself thinking that no matter what type of attire Alan Reynolds chose, it would always appear baggy. He really was skinny!

'Tomorrow evening? Are you feeling up to it?' inquired Reynolds solicitously.

'I'm in,' Chas responded sturdily.

'Food bank, Vicar!' Elsie strode, flat-footed, into the conservatory, a huge, bulging carrier bag in each hand. 'Missis Roseberry asked me to sort out things near to expiring and to give 'em to you!'

'How kind.' Reynolds, standing up in readiness to leave, wondered how he could manage two carrier bags whilst riding his bicycle.

'Strange that in this day and age we still need things like food banks and soup kitchens,' Chas commented.

'They're needed so very much. You can help with the food bank whilst you're on sick leave,' the Vicar suggested, a mischievous twinkle in evidence.

'No thanks,' was the hasty response. 'I don't intend to be away from the place for very long. But since I suspect you've cycled here, I'll ask the girls to load those into a wheelbarrow or something and take them to the vicarage.'

Sara and Tracy materialised, both wiping their hands on what appeared to be pieces of ancient towelling.

'We saw you getting ready to leave and came to say goodbye,' explained Sara. 'I have a lot of dill... it's getting out of control. Would you like some?'

Reynolds found it unsettling, looking into that youthful face... a face too wise for an almost thirteen-year-old.

'No, thank you,' he managed to reply affably. 'I wouldn't know what to do with it... not sure if my wife would either!'

In that moment, looking into that youthful face, he suddenly realised why Chas and Jennifer, whilst wanting their daughter returned to them, were coming to terms with this unusual situation. There was nothing but goodness in the face which was calmly, peacefully, scrutinising him.

'I could show her,' smiled Sara. 'Be glad to! It's lovely with fish. If you want to cycle ahead, Tracy and I will follow with the other stuff.'

Somehow, when she smiled broadly, showing a fleeting glimpse of her brace, she was a child again. *Well*, he inwardly amended, *an adolescent*.

'Perhaps we can arrange that dill tutorial sometime,' he agreed gently.

'Tracy can teach her to make woad,' Elsie declared heartily, still clutching the carrier bags. 'She was telling me about it just last night.'

Bemused, Reynolds wondered what on earth would his

wife do with woad? But then Jilly was very "into" arts and crafts. It might be just up her street.

'Tell me what happened next between you and David Royale?' begged Jennifer after dinner was consumed, the table cleared and the dishwasher loaded.

Chas was sprawled in a reclining chair, a mug of coffee cradled between his hands. Outside it was grey and overcast, likely to rain at any moment. The sitting room, where they were relaxing, was cheerful however; Jennifer's collection of table lamps were all lighted, giving a cosy glow.

'Oh, and I would like to know what happened to Victoria? Did she ever get married?'

'Ooooh, Victoria,' sighed Sara, running her fingers thoughtfully through her hair.

She was sprawled on the hearthrug, somehow managing to appear graceful, instead of the gawkiness of old which Jennifer had once so disliked in her daughter, but now, somehow, she would love to see again.

'Victoria behaved like a true lady. We met at the launching. I later found out she'd come to suspect that David Royale was no ordinary man. In fact, she eventually admitted she was becoming uneasy because of it. And somehow or other she guessed that I was "odd" in much the same way. It took very little time for her to know that a bond existed between David and myself, which she could never have, and she released him from the engagement quietly. She never married unfortunately. It was different for women then. If an engagement was broken it was invariably construed that the woman was perhaps not virginal… or was flirtatious. Or quite simply not good enough.

She never married, but David and I ensured she was always financially compensated at least. She obviously inherited some money from her parents, for although they weren't seriously rich they were comfortably situated. We sent money – anonymously – to her. I'm sure she knew where it came from, but she had no address for us and so could never return it! She retired to Bournemouth and lived a respectable life, doing many good works, until she died when she was somewhere in her late thirties,' Sara mused aloud.

It had not been the best of beginnings for herself and David, but matters could have been more complicated still. Supposing he had been married... and with children too? What would they have done under those circumstances? Nancy sharply reminded herself she ought to be grateful the situation was no worse than it was. Even so, a scandal was created, and the only solution was to quietly move to London.

David very quickly transferred to St Thomas's. Sir Frederick, furious that his daughter had become embroiled in a situation which was anything but respectable, made it clear that nothing else would suffice other than she should marry David Royale, quickly and quietly. Even though it was a respectable marriage – Royale came from an acceptable background – it was made clear to Nancy that her reputation was ruined and she had brought shame on the family name. At least Lady Denley was delighted; she thought it so very romantic and totally failed to see any disgrace in the situation.

Yet the following years were fulfilling. Encouraged by David, she studied to become a doctor, causing more scandal as she did so. A married woman... studying? It was unheard of. She had to apply as "Miss Denley" in order to be accepted. But at least she could console herself that any further scandal remained within the confines of London. It did not affect Sir Frederick and his family.

Five years passed, then an unexpected but peremptory summons arrived from Sir Frederick, instructing Nancy to return home immediately. Lady Denley was very ill, stated the letter. Reading between the lines, Nancy substituted *ill* for *dying*. Poor Lady Denley; following the birth of her twins, she had endured several pregnancies, none of which had reached full-term. Suspecting the second Lady Denley was following the path of the first, Nancy prepared to depart from London.

'I would accompany you, but...' began David.

'You cannot; you have work to do,' Nancy interposed. 'No, you must remain here. I shall return as soon as possible.' She briefly glanced around the small but comfortable home they shared together.

It was a pleasant place, the first dwelling she had regarded as home since that first marital residence she had shared with Gilbert, all those centuries ago. It was not grand, they employed only a small staff of servants, and she had soon realised there was a certain snobbery amongst serving folk. It had not been as easy as expected to find a cook, or a maid, who would remain with them for any length of time. This, she learned, was because of her own reputation of being an *unwomanly woman*. She had earned notoriety, and servants did not care to admit to be working for such a person. Consequently, the servants they employed were not of the finest calibre; they needed training, and also supervision. Household items often mysteriously went missing... and so did the servants.

David observed her glance of regret. 'You dislike leaving this place?' he stated needlessly.

'Yes,' she gave a brief nod.

'But we shall be leaving it permanently in the near future,' he squeezed her hand.

'Yes,' again she nodded.

She and David had made plans for the future. Together they would have an adventure. Travelling by ship was a perilous thing for an incubus, although David had chanced it numerous times during the days when he had fought in Europe. Nancy had never ventured from English soil. The very thought of it terrified her. If the ship sank what would become of them? But they each felt a need to "spread their wings", as David described it. They would visit another land, and whilst there would serve the British troops who were embroiled in the skirmishes in South Africa. They were still young, and so far Nancy had given birth to no children. So, being childless, they were free to be of use to their country.

And so she returned to the home where she had lived as Nancy Denley. It was a sad return, for Lady Denley was clearly dying. Taking one quick glance at the sunken cheeks and wasted frame, Nancy realised her frivolous, helpless, gentle little stepmother was suffering with something more than being worn out through childbearing. The sick room was filled with the stench of decay. She had cancer.

'The boys are now at boarding school,' Lady Charlotte Denley informed her.

'Already? They are so young!' Nancy heard a note of disapproval in her voice.

'Sir Frederick thought it best; they are both very boisterous, and he decided it would make them grow up,' Lady Denley explained sadly.

'But they are not yet seven years old,' protested Nancy, rolling her sleeves up and gently pressing upon her stepmother's abdomen which bulged suspiciously.

'I look as if I am pregnant, but the doctors say I am not,' whispered the sick woman.

'No, you are not,' agreed Nancy, wondering what to say. How could she tell this sweet woman, who had never knowingly hurt anyone, that she would never see her sons grow to manhood and would, in all probability, be dead within a few weeks?

'My hands are a strange yellow colour. I knew a girl, years ago, who had a fever, and she went all yellow… like me. She was ill for some months; I hope I do not have that fever!'

'I fear you might,' Nancy lied. Better her stepmother thought she had a fever, which was curable, than something more sinister.

'I miss you, Nancy.' Charlotte Denley held out her hand and grasped that of her stepdaughter. 'I missed you sorely when you left, yet at the same time I was glad you did. I wanted to you to be free and not tied to looking after this house – looking after me. I was delighted you married David because I knew you loved him, and I knew he would ensure you would have the future you desired. And it has happened, has it not?'

'It has,' Nancy confirmed.

'You are a doctor. I was so proud of you when I heard.'

'Most people think I am a nurse,' shrugged Nancy. 'They think it is more suitable for a woman. But I wanted to know more. To do more. To go further. However, I don't think I shall ever be able to have a general practice, as men do.'

'I should think women would prefer to see a lady doctor, once they get used to the idea,' mused Lady Denley. 'I think I would. It would be less embarrassing!'

'I think you need to sleep now,' Nancy suggested, noting the drooping eyelids. 'I shall bring you a cup of tea in an hour or so, and we shall talk again.'

'Sir Frederick has sent for the boys; I think he believes they shall cheer me somewhat… but I hope I won't infect them.' Lady Denley looked alarmed.

'Do not worry, they are young and strong. They shall not catch anything from you. Be assured of that,' Nancy informed her truthfully.

'Darling Nancy. It is good to have you here, and I also shall have the pleasure of seeing the boys again very soon,' sighed the sick woman. 'I look forward to some tea and a cosy chatter.' Her eyes closed slowly.

Nancy, entering the room an hour later, found her stepmother peaceful but dead. The promised tea and chatter was to be unfulfilled.

Within six months, she and David were bound for Cape Town, South Africa. A terrifying, yet exciting journey for them. Had they produced children, such a venture would have been complicated, and she was relieved not to have to prepare herself to accept outliving her offspring yet again. Nevertheless, her feminine instincts prevailed, making her long to carry David's child. The fact was, her "infertility" was due to something Nancy had never considered before and only dimly knew about, in spite of her long existence. It was due to contraception. Something respectable women did not consider. On their wedding night, when David had proposed it, she had been shocked. Yet it was so simple.

'So, what do I do to stop myself becoming pregnant?' she had questioned, shocked beyond belief. Prostitutes used sponges soaked with vinegar, she knew that. But it was, allegedly, not very effective.

'It is not something *you* use. It is something *I* use,' David assured her, amused by witnessing this unexpected naivety.

'I don't know what to say,' she gasped.

'What is there to say? You are my wife. We are lawfully married. So, let us do what is customary for married people to do.'

Except without the pregnancies. Yet it seemed wrong somehow. Pregnancy was the natural course for women –

wasn't it? Yet without it she came to know freedom. Being free of pregnancy enabled her to travel to South Africa with her husband, unencumbered, to care for those injured through the conflict between Britain and the Dutch farmers, the Boers.

During the long voyage to Cape Town, Nancy discovered – to David's concern – that she was, in spite of the contraception, actually pregnant. Obviously, it was not infallible. But to her bitter disappointment, she miscarried. After discovering she *was* pregnant, she realised how deeply she actually wanted to carry David's child, and was disappointed by his frank relief when she miscarried.

'I don't know how I managed to be so careless; obviously at some intimate moment I omitted to use any protection. But I was fearful for your safety when you discovered you were pregnant,' he informed the weeping Nancy. 'I know you are saddened but, truly, a pregnancy in a strange country is far from ideal. Nor shall the hygiene we encounter be anything akin to the standards we are both used to,' he earnestly assured her. 'It will be no better than it is here on the ship! In other words, a baby would be very much at risk. Whilst we are aboard ship at least, you have time to recover your strength.'

Nancy agreed, albeit reluctantly. He spoke truly. A pregnancy *would* be dangerous. David, though, had discovered that his wife might be a succubus but she was also physically and mentally desirous of giving birth.

Arriving at Cape Town, initially they felt insulated from events. Mostly this was due to the fact that they were both employed in a hospital which prepared wounded soldiers for their long journey home. The injuries were, for the most part, horrific: missing limbs, parts of limbs, people who were blinded or had massive abdominal wounds due to shrapnel.

'Very few sights we have never seen before,' David noted grimly. 'Although, due to improvements in weaponry – if you can call it that – and the soldiers using small calibre handguns, we are seeing differences in wounds and damage.'

Nancy could only agree but was indignant to be employed as a nurse, not a doctor, as soldiers did not expect to have dealings with female doctors. Females were nurses. Nancy *had* to be a nurse – although, due to a shortfall of surgeons, on more than one occasion she was required to perform surgery. The patients were in no position to object, and she had the satisfaction of discovering she was as good as any male surgeon. As David had said, weaponry was changing. The Boers used Mauser guns and, thanks to the smallness of the bullets and the style of casing, Nancy and David saw that wounds were healing better than they would have thought, even though the human carnage was as shocking as ever.

The Transvaal seemed so very far away. Over the passing months they heard reports of clashes between the President of the Republic, Paul Kruger, and Cecil Rhodes, a leading figure in the De Beers Corporation and a member of the Cape Assembly, who desired British control throughout South Africa. Nancy remained neutral, sympathising with the Afrikaners yet experiencing national pride in the Cape colony. As the 1890s inexorably progressed, Nancy and David became increasingly aware that they would not be unaffected by hostility; a declaration of outright war between the British and the Boers was inevitable. It took longer than either of them expected but came in October 1899, when war was declared between the British, the Boers and the Orange Free State.

Agreeing with David that it was their duty to move to where they could be of most use, near to the front lines of battle, after arduous travelling they found themselves in a hospital camp at Bloemfontein. Previously they had been working in a permanent building, one of a number conveniently placed near to a railway, but this camp was something different, consisting mostly of bell tents and larger marquees. Whilst unpacking, they were informed of the latest prediction regarding the presumed date for the end of the war – October 1900.

David was dubious. 'The Boers are determined fighters,' he remarked. 'And the fact they use guerrilla tactics is not good for the morale of our troops.'

'But our men are well trained,' Nancy declared loyally.

'I agree… but the Boers are not to be underestimated,' he assured her.

The camps created for them were lacking in sanitation and the food was of poor quality – for everyone. As for the stench of decomposition and effluence, it was overpowering. In consequence, many patients died and many staff were ill. Nancy was amongst those who sickened with typhoid. During her illness she again miscarried – until that moment neither of them had realised she was pregnant. But her illness, and the possibility she might not survive it, was a situation she and David had prepared for: the inevitability of death. Both of them had identified bodies they might choose to use when either of them perished, but on this occasion Nancy survived, thanks for this being entirely to David's knowledge and care. But the dire lack of sanitation, and decent food, remained, and even Nancy agreed it was no place to rear a child. A baby would require her return to England.

The experience of being in a different country, witnessing a totally different culture and enduring a new climate and landscape was worth the danger of an ocean voyage, along with the rigours of travelling. It was invigorating.

However, during the months following Nancy's illness, it became evident she was no longer as strong as she used to be. The only solution *was* to return to England.

'We must leave,' David insisted. He was newly returned from spending nearly twenty hours in surgery, and Nancy had assisted him with much of this. His apron bore gruesome evidence of his work. He had returned to their tent to find her lying, pale and exhausted, upon her narrow camp bed.

'If I die, we know what to do next. We have arranged it,' murmured Nancy. 'We must do our duty,' she stated firmly.

'We have done our duty. I am not as energetic as I used to be. Actually, I think I shall change my mind about whom to use next. I am thinking of Roger Vernon Kepier.' His eyes twinkled mischievously.

'Roger Vernon Kepier!' Nancy echoed, well knowing her horror pleased him. 'He is a fool! He only received a commission because he is the illegitimate son of a noble and wealthy duke! And he gambles and drinks too much!'

'He is very young; he might improve before I perish. If he doesn't... well... he will when I move in,' grinned David.

'Okay, you win. Let us go home now, before you inhabit Roger Vernon Kepier,' she acquiesced, adding, 'but he is very good-looking. And rich. That I admit!' It was such a pity the man was an arrogant fool.

In consequence, they departed from South Africa and returned to England, arriving there in March 1901, a year before the war ended. Much to David's amusement and Nancy's chagrin, amongst the other passengers onboard their ship was Roger Vernon Kepier, recovering from a compound fracture of his leg. He therefore required the care of David during the long voyage home. Injury did little to stem his folly. Long before the voyage ended he was heavily in debt through gambling, and tried – unsuccessfully – to borrow money from David and Nancy, amongst numerous others.

Once back in London, picking up the threads of their old lives was not as easy as they had contemplated. The city had altered during their absence. Unlike South Africa, progress was moving apace in England.

The most obvious thing Nancy noted, whilst peering from her carriage window, was the fashions. It hardly mattered what she wore in Cape Town, or anywhere else in South Africa. London was far more sophisticated.

'I am going to need a whole new wardrobe,' she announced with a large degree of pleasure.

She was going to need more than clothing. Water closets and telephones had grown in popularity. In fact, their latest house, situated near to St Thomas's Hospital where David was now working, had two indoor closets and a bathroom. David's first action was to arrange for a telephone to be installed. 'More useful than fashionable clothes,' he informed his wife.

On the streets, the bicycle was very much in evidence. Before departing abroad, the bicycle had been in existence, but upon returning they realised just how clearly popular they had become. The earlier style had been likely to mercilessly jolt the rider, but the newer versions were much improved and comfortable. Within a week of her return to England, Nancy was self-consciously riding her own bicycle. It was fun. It was exhilarating. No mode of transport had ever been as exciting. Not even a horse! Within days, David, who had laughed at her determination to try one, succumbed also. He required more than a bicycle, though. Before many months passed he owned an automobile. It was a foolish indulgence, in Nancy's opinion, but he was so enthusiastic about these new-fangled contraptions.

'They won't catch on,' predicted Nancy. 'Nothing is as reliable as a horse… or perhaps a bicycle. We have been using horses for years! Why buy such a noisy machine?'

'Come out with me and you shall find out,' David predicted.

She did. The car broke down. But this did not dim David's enthusiasm.

The telephone was becoming common too. As with the car, Nancy was uncertain of the use of a telephone.

Why have a telephone?' she questioned. 'No one we know has one... There is no one for you to chat with.'

'Aha, but soon there shall be!' beamed David. 'Within a few years everyone will have one. Also, the hospital has a telephone, so it means I can be contacted easily.' He gave an emphatic nod. 'Wait and see,' he warned.

Electricity, they both realised, was a favourite topic of conversation. There were those who felt it was the energy of the future, whilst others felt gas could not be surpassed. There was a certain refinement in Britain which was currently lacking in South Africa. Also, they possessed a sense of belonging to an old and established country, which they had never realised prior to their time abroad. Certainly, South Africa was a beautiful country, they had never pretended otherwise. Neither of them would ever regret the years spent there, not even the time spent amongst the carnage and debris of war. But they enjoyed the sense of homecoming, of returning to their roots. In addition, they returned to their home country at the beginning of a new era.

Queen Victoria had recently died. A new king now sat on the throne, Edward the Seventh. His wife, Queen Alexandra, was regarded by many as a long-suffering martyr, enduring her husband's love affairs and roguish behaviour. In spite of this, the new king was popular. Of particular interest to the Royales was the fact the King had undergone the removal of his appendix shortly before his coronation.

'Surgery,' David informed Nancy, 'has moved forward in this country since our departure. The King, a man who is neither young nor fit, endured invasive surgery, with a general anaesthetic, and made a good recovery! I tell you, we have returned at an era of advancement. Surgical instruments are sterilised as a matter of course; post-surgical deaths are diminishing. And we are amongst it all, working within the changes.'

'*You* are,' Nancy smiled.

She now no longer worked; her stamina was not equal to it, much to her regret. She consoled herself that it did not prevent her from listening and learning.

In fact, they both wished for a quiet life now. Within five years of their return, they settled at Bowness in Cumbria, in a large, slate-fronted establishment called Time House, the name being taken from a sundial on the front lawn. There was a purpose in this. They had been together as David and Nancy Royale for a long time. They had worked hard and led useful lives, but that time would end. Perhaps soon. David was prone to dizziness and palpitations. Serious symptoms. Nancy realised it was possible David might well succumb before herself. With her post-typhoid weakness, she had always assumed she would be first to die. Change, she reflected sadly, was approaching. They had been happy and content together. They would be happy again. It just would not be the same.

———

'And so we made our preparations,' Sara explained quietly. 'We were so used to each other, it was painful to confront the fact the end was near.'

'Did David die first?' Jennifer wanted to know.

'Yes,' she nodded. 'But yet again that will keep for another time. It's getting a bit like a saga! Oh dear, I've bored Chas. He's fallen asleep.'

'Well, he has an excuse.' Jennifer failed to notice the use of "Chas" instead of "Dad". 'Come along, invalid. Bedtime.' She shook his arm. 'I'll hear the next instalment another time.'

CHAPTER TEN

CHAS WAS NOT ENJOYING THE COACH TOUR. THE COACH was luxurious; the hotels had been excellent so far. He had to admit that really there was no reason why he should not be enjoying himself. Apart from the fact, of course, that he was not in charge of the vehicle. He preferred the freedom of driving a car and deciding where to go. Jennifer was clearly enjoying herself, as was Sara. But he wanted to be driving his new Alfa Romeo, and thanks to having had recent surgery, a long car journey – with him behind the wheel – was not an option. He *could* now drive but short distances only. As for Jennifer, she preferred to leave the driving to him – or someone else. So, they were trying a coach tour for the first time. *And the last,* thought Chas.

'You do get a superb view from this height,' observed Jennifer, peering eagerly out of the window. 'Better than in a car.'

Chas gave a grunt.

'You have to admit that, Chas… Look, there's the River Severn. I can see it glinting in the sunshine.'

Chas gave a stage yawn.

Sara was looking around eagerly, trying to recognise familiar scenery but finding nothing. Well, it was bound to have changed; she hadn't visited for over a century. Upton Manor, her first marital home, which she had not visited for nearly two centuries, was next on their tour itinerary. Part of her strongly desired to revisit, but perversely part of her was reluctant. She had looked at it on the internet, and the old chapel, her chapel, was still there. But like most of the building, she presumed it had no doubt been "improved".

'Here we are,' Jennifer cheerfully disembarked. As always, she was a vision of feminine prettiness. Gleaming curls tied up in a ponytail, secured with a white scarf, combined with lemon shirt tied in a knot at the waist, white cropped trousers, and bejewelled sandals which glinted in the warm morning sunlight.

Walking beside her, Sara remarked, 'I don't think there is a male on this coach who would say "no" if you offered to do their root canals.'

Chas, deciding to make the best of the day, gave a quick honk of laughter. 'I would.' He gave his wife a playful nudge with his elbow.

'This is Upton Park,' the guide announced needlessly, handing out information leaflets. 'It's still privately owned; the current family have lived her for over three hundred years,' she chirped brightly.

'Not the same people, I hope,' mumbled Chas as Jennifer gave an amused giggle.

'Until the Civil War it was owned by the de Laiche family. They lost it when Charles the Second came to the throne because they supported the Roundheads, the wrong side as far as he was concerned.'

'Typical of the de Laiche family,' snorted Sara. 'Always supporting the wrong side!'

'It is one of the most unchanged parks in the country, and the house has been the same for seven centuries!' The guide's voice rang with pride, as if she was personally responsible for this fact.

'I don't agree with that,' muttered Sara.

The guide overheard. 'Have you been studying it at school?' she questioned.

'Sort of. But it was seriously altered during the time of George the First.' Sara nodded towards the house which was now visible through the trees. 'Admittedly, the south face still retains a bit of black and white Elizabethan timbering.'

'Ah yes, but the old Norman brickwork is still there at the back; you just can't see it from here.' Deflated, the guide eyed Sara with distaste.

'It's a bit like the house that Jack built,' Jennifer remarked. 'It's an eclectic mix of several eras.'

'Well, it's old,' the guided stated unnecessarily. Then, suddenly looking pleased, she added, 'It's also said to be haunted! Yes, really! Someone was murdered in one of the bedrooms... I think she was called Ethel or something,' she said, flustered as she tried to recall the name. 'Or maybe...?'

'Alice?' supplied Sara. 'That's what is says on the website.'

'That's my girl,' grinned Chas, thoroughly fed up with the guide. She was – silently he sought for an adequate description. Over the top. Irritating. A pain in the butt. It was like having a holiday with a hyperactive parakeet. She chattered all of the time. Come to think of it, she looked like one, being small and slender, with huge lime green spectacles and a beaky nose.

'Oh yes, Alice, thank you,' the guide shot a glance towards Sara which was anything but thankful. 'Yes, Alice was murdered in the house and buried somewhere nearby, but no one knows where. You have two hours here, and there's a lovely coffee shop in what used to be the stables. I recommend it. And don't forget to light candles in the chapel; St Gilbert and St Maude are famous for their miracles!'

For Sara it was a strange experience. Obviously she had never lived in the Tudor part of the building, or the Georgian.

But the old Manor was still there and, in part, recognisable. It took her a while to orientate herself to it – after all, it was now two centuries since she had visited the place. But her old home was still there, buried among the new buildings. The room where Maude de Laiche had died and where Alice had been murdered was still familiar. It was furnished in the style of the fifteenth century, the bed being far more luxurious than anything Maude Dubreise – later Maude de Laiche – had ever known. Yet it was still her room, and before that it had been the chamber used by Gilbert's forefathers. It was the place where she had shared nights with Gilbert, never refusing to give her body to him, then stoically giving birth to his offspring. They *had* been happy together. Their union had been arranged, but it had been happier that many romantic marriages. Gilbert had been kind, gentle, and eager to please his wife. If it was possible to be forced to relive those days, she would do so gladly.

Solemnly she gazed out of the window, looking at the totally unfamiliar landscape. In spite of the guide's dialogue, that had certainly been altered. What had once been mostly farmland and kitchen gardens, was now a combination lush flowerbeds and rolling parkland. Disappointingly, her little solar had been swallowed up somehow; she couldn't trace it anywhere. The kitchen was now situated in the Tudor building, but the old kitchen was recognisable to her, although it had long since been used as a pantry and cold store. The buttery was still a buttery. She might have been the lady of the manor, but she had often been obliged to take her turn at the butter churn. Through assisting with the Lancastrians during the Wars of the Roses, she and Gilbert had so very often struggled financially and had not been able to afford to be people of leisure. In truth, few people at that time had been able to achieve that desirable state.

En route to the chapel they passed through a picture gallery. Most of the portraits were relatively recent, dating from Victorian times. But near to the chapel was a portrait of Gilbert and Maude de Laiche.

Reading aloud from his leaflet, Chas intoned, 'This portrait is a faithful copy; the original dates from the fifteenth century and now hangs in the National Portrait Gallery, London. The images are said to be very alike. Pity,' he shook his head. 'Neither of them looks particularly glamorous!'

Smiling to herself, Sara shook her head. Maude looked buxom, which was true enough, she supposed. But the fact was, this portrait actually *did* flatter both of them! 'Maude had nice hair as a girl and lovely teeth – until her teeth blackened and fell out a result of childbearing!' she explained to him. 'Plus, no one every painted our portraits whilst we were alive, so they can hardly be accurate,' she added.

Years of pregnancy and breastfeeding had been unkind to her. As for Gilbert, it pained her to realise that she could only dimly recall what he'd looked like. He had not been a handsome man, but on the positive side he had not been hideously ugly either. She searched the picture closely but could see nothing recognisable in those stern features. What she could recall, however, was that Gilbert always looked as if he was about to smile or laugh. He had such good humour, a trait which was not evident in that grim portrait.

Her chapel, which Gilbert so proudly had constructed for her, had been engulfed somehow in the Tudor building but, inside, the stonework had been retained. Probably because it was believed to house two saints. It was no longer quite the simple construction she had used for worship, though. The walls were no longer roughly hewn – someone had obviously seen fit to smooth them over at some point.

Maude de Laiche had been Roman Catholic; there was no other faith she could follow. Therefore a statue of the Virgin Mary, holding the infant Jesus, used to stand in a corner. Since the chapel had been Anglican for nearly five centuries, the image had long since vanished. Maude had embroidered some Biblical images and hung them on the walls, but they too had disappeared. Probably devoured by Tudor moths, she assumed. The pews were twentieth century, not that there was room for many pews. It was a small, intimate space. The arched windows, which once were filled with plain glass – Gilbert could not afford stained glass – now did possess stained glass, sending shafts of multicoloured light into the place.

On the stone-flagged floor, in front of the communion table – which hailed from the same era as the pews – was a well-worn stone, the carving on it barely legible. Maude and Gilbert's burial spot still had its original burial slab. Not far from this was the burial place of Alice. The grave which the guide had declared to be unknown. It was unmarked, and over the years had been forgotten. Beside this was a black iron stand, where votive candles burned. *It's different, but it still feels like my little chapel where I used to pray.*

'Do you want to light one?' whispered Jennifer, nodding towards the candles. She was holding a lighted taper and was about to light a candle herself.

Sara mutely shook her head and then sat in one of the modern pews. Somehow this place moved her deeply, more so than any other part of the house. The Tudor and Georgian buildings were alien to her. None of the original staircase remained; she couldn't even picture where it had been, yet in spite of feeling disorientated sometimes, she felt as if she was encountering some sort of homecoming. She had enjoyed walking around it. But here, in this chapel, she could feel old memories stirring. It had been a gift to her from a kind husband. Gilbert had known nothing would please her more than her own place of worship, plus her own personal priest. And how delighted he had been to present her with it!

'It is Gilbert who is the saint,' she whispered to Chas, who was sitting next to her. 'I *shall* light a candle after all.'

Sara looked emotional, Chas observed, but didn't know what to say to her. He felt out of his depth.

He had been interested, if not eager, to visit Upton Manor. In reality, he was unsure of his actual motive for this. Sara had told them of her early years there; that she had worked hard, been content, although sometimes fearful, owing to the fights and skirmishes which made up the Wars of the Roses. Her marriage had been happy, and as for rearing a large family, well, it was just one of those things women did. Children were a blessing, a source of security. Sitting once again on the bus bound for their next destination, it occurred to him that perhaps he'd half expected the succubus might decide to remain at Upton, whilst Sara – *his* Sara – would be restored to him, a gangly adolescent, uncertain and ungainly.

Perversely, the Sara who was now seated in the coach next to a window was graceful; there was something so ladylike about her demeanour. The body of his daughter was there, she still had braces on her teeth and a light splattering of freckles over her nose, but his daughter had never looked so elegant, which currently she managed to achieve even when wearing shorts and a tee shirt.

'Don't you wish you could live here again?' he enquired quietly, managing to adopt a casual tone.

'No, it wouldn't be the same. Everyone I knew here is long gone,' she replied logically.

'Of course,' he nodded. Well, they would be. They'd died something like six hundred years ago. He couldn't think of anything else to say. Jennifer, meanwhile, the other elegant lady in his life, was combing her curls and then retying the scarf which was holding them in check. Giving him a sideways glance, she smiled knowingly. Trust Jennifer to know what had been going through his mind.

In their hearts, they knew that the Sara they had known her, would never return. Accepting it was the issue. Sometimes, for an hour, if not a day or so, he could assure himself that there was nothing wrong with the situation. As he'd recently told Alan Reynolds, he had the security of knowing that Sara would be able to look after herself. She wouldn't die no matter what ailments life threw at her. At times he believed that, and felt all was well. At other times, he desperately wanted his girl back again – young and innocent, his sweet, uncertain, bashful daughter. Jen, he knew, felt likewise. But ever since Alan Reynolds had arrived at their house, bringing with him his friend and colleague, a man who was experienced in exorcism and the paranormal, their gut feeling that the succubus who resided in their daughter was here to stay was reinforced.

Appropriately enough, Alan and Jilly had brought their friend, Terry Richards, to see them on a wild night. The wind had raged, tipping over pots in the garden, breaking the stem of a towering sunflower which Chas had been particularly pleased with. Thunder rumbled in the distance and, as Jennifer opened the door to admit the visitors, lightning cracked overhead, and the rain, which was already falling copiously, suddenly became torrential. A fittingly atmospheric evening to chat with someone skilled in matters supernatural, Chas decided.

'Oh dear, come straight in; you're soaked already!' exclaimed Jennifer, opening the door to find three wet individuals on the doorstep.

'We've only walked from the car to the house,' Jilly breathlessly remarked, as Jennifer helped her to remove a bright yellow plastic poncho, the hood of which had a Donald Duck beak instead of a peak. 'It's from Disney World, Florida,' she explained, noticing Jennifer's amused glance. I've had it for years.'

'Very practical,' Jennifer approved, although inwardly admitting she would never wear such a garment. Well, not with that Donald Duck beak. 'Maybe we should invest in a canopy over the porch door, to save people getting wet.'

'Oh, we'll soon dry off,' beamed Alan, cheerfully divesting himself of a long plastic raincoat which contrasted oddly with his cropped cargo trousers. 'Allow me to introduce my old friend Terry Richards.'

As she and Chas shook hands with him, Jennifer realised she'd been expecting someone who looked as eccentric as Alan, who on this occasion was wearing a navy blue Led Zeppelin tee shirt, with one frayed sleeve and a hole in a shoulder seam. On the front was a picture of a Zeppelin, along with the logo "Led Zeppelin", spelled out in large letters. It occurred to her that the tee shirt had possibly been around as long as the band itself.

Terry Richards, however, was totally conventional. His mop of dark blond hair was neatly trimmed, as was his moustache. He wore casual trousers and a polo shirt, plus a conservative, but decidedly damp, grey sports jacket, which she hung over a radiator to dry off.

'My spectacles are steaming up,' he stated wryly, removing gold-rimmed glasses and polishing them with a handkerchief.

Somehow this broke the ice. 'Coffee, everyone?' asked Jennifer.

Coffee sorted, Terry became businesslike. 'Where *is* your daughter?' His eyes, brown and kindly, regarded Chas and Jennifer from a benign, calm face.

'She's upstairs,' replied Chas.

They hadn't mentioned the expected arrival of Terry Richards to her. Sara had requested Tracy might stay overnight, but he and Jennifer had refused, not giving any reason why. The fact was, they felt that two girls, each possessed by a succubus, would be something of an imposition; after all, he was only expecting one. Also, Elsie had no suspicion – or so it appeared – of anything being amiss with her daughter. Therefore, it would be wrong of them to make arrangements for her to be interviewed by an exorcist.

'I'll ask Sara to join us.'

Jennifer headed for the stairs, wondering what on earth she could say to her. Slowly she headed for Sara's room, from where she could hear the sounds of a Foo Fighters CD being played. She recognised it as being their *Sonic Highways* album; it was one of Chas's favourites.

'We've missed seeing them at Glastonbury this summer,' remarked Sara, as Jennifer entered her room. 'I think they would have been excellent to see live,' she gave a descriptive nod towards the CD player.

'I suppose so,' Jennifer agreed cautiously. 'Actually, I would have preferred it when Dolly Parton was there. I know,' she managed a smile, 'I'm a bit old-fashioned when it comes to music.'

'You are *a lot* old-fashioned when it comes to music,' smiled Sara, briefly showing her brace. 'But it doesn't matter, does it? Taste is subjective. That's how it should be. And now you want me to come downstairs with you to chat to the paranormal investigator–cum–exorcist whom Alan Reynolds has brought to the house?' She was making it easy for Jennifer.

'Why, yes – how did you know about that?'

Had Sara been peering into her mind again? she wondered anxiously, not feeling at all comfortable with that notion.

'I heard the vicar talking about it with Chas,' was the resigned response.

'Oh,' Jennifer breathed out with relief. 'I'm sorry, but, you know…' her voice trailed away.

'You want your daughter back.' There was genuine sympathy in Sara's tone. 'I'll talk to him, but you *are* wasting everyone's time. Including your own,' she added gently.

Jennifer nodded mutely. Yes, it probably was a waste of time. Her gut instinct agreed with that. But if there was a way of getting Sara back, unscathed, she was going to find it.

'You know, Maude, or whoever you are, I do like you, weird though it might seem. So does Chas. You're a good and seriously nice person. There's nothing evil or awful about you at all, and I know you have to go somewhere. But you chose my daughter, and I want the original daughter, not the one who's six hundred years old!'

'I demonstrated to you what will happen if I leave,' sighed Sara, her demeanour weary. 'But let us go and see this investigator, if that's what you wish,' she acquiesced.

Together they joined the others in the sitting room. Once introduced to Terry Richards, Sara calmly shook hands, poised, calm, totally in control.

'Sara knows why you're here,' explained Jennifer, admiring her daughter's composure and wishing at that moment that she too could be so quietly self-assured.

'I see.' Terry Richards drew out the words, seeming to endow them with a great deal of meaning. 'Perhaps we should all begin with a prayer,' he suggested, acutely observing Sara's reaction.

She remained calm. 'I would like that very much, Reverend Richards,' she assented demurely. 'Shall you pray alone, or may I join in?'

'Oh.' Momentarily he was taken aback. 'Of course you may join in. Everyone may join in. Also, I must stress, everything which occurs here, everything which is said, is totally confidential.'

Nearly an hour later Terry Richards found himself utterly bamboozled. Sara Roseberry was outwardly a twelve-year-old girl. In just a few weeks she would be thirteen, a teenager, but she was no ordinary adolescent. She had made no attempt to act as an adolescent ought, since he would clearly not be taken in by it.

'Who... what... are you? I know your story. You're not a soon-to-be-teenage girl.' Distractedly, he took off his spectacles and polished them unnecessarily. 'I know there's nothing *evil* possessing you, but clearly *something* is!'

'I am − was − Maude Dubriese, Maude de Laiche by marriage. I was born at the time of the Wars of the Roses. There are no records of my birth; they didn't bother about those things then. Well, not very much,' she amended. 'I believe there *was* a record made of the birth of my brothers, though.'

'There's a Saint Maude and a Saint Gilbert de Laiche,' frowned Richards.

'I am that Maude, and it never fails to amuse me. They canonised me! Gilbert, my husband, was a good man. More saintly than myself, I suspect. Did he deserve canonisation?' Sara laughed in genuine amusement. 'Seriously, I think not,' she replied to this question herself. 'After my death... well, after my original body died, people reported seeing lights over my grave, acts of healing carried out and so forth. Trust me, Reverend, I was no saint. But I was a nice woman, I admit that.' Pausing, she looked directly into Terry Richards' eyes. 'You know what I am, Reverend. I am a succubus. A female incubus, if you like. More people have heard of the incubus.'

'And you may leave that body anytime you wish?' he demanded.

'You wish me to demonstrate?'

Mutely he nodded, wondering what he would see.

'As you have said, this meeting is strictly confidential?' she stated gravely.

'Of course,' he nodded, suddenly feeling apprehensive.

This was new territory. This was unlike any case of possession he'd every contended with. Genuine possession was never as peaceful as this.

Sara lay back in her chair, closing her eyes, and in the cosy but dim lighting of Jennifer's sitting room, he saw nothing at all, just a young girl who appeared to have fallen asleep. It was Jennifer who all but jumped out of her chair and switched the overhead lights on. Having witnessed an issue of vapour drifting from Marilyn Hamilton's head during that fateful hospital visit and, later, having seen what had happened when she'd asked the succubus to leave Sara, she knew what to expect. The subdued lighting was inadequate for Terry Richards to see all he needed to see. She indicated towards what looked like a steamy column standing in front of the fire. It was taking on the shape of a woman.

'She's still breathing,' gasped Jilly Reynolds, shaking Sara and trying, but failing, to evoke a response.

'Sara?' Chas took Sara's wrist, checking her pulse. 'It's steady,' he averred.

'That is what happens when she leaves,' Jennifer explained.

'I command you to return Sara Roseberry to this body, and she alone,' instructed Terry Richards, his voice ringing with authority.

For a brief moment, such was the confidence of that voice, Chas was positive the succubus would obey. But the column of vapour, which had increased in density and was facing Richards, lifted its hands helplessly and gave a shrug and a shake of its head.

'What has happened to Sara?' It was Jilly Reynolds who spoke. 'Why is she unconscious? I'm going to call an ambulance!' Rummaging in her cluttered handbag she produced her mobile phone.

'No,' Jennifer's hand swiftly closed over hers.

'But she's out like a light,' protested Jilly.

'When the succubus returns to her, she'll regain consciousness. It is bound to her. I don't think they can be separated now. It's too late.' There was a suppressed sob in Jennifer's voice.

'This is what happens if that,' Jilly pointed to the vaporous figure, 'leaves her?'

The figure gave a brief nod and another helpless shrug. Jilly felt there was something apologetic about its stance. She could pretty much make out something of the features, irregular and plain, plus a sturdy figure, which she would describe as lumpish, for want of a better description. There was also the outline of two long plaits. Definitely a being from a bygone era, she decided. Jennifer, also staring at the apparition, found herself irrationally wishing it would at least give the impression of wearing some medieval dress or something.

'Perhaps you should return to Sara,' Jennifer eventually suggested, as they'd all been gaping at the apparition, perplexed, for quite some time. Terry Richards was silent. Probably lost for words, she assumed. Well, it was hardly surprising.

The figure gave another brief nod and began to disintegrate. A fine trickle of vapour began to enter Sara's mouth, and almost immediately the girl regained consciousness, and it was as if nothing had happened to her. The vaporous apparition had seemed to be of almost average height, noted Richards. It had also been the figure of a well-built woman, yet only a thin stream of vapour appeared to enter the girl's body. It was most peculiar, he decided inadequately as the apparition now totally dispersed.

'Are there others such as yourself?' he quested, more sharply than intended.

'Yes,' Sara replied quietly.

'So, who and where are the others?' Terry Richards requested more gently.

'For the most part, I don't know. We don't huddle together in a little community,' was the equally gentle, but final, reply.

'But don't you become weary? You go on and on; you must feel jaded sometimes. Don't you wish you could die?' persisted Richards.

'Do you?' was the simple but logical response.

The evening with the paranormal expert had been something of a let-down, Chas mused. A bit like the coach holiday. He had enjoyed it, after a fashion. As for Jennifer, she felt likewise. They'd tried it but preferred the independence of travelling with their car and going where they wished. There would be no more coach trips in the foreseeable future. However, he couldn't have managed the driving, and Jennifer would have hated having to do the bulk of it, but at least they'd stayed in nice hotels, and the people on the coach – apart from the irritating parakeet of a guide – had been pleasant enough. Sara had appeared to enjoy it too, so it hadn't been a total waste of time.

They arrived home to find three postcards awaiting them. All from Vi. Shortly after his surgery, she'd announced she was going to visit Kotu Beach in Gambia for a couple of weeks' relaxation. Alone. It was, he felt, a rebuke for not inviting her to join them on their coach trip. The prospect of taking a coach trip had been a step into new territory for him – including Vi would have been just a step too far.

'She must be due home in a few days,' he speculated, as Jennifer categorised the postcards in order of date.

'She's been away ten days so far,' she replied, holding the now organized cards, in readiness to read them aloud. 'Hello, everyone, just to let you know have arrived safely. Hope you all enjoyed your holiday. Hotel lovely, plenty of friendly people to talk to.'

'I'm surprised the cards have arrived in the UK before her,' Sara remarked. 'I'm impressed.'

'I am too,' nodded Jennifer. 'This second one says, "Having a lovely time. You would enjoy this place, have made a new friend, we get on well, so am not lonely, Love Mum".'

'Her new friend will soon scarper once she gets to know her,' Chas muttered audibly.

'This card says she won't send any more cards because she'll be home before they arrive. The friend is not a *she* but a *he*!' Jennifer sounded alarmed. 'He's called Randall Olongu; they get along so well they're staying in touch. In fact, he plans to come to the UK to see her in the near future. Chas! You don't think he's one of those predatory males we've read about, who target women of a certain age, marry them and use them to obtain British citizenship?!'

Chas was about to declare that anyone who planned to marry Vi deserved his British citizenship. Noting Jennifer's tense face, he thought better of it.

'Why not try texting her to find out?' he suggested. 'I know she's not known for using her mobile, but it's worth a try.'

Vi was notorious for not switching her phone on. As far as she was concerned, she hated the thing and it was for emergency use only. Unfortunately, it meant that although she could contact others in an emergency, in a similar situation others couldn't contact her.

Jennifer did so and, as expected, received no reply. They would, in all likelihood, have to wait until she returned to the UK to find out.

'Could it be she's just trying to be dramatic?' Sara suggested quietly. 'She loves to cause a sensation.'

'I hope that's all it is,' Jennifer agreed fervently.

Later that evening, with cases unpacked and the washing machine working energetically, the three of them sat in the conservatory, Jennifer and Chas both nursing a large glass of wine apiece, Sara clutching a glass of mineral water. Chas had just returned from visiting the neighbours, having called in to give them a couple of bottles of wine for watering the garden whilst they were away.

'Young Simon showed me his little cat, Sugar, and says to tell you she's had all of her vaccinations,' he informed Sara. 'He also says he hardly sees you now.'

'I know.' She felt guilty. 'I'll go and visit him tomorrow,' she promised.

'He also says you're too grown-up for him now,' grinned Chas.

'You know,' Jennifer leaned forward seriously, 'I was wondering… have you used the internet to try and find David, your husband?'

'Yes,' Sara replied slowly. 'At present I don't have a social media account. But for the past few years I've been using Facebook and Twitter. Marilyn Hamilton, being well-known, was a good springboard for making use of the internet, and she had a lot of followers. Sadly he wasn't one of them.'

'We can soon sort out Facebook for you,' Jennifer suggested. 'I have an account but hardly bother with it. Chas closed his due to his own lack of interest. Your school friends must surely be users. We always hesitated about permitting you to open an account due to internet grooming. We thought someone might seduce you or something,' she managed a half smile. 'I now think you're wise enough to avoid that!'

'Perhaps,' was the thoughtful, half joking response.

'How did you get separated?' Chas enquired. 'I'm sorry, but I fell asleep when you were telling us the story. It wasn't long after my surgery. That has to be my excuse!'

'It was all too easy,' was the simple response. 'David Royale died suddenly,' she explained. 'But afterwards, we still had a lot of years together using different bodies. We had a very deep relationship, partly because we both had centuries of experience, and that's uncommon, to use the fabled English understatement. But we were happy because we were so similar in ideals, temperament and outlook. He was – and, God willing, still is – such a *good* person.' She brushed some troublesome tears away from her eyes, then continued to explain.

They had been together as David and Nancy for a long time, and had lived in a Victorian villa, Time House , in Bowness, for four years. Barely had he established himself as a doctor in his new community than his palpitations and dizzy spells significantly increased. Their plans for substitute bodies – for both of them – were in place. David had employed an assistant, Joseph, a newly qualified doctor much in need of experience. Nancy had been observing Jemima, the vicar's daughter, at present a young woman of nineteen years, gifted with intelligence and grace. These were to be their replacement bodies. Then they discovered they had a new neighbour. Just a five-minute walk from Time House stood a mansion called Bowness House. A desirable property, it nestled grandly within its own park. The owners had been abroad for a number of years and it had been placed on the short-term rental market. David learned from one of his patients that it had been taken for the summer. With ill-concealed amusement, he delivered this information to Nancy.

'You are aching to tell me who it is,' she declared. 'Come on. Tell!'

'Can you not guess?' he drew out the anticipation.

'How am I supposed to guess? It could be anyone. Oooh…' exasperated she proclaimed, 'Queen Alexandra!'

'No,' he smirked teasingly.

'Oh… well… the Duke of Norfolk!'

'Less improbable than Queen Alexandra, I suppose. You're getting there! Now, woman, I shall tell you, it is Roger Vernon Kepier!

'*The* Roger Vernon Kepier? The pulchritudinous, but idiotic, illegitimate son of an aristocrat, whom we met in South Africa?' She shook her head. 'If it is he, I hope he doesn't come calling on us.

'The very one,' beamed David. 'I think he *shall* come visiting, however,' he predicted. 'After all, I looked after him during the long voyage home from South Africa.'

'Since he did not have the good manners say "thank you" when we parted company with him, I doubt if he will come visiting,' Nancy speculated optimistically.

'Oh, and, by the way, he is now *Sir* Roger Vernon Kepier. He received a knighthood a year ago,' David added gleefully, enjoying his wife's irritation.

'Well, he didn't receive it for having good manners! Honestly, he did not even have the decency to shake your hand!' Nancy stated explosively.

A week later, Sir Roger Vernon Kepier indeed paid a visit, limping into the Royales' home as if he owned it. Nancy, who had watched him dismount from his horse, was disinclined to be effusive with civility where he was concerned. Sourly she commented upon his impaired gait, suggesting a walking stick might be of use to him. Sir Roger had other matters occupying his mind.

'I've just seen the most gorgeous young filly in the village,' he announced cheerfully, as if it was merely days since he had last spoken with the Royales' instead of years.

'You are obviously referring to the vicar's daughter,' replied David.

'I thought he was referring to the vicar's horse. It too is a fine filly,' Nancy observed drily.

Sir Roger, far from being offended, roared with laughter.

'Local gossip has it you have been recently widowed,' David remarked quietly.

'Yes. Shame. Fine woman.'

Having dismissed his recently departed wife, Sir Roger accepted a chair and flopped into it. No longer the slender man who had fought in the Boer War, his chair gave an ominous creak.

'So, she is the vicar's daughter,' he nodded, digesting this information.

Observing him closely, Nancy considered him to be still a handsome man; his complexion was clear, as were his eyes, leading her to assume he was now not given to partaking of excessive amounts of alcohol. David, she realised, was observing him avidly. Asking questions, inquiring of his political opinions, how he spent his time, did he enjoy reading? Music?

The visit was relatively brief, or at least as brief as David's interrogation would permit. As the visitor departed, Nancy faced her husband, hands resting on her hips.

'You are considering him as your next body,' she stated flatly.

'Yes,' was the calm reply. 'There is nothing terrible about him. He is not exceedingly intelligent, but I can remedy that in a very short space of time! But don't you see, my dear, he is rich. Through him, I can ensure you are well looked after.'

CHAPTER ELEVEN

David's death occurred quickly. In spite of her vast multitude of encounters with death and dying, somehow Nancy anticipated it would occur in her presence. It was Joe, the assistant doctor, who rushed to the house to break the news, giving assurances that it had been quick, peaceful and painless. It had occurred, apparently, whilst Doctor Royale was visiting a patient and lancing an abscess. Nancy studied Joe closely, wondering if, after all, David had decided to use his body. But there was no indication of David's presence – at least not yet. From experience she knew it took a while, a few days at the very least, for an incubus to actually totally bond with and inhabit a new person. However, from the beginning, there were always small signs of change taking place.

David's body was transported by cart to the home where they had been happy together, and her grief took her totally by surprise. Knowing, as she did, that he would move on into someone else, had always led her to imagine she would have to actually *act* the part of the grieving widow. It transpired that no acting was required.

This was the body of someone whom she had loved, worked with and, during their younger, fitter years, enjoyed a passionate physical relationship with. Together they had travelled a vast distance to share in an adventure. Travelling by sea was safer now than it had ever been; but for them, should the boat have sunk, it could have been the means of ending their existence permanently. This, of course, was uncertain but decidedly possible. Yet because they were together, they had embarked upon a voyage, knowing that should a calamity occur they would perish together. Would everything be the same with David inhabiting another body, another mind? Not only would the David she knew so well be lodging there, but also the past experiences of the newer person. Although intrinsically, of course, the vast part of the new person would inevitably be the centuries' old spirit of the man whom she loved. Desperately, she clung to that comforting thought.

'Perhaps I should give you some laudanum,' suggested Joe solicitously.

'No.' Unable to find a convenient handkerchief, Nancy wiped away her tears with the frilled cuff of her blouse. 'But I thank you anyway. I know he has been ill for some time, but so am I. I now realise that, in spite of his cardiac issues, I have been clinging to the belief that he would outlive me after all. Foolish, I know.' Again she wiped her eyes with her cuff.

Joe steered the fragile, elderly lady to an armchair, wondering how would she cope alone? Of course, she might be stronger than she looked. In his opinion women usually were.

'Try some brandy wine instead,' he compromised, pouring out a generous measure of the liquid. 'If you don't mind, I shall have some also. I find myself somewhat stunned. He was such a supportive, wise person, with vast knowledge... I have never met anyone like him!'

'Neither have I,' Nancy replied truthfully, whilst inwardly she railed against David's decision *not* to use the body of this dependable young man who, conveniently, lived in a small cottage only a couple of hundred yards away.

 She spent the evening sitting in an armchair beside the fire, telling Milly, the maid, to take herself out into the village, since she was courting a steady young man whose occupation was repairing drystone walls. Marriage was looking very much a probability. Cheered by the look of gratitude in the girl's eyes, Nancy remained in her chair, constantly aware of the body of David lying on the dining room table nearby. What would happen now? This was new territory, something that had never happened to her before. She was used with loss, but this was totally different. This time there was would be a reunion, yet at the same time there was still that familiar sense of loss and change. After all, nothing would ever be the same again.

 She was still in the armchair when Milly found her early the following morning, when she walked into the kitchen to begin her work. Stiffly, Nancy rose from the chair, suggesting Milly should make some tea.

 'I'm going upstairs to wash and put on a clean blouse,' she murmured.

 She was barely halfway up the stairs when a tentative knock could be heard at the front door. Pausing, she heard voices, the voice of Milly, with her Cumbrian accent, and a male voice, well bred, clipped and assertive. She knew who it was. As swiftly as she could, she descended the stairs again, directing Milly to usher the new arrival into the parlour. Once she was face to face with Sir Roger Vernon Kepier, his assertiveness evaporated abruptly, as did her own voice. A question hovered on her lips but remained unspoken. Milly's rosy face peered through the half open door.

 'Excuse me, ma'am, sir, but do you *both* want tea?'

 'Yes please, Milly,' Nancy found her voice again.

Sir Roger was staring at her, transfixed yet clearly bewildered.

'I came because your husband... the doctor... Well, ma'am, he tragically died. I know it is early, but I have spent the night trying to keep away, such is the compulsion I have to visit you. My apologies, ma'am, for arriving at this unearthly hour!'

As she indicated towards a chair, he seated himself heavily, a man clearly undergoing mental turmoil.

'I see you have a well-used pianoforte, ma'am.' Having only been seated for a few seconds, he stood up and, as if sleepwalking, headed with his customary limp towards the instrument and began playing *The Barley Break*. 'I don't know where that came from,' he muttered, bemused and embarrassed. 'I didn't know I could play the pianoforte.'

'Well, you certainly can now,' Nancy rejoiced.

Only David knew the significance of that tune. The first music he had ever played in her hearing. It had worked. David was there, bonding with Sir Roger. That was all that mattered. They were still together. If all went according to plan, she would, in due course, take over Jemima, the vicar's daughter. Of course, she could always leave her aging body now and take it over forthwith. It was something to consider, but she preferred to remain in a body until the very end, if possible. There was also the fact to consider that Jemima seemed to be growing close to Joe. *He should have used Joe*, she sighed inwardly. *It would have been so simple!*

A few days after David Royale's funeral, the village nodded approval at Sir Roger's magnanimous gesture, when he took Mrs Royale into his home. He also gave a dowry to Milly, the maid, honouring a promise David Royale had made to her, which further enhanced his stature in the local community. Everyone was talking about how wonderful it was that a man who looked and acted in such a foppish fashion should be wise and caring beneath the pomade and fine clothing. Nor was he profligate with money – for such had been his reputation. He now invested wisely, and also married wisely – a local girl, which further delighted the villagers: Jemima, the vicar's daughter.

Jemima had looked set to wed Joe, Dr Royale's young assistant. However, it became public knowledge (knowledge mentioned in whispers combined with much nudging) that a local girl was "in trouble" and that he was the cause. The two were married very quickly and quietly. Jemima was quick to distance herself from him and soon accepted Sir Roger's advances. For Nancy, this was all very convenient.

Shortly after their wedding, Nancy Royale died. Everyone said she had never been the same since the death of her husband. She complained of chest pains which radiated down her left arm and upwards into her jaw. Her lower legs were considerably swollen, and her complexion held a bluish tinge. And so it was that just four months after the death of her husband, and just two weeks after the marriage of Sir Roger and Jemima, she died quietly one evening, alone and peaceful in her room.

'And so I took over Jemima's body, according to the plans we had agreed upon,' Sara explained quietly, to her enraptured audience.

Jennifer had been clutching a glass of wine for some time, untasted. Chas also had a glass of wine beside him near to the arm of his chair; it was barely tasted.

'So, how it was that you were separated?' Jennifer demanded finally taking a generous gulp of her wine, leaving a red stain at the side of her mouth. 'I don't know the whole story.'

'It was just so easy!' She explained. 'We were separated during World War Two. During the 1914–18 war, we both felt we ought to do our duty, yet again. Roger worked in espionage; I worked as a nurse with Harold Gillies, the plastic surgeon. Initially I was in France and Belgium, then, towards the end of the war, at The Queen's Hospital, still with Gillies and still specialising in plastic surgery.

Roger was killed, shot by the Germans, but in his new body he returned to our home in Bowness. We had planned for this happening; such is the outcome of war. What was unplanned was that prior to the war I had given birth to a son and a daughter; obviously we were careless when it came to contraception! But I so wanted to have those children, neither of whom was an incubus. Whilst we were away the boy was at boarding school, the girl cared for by a governess, as was typical of the time.

'And so World War Two arrived. Well, again, we knew we had to do our duty, and we were often separated during the conflict. But we managed, throughout most of it, to keep in touch, and even contrived to meet sometimes. He was in the army, his espionage skills were noted, and he was headhunted by the SOE. I was a doctor; I worked in London throughout the Blitz.

'I had better explain. By the 1930s we were both inhabiting new bodies, and the house at Bowness belonged to the children I had borne. So, before the war began, I was working at St Bart's. Then a marvellous surgeon called Archibald McIndoe devised techniques to help badly burned airmen. Units were set up for them, and I was eager to be a part of the process of enabling these men to regain their lives. So I transferred to a unit near Oxford. My husband – yet again he was called David – was killed. Our marital home was in London, Willesden Green, where, of course, we expected to meet up at some point. But it was bombed.'

'No contingency plan?' queried Chas, indicating to Jen that she had a red wine moustache.

'Yes, of course we did. Our home was a lovely detached house near Blenheim Gardens. After the war, I spent a lot of time in the area, hoping he would be loitering there also. Anyway, another of our "just in case" plans was to meet on my birthday. The person I was then had a birthday on 22nd July. We would meet at St Swithun's Church, Canongate, which had been our place of worship for years. I kept going there until it was demolished in 1962. Yet another plan was to use Highgate Railway Station, meaningful to both of us as we'd set out on many journeys from there and of course had returned there. It would be an excellent meeting point, in the waiting room, so I often loitered there too.' Sara ran her fingers distractedly through her hair. 'It closed around 1970.'

'It can't be easy if you don't know who you're looking for,' Jennifer presciently commented.

'That is so true... That was the problem. I had to change bodies soon after the war. I contracted hepatitis B from a patient, due to blood contamination. So, obviously, if David returned he didn't know who he was looking for. Obviously I didn't either,' nodded Sara, wondering how many days and nights she had spent in and around St Swithun's Church, how many times someone had approached her, wishing to know if she was a "lady of the night"? On more than one occasion she'd been threatened with police intervention if she didn't remove herself from Highgate Station waiting room – when it existed.

'I thought Highgate Station was still in use,' Chas frowned in concentration. 'I'm sure it is.'

'It's part of the Underground. One of the original buildings survives; it's now a private house,' agreed Sara. 'I have hung around there, but without success.'

'How about the house at Bowness? Is it still there?' Chas queried.

'Yes, I have tried visiting it,' Sara shrugged. 'To no avail. We seem to have some sort of intuition when we meet one of our kind. I wonder if I *have* seen him and have been too intent to actually realise who he was. Do you understand my meaning? I'm explaining it badly.'

'You mean you've been so intent on finding him, you can't see the wood for the trees,' Chas stated.

'Yes, that's it exactly,' Sara agreed.

'I'm sure social media is the answer,' Jennifer affirmed.

'Well, as Marilyn Hamilton, I wrote a book about Maude Dubreise. I finished it shortly before I died, and it's about to be published posthumously. You see, when I commenced the work, I was sure that David, or whatever he's called now, would see it advertised and contact me. I didn't realise I was so very ill. It came about pretty quickly, you see.'

'Maybe if you'd taken over one of your daughters, he would have contacted them as next of kin.' Jennifer wondered if she sounded a little caustic. If Marilyn had taken over one of her own daughters, Sara would have been left alone!

A knowing expression flitted quickly over Sara's face and was gone in an instant. 'I realise what you're thinking but, you see, as Marilyn I didn't have children, the girls weren't mine but belonged to my husband from a previous relationship. As I was dying, well, Sara was "just there", and I acted more spontaneously than perhaps I should have done,' she mused aloud.

'Have you ever taken over one of your own children?' Jennifer wanted to know.

'Mmmm, well, a few times actually. It wasn't always convenient or advisable to do so. Sometimes I only gave birth to sons; so, since I seem to be a very feminine entity, I don't feel any eagerness to occupy a male body. Invariably, I use a body I've targeted and vetted.' Sara hesitated. 'When I saw you visiting with your daughter, I decided, very quickly, that here was an intelligent girl, a bit young perhaps, but who came from a family who could help me through university and enable me to carve out a decent career. I haven't worked in medicine for a number of years; I could try that again. History is obviously a good subject for me to study, for obvious reasons, but I've just done that. Law interests me too. As yet, I am undecided.' Sara shrugged helplessly.

'You see,' she continued after some hesitation, 'Marilyn Hamilton's stepdaughters were not bodies I wished to use. Tragically, one of them has cystic fibrosis, although she's relatively well at present. At least, as well as she can be. The other had meningitis when only four years of age. She's severely disabled, and I doubt if she will live for very much longer.' Just as she was explaining this, Jennifer's mobile range. It was Vi.

'I can only just hear you, Mum... You're breaking up. What...? He's coming to the UK with you? Are you sure that's wise? Where is he going to stay? He might burgle your house! Mum? Mum!' Jennifer flung her phone on the sofa in exasperation. 'Damnation!' It was unusual for her to swear. 'Damn... The signal was breaking up. She's coming home, and this Randall man, I gather, has managed to get a fight alongside her! She must have paid for it! I can't believe she's so foolish with her money. At her age!'

'Poor dude.' Chas gave an impish grin. 'Look, she is of age. Well and truly of age; she's over sixty. If this guy is going to fleece you of your inheritance, well, so be it. As long as she enjoys herself.'

'Chas! I wasn't thinking about my inheritance,' gasped Jennifer.

'Maybe you should,' Sara chipped in, suddenly relieved to be discussing a new subject.

'I know she's annoying—'

'Putting it mildly,' Chas interrupted.

'She's annoying,' Jennifer persisted. 'But I don't like to imagine her being hurt or made to look foolish.'

'Invite her to bring him to dinner one evening – as soon as possible. It's the only way to assess the situation,' Chas advised, suddenly serious.

A week later, on the Friday evening, Vi was expected to arrive, bringing with her Randall Olongu. Chas, who'd finished work early, was cheerfully loading charcoal onto one of his barbeques, proclaiming it gave a better flavour to the food than the gas model. Jennifer was still at work. Sara was pressing balls of spiced, minced lamb into firm balls to make koftas. Tracy was piercing chicken and peppers onto skewers, her eyes watering because of the raw onion mixed into the ingredients. Watching them, Chas pronounced that he hoped this Randall dude wasn't vegetarian, or he would go home seriously hungry.

Glancing towards plates of defrosting rump steaks and tuna fillets, Sara nodded in agreement. It would be a meat feast. But at least there was a bowl of mixed green leaves, cucumber and some tomatoes – produce from a neighbour's greenhouse. Randall Olongu, if vegetarian, would have to eat salad with buns or naan breads. Giving a wry smile, she suggested she could make him an omelette in an emergency.

Tracy, who had spent a week in Majorca with her parents and brother whilst the Roseberrys were engaged with their coach trip, was suntanned. This was highly noticeable since both Sara and Chas were quite pale. The summer had been poor and, although their holiday weather had not been a total washout, it wasn't memorable for being hot.

Observing the two of them, Chas reflected that at least Sara had the companionship of someone akin to herself. Tracy, he decided, was a thoroughly decent person, more adventurous than Sara, but somehow there was something – he searched for a description – there was something remarkably *pure* about Sara. And he was certain this opinion didn't stem from the fact that biologically the girl was his daughter. Jennifer saw it too.

It was sad she'd lost her soulmate. He found himself pitying her, imagining how he might feel should Jennifer be erased from his life. It was a painful notion and he preferred not to think about it. Sara had lost someone with whom she had clearly been in harmony for decades.

'You'll be thirteen soon,' he stated aloud to Sara. 'A teenager. We need to think of what to do to celebrate it.'

A new term would be commencing very soon. Sara would be thirteen on the tenth of September. It would be strange if they didn't celebrate it, and truthfully he did want to celebrate. She was still his daughter, after all, even if she was mentally over six hundred years old, he reflected ruefully. He and Jen had always held birthday parties for her, although the parties had always somehow or other ended up including more of their friends than Sara's.

'Not a schoolgirl's party, spare me that,' she replied after a moment of reflection.

'It is the downside of using a young body,' smiled Tracy, wiping her streaming eyes. 'Dratted onions! But at least we don't stay so very young for a long time!'

Sara was silent for a while, them remarked, 'I know I shall have to attend some schoolgirl parties, I accept that. But for my thirteenth, what I would really like to do is go to see VPL with… well, you Chas, plus Jen and Tracy. They're on at the

Metro Arena at the end of September... but I doubt if there will be any tickets available,' she reflected.

'I know people who can arrange things,' Chas stated smugly. 'I have contacts, you know! Stick with me, and who knows what could be arranged!'

'Except I heard today on the news that the VPL concert won't be taking place.' Tracy again wiped her eyes. 'Honestly, I hate these onions! 'I have never known such an accident prone band.' Gentian de Barke fell downstairs – she denied being drunk or otherwise chemically inconvenienced – broke her leg, compound fracture apparently, and dislocated her shoulder. In a separate accident, Paradise, the drummer, broke her arm. Fell off her motorbike apparently. She admits to being chemically inconvenienced at the time but didn't state the nature of the chemicals. Refunds are being offered to those who have purchased tickets, or they can be used at a later date.'

'Presumably when the drummer has two arms,' Chas stated drily. 'But just to show you I sometimes can be in with the in-crowd, that other heavy metal band you both like – and I'm actually beginning to *kind of like* – Queen Anne's Revenge, is doing a gig at the Durham cricket ground at Chester–le–Street on the sixteenth of September... a week after your birthday.'

Sara nodded. She'd known about that. Musically she preferred them to VPL. But the cricket ground was a greater distance to travel than the Metro Arena, Gateshead.

'Well, it's not that far,' Chas responded after she'd voiced her reservation.

'Can you arrange tickets?' she asked eagerly.

'I know who to get in touch with,' nodded Chas. 'I even know the name of a band member!' He gave a schoolboy grin. 'Warlock!' he stated triumphantly.

'What about the other five?' demanded Tracy. 'They all use just single names, you know.'

'That should make it easier,' piped up Sara.

Chas stepped back after lighting the barbeque.

'I only know one... and am impressed about that, I have to say! I rather hoped you two would be likewise impressed.' Unsuccessfully, he tried to arrange his features into an expression of disappointment.

'Oh, we are, indeed we are!' smiled Sara. 'The rest include Castor and Pollux – as in the twin gods. Except they're brothers, not twins,' she explained

'Why allow facts to get in the way of a good name?' nodded Chas. 'At least they're related.'

'Then there's Horatio (a fan of Horatio Lord Nelson) and Swordfish,' Sara continued.

'Swordfish is apparently clean of addictive herbal substances now. Has been for nearly a year, I read.' Tracy wiped her eyes yet again. 'In fact, their new album, which is released this week, consists mostly of his work. I suspect he might be leaving the band soon and going solo, if this new album is a massive hit,' she speculated.

'You really are a mine of information.' Sara placed yet another neatly formed kofta on the tray. 'And then there's Artemis,' she concluded.

'But Artemis is a female deity. Otherwise known as Diana of the Ephesians. Some sort of fertility goddess, I seem to recall.' Chas proudly displayed his classical knowledge. 'She was depicted with lots of bosoms!'

'He's gay,' nodded Sara. 'I get the impression you already assumed that!'

'Well, it was either that or he has a fixation with bosoms,' Chas reflected. 'So... you would like to go to the Queen Anne's Revenge concert, then?' he demanded, suddenly businesslike.

'If it can be arranged, I'd love that. They're very original, and I think you and Jennifer will enjoy them more than VPL,' beamed Sara. Admiring the sight of her neatly arranged koftas, she shook her head in amusement. 'Tracy, I think you must spend hours surfing the net. The things you seem to read about!'

'Well, there's only one television set in the house, and the family are addicted to soaps. I'm not, so I stick with my iPad!'

Jennifer returned home from work and was informed of the Queen Anne's Revenge concert, and although less enthusiastic than Chas she gave a feeble smile and nodded in agreement. After all, Sara would only be thirteen once. A teenager. As long as she, like Chas, ignored the extra six hundred or so years.

She disappeared into her bedroom to quickly shower and get changed, rummaging through her substantial wardrobe, wondering what to wear. It was a barbeque, so casual was the obvious choice. Skinny cropped jeans, she decided. But which pair? Red, orange or blue? Or yellow? White? She pushed hangers back and forth, finally opting for red. To be combined with a lemon and white finely knitted top.

Chas, coming into the bedroom, gave a wolf whistle, signalling his approval.

'I didn't hear you come in,' she smiled.

'I hoped to catch you wearing a few items less. Too late, though,' he shrugged, disappointed. 'But I have to say your rear looks great in those. Look, you're not uptight about tonight, are you?' he demanded. 'I mean, we can tell them not to come…'

'I'm fine,' she interrupted gently, patting his face fondly. 'As I've said, my only hope is that she's not made to look a fool.'

'Okay.' Chas gave her a bear hug. 'But one thing…' He began extracting pins and slides from her hair, which was fastened into a bun, her favoured workplace hairstyle.

'I was going to leave it up,' she protested gently, pleased with his obvious admiration.

'Don't,' he advised. 'You're not at work now. Look, I'm going to be slaving over the barbeque, so I need a glass of wine. In fact, I deserve it.'

'Pour one for me... and I don't believe you're overworked. I know for certain that Sara and Tracy have been busy all afternoon!'

Tracy was staying overnight, which meant she and Sara would attend to all of the drudgery: loading the dishwasher, unloading the dishwasher, clearing tables, making tea and coffee, and filling wine glasses. They were more efficient than any waitress she'd ever come across.

At seven o' clock prompt, Vi and her man friend arrived. Peering eagerly out the porch window, whilst trying to be discreet, Jennifer could make out what seemed to be a grey-haired man at the wheel of a Vauxhall people carrier. *That's a relief*, she thought. At least Vi wasn't running around with a young man and fancying herself as a cougar.

Shouting for Chas, she opened the front door, watching in amazement as a tall man, of medium build, climbed out of the driving seat. He was intellectual looking, wearing half-moon gold-rimmed spectacles and an expensive looking suit, complete with a well-coordinated shirt and tie. Walking round to the passenger side, he courteously opened the door for Vi. Trying to appear majestic, Vi stepped out, unfortunately exposing a great deal of leg, complete with varicose veins, as she did so.

Turning to the stunned Jennifer and Chas, he uttered the words, 'Good day; you must be Jen and Chas?' with a definite Australian accent.

'Indeed, yes.' Rallying his thoughts, Chas stepped forward, his arm extended to shake hands. It was gripped in a vice-like hold.

'Randall Olongu. Well, pleased to meet you.' Turning to Jennifer he treated her to a less firm handshake. 'What do you think of my hired wheels? Brand new – I'm its first customer!' he declared proudly. 'Prefer that one, though,' he nodded towards Chas's Alfa Romeo, which had not yet been garaged for the night.

Chas was all but purring, decided Jennifer. Anyone who gave a compliment to his car won his esteem. Sara and Tracy were duly introduced, then immediately afterwards Randall opened the boot of his car and produced a crate of wine. Clearly he was set to enjoy the evening. Noting Chas's casual attire, cropped trousers and a tee shirt, he returned to the boot of the car.

'I didn't know what threads to wear. Vi said a suit and tie, but these strides are hot and uncomfortable. Since you're both casual, would you mind if I nipped into the dunny to put on my shorts? Brought them, just in case!'

Vi sighed. It looked as if the evening was not going to proceed in the genteel manner she had envisioned. It was always the case with Chas. He always lowered the tone of any party, in her opinion, and he encouraged others to do likewise. Poor Jennifer, she seemed to have resigned herself to his "gung ho, let's all have a good time" attitude.

'You're welcome to wear whatever you feel comfortable in… but it is a mild evening, although not red hot. Clearly, you're not used to the northern climate,' Chas informed him affably. 'But we do have some patio heaters should you need warming up.'

'Lovely to see you, Mum.' Jennifer gave her mother a gentle kiss on the cheek. 'You look wonderful!' she stated truthfully. 'Your hair is lovely.' The concrete waves were gone. In their place was a shorter, more casual style. It made her look years younger.

'Just had it done yesterday. It was Randall's idea. He thinks I spend too long doing my hair of a morning.' Vi patted her hair complacently. 'Must admit I like it enormously!'

'She's a fine-looking Sheila,' intoned the visitor. 'Obviously good looks run in the family,' he added gallantly.

Once seated in the garden, Jennifer studied him covertly. His hair was grey and frizzy, the bridge of his nose was wide, his eyes were dark – obviously some native Australian there somewhere, she noted. He was decidedly attractive. Tall, even taller than Chas, lean without being scraggy; his casual cargo shorts and tee shirt suited him.

'It's an unusual name – Olongu,' Sara observed gently, noting her mother's scrutiny. *She's dying to know what sort of background he comes from,* she speculated mischievously.

'Great-grandfather was native Australian. Aborigine,' he explained cheerfully. 'He was the real deal. Used to go walkabout regularly. Apparently my great-grandmother was not a happy woman; spent a lot of time weeping. Thanks a lot!' Eagerly he accepted a substantial glass of wine from Chas.

'I suppose she never knew when she would see him again,' Jennifer guessed.

'Oh no… she wept when he returned home,' was the placid response. 'Eventually she turned to drink. She was a lot more cheerful after that.'

'Would be, I suppose,' nodded Chas. He was just about to bring the conversation around to Randall Olongu's mode of employment, but was forestalled.

'Vi tells me you're a lawyer feller,' Randall commented affably. 'And she says Jen is a dentist.' He pronounced it "dintist". 'By the look of them, she must do your teeth.'

'She even gives me an anaesthetic!' Chas stated drily.

'And as you can see, I have a mouthful of metal,' Sara added. 'No misshapen teeth in this household, Mr Olongu!'

'Call me Randall,' he invited. 'I don't stand on ceremony. Did I get it right? You're Sarah?'

'Sara. It rhymes with Clara.'

'Or tiara,' added Tracy, who was hugely enjoying herself.

'Are you still working?' Chas wondered if he was being tactful enough, but he wanted to know about this man's profession – or lack of it.

'Pilot. Commercial flights. Took early retirement a few months back. Hence I get a certain number of free flights as part of my retirement package, and when I run out of them I get fifty per cent off. So do my next of kin. Got a daughter from my first wife, cracker kid; she's a surgeon in Sydney. Twin sons from the second; one is a newly qualified engineer, the other is also a pilot. Have a twenty-year-old son from my third wife; seems to want to do nothing but surf. Not studious like the others. He's a surfing instructor. But as long as he's happy that's all that matters.'

'I would agree with that,' Chas affirmed, digesting this information. He got up to tend to the barbeque.

It was a mild evening, but even so they still needed to use the patio heaters. It was far from being hot. There was a light breeze, wafting the smell of cooking food towards the patio where everyone was seated.

'Do you need help, Dad?' Sara was always careful to refer to her parents as Mum and Dad when in company. Otherwise, she'd slipped into the habit of calling them by their Christian names in private.

'I'll help.'

Randall Olongu eased his long frame from his seat. He even towered over Chas. Making himself at home, he refilled his glass before wandering over to the area put aside for barbequing. Side by side, the two massive barbeques were covered by a three-sided wooden structure, enabling Chas to cook even when it rained.

'You seem to take this seriously,' observed Randall. 'Only right too; I love barbies.'

'In this country we assume Australians eat nothing else!' Chas gave his wicked grin. 'You must have handed out a lot of cash to ex-wives,' he noted, suddenly serious.

'My, yes,' nodded Randall. 'Especially wife one. I was living with her, married, and shacked up with number two at the same time. One found out about two and threw me out, and I had to support her for years, until she finally married a teacher. Two left me for a plastic surgeon. Three, well, we didn't get on together. She left me for a businessman. She maybe should have been the one who married the plastic surgeon, though. The amount of stuff she's had done! Honest to goodness, she has so much silicone in her, if I was her husband I'd be scared to let her near a barbie in case she melted!' He pronounced it *milted*.

Chas gave a roar of laughter. 'She must be insecure about her looks,' he speculated.

'Don't see why she should be. After all, no man looks at the fireplace when he's stoking the fire,' shrugged the Australian pragmatically.

Chas gave another hoot of laughter.

'Your wife is a grand-looking Sheila. She your first or second?' Randall demanded frankly.

'The one and only, I hope,' was the serious reply. 'We make a good team.' Chas flipped some koftas over with a spatula.

'If I'd only had one, I would have been a rich man.' Randall Olongu was suddenly serious. 'I have kids, and kids are costly. They're a responsibility, and you have to pay for them. I accept that, and whilst I'm financially comfortable I would have been even more so if I'd been less, well, intent upon pursuing every Sheila in sight! And they do seem to be intent upon breeding. I could have done without that!'

'Whilst we're here chatting,' Chas, with some deliberation, placed his spatula on the workbench, 'Vi and I are often at odds. In short, we don't sing from the same hymn sheet. But I don't want her to be made a fool of—'

'Aaah,' the Australian interrupted, 'I know what you're gonna say. I'm not taking advantage of her. She and I *are* singing from the same hymn sheet, you see. Neither of us wants anything from the other. We just want to enjoy each other's company. I'm lonely sometimes. So is she. We get along very well! I'm arranging a flight for her to visit me in Oz soon. Say… you weren't hoping she would marry me and move permanently to Oz?' There was a gleam of humorous understanding in Olongu's eyes.

'I'm not that optimistic,' grinned Chas. From that moment on, he had huge respect for the Australian visitor.

Vi was watching Sara critically, lips pursed in her customary fashion when registering disapproval. The girl seemed to have matured beyond all recognition this summer. Her hair was longer. She no longer had a full fringe; she'd swept it to the side whilst growing it out. The style flattered her face. Her ears were newly pierced, and the presence of earrings seemed to give an added maturity too. The slouching schoolgirl was now gracefully seated in her chair, shoulders straight, legs elegantly turned slightly to the side. Even the way she held her glass of mineral water, fingers gently holding the stem of the glass, showed a new sophistication. She determined to try and manoeuvre Jennifer away from everyone to speak with her alone. Jennifer must surely be aware she was forcing the girl to grow up too quickly! She was such a perfectionist, she was surely pushing Sara towards being an adult long before she was ready to be one.

'Where are the plates?' shouted Chas, deciding that everything was cooked to his satisfaction.

He was using both barbeques due to the volume of food, although the bulk of it was being done over the glowing charcoal.

Sara jumped up from her seat, lithe and graceful, Vi noted, still disapproving. Maybe Jen was sending her to dancing lessons; Sara had never been interested in learning to dance.

'They're in the gas side, inside the cabinet!' She hurried over to demonstrate where the required items were.

'In that case, food is served!' bellowed Chas. 'Come and get it!'

Vi turned her attention to Tracy. The girl was older than Sara; maybe she was to blame for the surge of maturity. Certainly she seemed a nice girl. She was well-mannered, quiet, unassuming, everything she ought to be. Jennifer thought that she, Vi, personally disapproved of the friendship simply because Tracy was the cleaner's daughter. But she was wrong, decided Vi. She disapproved of the cleaner, not because she was a cleaner, but because she was Elsie. Elsie was *not* refined or ladylike; she had some awful habits. One of them was steeping her false teeth in a glass, which she would leave on the kitchen sink whilst doing the housework. She never did this when Jen was around. When she, Vi, had informed her daughter of this disgusting outrage, Jen had merely laughed and said that if she ever saw those teeth grinning at her, she'd request Elsie to at least place them somewhere a bit more discreet. Jen's attitude – unbelievable given how proper she could be – was one of relief that Elsie at least steeped her teeth thoroughly!

There was more than enough food, causing Vi to remark that it was shocking, simply shocking, to be so extravagant, when people abroad were starving. Jennifer, more sharply than she intended, pointed out that nothing would be wasted because it could be put into the fridge to be served up tomorrow. Once everyone had finished eating, Vi suddenly realised that Randall had consumed more wine than – in her opinion – everyone else put together.

'You surely cannot be thinking of driving with that amount of wine in your body!' she accused.

'Thought we would be staying over,' was the placid response.

'Plenty of room,' Chas stated, as Vi grumbled she'd not brought any nightwear or toiletries with her. He felt Jennifer tugging at his arm, signalling he should accompany her into the kitchen.

'Do we assume they'll both stay in the room Mum uses... or should I give them one each?' she whispered.

'Not a problem,' Chas whispered in return. 'I'll tell him we're being tactful, putting him next door to her, and if they feel like behaving like a pair of randy geriatrics we won't be listening for creaking floorboards!'

'Chas!' Jennifer reproachfully gave him one of her kittenish swipes. It made her faintly uncomfortable to think of her mother sleeping with Randall Olongu. Or anyone else, for that matter. 'Anyway, technically he is not a geriatric. He's only in his mid-fifties! He took early retirement.'

'Which definitely makes her a cougar; she's older than him!' Chas gave a low theatrical growl, earning him another kittenish swipe. 'Anyway, technically we shouldn't tolerate her sharing a room with him. Do you remember how she always insisted we used separate rooms before we were married, when I stayed at your house?'

'I do,' smiled Jennifer. 'Nor did she approve when we went on holiday together, even though we were engaged!'

'Well, it's payback time,' Chas assured her with mock-seriousness. 'I shall tell her we're having no hanky-panky in this house, thank you very much! We shall tolerate nothing more intimate than a handshake on the landing!'

Sara and Tracy had retired to Sara's bedroom; Tracy would be using a sleeping bag on the couch settee. Vi and Jennifer had gone upstairs to sort out a nightgown and toiletries. Randall accepted yet another glass of wine, whilst Chas wondered how he managed to remain so sober. He could certainly hold his liquor.

'Those two girls; they're unusual.' Randall was deadly serious. 'I have to tell you, I'm not looking at them like I'm some kind of weirdo. I don't go for little kids. You see, my great-great-grandmother, and my great-grandfather, and also my dad, had what my family call "a knowledge". I don't know what it really is, or what it's really called. We've never had anyone explain it to us. I've got it, but not as much as they had. But we know… well, we know when something is amiss. We know when something is wrong, when a spirit is troubled, or maybe even… an unusual spirit. We also sometimes sense when something is going to happen.'

Chas was still, his eyes fixed intently on the Australian's face.

'So, what are you seeing with Sara and Tracy?'

'I'm only mentioning this to you, no one else.' Randall Olongu was deeply serious. 'Not even Vi. But I'm telling you, those two girls are not girls. Only in their bodies. They are ancient, mate, and that's a fact!'

CHAPTER TWELVE

'I'VE BEEN TALKING TO RANDALL,' WHISPERED CHAS, IN response to Jennifer wondering where he'd been.

She was in bed, as ever looking very fetching in one of her pretty silky nightgowns, smelling of a mixture of toothpaste and scented body lotion, her long curls draped seductively – in his opinion – over the pillow. Quietly he delivered an account of their conversation.

As he concluded, Jennifer sat bolt upright, alarmed. 'But he might tell Mum! I don't want her knowing; she'll tell everyone!'

Chas shook his head vehemently. There was something honest about the visitor. He definitely possessed integrity, in spite of his admittedly colourful past. Randall Olongu had ventured to declare that whilst he sensed both girls were ancient people, there was only much goodness there, especially in Sara. 'They are nothing to be fearful of,' Olongu had concluded, after Chas had explained what had happened to his previously "normal" daughter, and admitted he and Jen had actually approached the vicar and an exorcist to try and deal with the situation.

'So, he gets this insight thing from his Aboriginal ancestors?' Jennifer asked.

'Seems so,' stated Chas. 'I think he said it came from his great-grandfather... or maybe his great-great-grandfather? I lost count of the "greats", but I don't mind admitting, a few months ago if someone had told me that he or she had some sort of strange knowledge, I wouldn't have believed it. This has made me more open to oddball things.'

'Me too,' Jennifer agreed. 'Mum likes him. I had a chat with her. But she says she just wants a friend.'

Chas ached to admit that this evening he'd hoped Olongu would take Vi to live with him in Australia, permanently. During the evening Vi had commented on the number of lights in the garden, what a waste of power they were. Then there was the furniture in the living room. She preferred lots of ornaments and to have furniture crammed into every nook and cranny. He and Jen preferred the minimalist look. Vi had spent some time explaining to her new man friend how much she could improve the room given the opportunity to do so. In fact, most of the house needed her expertise, apparently. She also disliked Jennifer's enthusiasm for candles, especially the scented candles she placed in the downstairs cloakroom. Privately, Chas wasn't fond of scented candles either, but it irritated him to hear his mother-in-law criticising them. It was Jen's home – if she wanted smelly candles she could have smelly candles.

'Sara seems to have been discussed by everyone,' Jennifer informed Chas. 'Mum had a word with me. Apparently she thinks Sara is growing up too quickly, and it's entirely my fault. I'm being too controlling and demanding.' A note of irritation had crept into her voice. Chas took advantage of it.

'I hope Randall coaxes her to move to Australia,' he stated waspishly, putting his arm around Jennifer as she cuddled up to him. 'They're certainly not just friends. When we came upstairs together he asked which room she was using. I pointed to it and that's where he's gone! Your mother is definitely a cougar, and I hope it's not hereditary!'

'She's not that much older than him,' Jennifer rebuked mildly.

Over breakfast, Chas noticed Olongu covertly observing Sara and Tracy. Somehow, last night's conversation with the Australian had given him a feeling of peace. Olongu, having mentioned knowing that both girls were ancient spirits, had proceeded to listen sympathetically to Chas's feelings about the subject.

His emotions were, at best, mixed. Yes, Sara would be well educated, have a good career and would live on long after he and Jennifer were dead. But at the same time, he still so very much wanted his daughter back. His almost teenage daughter. But there was something cathartic about that talk with Randall Olongu, something so very healing, which was strange, since Olongu himself had said very little, other than advising acceptance as the only way to deal with it.

So, he'd suggested to Jennifer that perhaps she too should open up to Olongu about the situation. They were both due to have another appointment with Alan Reynolds and Terry Richards, which Sara herself was refusing to attend. She'd had enough of him. Chas felt he'd had enough too. In fact, he wondered if he'd been wise in involving the clergy in his domestic problem. But, perversely, he also felt he owed it to his daughter to have her restored to her previous self.

After breakfast, Jennifer offered to show Olongu some guidebooks on Northumberland, since he'd expressed an interest in visiting some local points of interest. He didn't seem to be worse for wear at all following his enthusiastic wine-tasting of the previous night – unlike Vi, who had only partaken of three glasses of white wine and now had a headache. But, Jennifer had pointed out, they had been very large glasses.

As far as Vi was concerned, three glasses were three glasses, irrespective of size. She hadn't drunk very much. Therefore her current malaise must originate from catching some bug or other. She also waspishly pointed out that Chas had left the garden lights on overnight.

'They're LED so it won't bankrupt us or cause a huge drain on the national grid,' he explained through gritted teeth, whilst at the same time he was thankful he'd not tried to keep up with the Australian's wine drinking. Changing the subject abruptly, he enquired of his mother-in-law, 'Does he always drink so much?'

'Well, I haven't known him very long, but so far he's not done anything more than share a bottle with me over dinner.' Vi looked irritated. 'You aren't implying he has a drink problem, are you?'

'No, not at all,' Chas assured her. 'I just wondered if that was his usual nightly intake.'

'Well, it isn't,' was the tart response. 'You're a bad influence.'

With quiet satisfaction, Chas informed her, 'Well, it has to be said, Randall did arrive armed with a crate of wine. He clearly didn't need any influence from me.'

In the next room, with a map of Northumberland in front of them, Jennifer mentioned to Randall that Chas had informed her about him knowing Sara was more than a mere adolescent. She found him sympathetic about it, frankly admitting he would find it difficult should he ever be in the same situation.

'How did you realise they're both, well, different, for want of a better description?' Jennifer wanted to know.

'I don't know myself.' Randall seemed to spend a few moments musingly studying the map. 'I guess I've inherited some strange ability from my ancestors. I've never consulted anyone about it. I seem to pick up vibrations or something. Not a very good description, but the best I can offer. As for my eldest son, he's got something strange going on. He can walk past a computer and it acts all weird. When he goes to a checkout in a shop the tills go crazy. Sometimes he passes a light and it just switches on! Then it goes off when he leaves the room. If he warns us about anything, we know we need to take heed, as he's never wrong. Neither his mother nor I ever made a big deal of it; we never wanted him to think he had something wrong with him. And he's grown up to be a fine, decent man. Sometimes people have to be left to be themselves, in my opinion. But obviously parents all have to do what they feel is appropriate. And of course it depends on the problem. Your situation is not the same as mine.'

'No,' mused Jennifer.

His accent was soothing, she felt. It was warm and cosy. Perhaps even hypnotic. He was truly a nice person, which was a relief to know. He would be a good companion for Vi. She found his Australian terminology amusing too, the way he called the toilet "the dunny". Clearly Vi didn't approve of that one, her lips pursed whenever he said it, but it was harmless enough. Jennifer could only suppose her mother felt it was vulgar or something. Then he referred to his trousers as his "strides". As for his vowel sounds, they were attractively different to those of everyone else she knew.

'How long did it take you to find out she'd changed?' queried Randall.

'Not very long. A few days. I noticed she was talking about things she was too young to know about.' Jennifer proceeded to explain about listening to conversations between Sara and

Tracy, and then making a recording of them. 'It was a bit sneaky, it felt wrong, but I needed to know what was happening. In the end, I cornered Sara and she told me. As the saying goes, beware of asking for something, as you might actually get it.

'Elsie, Tracy's mother, seems unaware. Same goes for her father. But I sometimes wonder if it's not just a case of them being really determined *not* to know. They're good parents, not academic, but both are far from being stupid or foolish. I think perhaps it would be wise for Chas and me to follow their example.'

'I think you both know what to do.' Randall patted her hand paternally. 'And I hope you find peace with it,' he added.

'Yes.' Jennifer twirled her engagement and wedding rings about thoughtfully. 'At least she's a good spirit. I only hope she's okay with school, though. She knows more than the teachers... but she tells me that technology and science are always interesting; they keep moving on, so there's a lot out there that is new for her. I know she finds it difficult to act like someone who won't be a teenager for a few days yet. But girls are so grown-up these days, perhaps no one will notice!' Jennifer managed a smile.

'She'll manage,' nodded Randall, adding, 'as will the other one.'

It was with regret that Chas and Jennifer waved farewell to their Australian guest. He had agreed to join them for Sara's actual birthday, though, which was on the ninth of September, the week before the concert. He even initially seemed agreeable to actually attending the concert with them, but Vi was strongly opposed to the suggestion. She hated modern music.

The birthday party itself would consist of a barbeque – naturally. Jennifer's brother would be coming, plus five of

Sara's long-time school friends, along with Tracy of course. Alan and Jilly had also been invited.

Jennifer and Chas had wondered whether to invite Terry Richards too. They'd talked at length as to whether or not to involve him any further, then had mutually agreed not to. What was the point? All of them, those who knew of Sara's story, realised there was now no going back. The succubus was firmly rooted. Driving it out would destroy Sara herself. That was unthinkable. But it had been kind of Terry Richards to at least attempt to help them. So, having spent time pondering the matter, they decided to write a thank-you letter to him, ending it with an invitation to visit on the evening of Sara's thirteenth birthday. After all, he was so very friendly with Alan and Jilly. Not only that, they were certain Terry and his wife would decline the invitation. The letter had been posted first class, and a couple of days later Chas received an email thanking Jennifer and him for the invitation and stating that he and his wife would be very pleased to come to the party.

'Ah well, the more the merrier,' shrugged Chas.

He and Jennifer had just arrived home from work and were seated in the conservatory, looking out at a dismal grey garden, a scene of pouring rain and brisk wind.

'Mum will be pleased. With a couple of members of the clergy around, she'll consider herself to be in refined company!' said Jennifer, adding, 'As for Randall, I don't think he cares whom he associates with. I think he's totally himself. If we invited the Duke of Northumberland, he would just offer him a beer and tell him where he could find the dunny!'

'The Duke is not one of my clients, so I've never met him. The Duchess neither, so I can't invite them, even though your mother would love it!' commented Chas, whilst busily counting up how many would attend and reckoning how much food to prepare.

The guest list had increased because he'd begun inviting work colleagues. So had Jennifer. Just as well they had two barbeques, he reasoned. And to think Jennifer had laughed at him for getting a second one. No one could manage with just one. He hadn't introduced the subject yet, but he'd just bought another one, half price, in the end-of-season sale at the local garden centre. It was to be delivered well before the party. The gas barbeque was excellent, he wouldn't want to be without it, but for flavour, well, the old-fashioned way was best. It was time to inform Jennifer of his purchase... not that she would be irritated. She was a reasonable woman. Most of the time.

'Well... I've had dealings with some of the family,' smirked Jennifer. Chas seemed to meet a lot of well-known people; it was pleasant to be able to act superior for a change.

'Really? You've crowned the duke's teeth?' chuckled Chas.

Jennifer gave him one of her kittenish swipes.

'And drilled the duchess's cavities?'

'Professional confidentiality... I can tell you nothing,' she stated primly. 'But they are nice people, although very busy, and I doubt if they could accept an invitation to the barbeque, especially since it's such short notice.'

Summing up the guest list, Chas observed, 'Well, it's just as well the aristocracy can't accept. With our combined work colleagues, plus their spouses and partners, the list is approaching forty.'

'Elsie's agreed to come and help with the cooking and cleaning up. Her husband is coming too, to lend a hand. After all, there's going to be quite a crowd. The barbeques shall be well and truly overworked,' Jennifer informed him.

'Whose party is this... yours or mine?' demanded Sara, newly returned from her first day of term at school.

'Well... I gave birth, so I have to have a part of it. And don't you say anything, Chas, we all know you were present at the moment of procreation, plus the moment of delivery.' Jennifer fluffed up her curls and rearranged her tortoiseshell combs. 'You did the easy bits!'

'Well, I shall be slaving away at the party.' The moment had come, Chas knew it. 'And talking of slaving away, I came across a bargain, a half-price barbeque at the garden centre; it'll be delivered sometime on Friday.' There. It was said, and Jennifer didn't even seem surprised.

'I knew you were angling for another. I heard you tell Randall how sometimes even two barbies aren't enough,' Jennifer stated mildly, turning her attention to Sara. 'How did your day go, darling?'

'It was everything I expected it to be.'

Sara flung herself onto a chair, her bulky school bag balanced on her knees. Her school friends, those whom she had been exchanging occasional emails with through the summer holiday, had already commented upon how grown-up her messages sounded. Today they'd exclaimed over how grown-up she appeared. She'd expected that, and it didn't worry her unduly. But she did feel she'd gained the dislike of the history teacher.

He'd made the mistake of remarking that the Battle of Neville's Cross had taken place during the Wars of the Roses. Sara had put up her hand and stated that she'd read it was earlier than the Wars of the Roses. Clearly offended, the teacher had given the date for the battle as being 1446. To this, Sara had informed him it was actually 1346. And it was not the Wars of the Roses, but a battle between the English and the Scots.

It took just a few seconds to check the date, and Sara was indeed correct, to the delight of her classmates, who were overjoyed to see the teacher proved wrong. Sara herself felt a little ashamed. He wasn't a good teacher; he was arrogant and had a huge ego. Clearly he thought every female he met was impressed by him. At the last parents' and teachers' evening, he'd very obviously been taken with Jennifer and had totally failed to notice she was utterly unimpressed by him. But it was wrong of her to humiliate him in front of her classmates... or was it? He was, after all, there to deliver accurate information. It was surely part of his job description! To ease her conscience, she apologised to him in front of her classmates, all of whom would have preferred it if she hadn't.

'My day was much the same as I expected,' she explained to Chas and Jennifer quietly. 'I've done it all before, and it brought no great surprises. And I have a mountain of homework!'

'Excellent,' approved Chas. 'That's what other parents pay the fees for!' he exclaimed, remembering, with satisfaction, Sara's scholarship.

———

On Friday evening, the three of them were gathered in the sitting room, Chas and Jennifer debating over whether or not to open a bottle of wine. After all, there would be wine flowing at the party tomorrow. It was Jennifer who solved the issue by commenting that neither of them would be drinking very much at the party since it was ill-mannered to have a drunken host or hostess. Within seconds, Chas produced a bottle of wine, two glasses and a corkscrew. He loved bottles of wine which had a genuine cork. He was deft with a traditional barman's corkscrew and made no secret of his delight that Jennifer was totally incapable of using one.

Jennifer, meanwhile, switched the television on, announcing she'd like to watch a film. A nice film. Something that didn't contain bad language or too much violence. Chas remarked that he didn't want to watch anything with Doris Day in it, if that was what she was fancying.

'I just want to watch something with reasonably clean language,' protested Jennifer. 'I'm not suggesting we watch *Annie Get Your Gun*!'

The screen flickered into life, and a chat show host was announcing his guests for the evening, the members of the heavy rock band Queen Anne's Revenge. Tracy had recently commented that the band were everywhere on television, thanks to their new album – out that very day – and their current national tour. Succumbing to curiosity, since they were going to see the band live in just over a week, the three of them sat forward and prepared to hear what was being said.

Six young men were arranged on a semi-circle of chairs, the central, biggest seat being occupied by the interviewer. The young men, all aged between twenty and twenty-five, were varied in appearance. Two, the brothers Castor and Pollux, wore their hair cut neatly short and were attired casually, but neatly enough to win Jennifer's approval. Another band member had his head totally shaved and a tattoo of a crow stained the top of his head, the beak dipping towards his left eyebrow. This was Horatio, who was clearly inclined towards being a goth. He wore a black ripped tee shirt, black jeans and plenty of studded bracelets. Artemis sported a man-bun and a long, forked beard, eyeliner (but only on one eye), and his choice of attire was an army uniform, circa World War One. Warlock had a jaw-length mop of cherubic blond curls, which Chas thought to be at odds with his choice of name. However, they were mostly obscured by a leather top hat with a stuffed bat attached to the side of it. Shirtless, he wore a black suede waistcoat and dark red leather jeans. He clearly liked bats; in case the bat on his leather top hat was lonely, there was another one tattooed onto his chest. The sixth band member wore skin-tight black leather jeans, knee-length boots and a ripped grey tee shirt. He possessed a luxurious mane of dark brown hair, hanging past his shoulders, lightly waved and framing an almost gaunt face. It was he whom the interviewer was initially focused upon. This was Swordfish, who had, according to journalists, written most of their new album.

When asked if he was indeed clean of drugs and alcohol, the young man nodded his affirmation. Yes, he was detoxed of all impurities. He was almost teetotal, had given up smoking and hardly ever touched tea or coffee, although he confessed to a craving for caffeine and thought he would, in the near future, succumb to that on a daily basis. But everything else was in the past, he assured the television audience earnestly, adding musingly that he did have one huge vice; he loved beef and eschewed vegetarianism, much to the disgust of the vegans, Castor and Pollux, who were shaking their heads sadly. There was a ripple of laugher, before the interviewer enquired as to how difficult had it been to turn his back on his old habits?

'I was determined,' Swordfish intoned slowly, his voice holding a slight, musical Welsh accent. 'I think I suddenly grew up overnight. It was as if some new spirit took over me and told me to stop killing myself. I checked into rehab, had a few bad days of the shakes, but the urge had gone to return to the old ways. I'm reliably informed I'm not so much fun to socialise with anymore. Thankfully, my family, plus these band mates of mine, are, and always have been, supportive.'

The interviewer turned his attention briefly to Horatio and the two brothers, one of whom was to become a father in the near future, before turning again to Swordfish. Was it true his marriage had come unstuck because he wife thought he was utterly boring nowadays?

Swordfish gravely acknowledged this. Yes, it was unfortunate, but then he and his soon to be ex-wife had sadly shared a penchant for drugs and alcohol, and in fact had known each other only for six weeks when they were wed. Both of them were totally unable to recall the ceremony.

'It seemed like a good idea at the time, I think,' he stated softly. 'We both enjoyed a good party; we had a blast during the six months of our marriage. But I wanted to dry out and she didn't. I wish her well, but it's the end of the road for us as a couple. Thankfully there are no children to be traumatised by our actions.'

'So, now you're turning your attention to being creative… and this new album is, in sound, something totally different to the band's previous recordings, being almost entirely your own work?' the interviewer enquired eagerly.

'Mmm, I guess so. Our signature sound has always been of heavy percussion – a lot of our work requires two drummers, two drum kits. Some of the album tracks are true to this. But previously I've been too out of it to actually contribute very much. This is my apology to them for being so stupid, I guess.' Swordfish managed a tight smile. 'I'm surprised they didn't kick me out long ago.'

Horatio chipped in with a remark that they couldn't throw him out because he was an ace guitarist, and recently they'd discovered that he could actually play keyboards. They'd previously been unaware of this. The others all nodded enthusiastically. Yes, it had come as a total surprise, they agreed. Swordfish had been hiding his light under a bushel. Whatever a bushel was. He was a fantastic piano player and, furthermore, his voice had improved since he wasn't chain-smoking anymore. He was actually singing on all the tracks. Sometimes solo, sometimes with Warlock and Artemis, who were the most frequent vocalists.

'There are surely some undercurrents here,' snorted Chas. 'If there's no professional jealousy there, they're a saintly bunch!'

But Warlock and Artemis were nodding approvingly, whilst the others smiled benignly. Yes, Swordfish was proving to be an excellent vocalist, which was the cue for the band to play one of the tracks from their new album, with Swordfish on keyboards and vocals.

'This song is not an original. It's actually by the Elizabethan composer William Byrd. He called it *The Barley Break*,' explained Swordfish. 'I've always had a sneaky liking for this sort of music, but of course we've fired it up a bit. You know, plenty of percussion and so forth. My take on Byrd, I guess. It's called *The Barley Break*.' Rising from their seats, the band took up their instruments.

Jennifer suddenly realised Sara was sitting totally still, seeming to be barely breathing, transfixed by what was happening on the screen.

There was a gentle opening, several bars of a piano solo, before the drums and guitars came in, then Swordfish began singing.

'My sweet Victorian lady,' he intoned his voice husky and pleasing. 'I see your image before me, looking out from an aging photograph…'

'Sara!' Jennifer gasped anxiously, jumping forward to attend to her daughter.

Sara had fainted.

'Chas, bring some cold water,' Jennifer instructed, rolling Sara onto her side on the floor, into the recovery position; but although deathly white, Sara was already recovering.

'Please… record it. Set it to record,' she gasped groggily, trying to raise herself up onto her elbow.

As Jennifer urged her to remain flat, Chas quickly returned with the water, demanding to know if it was to throw over her or for drinking purposes. Reaching up, Jennifer took hold of the glass, supporting Sara's head to give her a few sips.

'Set it to record,' she repeated. 'Please!'

Chas took up the remote control and set it to record.

Jennifer had never known her daughter to faint, but then she was an adolescent. She herself had once fainted at that age whilst having an oddly heavy period.

'Sara,' she murmured, close to the girl's ear, 'are you having a period? Do you need some tablets for the discomfort?'

Sara shook her head, struggling to sit upright and now clutching the glass of water. Some colour was returning to her cheeks.

'Do you hear what he's singing?'

Chas and Jennifer both shook their heads. Muttering about the usefulness of digital TV, Chas turned it back to the beginning of the song.

'It's him,' Sara informed them. 'He's singing of things only I could know.'

'You move through time, endless, timeless, bewitching me over and over again,' intoned Swordfish. 'Come back to me, come back to me…'

Sara felt faint again.

Later in the evening, she was clutching a glass of well-diluted brandy, which at least seemed to be keeping the colour in her cheeks. They had now watched the show three times, and throughout Jennifer and Chas had anxiously noted the colour coming and going from their daughter's face.

The band had demonstrated three of their songs from the new album, and each song title, apart from The Barley Break, was the name of a woman. They next chose to pay *Ode to Nancy,* followed by *Anthem For Jemim*a. The latter two were entirely original, Swordfish emphasised. There was no doubt about it, Sara declared. This man *was* her David Royale.

'He's singing about things only I could know,' she assured the anxious Jennifer and Chas. 'Also, I think I've mentioned this to you, when first I met him he played the piano for me.

The tune he chose was *The Barley Break* by William Byrd. I suppose you could say *The Barley Break* is our song.'

The ninth of September was at least a dry evening, although cooler than expected for the first part of September. From the garden the aroma of cooking food wafted into the house. Randall, having arrived with Vi half an hour earlier, and who anticipated being permitted to stay overnight again, was already enthusiastically drinking wine and assisting Chas in the barbeque shelter.

Sara felt like an automaton, her mind now totally fixated on the upcoming concert. The prospect of waiting for a week before the concert seemed endless. A unique situation for someone who had been round for centuries, and was used with waiting. Spotting Tracy, she pulled her aside to inform her of the startling outcome of the previous evening. Nearby, the girls invited from her school class were seated around a garden table, excitedly chattering and drinking cola, all of them clutching smartphones, taking "selfies" and energetically texting as they chatted.

Briefly she envied them their freshness, their youthful joy and their as yet relatively uncomplicated lives. But one day soon, they would grow up and no longer be carefree. She smiled gently in their direction, silently praying they would enjoy their carefree youth for the short time it lasted.

David had made himself known, but now she had to decide how on earth she was going to get near him and make herself known. Well, she had a week to think of something. If only she could find out which hotel the band was staying in. That might help. The cricket ground was situated near several excellent hotels.

Tracy herself was excited. At the end of the month, her historian-cum-television personality incubus friend, was going to be in the region for at least a couple of weeks, working on a documentary on Warkworth Castle in Northumberland.

'We're working out a means of seeing as much of each other as possible,' she informed Sara. 'His wife and family are remaining in London, which makes things easier for him.'

Sara, wrapped up in her own sheer delight that David (as she always thought of him, in spite of the string of names he'd acquired during their time together) was trying to make contact, tried to make a determined effort to share in her friend's pleasure. But her delight was mingled with anxiety. Her mind was buzzing.

Would things be the same for them? After all, they'd been apart for about as long as they'd been together. But he was clearly as desperate as herself to be with her, otherwise he wouldn't have thought of such an ingeniously public platform to make himself known to her. Her own discreet efforts, especially when she used the body of Marilyn Hamilton, paled into insignificance. But communication methods had literally exploded over the past decade and a half; social media, mobile phones and email made it so simple to keep in touch. But David was using global fame as a means. The band, Queen Anne's Revenge, was hugely popular in Australia, New Zealand, China and Japan. They were known in the US and Canada too, although the adulation level was lower there. However, now she knew who he was, and also more or less *where* he was, she was aflame with eagerness to meet him again.

'Someone's obviously impatient to meet you.' Tracy nodded over Sara's shoulder towards an approaching man who'd arrived with Alan and Jilly Reynolds, plus a woman whom she presumed to be his wife or partner. 'I don't know who he is, but he's definitely coming this way,' she murmured.

Turning to see whom Tracy was referring to, Sara realised it was Terry Richards.

'Oh dear, it's that exorcist fellow,' she whispered, hoping he wasn't intending to delve again into her long history.

She'd seen enough of him on that single evening she'd spent in his company. He was a nice man, she excused, but tiresome. Over the centuries she'd endured wearyingly long amounts of time with such people. This current body would be her home as long as it was able to breathe. There was nothing else to be said really.

'Oooh, introduce me; let's see if he realises we're the same,' Tracy responded mischievously.

Sara did so, and much to her relief he was pleasant and kindly and, having been assured of Chas and Jennifer's desire to "just get on with their lives", merely wished Sara a very happy birthday.

Tracy, who, after exchanging pleasantries, politely suggested she bring some drinks over. Once alone with Sara, he quietly assured her that should she need advice, as a clergyman he would always be available.

'I know you teenagers have such complicated lives,' he stated benignly.

'I keep forgetting I'm a teenager now,' Sara replied demurely. 'I feel ancient!'

'Wait until you're my age,' the newly returned Tracy remarked demurely.

'And you are… how old?' Terry Richards prompted gently, regarding both girls paternally.

'Fifteen – in a few weeks' time.' Tracy's smile was cherubic.

Terry Richards chatted for a short while before excusing himself, explaining he knew, as the birthday girl, that Sara would have to circulate and talk to everyone, so he'd speak with her later if they had the opportunity. Meanwhile, he and his wife had left a card and parcel for her in the dining room.

Sara and Tracy exchanged knowing glances. He hadn't suspected Tracy of being a succubus, and there was no reason why he should. Only Randall Olongu had spotted it.

'I'm going to have to write ever so many thank-you letters,' Sara remarked to her friend. 'People have been so very kind. But come and meet my school friends… I know you're aching to meet up with them.' Mischief tinged her voice.

'I refuse to pose for "selfies" with them,' protested Tracy. 'As birthday girl, you have no choice. You cannot refuse. I can.'

'Oh yes I can,' muttered Sara. 'I hate them. So unflattering. I shall ruthlessly use that as an excuse to avoid it.'

'I have come to hear all about her misdemeanours in school,' grinned Tracy, having been introduced to the schoolgirls.

Jennifer, a dutiful hostess, was circulating and ensuring everyone had drinks and nibbles to keep them going until the food was ready. She reached the schoolgirls' table just as Sara's friends were regaling Tracy with an example of how Sara had managed to all but silence a teacher.

It had occurred during current affairs, when they were required to choose a topic and use it for debate. Sara had suggested they debate whether or not there was still free speech in the United Kingdom, since she was certain it didn't exist anymore. Squealing with high-pitched laughter, they set Jennifer's teeth on edge. How did teenage girls manage to have such a high screeching laugh? They were like banshees, she decided irritably. She learned that Sara had successfully led the side of debate which considered free speech to be no longer evident in the UK, and she'd totally silenced the teacher, who believed free speech did exist, into the bargain.

Jennifer was feeling stressed and weary. Chas, she knew, was also feeling anxious. Sara was thirteen. An adolescent. She was their daughter, yet really they didn't actually *know* her now. There was so much depth to her, so many layers.

Supposing she was reunited with this David, as she called him? There was no way she or Chas would permit her to go running off with him; after all, theoretically she was only a minor. All of her protective maternal instincts rushed to the surface as she contemplated such a possibility. She'd been awake all last night thinking about it. Why oh why had they invited so many people to the party? All she wanted to do was sit in the conservatory with Chas's reassuring company and a glass of wine.

'Mum, you're daydreaming.' Sara was tugging at her arm. 'Sabrina wants to show you the pictures she's taken.'

Feigning interest, Jennifer obediently looked at the "selfies" Sabrina was holding in front of her. Another girl, Chloe, wanted to show her "selfies" too, mainly to display her new phone. The girl flicked her finger deftly across the screen, showing one picture after another. There was something reassuring about seeing Sara's classmates out of their school uniforms. They all looked so sophisticated, with their off-the-shoulder blouses – *They must be freezing,* she thought briefly – and short skirts. Two girls were wearing over-the-knee socks, which somehow added to their adult appearance. As for their hair, all of them were groomed to perfection. If anything, Sara was the most modestly clad of the group. As for Tracy, she could have easily walked into a pub and bought a glass of brandy for herself without any problem at all. Sara looked modest, demure and infinitely more sensible, more adult, in her behaviour. She stood out from the others, including Tracy.

At the barbeque Randall Olongu was assisting Chas.

'You certainly like your barbies,' he observed, nodding towards the latest acquisition.

'Jennifer calls them my man toys,' Chas informed him.

Eyeing Chas quizzically, Randall commented, 'You a bit stressed, mate?' He pronounced it '"strissed". Deftly he flicked a burger over and then proceeded to do the same with a series of sausages.

'Yes, I'll tell you later. I'm worried, shall we say, but it's not a life or death drama.'

The first batch of barbequed food was ready to eat, Chas decided. Time to bang the dinner gong. In spite of having his new third barbeque, he wasn't enjoying himself as much as he usually did when cooking al fresco.

'So, is it your missis?' Randall nodded in Jennifer's direction. She'd moved away from the schoolgirls and was now refilling the glasses of some of Chas's colleagues. 'She's putting on a good show, but something is amiss.' He took a deep drink of rose wine. He wasn't fond of rose, but it'd been the nearest bottle for him to get hold of. 'I'm thinking it's your girl who worries you, and I can tell you this. She's going to be okay. The little miss is lit up like a Christmas tree; if you switched your garden lights off she'd give off a glow, I tell you. Well, maybe that's an exaggeration. But she is all lit up, and I have a good feeling about it.'

'Then I hope your good feeling is correct.'

Chas wondered what would happen next Saturday evening. He thought that Sara seemed to have resigned herself to waiting for the concert before meeting Swordfish, although how that could be arranged was beyond him. She'd spent some time last night trying to figure out which hotel he might be staying in, but currently the band wasn't even in the north east. They had a concert in Cardiff tonight, and on Wednesday were playing at Birmingham.

'Do me a favour, Randall.' He looked at Jennifer still gamely refilling glasses. 'What you've just said… Tell it to Jen.'

'Will do,' the Australian agreed cheerfully. He was having a good time, he reflected contentedly. It was a good party, everyone seemed friendly and he was free to have a glass of wine or two. Or more. He'd been totally dry since last weekend. As a pilot he had been disciplined where alcohol was concerned, although Vi claimed she couldn't believe it. But a dude had to let his hair down sometimes, he excused.

Terry Richards observed Tracy whilst conversing with one of Jennifer's dentist colleagues; somehow the subject had drifted onto dental veneers, which didn't interest him at all. He knew Sara had admitted to knowing someone who was a fellow incubus – or succubus. Surely that person must be young Tracy? She had smiled innocently, but there was nothing girlish about her. However, there was nothing sinister about her either, and he would have surely sensed it had it been there. He wished he could talk with her, try to find out something about her background. But, he sighed inwardly, tonight was not the occasion to do so.

The party was moving on apace, and Jennifer thankfully noticed guests were beginning to drift away. Sara's school friends had gone, the embers in the two charcoal barbeques were almost dead and the gas barbeque was switched off. A huge quantity of food had been consumed, alcohol likewise. Elsie and her husband, helped by Sara and Tracy, had all worked hard to keep the food circulating and the glasses and dishes washed. They'd also kept a constant stream of tea and coffee going for those who desired it. Rick had also come to help, but had begun to join in with the party instead.

Early that morning Jennifer and Chas had visited the supermarket and purchased numerous bottles of wine, plus cans of beer and lager. But, as often seemed to happen at parties, so many people had arrived carrying at least one bottle and many had brought two, along with cans of beer, they had nearly as much alcohol at the end of the evening as they had at the beginning.

Their neighbours were very much present, seated on the patio, cheerfully warming themselves beneath the patio heaters. It was always a good idea to invite neighbours, in Chas and Jennifer's opinion. It meant they couldn't complain about the noise. Jennifer had noted approvingly that Sara had spent some time chatting with Simon. The latter had long since returned home and gone to bed, but at least Sara, along with Tracy, had included him and kept the lad amused.

Susan, Simon's mother, who was now drinking coffee as opposed to wine, caught Jennifer's eye and nodded towards Sara and Tracy.

'Girlsh mature so much more quickly than boysh, don't you think?' she observed. 'Those girlsh from Sara's class at school were pure goal bait! Am I allowed to shay that?' Her voice was slurred.

'Hmmm, apparently Sara's class held a debate at school as to whether or not there's such a thing as free speech in this country at the present time. I think they decided it doesn't exist anymore.' Jennifer sank gratefully onto a seat, then immediately jumped up as someone came to say goodbye.

'I told you, girlsh are more mature than boysh... I shuppose I should go too.' Susan looked around for her husband, only to be informed that he'd returned home half an hour ago.

'Ah well, I had better shay goodnight too then.' Susan drained her coffee cup. 'Poor guy, I think he was pole-axed when that Australian man gave him a tot of rye whisky. His doshn't drink spirits usually.' Unsteadily she wove her way out of the garden. 'It would be a good idea if we had a gate adjoining our two gardens,' she observed brightly. 'Make things eashier.'

'Take my arm,' Sara suggested. 'I'll see you safely home.'

'You alwaysh have such lovely manners,' beamed Susan. 'Girlsh are more mature than boysh,' she repeated.

'Thank goodness they've all gone.' Jennifer kicked off her shoes having escorted the last of the guests from the house. 'I need a cup of tea.' She massaged one of her feet and then turned her attention to the other. 'Maybe I should have worn flip-flops.'

'Been a bonzer good night, though,' Randall Olongu reflected, eyeing his empty glass. Room for one more? There probably was, he decided.

Sara and Tracy had now gone to bed; only Jennifer, Chas, Vi and Randall were seated in the conservatory, surrounded by the detritus of empty glasses and plates, crumpled paper napkins, scattered cutlery (disposable, for ease) and empty bottles and cans. Elsie had said she would arrive early in the morning to clean up the bulk of the mess. Sara and Tracy had been excellent, and had already made inroads into the clearing up. They had put yet another load into the dishwasher before going to bed, but the place still looked a mess.

Vi was being heavily critical of the five school friends who'd been invited to the party. What kind of party did they think it was going to be? Her lips were disapprovingly pursed. They looked like they'd stepped out of some sort of vice club.

'That's how they dress, Mum,' Jennifer stated wearily. 'At least you can't now tell me I've made Sara grow up too fast… She was the most covered up out of the group!'

Vi pursed her lips even tighter and decided she would go to bed.

'Well, you both survived the evening, and did it very well,' Randall observed gently as Vi's footsteps could be heard going upstairs. 'No one would have guessed you were both feeling stressed.'

'You did,' Chas stated mildly.

'Aaaah, but I have inbuilt radar.' Randall raised his refilled glass in salute. 'You are two feisty Poms!'

'Two anxious and stressed Poms,' Chas declared, declining to have his wine glass refilled. 'Now we're alone, Jen and I can tell you what happened last night.'

'Bonzer!' Randall exclaimed happily, settling himself into a chair like a child awaiting a nice story.

CHAPTER THIRTEEN

'Look, I can't say this without sounding totally gooey, so I'll just let it out. I truly love the pair of you and will never intentionally do anything to cause trouble,' Sara affirmed sincerely.

Jennifer felt her eyes misting. Her daughter was still there, entangled of course within numerous layers of other personalities, but she *was* still there. During the past few months, though, she'd felt an inner niggling of guilt and regret because she'd never been a mother who regularly declared love for her daughter. Chas too had been equally restrained. She and Chas were very open with each other, ending phone calls with the words 'Love you,' and saying it every night before going to sleep. But with their daughter they'd behaved differently. Why? She could think of no satisfactory explanation. They loved her – she loved them in return. Perhaps they'd been content to take that love for granted? Even now she felt awkward declaring her feelings for her daughter. But come to think of it, she and Vi had never been sentimental towards each other. In fact, when had she ever told her mother that she loved her? Certainly not during the past decade.

'I will always love you, you know that,' she assured Sara. 'We both will.' She looked towards Chas who nodded in affirmation. 'Maybe we *are* still coming to terms with what's happened to you, but our feelings won't change. And we were obviously concerned that having found this David, or Swordfish as he is now, you would elope or something.'

'I won't run away or do anything illegal.' Sara's smile was seraphic. 'As for your feelings, I know how deeply you care, I always did,' she added gently.

Jennifer seriously wondered if her daughter was reading her mind.

They were all pretty much ready to set out for the concert. On the coffee table lay the detritus of a recent meal, which, unusually, they'd casually eaten whilst watching the news on television. Both Chas and Jennifer invariably avoided combining dining with television. Chas had suggested a refill of coffee for everyone; it might help them keep warm, he supposed. Jennifer had shaken her head, wanting to avoid using the lavatory during the show. Sara had likewise shaken her head, for the same reason. Chas was drinking coffee alone.

Having heard the song *The Barley Break* numerous times during the past few days, he manoeuvred his mind towards other matters. He had initially been concerned lest his daughter should decide to run away with this rock star, Swordfish. Having now received her assurance that this wouldn't happen, he wished to know what a *Barley Break* was anyway. Since it'd been downloaded, he felt he was more familiar with it than the original composer.

'Well, it's a sort of chasing game,' Sara enlightened them. 'Six people; three couples of men and women. The two in the middle keep their arms linked and chase the other two couples, who do *not* keep their arms linked. It's a bit complicated, I suppose,' she explained musingly. 'I think the rules perhaps changed from country to country, and generation to generation. As I know it, you need a long field – such as a barley field just after harvest time. The middle bit of the field, where the "linked" couple begin the game, is called "hell". The two free couples sort of dance around to tease the linked couple; when one of them is caught, he or she must remain in hell until the other person is caught. When a man and a woman of the same couple are caught, then the linked couple can break – a barley break – and a new game begins. It's more fun than it sounds,' she half smiled in reminiscence, adding, 'Of course, there can be more than three couples playing, but that's the minimum, obviously.'

Chas tried to imagine it and failed. 'I think you and I shall stick to tennis,' he suggested to Jennifer.

'I don't know,' Jennifer replied slowly. 'A young, courting couple; they might enjoy it, you know.'

Chas wanted to know why the middle strip was called hell.

Sara shrugged expressively. 'I don't know why. Maybe because it was difficult to catch people sometimes? I never thought to question it at the time. But the game could become quite bawdy,' she admitted, giving a knowing smirk. 'Country folk were anything but prim, even during Queen Victoria's reign. They had a healthy, uninhibited approach to lovemaking.'

The weather for the concert was damp and cold, more like late November than mid-September. All of them were wearing trousers and trainers and had elected to wear anoraks, much to Jennifer's disappointment. Trousers with trainers was her least favourite look. She much preferred to go to the theatre, which meant she could wear a glamorous dress, killer heels, and show off some nice jewellery. The county cricket ground was not the place to do that. Not for a Queen Anne's Revenge concert, at any rate. Much to Chas's amusement, she'd tucked a pair of yellow fluffy earmuffs into her bag, along with some fingerless mittens. She'd also considered taking a flask of hot soup, then wondered if they would be allowed to actually taken that into the grounds. Probably not, she answered this question herself. But no doubt there would be plenty of food and drink stations at the cricket ground. As well as wearing the anoraks, Jennifer had placed some fleecy blankets into a rucksack (for Chas to carry), since she wished to be well prepared.

Sara was in a state of excitement, which meant she was all but impervious to the cold. Her excitement, however, was combined with anxiety. Obviously David – or Swordfish – wanted to get in touch with her. But always she wondered: how would things work out between them? She gave herself a mental shake. As long as they were reunited and could keep in touch, everything would fall into place, surely.

Just as Sara was loading up the dishwasher and Jennifer was adding a new layer of eyeliner, Tracy arrived. Her attire was much the same as everyone else's, with the addition of a knitted hat with a large pom-pom. 'Good idea,' approved Jennifer, now wondering whether or not to follow suit. But, she reasoned, surely the hood on her anorak would suffice.

At that moment it occurred to her that she'd never once asked Tracy anything about her past. Tracy's story would be every bit as gripping as Sara's, she supposed. Yet it had never occurred to her to enquire. Of course, they'd been very wrapped up in trying to regain their former Sara, but a niggle of guilt persisted. She ought to have talked to Tracy; especially since it was unlikely she could talk about it with her parents. Still, she excused hopefully, at least Tracy had Sara to communicate with.

'Since they're called Queen Anne's Revenge, after Blackbeard's ship, how is it none of the band has called themselves after the man himself?' Chas wanted to know, as he set the burglar alarm and locked up the house.

'No idea,' Sara and Tracy chorused.

Soon they were all in the car; Chas was wearing his latest baseball cap, which carried an Australian airline logo. Obviously it had been given to him by Randall. Quickly he began typing the coordinates for the park-and-ride into his satnav. Since none of them was familiar with the cricket ground, and the website recommended using the park-and-ride, they'd decided to adhere to this advice. In the rear-view mirror he glimpsed Sara's face. She was outwardly composed, he noted. What would happen to his daughter once she was reunited with her several-times husband? He could only hope she wouldn't be disappointed.

'How did we manage without satnavs?' questioned Jennifer. They seemed so much a part of modern driving, like rear cameras for parking, and heated seats.

'You mean how did *you* manage without satnavs,' grinned Chas. His wife's lack of a sense of direction was the stuff of legend.

Jennifer gave him one of her swipes. 'Cheeky,' she reproved. 'I have never been disgustingly lost.'

Chas gave a guffaw of disbelieving laughter, then reversed the car from the drive.

'Well, we're off. Queen Anne's Revenge should be something of an experience. Hopefully a good one.'

'Well, you liked the songs they showcased on TV,' Sara retorted mildly.

'I think they'll be awesome,' nodded Tracy. She too had misgivings. What if Sara's long-time partner was totally different to the person he had been? An incubus could change, in fact did change, with every body he or she took over. Plus, he and Sara had been apart for years. She sincerely hoped her friend wouldn't be unhappy about those changes. For that matter, she also hoped he wouldn't be offended by *her* changes.

Their journey was smooth and without incident. As Chas drove, Jennifer sat quietly as Sara began to deliver to them her plan of how she might be able to get backstage to see this Swordfish person. But first of all, she had stated, they needed to get to their seats and obtain a general idea of the venue. Once she'd finished speaking, it seemed a simple idea, so certainly nothing could go wrong; Jennifer was as certain as she could be of that. However, she couldn't help but feel a few twinges of apprehension. Like Chas and Tracy, she was worried in case Sara was disappointed with the outcome of the evening.

The cricket ground was new territory for all of them. Chas and Jennifer had only glimpsed it occasionally on *North East News*, when sport was reported. They were totally uninterested in cricket, even though Chas had been very good at it (according to Chas) when he was at school. Tennis was basically the only sport which captured their interest.

All too soon – for Jennifer at least – they'd parked the car at the park-and-ride, taken note of where the car was placed and were riding on the bus for the short journey to the cricket ground. Delving into her handbag she produced a couple of small cellophane bags, tucked one of them into her coat pocket and presented Chas with the other.

'Earplugs; put them in your pocket,' she instructed, much to the hilarity of two male youths who were seated opposite, and who, until that moment, had been shamelessly ogling Tracy and Sara.

Chas needed his earplugs. The "warm-up band" hailed from nearby Darlington and were the loudest he'd ever heard. They consisted of five young men and two women; the latter were so heavily made up he reckoned they could be anywhere between the ages of eighteen and fifty.

'They're certainly flaunting their assets!' he shouted in Jennifer's ear.

He gave them all top marks for bravery, though. The males were either shirtless or wearing brief vests, and the girls wore indecently skimpy clothing; yet there they were, standing on a stage on an autumnal evening. 'They're true northerners!' he approved.

'I'm going to go now!' Sara shouted into Chas's ear.

They'd discussed it in detail. During the warm-up act, Sara intended to leave her body, slip into the backstage area and there find Swordfish. It would be easy to do so, she'd explained. She would simply go into his mind and let him know she was there, then try to impress upon him her name and address. Jennifer had initially been concerned regarding the vapour trail Sara seemed to emit whenever she left her body – would it be visible?

'I'll keep low,' Sara had assured her. 'I doubt if anyone will be looking downwards towards the floor. You know, when I first began, I hardly left any trail at all. It became more noticeable as time went on and I became stronger. Anyway, the plan is so simple, nothing can go wrong.'

As Jennifer looked on anxiously, as had been arranged Chas wrapped an arm supportively about Sara as she slumped against him, her head resting on his shoulder. They both looked relaxed, Jennifer decided; so, if Sara was quick, no one would consider anything was amiss. Glancing towards the floor, she briefly observed a quick-moving flash of vapour. Sara was right; it was so low to the floor it was barely discernible in the gloom. Had she not known what to look for, she would never have seen it.

Chas was finding Sara's head lay heavily against his shoulder. It wasn't uncomfortable, but it was surprising how much the human head weighed, he reflected, whilst trying to make sense of the warm-up band. They really were lousy, he decided, wondering if his distaste was because he was getting old. It was more than probable, he mused inwardly. Certainly the younger members of the audience – and the majority were, he calculated, under the age of thirty – appeared to be enjoying it. The more mature people, such as himself, merely looked bored. Then he became aware of someone from the row behind tapping him on his other shoulder. He managed to half turn and found himself looking into the moon-like face of an extremely large woman. His first reaction was to wonder if she'd paid for two seats instead of one. The woman was mouthing something; he couldn't make out what she was saying. He took out an earplug.

Determinedly, the women placed her mouth against his now unplugged ear. 'I think she's ill,' she gave a nod towards Sara.

Guessing what was happening, Jennifer, who was two seats away from Chas – Sara and then Tracy being between them – bellowed, 'Oh, she's okay, just excited about seeing Queen Anne's Revenge!'

Chas, having thanked the woman for her concern, managed to turn to sit squarely in his seat again, only for Sara's head to slip from his shoulder to his lap. As deftly as possible he heaved her upright again, hoping everyone – including the concerned lady behind – was absorbed in the show. But Tracy reached across Sara and touched his arm.

'She's going somewhere!' she shouted to Chas.

Turning his head, Chas saw her forcefully making her way along the row of seats, forcing her huge bulk between people's knees and the seats in front, obviously on some sort of mission.

'Maybe she needs the bathroom!' he shouted optimistically. 'Or maybe one of the burger vans outside!' He wasn't feeling very politically correct at that moment. 'She looks as if she eats a lot of burgers!' he added waspishly.

Unable to hear what he was saying, Tracy gave a vague nod of agreement, whilst desperately hoping Sara would complete her operation quickly.

Unfortunately, moments later, two paramedics arrived. Clearly the helpful lady had been overly helpful. Their seats were, unfortunately, in the middle of a row, making it as difficult as possible for everyone. But with remarkably deft efficiency, the medics soon extracted Sara from her seat and laid her, unresponsive, on a stretcher. The helpful lady, meanwhile, was telling everyone who could listen, above the noise, that she hated modern, laid-back parents. Just fancy, the girl's father hadn't even realised she was unconscious! Mercifully few people were able to hear.

'You two go with Sara; I'll stay here and wait for her!' Tracy bellowed into Jennifer's ear.

Where is Sara? Desperately, Jennifer looked around for a sign of the succubus returning to her daughter. The medics were shaking their heads and signalling to her and Chas to follow them; they hurried towards a waiting ambulance. Even in the parking area where the ambulance waited, the warm-up band still sounded unbelievably noisy.

'We're taking her to hospital!' shouted a young, female paramedic. 'We don't know what the matter is – she's unresponsive, but her vital signs are there. She has reflexes, her pulse is steady, her pupils react, oxygen levels are good… She's quite simply unconscious.' Deftly, she attached an oxygen mask to Sara's face. 'I'll get an I/V into her, just in case,' she added efficiently.

Jennifer and Chas looked at each other helplessly. 'Which hospital are you taking her to?' Chas inquired.

Upon being informed, gathering his wits about him, Chas instructed Jennifer, 'You go with Sara. I'll get back to Tracy, and we'll to the park-and-ride and follow in the car,' he assured Jennifer. Surely Sara would be back with Tracy now? She *had* to be. 'I'll be with you as quickly as possible, darling.'

At that moment they heard one of the paramedics – he seemed to be in charge as he'd been directing the medics dealing with Sara – talking into his mobile.

'What? One of Queen Anne's Revenge has collapsed? Yes, we'll get a crew backstage immediately,' he spoke in clipped, no-nonsense tones. 'Crew backstage!' He waved a beckoning hand towards some nearby green–clad medics. 'Follow me!' Clutching their equipment, they sped away.

Jennifer, looking pale and vulnerable in her fluffy earmuffs and bulky anorak, gave Chas an anxious look. What was happening backstage? Was it something to do with Sara managing to get to Swordfish? *Just imagine you're at work,* she told herself. *You have to remain calm.* She took a deep breath.

'We'll be fine; these people know what they're doing,' she assured him.

At that moment the driver shouted to have the rear doors closed. Chas stepped out of the vehicle and dashed back to their seating area, where Tracy was sitting alone. Momentarily, the noise had calmed, and the lead singer was speaking, introducing a new song. As he approached, his heart sank. Tracy was looking around anxiously… surely an indication Sara hadn't returned yet. The large, helpful lady – whom Chas desperately wanted to throttle – was now tapping Tracy on her shoulder. No doubt she wanted to know if Tracy was in danger of collapsing too.

'Is she here?' he demanded anxiously, trying to ignore the overly helpful lady.

'No.' Tracy looked concerned.

'Something's happened backstage. I overheard a paramedic taking a call; someone's collapsed. They said it was one of the band,' Chas explained.

'Swordfish?'

'No idea – obviously because of confidentiality he didn't mention any names!' Chas had to shout again, as the band had begun a new song.

'But I have an idea!' Tracy shouted above the scream of two electric violins. 'They've taken her to casualty, right?'

'Right.'

'Which one? You have to go there obviously. You need to leave me and go and get your car. Follow Jennifer to the hospital.'

'Just what I've been saying to Jen. But I can't leave you alone; you have to come too!' he bellowed. *My, it was hard work holding a conversation in the midst of this noise.*

'No. Leave me here. I'll be okay. I know what I'm doing; I'm older than I look.' She gave a wry smile. 'If anyone asks my age, I can pass for eighteen or nineteen with this make-up on.'

She spoke truly. With her smoky eye make-up and expertly applied blusher, she could indeed pass for being of age.

'I have some money, so when Sara returns I'll get a taxi and bring her to casualty. Keep in touch with your mobile!' Tracy screamed, her throat feeling raw with the effort of holding a conversation.

'With what?.....I mean, how will manage to do that?' bellowed Chas. After all, the Sara backstage was simply a stream of vapour.

'I have an idea of how I can do it,' Tracy pulled her phone from her pocket and waved it in front of him. 'Plus I have Sara's number in it but not yours. Use her phone. I saw Jennifer carrying Sara's bag!' she shrieked. This was murder, she decided, anxiously peering at the floor, looking for signs of Sara returning.

Comprehending, Chas gave a brisk nod, and pulling out his wallet extracted two twenty-pound notes and pressed them into Tracy's hand. 'Take them. Just in case,' he advised, and was about to leave, when the large lady tugged at his arm. Pulling him down to her level, she shouted into his ear, 'Is she okay?!'

Restraining himself from being rude, Chas gave her a thumbs-up sign, then hurried from the concert ground.

As he looked around for a means of transport to return to the park-and-ride – the buses wouldn't be returning for hours, as the show had only just begun – he pulled his phone out of his pocket to call for a taxi. The air was pungent with the smell of cooking burgers and hot dogs from the snack vans, the acrid smell of frying onions being uppermost. The onions made him feel nauseous. They seemed to be doing a roaring trade, he noted absently. Just at that moment a taxi drew up and a group of excited youths spilled out. Eagerly he rushed forward, thrusting his head through the front passenger door of the vehicle.

'Can you get me back to the park-and-ride?' he demanded anxiously.

'Get in,' the driver cheerfully instructed.

Thankfully, he sank into the passenger seat, automatically glancing at his wristwatch. Jen and Sara would be well on their way to the hospital by now. In that instant his phone vibrated and then gave a bleep. It was a text from Jen; they were already entering the hospital car park, siren blaring. If only he could attach a flashing light and a siren onto his car, he sighed.

In the cricket ground Tracy kept looking around anxiously for Sara returning. When she did arrive, she was barely noticeable. In fact, it wasn't until she actually felt Sara herself nudging at her mind that she realised she was there at all.

'It's all gone wrong,' she informed Sara.

Cleverly, Sara had spread her fine vapour trail so thinly it was totally invisible. It was nearly dark now; the air of anticipation in the ground was palpable. Everywhere seemed to bedecked with lights. Soon Queen Anne's Revenge would take to the stage – providing Swordfish was conscious, of course. It appeared the warm-up band had done what they were supposed to do. The audience was a seething mass of waving arms.

'You need to come with me, literally with me,' she explained to Sara. 'It's just for a short while; we won't bond permanently…' Tracy paused; could a body hold more than one succubus? They could "nudge" each other mentally, but to actually accept an entire succubus… could it be done? In all of her many years she'd never tried it. It seemed a distasteful thing to do, a total invasion of privacy. Anyway, she'd never met anyone who'd suggested such a thing.

'A sort of piggyback?' Sara's voice rang in her head.

'Yes, give it a try. At least until we can get into a taxi.'

It worked. It felt strange, but it worked. Jumping from her seat and firmly clutching her bag, Tracy ran from the showground into the car park where Chas had found his taxi just a short while ago. Unlike Chas, she barely registered the smell of cooking burgers and onions.

'I need a taxi.' She clutched the sleeve of a nearby elderly attendant who was wearing a luminous baseball hat and a high-vis jacket. He was unmissable. 'My mother is ill,' she lied blatantly without a twinge of conscience.

'Come this way.' The attendant led her towards a gate, where already yet another taxi was approaching. 'Where to, miss?' he asked kindly.

Warming to his benevolent manner, she replied truthfully that she wanted to get to the hospital as soon as possible.

'University Hospital of North Durham,' she explained as

he opened the rear door for her to climb in. 'Thank you for your assistance.'

'You are most welcome, and I hope your mother gets well soon,' he beamed benignly at her. *It was lovely to know there were some polite teenagers around these days.*

Leaning back in the seat, she felt Sara making an exit. In the darkness, the manoeuvre was totally invisible. But during that brief time, wedged together in one body, she had discovered what had occurred backstage at the cricket ground.

Getting backstage had been no problem at all. Finding Swordfish had also been very simple. But as Sara had known, there was no chance he would be alone. She could hardly show herself in her shadowy form of Maude Dubreise. The scene was one of immense bustle. People were milling around; sound technicians checking out instruments and amplifiers, electricians anxiously chatting about lighting. Two young female goths had managed to inveigle their way in, hoping to gain an introduction to Horatio, who was nowhere to be seen at that moment. A roadie, exchanging a lewd, knowing glance with a bouncer, explained that Horatio was *resting* in his changing room, as the bouncer ejected the protesting young goths from the area. A blowsy looking professional photographer, who also happened to be Castor's girlfriend, was swiftly moving around, taking pictures. With purple hair and surgically enhanced breasts and lips (looking suspiciously akin to the infamous "trout pout"), she was clearly a familiar figure to most of the people there. She was shouting names and demanding they face the camera and strike a pose.

Castor and Pollux were performing what looked like Pilates. Swordfish himself, looking calm and relaxed, was conversing with a fellow band member whom she recognised as Warlock, who clutched what looked like a very large glass of whisky. They were deep in conversation; clearly an earnest but amicable discussion was taking place.

But Swordfish was *her* David; in the strange way their kind had of knowing one another, she recognised that he was *definitely* an incubus. She'd not been misled by his songs. This was something which had worried her over the past week.

Keeping, for the most part, very low, she extended a thin tendril, embracing his mind with it – much as Tracy had done to her when they'd first met. Whilst so doing, she told him her present name and her address. It was the first time she'd actually tried to give information in this way to a fellow incubus. Would it work? The effect was startling. Swordfish staggered backwards, falling against a guitar stand. Man, guitar and stand toppled over. It was all over very quickly, and Swordfish instantly sat upright, but the damage had been done, not only to the guitar and stand but to the man himself. He'd bumped his head and blood was streaming from a cut on his brow. Amid assistants shouting for paramedics, Swordfish was quick to sit bolt upright, as Sara retreated a short distance from him. Artemis grabbed a handkerchief to stem the flow of blood, but, seizing the piece of cloth, the injured man immediately stood upright, looking eagerly around and shouting, 'Sara Roseberry! Where are you?'

It had worked. He knew who she was! Elated, she knew she ought to return to her seat, but she so wanted to ensure all was well here.

The band were aghast, and a manager suggested the show should be cancelled. Swordfish managed to shout there was no need, as he wasn't badly hurt. He merely needed a plaster to cover the gash on his head. And, most importantly, where was Sara Roseberry?

Again extending a tendril towards him, Sara informed him she was about to return to her seat, and then followed this information by repeating her home address, just as Horatio finally appeared.

'Man, you are one confused dude. Bit like the old days,' he drawled.

'I'm not confused,' protested Swordfish.

By the time paramedics arrived, Swordfish was giving every impression of being of sound mind again, and insisted the show wasn't going to be cancelled. He'd not received a hard knock; the damage was simply due to him having had contact with a sharp edge. Nor was he confused. All he needed was a plaster. And a clean shirt, since he'd bled onto his current one.

'Tho, who ith this Thara Wosebewwy, then?' Castor's girlfriend demanded, speaking with a marked lisp. She was loath to admit it, but she had, just that day, had some cosmetic dentistry performed, hence her speech impediment. Her enthusiastic photography had ensured the entire incident had been caught on camera. Taking a final shot, she turned her attention to reviewing her photographs. More professional than she actually looked, she would shortly be taking official photographs of the gig itself.

'A girl in the audience. I can't explain now. But she's in the audience.' Swordfish had regained his composure. 'I need to go to the dressing room for a shirt.'

'Brought one.' Artemis was brisk, efficient. 'Go on stage with your current shirt on and you'll frighten the audience. Look, dude, you seem okay. Put this on and let's get on with the gig. The warm-up band is all but finished. You can collapse later.'

Somehow, Artemis had calmed the situation. The paramedics were still eager to take Swordfish to hospital, but accepted his refusal. They had no other choice.

'Did you say Sara Roseberry?' One of the paramedics frowned, perplexed. 'I know that name.'

'Course you do,' the senior medic informed him. 'She's the young girl we just sent to hospital.'

'You see? I'm not hallucinating,' said Swordfish.

Alarmed upon hearing her name mentioned by the paramedics, Sara realised it was definitely time to leave, but was temporarily stalled by the purple-haired pouting photographer.

'Damnation,' the young woman exclaimed, shaking her head at a picture she was reviewing. 'Oh thit... a few are wuined. I don't know what'th happened. Look,' she shoved her camera viewer into Castor's face, unaware he was more interested in eyeing her enhanced cleavage, shown very much to advantage in a black patent-leather boned corset. 'There'th a mitht about Thodrfish's head. And on thith one. And thith one.' Pressing the review button, she flashed pictures on the screen. 'It'th really spoiled them,' she grumbled. 'It would have been good footage of hith accident.' She suddenly brightened. 'But I thould be able to eliminate it on my PC,' she said optimistically.

'Your lisp is so sexy,' Castor approved. 'But it's time to clear the area and get this show on the road. Okay, Swordfish? Good to go?'

'I am now.'

Cleansed of bloodstains and wearing a clean shirt, Swordfish looked ready for action. Those who were more observant noticed he seemed to be distractedly looking around for something. Sara moved away. It was time to return to her body. But... there must be someone else in the audience called Sara Roseberry. How could it possibly be that she would require hospital treatment?

Chas rushed into the casualty department, wildly looking around for Jennifer. There was no sign of her. Just as he was texting, "Where are you?", she appeared, looking stressed and frightened. Sara, it transpired, was still in an ambulance. There was a queue; the ambulance crew were waiting for a cubicle to be freed up so she could be brought in to the actual department.

This is what we've been hearing about on the news, thought Chas. *Ambulances being stuck at hospitals and unable to go about and do what they're supposed to do!*

'I've spoken to a member of the casualty team; he was very professional and capable. In fact, everyone is so very nice. Sara's not in any danger, and the next cubicle that's freed up is ours. Tracy texted on Sara's phone to say they're okay, both together and are going to find a taxi. And I've been in touch with Jilly to put us on the prayer chain.' The words tumbled out in a bewildering rush. Pulling a tissue from her pocket, Jennifer dabbed her eyes, vaguely noticing it was stained with mascara, but smudged mascara was not her priority at present.

Chas hugged her, rubbing his cheek against her hair. 'They'll be here soon, and then we'll have Sara back again—' he paused abruptly. 'What on earth is a prayer chain?'

'Oh, Jilly runs it. I read about it in the church magazine,' again Jennifer's words came tumbling out at rapid speed. 'Apparently you phone someone who's a member of the chain… I only know Jilly at present. And that person phones another, and that person phones the next on the chain, until it goes around. So they're all praying, and I can't tell you how much better I feel just knowing that! Chas, how could things go so wrong? It initially sounded so straightforward!'

Releasing her, Chas shook his head. *It had indeed seemed so straightforward.* 'It's the fault of the nosy fat woman,' he grumbled. 'Why couldn't she mind her own business?'

'Don't call her fat,' Jennifer objected mildly. 'She might be big because she has cancer or something. They're often given steroids now for that. I suppose she thought she was doing her civic duty.'

'I call it interference,' Chas objected.

The casualty department wasn't as busy as he would have expected for a Saturday evening, but there was a notice on the reception desk saying "approximately 4 hours waiting time". He suddenly blinked in amazement; a very small girl – she looked barely older than Sara – was approaching, pushing a wheelchair holding a very substantial looking man. He baulked at using the word "fat" following Jennifer's rebuke. He could hear some of their conversation as they drew near.

'… a proper nurse, then?' the man was asking.

'Naaah, I'm a healthcare assistant. Not qualified like a registered nurse,' the girl replied.

Chas gave a sigh of relief; she didn't appear old enough to carry responsibility.

'So, you going out after finishing your shift? Shame not to on a Saturday.' The man, Chas absently observed, was attached to an oxygen cylinder.

'Naaah,' the assistant replied. 'Ah were asked to work a few extra hours the night. Ah need the money, plus me hair's mingin' so mebe it's just as well. Ah want to…' Her voice trailed away as she walked past Chas and Jennifer, coping very well with the wheelchair in spite of her diminutive size. With relief, Chas noticed she didn't look quite so young at close range.

At that moment their names were called. Sara was to be moved at last to a cubicle. They heard one of the paramedics remarking that this was relatively quick; often they had to stay in the queue for much longer. Chas, who was still feeling inclined to be grumpy, found his mood not improved when Jennifer explained that whilst she was standing at the reception desk giving Sara's personal details, she heard the person at the next station telling the reception clerk that she had sinusitis and had come to casualty because she couldn't obtain an appointment with her GP that fitted in with her commitments.

They were shown to the cubicle where Sara was to be placed, all the while Chas muttering truculently about people who used the NHS inappropriately. As they waited, they heard someone's authoritative tones instructing people to stand aside unless they wanted their feet to be squashed by trolley wheels.

'They're bringing Sara,' Jennifer stated with relief.

At that moment Sara's phone, which she'd placed in her pocket, bleeped, indicating a text had arrived. It was from Tracy; they were in a taxi and on their way.

'Thank goodness,' Chas stated with relief.

'It's the work of the prayer chain,' Jennifer decided.

'Whatever it is, it's a relief,' Chas intoned fervently. He returned to the subject of inappropriate use of the NHS. 'How can sinusitis be an accident or an emergency? This is an accident and emergency department, not a GP's practice!' he persisted, as Jennifer shook her head, rolling her eyes upwards.

'Search me,' replied a paramedic. 'Folks these days have queer ideas of what is or isn't an emergency.'

With practised efficiency the trolley was steered into the cubicle, with Sara's slender form lying, still inert, upon it. Jennifer felt like weeping again, she looked so small and vulnerable. The scene was having the same effect on Chas, she realised. He had quit grumbling and looked as if he was fighting to retain his composure.

'Tracy is on her way,' he pulled Jennifer close and whispered into her ear. 'We'll have Sara back in no time.'

Jennifer nodded numbly. Nothing mattered at this moment other than having Sara conscious again. Even if the being that restored her was hundreds of years old. As for Tracy, her assistance this evening had been invaluable. Some time soon she really must find out something about Tracy's past. Her only knowledge was, that she was centuries older than Sara and had a male incubus friend who was a historian, author and television personality. Was her relationship with the television personality as deep and meaningful as Sara's was with Swordfish? She had no idea. During the past few months, being so focused on what was happening with Sara, she'd not spared a thought for Tracy.

Seated in the back of the taxi, Tracy recognised they were approaching the entrance to the hospital. It was time to give Sara a piggyback again. The driver, approaching the lights of the hospital entrance, glanced in the rear-view mirror. Was that a thin wisp of smoke he could see? There was no smell of tobacco…. 'hey, you lighting up?' he demanded abruptly. 'No smoking allowed.'

Tracy shook her head innocently. 'Never tried a cigarette in my life,' she assured him, adding inwardly, *Well, not in this body anyway.* She could feel Sara's amusement.

Having paid the driver, she pulled her phone out of her bag and texted: "Am in casualty entrance. Where are you?" Jennifer must have been clutching Sara's mobile, because the reply came instantly: "Coming to find you. Stay put."

The place was busy but not manically so. At least not yet. From ten o'clock onwards casualty departments livened up; she knew that from former experience. It was still only nine fifteen, which she found strange, as it felt so much later. Queen Anne's Revenge, in all probability, were barely finishing their second song. It had certainly been a very eventful evening. As she stood near to the automatic doors, glancing anxiously round for Jennifer, a girl approached with a dressing on her forehead and her arm in a sling. She was accompanied by an older woman.

'You got a tab?' the older woman demanded. 'I'm dying for a tab. Forgot to bring them.'

'Sorry,' Tracy shook her head, 'I don't smoke.'

'No, you probably take drugs instead,' snapped the woman, as her younger companion, embarrassed, urged her to be silent.

She spotted Jennifer hurrying toward her, weaving her way through the queue of people standing in the reception area, apologising as she did so. Reaching Tracy, with an audible gasp of relief, she reached out and gave the girl a hug.

At that moment, as she hugged Tracy, it occurred to Jennifer that there was no sign of Sara, and she had been imagining the girl would turn up with the shadowy form of Maude somehow hiding behind her.

'She's with me,' Tracy said, pointing to her head, adding, 'literally. With me.'

Taking her arm, Jennifer guided her towards the cubicle where Sara was situated, at least for the time being. They were going to take her for a CT scan at any moment. Chas had whispered to her that it would be better if Sara, the succubus, was reunited with her body before the scan. If the reunion happened afterwards, who knew what would happen? There wasn't much going on in Sara's mind at present, and he was guessing it was probable she would likely be moved to the Intensive Care Unit following the scan results.

'Distract them when you take me into the cubicle,' Tracy urged. 'Faint. Anything.'

'They might not allow you in,' Jennifer fumed. 'But I'll tell them that if anyone can get Sara back it's you, her best friend.'

Tracy gave a nod of approval. But, as Jennifer had predicted, the entrance to the cubicle was blocked by a tall, middle-aged, male nurse. Around his neck was a blue lariat, the badge dangling from it bearing the legend, "NHS. Charge Nurse", beneath which was a photograph and his name.

'This is Sara's friend, Tracy.' Jennifer gave him a captivating smile, as did Tracy. 'If anyone can help Sara, it's Tracy.'

'Things like that only happen in movies.' The charge nurse had the jaded appearance of someone who'd seen it all and had no illusions left. But at least he stood aside to allow Tracy to enter, adding warningly, 'Only a couple of minutes, miss.'

As Tracy leaned close to Sara, ostensibly pressing a kiss to her cheek, Jennifer took stock of a neurosurgeon, who had been summoned, and a clinical neurologist, both highly qualified doctors. Beside them stood a young nurse; young but very capable. Somehow she had to distract them, and she'd never been known for her acting ability. At New Year she and Chas had held a murder party. It transpired that her character, a dowager duchess no less, was the murderer. She took her part so badly, that when the guests were asked to name the murderer, everyone – apart from Vi – immediately pointed in her direction. If there was a visible cloud of vapour, questions would surely be asked. So, she had to do something, even if it meant summoning her non-existent acting ability.

There was a lot of equipment around: an ECG machine; a crash trolley complete with defibrillator and shelves containing syringes and medication; and an I/V drip was positioned to one side of Sara, the tube leading into her right arm; whilst at the other side a machine recorded her blood pressure and oxygen SATS. If she tried to fake a faint, she might damage something valuable. But drastic action was necessary.

'I need a chair,' she tried to sound faint and breathless. But since she was in fact absolutely overwrought, her voice sounded totally believable. 'I feel dizzy.'

'Jen...' Chas looked around for a chair, but owing to the amount of equipment in the small cubicle there was no chair nearby.

'Oooh.' Jennifer hoped she wasn't overdoing it. Being a dentist, she'd seen plenty of people faint. Dentists often had that effect. She flopped to the floor, more heavily than intended, managing not to yelp as her shoulder came into contact with the corner of the crash trolley. But at least she had the undivided attention of the two doctors and the nurse. Tracy remained with Sara, eyes closed with relief.

Chas pulled Jennifer into a sitting position.

'Head between your knees,' the nurse instructed. 'I'll get another blood pressure machine.' She disappeared momentarily.

The neurosurgeon reached for Jennifer's pulse, and the neurologist shone his torch into her eyes. 'Simple faint, I would say...'

'I didn't lose consciousness,' Jennifer protested, in case they sent her for a CT scan too. 'I just feel a little flaky.'

'Hardly surprising,' the neurosurgeon stated benignly. 'Been a difficult evening for you.'

'Facial colour is good,' the neurologist intoned professionally. 'No extreme pallor. Pulse steady. Just a simple stress reaction, I would say.'

Chas, not knowing of the latest conversation between his wife and Tracy, unconsciously bought more time for Tracy. 'She's not prone to fainting,' he protested. 'Do you feel sick or something?'

'I'm okay, Chas, but I do feel a bit sick.' Jennifer had been trying to think of something to say that might keep the attention focused on herself, yet wouldn't result in her being admitted as an in patient. Nausea seemed good enough.

The nurse, newly returned with a blood pressure machine, now thrust a vomit bowl under Jennifer's nose, whilst the neurosurgeon checked her blood pressure. The neurologist was tapping at her knees with a patella hammer.

'Reflexes present, just as I expected,' he stated approvingly.

'Blood pressure excellent.' Deftly, the neurosurgeon removed the blood pressure cuff. The nurse was still holding the vomit bowl under Jennifer's nose with one hand, her other hand clamped to the back of her head with a vice-like grip. Unable to move, she took some deep breaths, simulating – she hoped – the possibility of forthcoming sickness.

'You okay, Mum?'

Instantly, attention swung away from Jennifer. Sara was sitting up on the examination couch, fully restored.

CHAPTER FOURTEEN

THE MEDICAL TEAM WERE STUNNED INTO SILENCE; THE doctors and the nurse gazed at Sara, jaws hanging foolishly agape.

'Are you alright, Mum?' Sara repeated.

'Fine. I'm fine,' Jennifer's voice was a startled, unnatural squeak.

The neurologist was first to recover his wits, rushing to Sara and examining her pupils with his torch yet again. Jennifer wondered if this was the only piece of equipment he bothered with. But of course, she recalled, there was also his patella hammer. He seemed to love that too.

'I really want to go home,' Sara announced. 'And a cup of tea would be lovely.'

The nurse had momentarily disappeared, but she returned, pulling the jaded charge nurse with her. Tracy treated him to a beaming, triumphant smile. However, the charge nurse was not to be shaken out of his habitual pessimism.

'This young lady seemed to bring her back! I've never seen it happen before, but then I'm a lot younger than you,' the nurse tactlessly informed her superior. 'You must have seen it happen a few times.'

'Coincidence,' was the sour reply. 'She would have recovered whether or not her friend chanced to arrive.'

'Oh, I've known relatives and friends help stimulate the minds of stroke victims,' the neurosurgeon pronounced. He proceeded to state that he still required Sara to have a CT scan, after which a decision would be made as to whether she was fit to return home.

Jennifer anxiously wondered if this was a good idea… Would it not show up something strange? Surely the girl's brain couldn't give a normal pattern, occupied as it was with an ancient succubus. It seemed as if Tracy had read her mind and, addressing Sara, she proceeded to inform her friend that the scan was nothing to worry about. She'd undergone the same procedure a year ago, having fallen, bumped her head and ended up with concussion.

Jennifer flashed a thankful smile in Tracy's direction. *What would we have done without her this evening?* she wondered. At that moment a couple of porters arrived to wheel Sara to the CT scanner room.

Chas proceeded to inform the two consultants that he and his family were insured, so, if the scan proved to be satisfactory, perhaps Sara could be discharged home and followed up in the private consulting rooms?

'I'm not a doctor, but I *am* a dentist,' Jennifer urged. 'I know enough about monitoring vital signs, etcetera. She'll be safe with us.'

Chas distinctly felt they were saying all the right things. The consultants conferred, decided to head for the CT scanner and, following the procedure, they would made a decision. Certainly they'd both desire to follow her up in the very near future; her return to consciousness had been remarkably swift and unusual. The girl was alert, totally focused and unconfused, and her coordination was perfect.

It was as if nothing had happened. 'Very unusual,' they kept repeating.

'You've had a CT scan?' Jennifer asked of Tracy as soon as the consultants disappeared. 'And it was normal? I'm frightened it might look odd... you know, with...' her voice trailed away.

It hadn't occurred to Chas that the scan might prove to be unusual. 'You mean it might look strange because of the succubus?'

'Mine was fine, and I'm a lot older than Sara,' Tracy assured them.

Chas pulled up a chair, urging Jennifer to sit down in case she fainted again. Accepting the seat, Jennifer explained how she and Tracy had agreed to arrange some sort of diversion so Tracy could restore Sara to herself. Relieved, Chas laughed so loudly, the charge nurse popped his head around the door to see what was happening.

'We're just so thankful,' Jennifer assured him.

'Still, it was a good attempt at simulating a faint,' Chas informed her, and then added a caveat, 'but then I've not seen many people faint. *My* clients tend not to.'

'No, I suppose they do it at home. When they receive your invoice in the post,' Tracy quipped.

Time dragged as they awaited Sara's return. *How long did a CT scan take?* Jennifer wondered.

Tracy decided to go into the waiting room to find a functional vending machine, preferably one able to dispense coffee. At that moment, even vending machine coffee seemed an attractive prospect. She returned, managing to clutch three cartons of coffee, tightly pressed together. Some of the liquid had spilled out onto the floor during her journey, but the cartons were still relatively full.

'I hope no one slips on the coffee drips,' she stated anxiously. 'I'd better take some tissues and mop up.'

The coffee was disgusting, in Chas's opinion, but nonetheless he was grateful for it. It was at least strong and hot, although under normal circumstances he wouldn't have touched it. Jennifer glanced at her wristwatch... It was only eleven p.m. It seemed much later. How could so much happen in such a short period of time? Tracy, having mopped up the spilled coffee, returned and began to explain everything that had happened backstage.

'If it wasn't such a serious situation, I would say it sounds like some sort of black comedy,' Chas said. 'With Swordfish keeling over, Sara carried away on a stretcher... I thought it would all be so simple.'

Jennifer nodded soberly. 'How on earth could Sara tell Swordfish her address? I mean, she's a spirit, unable to actually speak.'

Tracy gave a knowing smirk. 'Easy. When you know how.' It was barely noticeable in the harsh overhead hospital light, but a small, thin streak of vapour emitted from Tracy's mouth towards Jennifer, then almost instantly returned to its source.

Jennifer gave an amazed gasp. 'You told me you're going to meet your historian television presenter next weekend!'

'See? Easy. That's how Sara gave him her address. We can send out just enough of ourselves to pass on information,' Tracy explained. 'I don't know how we manage to do so, or why we can do so. But then I don't know why we just keep on living either,' she gave a helpless shrug.

'But by just sending out a sort of feeler – for want of a better description – it means you don't flop unconscious? Sara should have done that tonight instead of flopping like a muppet,' frowned Chas.

'Hmm, I see where you're coming from,' nodded Tracy. 'But I find that when it comes to distance, and Sara had to get backstage, it's a case of having to make a total departure,' she assured him.

'She almost sabotaged the concert!' Chas commented drily, his lips suddenly twitching with amusement.

They heard the sound of an approaching trolley. So far they'd heard the sound of several approaching trolleys and each time had all leapt to their feet, anticipating it might be Sara returning. Each time they'd been disappointed. Peering out of the cubicle door, Chas realised that once again the trolley did not have his daughter lying on it. But just as he registered disappointment, he noticed a porter walking behind the trolley, and he was pushing someone in a wheelchair. This person *was* Sara. And if she was in a chair instead of recumbent upon a trolley, it must be good news. She still had the I/V in her arm, but the oxygen mask was missing, along with the blood pressure cuff; plus she was smiling broadly. Within seconds, the nurse appeared, clutching cotton wool, an antiseptic pad and a dressing.

'I'll just take this out, since you're drinking normally,' and she proceeded to remove the needle from Sara's hand. Chas noticed how steady the nurse's hands were. Obviously she'd done this many times before. 'She drank a good half litre of water after the scan,' she informed Chas and Jennifer.

'I needed it. I was choking for a drink,' Sara declared, adding, 'and I see you guys have been having a good time drinking coffee.'

'The consultants will be speaking with you shortly.' The nurse deftly disposed of the needle. 'But it looks as if you can all go home soon. I hope if you go to any more concerts, young lady, you won't be as overwrought as you were at this one,' she informed Sara.

'They think the scan is good and are just giving it a close inspection,' Sara explained. 'It seems I was just too excited.'

For the benefit of the nurse, she added ingenuously, 'After all, it *would* have been my first rock concert – if I'd actually got to see it.'

Nearly a quarter of an hour passed before the consultants finally did reappear, both explaining, in turn, that they'd minutely examined the scan, could find nothing amiss, and their explanation echoed Sara's. It was teenage excitement: her first rock concert; she was infatuated with one of the band; she was overcome.

'I've never seen such an extreme reaction,' the neurologist stated somewhat pompously. 'It's all very interesting. I'm going to commence a study of teenage infatuation and the physical reactions which can ensue. Meanwhile, I do need the scan to be reported on by a radiologist, just to obtain another opinion. I shall give your details to my secretary. She'll contact you on Monday morning. I have a clinic at a private hospital on Monday evening, so I'd like to review Sara then.'

'Meanwhile, should you have any problems, or notice any changes in mood or behaviour, please return to casualty,' added the neurosurgeon. 'I will wait for my colleague here to inform me of his opinion following Monday's appointment,' he said, nodding towards the neurologist, 'and should he deem it necessary, my secretary will be in touch to arrange an appointment at one of *my* clinics.'

Chas and Jennifer, beaming with relief, nodded eagerly.

It took nearly another half hour before the relevant discharge paperwork was prepared, which included a letter for their GP, plus an advice sheet on the subject of what to do should Sara lose consciousness. Stuffing them unceremoniously into her handbag, Jennifer linked Chas's arm, leaning her head wearily against his shoulder. It had been a traumatic night, on a par with the time Chas had needed his appendix removing.

'Home,' said Chas.

'Home,' she echoed.

Outside, the evening was chilly and damp, but the fresh air was welcome. The atmosphere in the hospital had been warm and uncomfortably stuffy. Jennifer had remarked more than once that she wouldn't care to work in such an environment… although of course it could be that perhaps something had gone wrong with their ventilation system. Hopefully they wouldn't be returning to find out.

It was nearly one o'clock by the time Chas turned the car into the estate where the Roseberrys lived. It had been a speedy, peaceful journey; there'd been relatively little traffic on the road, therefore the only hold-ups had only been at traffic lights. It had also been a silent journey; no one had spoken. No one really knew what to say. Jennifer wanted to hear Sara's own account of what had happened backstage but, since they'd received a report from Tracy already, it could wait until she'd had some sleep. Until they had all had some sleep, in fact. The girl was okay, she was in perfect health, and nothing else mattered.

As Chas rounded the corner leading to their house, the headlights illuminated two people on the drive, both leaning casually against a vehicle Chas recognised. It was Randall's hired car. One of the men was clearly Randall himself, the other he didn't immediately recognise. His immediate reaction was one of relief, that Randall at least hadn't brought Vi with him; it would have been just too much to have to make excuses to Vi about the events of the evening. Suddenly, he realised the other tall figure was the man he'd seen on television. None other than Swordfish himself. It wasn't until much later that Chas and Jennifer realised how composed Sara's reaction was.

As soon as Chas parked the car on the drive and switched the ignition off, Sara opened her rear passenger door and, upon climbing out, found Swordfish's extended hand waiting to assist her. Silently she stood staring up at him, taking in the face which was as unfamiliar to her as her face was to him.

Opening the front door, Jennifer ushered Randall and Tracy (who was spending the night with them) into the house, whilst Chas followed.

'Have you fallen out with Vi?' Chas demanded curiously.

'Nah, I felt something was amiss. So I told Vi I had a native Australian need to go walkabout... or drive-about I should say. She was okay with it, and here I am. And I was right, wasn't I?' he concluded triumphantly.

'Mum was happy enough to let you loose?' Jennifer was astonished.

Randall nodded. 'I just felt I should come here. Don't know how I'm going to explain it to her though... I'll think of something. But a strong feeling it was. Then what happens but I roll up, about fifteen minutes ago, then a taxi arrives with a lanky dude getting out of it. And he's the same as those two young Sheilas! Place is infested with them! We've been chatting like old friends ever since,' he stated with obvious approval. 'He's a good dude, though. Said he'd heard Sara had been taken to casualty. So he was uncertain whether to come here or try the hospital first. He opted for here, as he reckoned they wouldn't give him any information anyway in the casualty department.'

Chas and Jennifer shook their heads in unison. The evening was becoming yet more bizarre. Glancing out the window, Jennifer could clearly make out Sara and Swordfish, still standing staring at one another, illuminated by their security light. With an effort she turned her mind to practical matters.

'Anyone hungry? I left a selection of sandwiches in the fridge in case we wanted something to eat,' she suggested.

Chas realised he was ravenous. Plus a glass of wine wouldn't go amiss either. Randal was clearly up for both and followed Jennifer into the kitchen, whilst Chas selected a bottle of red wine from the rack. Tracy quietly began taking plates from a cupboard, placing them on the table as Jennifer pulled the plastic films from the plates of sandwiches.

'Chicken and pickle, tuna and mayo, beef and horseradish,' she indicated each plate in turn. 'What would you like to drink, Tracy? Tea, coffee…?'

Tracy eyed the red wine before replying, with obvious regret, that tea would be lovely. This was clearly a dentist's household; soft sugary drinks were kept to a minimum. Wine, obviously, was not.

Randall was munching with enthusiasm. Chas managed to avoid commenting that Vi was noted for being frugal with food. This was due to her determination to remain slim; she also tended to assume everyone else desired to be likewise.

'So, what's been happening, then?' demanded Randall.

Chas began explaining, then reached the point where Sara had flopped against him.

'This fat…' he noticed Jennifer shaking her head in his direction. 'This is my home,' he grumbled. 'I have to be politically correct at work, so in this house I shall say what I want to say! She was a *fat* woman!' He held his arms wide for emphasis.

At that moment the front door clicked shut. Sara and Swordfish finally walked into the house.

Her mouth full of half masticated chicken and bread, Jennifer mutely waved an inviting hand towards the plates on the table. Swordfish, clearly as ravenous as Randall, swooped, without ceremony, on the beef and horseradish. No one knew what to say; it was uneasily silent apart from the sounds of wine and tea being poured, and the clinking of crockery. Chas wanted to say something to the newcomer but nothing sensible sprang to mind. They all remained standing awkwardly in the kitchen.

Typically, it was Randall who broke the silence; firstly, he handed a glass of wine to Swordfish, then he opened a second bottle to refill his own glass – no one else had finished their drink – before he enquired affably, 'So, what happens next with you two?'

Chas's mind buzzed. This man, Swordfish, needed to know that nothing *could* happen. Not only was Sara underage, she had an education to finish. She was clever. She'd been clever before that succubus thing took over. Putting his glass of wine down on the kitchen bench, he opened his mouth to speak but was gently forestalled by Swordfish.

'We have a lot to talk about.' He paused to take a sip of wine from the glass Randall had thoughtfully given him. 'But obviously... Sara...' he spoke the name hesitantly. It sounded strange; she had never during their time together used a body called "Sara". 'Sara,' he resumed, 'is young and needs to complete school and university.'

Without realising it, Chas took a deep sigh of relief.

'I'll probably be able to go to university before I'm eighteen,' Sara informed him. 'My teachers are now saying I'm gifted and probably will sit my GCSEs and A levels all before time.'

'Obviously you chose well,' Swordfish mused aloud. 'You selected a body belonging to a home that can well support you financially. Sorry to speak so,' he addressed Chas and Jennifer, 'but it's a fact.'

'More than I did,' Tracy observed drily, though she was not unduly worried about this. She was determined to carve out a career for herself, and her male incubus friend would provide financial backup if needed.

'My new friend Randall informs me you're the same as Sara and myself. It must be some kind of record... three of us in a room together,' Swordfish addressed Tracy, before eagerly accepting another sandwich as Jennifer waved a plate in front of him.

'Oh, you two are youngsters,' smiled Tracy. 'I also have an incubus friend who is older than Sara and you. I expect you'll meet him sometime in the future.'

Whilst eating, Jennifer had been quietly appraising the newcomer. Like Sara, and Tracy too, his face was young, although obviously not as young as the faces of the two girls. A few months ago, although it seemed much longer, she'd detected something suddenly amiss, something unusual, about Sara's eyes. Her gaze was no longer young and girlish. Swordfish too showed something ancient in his countenance. *Wisdom*, she decided. It's wisdom. It was exactly the same with Tracy. Suddenly she realised no introductions had been made. It hardly seemed necessary now but, apologising, she hastily remedied this lack.

'I think we should all sit down,' Chas suggested, whilst Randall, as ever making himself at home, refilled his host's glass.

They all trooped into the sitting room, followed by Randall who had paused to help himself to the last sandwich. Utterly unembarrassed by the long overdue reunion between two people, who were now seated side by side on one of the sofas, he proceeded to ask, 'Well, you two going to stay together now?'

Silently, Chas blessed the arrival of the Australian. This was exactly the question he longed to ask, but convention somehow forbade it. Randall and convention didn't go together.

'Of course,' Sara and Swordfish stated in unison.

'We need to get to know each other again; we've both changed…' Sara informed Randall.

'But the core of the people we were remains,' Swordfish interrupted gently, squeezing Sara's hand. 'We're adaptable people. We have to be,' he added, as Sara nodded in agreement.

'Vi – my lady friend – and I were watching you dudes on TV just over a week ago,' Randal's eyes held a gleam of mischief. 'You said you had eased up on the grog, or something to that effect. Glad to see you're not tee total!'

'Moderation,' smiled Swordfish.

Seated opposite, on the other sofa, separated by a coffee table, Jennifer felt choked with emotion. They were so peaceful together. She had envisioned this Swordfish fellow storming into their lives, trying to drag Sara from them; yet here he was, sitting contentedly beside the girl, having just a few moments ago raised the subject of Sara's education! It was more than she had dared hope for.

'What about the past? I mean, how did you manage to lose each other? How did you lose Sara?' Jennifer's mouth felt suddenly dry.

As ever, as if reading her mind, Randall leaned forward from the depths of the armchair he was slouched in, to refill her glass. It was strange, she noted absently. Somehow or other, Randall, in a short period of time, had just slotted into their family circle.

'The war,' Swordfish informed her. 'World War Two.'

'The last I knew you were in the SOE,' Sara informed him. 'You were shot. I received a telegram informing me of that.'

'Yes, I was shot. By the S.S. So I searched for and found an SOE colleague and took him over. He too was shot – accidently. A member of the French Resistance thought I was a German plant.'

Swordfish went on to explain how he'd managed to do what he did best – by becoming an army surgeon. He managed to locate such a person, English, reasonably young and likely to live for some time. Unfortunately, he too was killed, by flying debris during combat. He took over another young army surgeon, and this time he survived the war. However, he was encumbered with a wife, five children, and lived in Canada.

'Obviously I had to support them afterwards…'

'Of course,' Sara agreed emphatically. 'I would not have permitted anything else.'

'I think I would have been inclined to leave them,' mused Tracy.

'No, responsibilities have to be met,' Sara disagreed, giving Swordfish an approving glance. 'Those five children needed financial and emotional guidance.'

Chas regarded Tracy thoughtfully. This was the difference between Tracy and Sara. Tracy was a decent person; he and Jennifer were becoming fond of her. But there was a sense of responsibility about Sara. Everything she'd told them about her past lives demonstrated this. She had huge integrity and it appeared that Swordfish was very similar.

'I wrote a lot of letters to you, which was the only real form of communication back then. But received no reply. I did travel to our house as soon as I could, but it was the mid-1950s before I could financially do so. I had a good job, but with a wife and five children, money just kind of disappeared. Like our London house, I guess. It too had disappeared! It had been flattened, and rebuilding was in progress when I visited it.'

Swordfish reflected upon that scene for a moment. The awful desolation of it all. Thankfully, he knew his soulmate would survive, even if she wasn't in the same body. But whose body was she using? Also, he too had another body. She might not readily recognise him.

'I lived a very long time in that body,' Swordfish explained. 'It died in 2008, aged ninety-eight! The longest living person I've used! I ended up telling my wife about myself – she lived just long enough to celebrate the millennium. She suspected something was very different about me and sensed it wasn't all due to my being traumatised by the war. I'd learned to trust and respect her, so I levelled with her. Like you guys – he nodded towards Chas and Jennifer – she found it difficult to take in. You must have found it difficult to come to terms with, when you realised Sara was as she is. But my wife came to accept it, and even accompanied me on one of my regular visits to England to find my soulmate.' He squeezed Sara's hand.

Jennifer surreptitiously dabbed at her eyes with a tissue. Noticing Randall was likewise moved, she passed one to him. She glanced at Chas, who was looking dry-eyed but stunned.

He was, in fact, totally taken aback by the level of understanding the new arrival possessed. This man approved of Sara needing an education and was not bent upon running away with her. He likewise approved of her decision to select a body which belonged to an affluent household. But he was also sympathetic to his and Jennifer's struggle to come to terms with the changes in their daughter. A thought suddenly struck him; Sara was giving no sign of being jealous of Swordfish's Canadian wife, and they'd lived together for a very long time. He and Jennifer would have personally been eaten up with jealousy by such a situation!

'I went to our church often. For years. Even until my last body, a historian called Marilyn Hamilton, died,' Sara informed him.

'*You* were Marilyn Hamilton?!' Swordfish's tone was incredulous. 'I had such a feeling about that.'

'Why didn't you get in touch, then?' she inquired logically.

'I did... then I discovered you'd died. You see,' Swordfish explained, 'it wasn't until early this year that I actually found out about her. Until then I'd never heard of her. You see, when my ninety-eight-year-old body died, I took over a young man.'

That young man, he continued, had been an affluent English tourist visiting Canada, and so by using this body he soon returned to the UK. Being young, it could be anticipated that this would be a long-term body. It turned out otherwise.

Last year, whilst travelling with friends to attend a Queen Anne's Revenge concert at the O2 Arena in London, he was involved in a horrific car accident and was killed along with his three companions. There were no survivors. But it had already occurred to him that inhabiting a famous body might be a springboard to finding Nancy (as he always thought of her). So, he reached the O2 Arena, bent upon using the body of one of the hugely famous band. Swordfish was chosen simply because he was the first band member he spotted. Unfortunately, it had never occurred to him that he might be occupying someone who was an addict.

'I tell you, I nearly moved out as quickly as I moved in!' he informed his audience. 'But there was potential there, I soon discovered. The guy was a seriously talented musician. So I took myself to a clinic to dry out and detoxify. I urge you, avoid drugs and alcohol; cold turkey is not a good thing. Anyway, I saw a book by Marilyn Hamilton lying on a table. One of her histories of the Wars of the Roses. Well, I read it, and she talked about Maude Dubreise. Maude, as only you, Sara, could know her. By the time I was fit to be seen, I'd learned that Marilyn Hamilton was terminally ill. I found out which hospital you – or she – had been admitted to and went to visit, but she'd died a few hours previously. So, having discovered she had two stepdaughters, Rosie and Alice, I managed to find them, just in case she'd taken over one of them. She hadn't. Anyway,' he stated defensively, 'what did you do to get in touch?' His lips twitched, trying to hide a contented smile. They were together. Thanks to modern communication, it was probable they always would be now. Or at least they would always be able to make contact.

'We missed each other by a few hours, perhaps less, in that hospital,' Sara's voice was a whisper, and her audience leaned forward, desperate to hear her words, whilst Swordfish rested his head against hers to listen. 'And, for your information, I didn't want to use my stepdaughters. Neither of them was – is – a long-term prospect. Neither has good health. I ensured my entire estate was left to them in my will, to keep them well provided for. But once I saw this body, which was near to me when I died, I knew it to be a wise choice.' Shaking her head incredulously, she continued, 'However, during those years, when I was trying to get in touch with you, I kept going to that church,' she explained. 'Plus I put adverts in lonely hearts columns, and suchlike. Looking for Harry Percy, and David Royale, things like that. I received a lot of replies... some of them pretty weird, but none from you. Obviously because you were in Canada!'

'I visited that church – well, what was left of it – several times a year. The problem was, I didn't know who I was looking for,' he sighed, shaking his mane of hair. 'We *are* able to spot incubi such as ourselves, but it's sometimes difficult... in a crowd, for example.'

'True,' Tracy nodded in agreement. 'I spotted Sara first, at a party here. But only because she was standing slightly apart from everyone else.'

Sara gave a nod of agreement. 'It's difficult in a crowded environment. And every time I saw a man standing alone I reached out – mentally – to see if he was an incubus. On more than one occasion someone took me for a hooker looking for business. I tell you truly,' she emphasised as Swordfish gave a chuckle of laughter. 'But whilst I tried to cling to the hope you would still be alive, I wondered if you'd drowned. It was logical that you might have been on board a ship that was torpedoed, or an aircraft that was shot down over water. You might not have been able to survive long enough to find a new body,' her voice gave a quiver of emotion.

'Yes, it's a problem... We don't know just how long we *can* survive. But when I quit my mangled car-crashed body, until I came across Swordfish I can state I'd been without a body for nearly four hours. And I was right, I *could* use his fame!' he grinned triumphantly. 'It worked.'

'Thanks to *The Barley Break*.' Sara's smile was seraphic.

'Talking of that – we have a routine to complete.' Easing his long frame from the sofa, he headed towards the piano which stood in the bay window. At first glance it appeared antique but it was in fact modern and electronic and, flicking a switch, he began to play the classical version of the old tune.

Chas, thoughtfully swirling red wine around in his glass with one hand, reached out for Jennifer with the other. Sara and Swordfish would go on for centuries. How would it be if he and Jennifer could be like that? What he did detect in the newly reunited couple was that their relationship was built upon a spiritual compatibility. Obviously they'd indulged in a physical relationship in the past, but that wasn't central to their connection. Perhaps he and Jennifer so valued their relationship because it wasn't infinite? They shared a mutual dread of a final separation, something they shied away from discussing. It was only because he was a lawyer that they'd made out their wills, such was their distaste for considering the inevitability of dying. As for his feelings towards Swordfish, they were complex. In just a few short years he would, no doubt, whisk Sara away somewhere. Yet some instinct told him Sara would always return to him and Jennifer. They would never lose their daughter. If either of them needed the adult Sara, she would be there for them. He looked down at Jennifer, whose head was now resting wearily upon his shoulder. How would he have felt if the being that had taken over Sara had selected Jennifer instead? He felt sickened to consider how he might feel if Swordfish had walked into his home, seeking to remain in contact with his wife. It was a situation he could not even have contemplated.

'There.' Swordfish, having finished playing, stood up and directed a wicked smile in Sara's direction. 'But there is one thing I really do need to know, Sara,' the name becoming familiar now. 'How long are you going to be wearing those ghastly braces on your teeth?'

As he seated himself beside her again, Sara, unconsciously imitating her mother, aimed a kittenish swipe at him.

'They are not in situ for much longer. A month?' she directed a questioning glance towards Jennifer, who nodded assent. 'I shall be beautified before Christmas!'

'A dentist's daughter cannot have wonky teeth,' Jennifer stated unctuously, trying to smother a yawn.

'Of course not,' he nodded in agreement.

'You ever been gay?' Randall asked unexpectedly of Swordfish. 'I mean, could you inhabit a gay body? And if so, would it remain gay?'

Jennifer's eyes widened briefly with surprise, but she was now too weary to be overly shocked.

'Well, I was just wondering, you know.' Randall had spotted her swift reaction.

'I know it's unfashionable to say so, but I'm a heterosexual being. So is Sara, and so I suspect is Tracy,' Swordfish assured him. 'Any body I inhabited would undoubtedly therefore become heterosexual. Although I'm certain there must be, somewhere, gay incubi and succubi.'

'No offence intended, dude,' said Randall, cheerfully taking a deep drink of his wine.

'None taken,' Swordfish amicably responded. 'Randall informed me that this is a very professional household,' Swordfish deftly changed the subject. 'You have a lawyer father and a dentist mother. Are you considering either of those professions?'

Sara shook her head. Medicine beckoned... perhaps. School wasn't quite as boring for her as her parents had feared it would be. There was always something to learn. Science was constantly moving on, medical research was fascinating, and she hadn't been a doctor for a few decades. It was an attractive prospect. Maybe.

'Not medicine again?' Swordfish demanded.

'It has some appeal. I think,' she replied hesitantly, adding, 'but perhaps something a bit different... forensics perhaps. Or biophysics.'

'I have an idea, for both of us.' He wriggled closer to her on the sofa.

'Oh no... no.' Sara was alarmed. 'You are not thinking we should become some sort of musical duo! Nina and Frederick. Peters and Lee. Renee and Renato. Dollar...!'

'I liked that blonde Sheila in Dollar,' Randall chipped in. 'Give it a go.'

Swordfish gave a hoot of laughter. 'Better than that. I'm leaving the music business; it has served its purpose. It's back to college for me. Archaeology! Or, to be precise, I fancy being a palaeontologist.'

Sara's face lit up with interest.

'No problems regarding funding digs. I am amazed how much money a bit of songwriting generates! When I first took over this body, I was seriously staggered to discover I was inhabiting a multi-millionaire. Just for belting out a few songs!' Swordfish gave a delighted grin.

'Better keep putting yourself in the public eye now and again,' Chas stated drily. 'I have an archaeologist client. Digs can eat up funds. Maybe you can keep re–releasing *The Barley Break*!'

Tracy's eyelids were drooping. Her head was resting peacefully against the wing of her armchair. It was nearly three a.m. Even Randal, who seemed indefatigable, was feeling weary. Before retiring to bed – he assumed he would be welcome to spend the night – maybe one more glass of wine would be acceptable?

Refilling his glass, Randal directed an amused glance towards Chas and Jennifer. 'Incubus people are rare, right?'

They both nodded in weary agreement.

'But there are *three* ancient people in this house; I've never felt so young, ever!'

Chas solemnly nodded his agreement. 'This is one seriously weird household, dude.'